一本でビッグになる

BIG IN JAPAN

A NOVEL BY
JENNIFER GRIFFITH

JOLLY
FISH
PRESS
Provo, Utah

Jolly Fish Press, LLC
PO Box 1773
Provo, UT 84603-1773
www.jollyfishpress.com

First Paperback Edition: July 2012
Second Paperback Edition: January 2014

For information on subsidiary rights, please contact the publisher at rights@jollyfishpress.com. For a complete list of our distributors, please visit our website at www.jollyfishpress.com.

Library of Congress Control Number: 2012938026

THIS TITLE IS ALSO AVAILABLE AS AN EBOOK.

ISBN 0984880119
ISBN 978-0-9848801-1-9

Printed in the United States of America

10 9 8 7 6 5 4 3 2

For my grandpa, BHS, who loved Japan first.
"Good night, sleep tight, see you in the morning light."

BIG IN JAPAN

KAGEMUSHA: SHADOW WARRIOR

DEAD OF NIGHT. FUKUOKA, JAPAN

Buck Cooper crouched into fighting stance. Nothing stood between him and his assailants but his thin kimono and the bitter winter air. Night enveloped him, but the sodium glow of the city streetlights hanging sparsely near the docks gave faint outline to the three black-pajamaed henchmen sent to do him bodily harm.

Buck's folds of flesh shook like a gelatin on his mother's holiday table back home—not so much from fear, but from the winter night. These trained fighters' eyes pierced the night in steely hatred of him, and Buck wondered again whose money they accepted in exchange for this assault under night's blanket of secrecy; which of his many recently-amassed enemies felt strongly enough about his demise to resort to this?

The tallest of the three advanced first. Buck knew from stories bandied about the stable that these kinds of hits almost always came orchestrated by the Japanese underground, the *yakuza*. Surrounded by the towering steel freight containers that slid in and soared upward, his world was this alley. Buck had never fought three men at once, except in days on the playground in Texas when bullies ganged up on him almost twenty years ago. If what he did then could even be called fighting. Certainly he had never triumphed in a three on one battle.

A gust of icy air made his throat constrict. The first hitman circled him at a short distance, and Buck rotated to keep him in sight, even though it meant turning his back on the other two.

Puffs of exhaled steam hung momentarily in the freezing air.

With blinding speed the first assailant attacked, and Buck struck out a hand in hopes of catching him by the throat. The impact seared through his shoulder. Protecting his own life was going to be more brutal than he imagined.

TWO YEARS EARLIER

DESERTION AT DAWN
SEPTEMBER. TEXAS

Buck Cooper squared his shoulders and tucked in the back of his damp shirt—again. In thirty seconds, Alison Turner would be off her phone, and he would do a strategic walk-by past her desk, the desk with the polka dot coffee mug and the eleven purple Sharpie markers and the picture of her vacation to South Padre Island last fall. Today was the day she'd shake her long hair and glance up when he passed, look at him with her melting chocolate brown eyes and finally really notice him.

The Eaglestone Pharmaceuticals break room stifled with heat, but it gave him a view of the receptionist's desk. He shifted his weight, no small task, and listened for her fetching Texas drawl of "buh-bye." It was almost go-time. He moved his stack of statistical analysis files into his right arm, just in case she wanted to give a high-five to his left hand as he passed. Not that she ever had before.

The water cooler bubbled behind him.

"Ooh, hoo-hoo, Mr. Buck. You watching that woohman again? Ar-har-har-har."

Great. Ranjit and his super skinny frame in the brown argyle sweater, the same one he wore daily. He wasn't even breaking a sweat, but he still smelled like curry.

"You know, of course, a girl with luscious hair like that is never going to be looking in the direction of a 400-pound man. Ar-har-har-har. Why are you discombobulating yourself over her?" the lothario of Mumbai sniggered. "Well, of course there's the luscious body."

"Ranjit. Didn't your mama teach you how to talk about a lady?" Buck got enough of Ranjit on his stats team. But the jerk was right about her hair. It was luscious, the way it cascaded in spun gold waves over her shoulders. She was the only bright spot in this pain cave of an office.

Sadly, Ranjit was right about the other thing, too. When in history had the enormous guy ever snagged the hottest girl in a five-mile radius? Worse, when had Buck ever snagged any girl in all his twenty-four years?

"Give it up, Mr. Buck." The Indian accent lilted and Ranjit bobbled his head side to side. "Take a look at yourself. Your body is a superstructure constructed entirely of junk food." Ranjit patted his own stomach and then Buck's before punching him in the arm.

That buh-bye should be coming any second now. He wished Ranjit would evaporate in the orange cloud of curry vapors that followed him everywhere.

"You should be more worried about getting laid off. Impending doom for all of us." Ranjit cackled all the way down the corridor to his cubicle.

Layoffs. Whatever. Buck pulled more than just his own considerable weight in the stats department. He pulled Ranjit and Gupta and all the other Indians' weight as well. Management should be considering Buck's application for the promotion just about now, not whether to lay him off.

Alison hung up the phone. Yes! Buck made his move. His damp shirt had come untucked again. Stupid heat. Somebody turned off the air conditioning again. Just because the calendar read September didn't mean Texas heat was done. It was probably one of those underweight exercise freak boys on the company soccer team, the kind who were perpetually freezing and wearing cardigan sweaters even in the dead of summer. The kind Alison Turner probably dated on weekends.

He attempted a swagger, but it came out more like a lumber. "Hi, Alison." Buck lifted a hello hand, but his greeting got swallowed up in the ring tone of her cell phone, which she snapped open immediately. She didn't even look up when he passed.

Thwarted. His smile faded.

He stumped back to his desk. Superstructure. He rolled a hand over the shoddy addition out front and winced. He just had to lose some of this weight—he *had* to. Maybe he would take the stairs today when he went to lunch. But it would be hard to take them on the way back, especially after a plateful of Charlie Unger's barbecue. Today was Thursday—Brisket day! But he would definitely take the stairs.

"Who left this window open?"

Buck walked up to his cubicle to find another Indian coworker, Gupta, complaining at Buck's desk. He had his head out the window across from the line of desks and was reaching for something.

"What's going on?"

"Some idiot left this window open and now my best collector card of Aishwarya Rai blew out onto the ledge and some stupid seagull is going to come along and use it to line its nest, and that is just sacrilege." Gupta had a piercing whine Buck knew too well.

Buck pressed Gupta aside and leaned out the eighth story window. Sure enough, the photo of the Bollywood actress was about five feet away, perched on the ledge and about to fall eight stories to the streets of Dallas.

"I was the one who left the window open. What were you doing at my desk, anyway?" Buck leaned farther, but the card was just out of reach.

"You always have a twenty-dollar bill in your top drawer, and it's lunchtime. Brisket day at Charlie Unger's. I forgot my wallet." As usual.

Buck leaned back in and gave Gupta a look of disbelief. "Give me that chair." He grabbed the steel chair from Gupta and stood on it, adding another eighteen inches to his already six-foot-six frame. With a long stretch over the lip of the windowsill, Buck procured the card and brought it back to safety. Gupta snatched it and kissed the card.

"I missed you, Aishwarya!" Another kiss. "Now, Mr. Buck, how about that twenty dollars? I'm good for it. I'm not going to be cut in the layoffs."

It was worth twenty dollars to Buck to see Gupta scatter.

Gupta called over the cubicle wall on his way to spend the cash. "You ought to keep your window shut, Mr. Buck. It's September already."

Right. Autumn. Of course.

Buck lifted his shoulder-length hair off his neck in a wad. He swiped at a lock of hair frizzing at his brow line. Cutting this mop would make sense—to help cool his head in this heat—but he hadn't had time. The quality control analysis of this latest drug trial kept him past eight every night for the last month. He could finish it up this afternoon, but then tonight he needed to look for an apartment. Mrs. Jenkins put him on notice two weeks ago. Her nephew was moving into the place, and Buck had to vamoose.

Plus, the Rangers game was on tonight, and Mays had first at-bats—

His phone rang, yanking him out of his field of dreams.

"Mr. Buck? Hi. This is Alison Turner."

Alison? Buck jumped to his feet. His pulse ratcheted up five notches.

"A-a-alison?" Over the tops of all the cubicles he spotted her head at the front desk. That hair—he could see it rippling over her shoulder from here, like metallic honey.

"At the front desk? Do you speak English?"

"Alison. Uh. Yeah."

Sort of. He sort of spoke English. Gack! He was being such a dork. Get it together, pal—this is your big chance.

"Oh, thank goodness. You do speak English." She gave a long whew. "I really need a favor."

"Sure, Alison," he stuttered. "Anything." Buck's heart thumped like a jackrabbit's leg. He knew it! He just knew *today* was the day. He stood up straight and tucked in that damp shirt—again.

"Fantastic. It's about lunch. Oh, shoot. There's my other line. Gotta take it. Can you just, like, drop by my desk up here in a few shakes? Whoops. Gotta grab that. Thanks. Buh-bye, Mr. Buck." The phone clicked off.

Yes! Buck danced a little jig. Finally, the nice guy was going to win. *Lunch!* She said it was about lunch. She wanted him to take her for the brisket, obviously. Cha-ching! He'd have to hit the ATM real quick. He could make that work. A plate of savory beef and Alison Turner. He plopped down in his chair and stared up at the popcorn ceiling in joy.

He'd always sensed Alison Turner was the one girl who had the X-ray vision that let her see through all Buck's outer layers into his inner goodness.

Most people had *more* than X-ray vision when it came to seeing Buck: they saw clean through him. How could someone who took up as much of the visible spectrum of light as he did still be utterly invisible, the fat guy no one noticed? Sometime he'd calculate and find a quantifiable ratio between a person's becoming less noticeable and reaching a certain body mass index.

Buck thought back. What marked the beginning of his invisibility? When he hit three hundred pounds? And he wasn't invisible just to women. Barely a handful of guys—mostly Ranjit's country-men—knew his name, and only as "Mr. Buck."

Suddenly it hit him—the reason Alison noticed him today. The promotion! It had to be the promotion. Management had been bandying his name about, Alison caught wind of it and called to congratulate him. Joy melted him into a puddle of grease.

Then reality resurged and bit hard, and he pulled open his desk's bottom drawer. Book titles stared out at him:

Body Fit.

You and Your Super-Slim Hardbody.

Ripped Abs Without Steroids the Dwayne Johnson Way.

Lose to Win.

Several promised quick weight loss with little effort. Others required vast amounts of dedication and time. None of them rec-ommended deep fried okra from Charlie Unger's five days a week.

A-ha. There it was—the fake "before and after" picture of himself he'd photo-doctored on a free website. It showed how he looked now at 375 pounds, beside a potential picture of himself at 220 pounds, the perfect weight for his six-foot-six height according to web experts. His Gold's Gym membership haunted him. Maybe if he hadn't avoided it so religiously for the past year, he wouldn't be sitting here cursing the sweat pool between the layers of flab on his back like some panting beached walrus.

"My, my, son. You have got to get that hair of yours trimmed." A woman's voice cut the air, and Buck snapped awake. Mom? "You're starting to look like Jon Bon Jovi. Or is it David Lee Roth? The blond one."

"Mom, what're you doing down here?"

She never came to downtown Dallas. She stood over him in her daisy sundress, clutching and unclutching the strap on her patent leather purse. He stood up and let her have his chair. He perched on the edge of his desk.

"Is there an emergency? Dad—" There'd been an accident at his lab—

"No, no, Buck. Everything's fine. Oh, look at that picture of your grandma and grandpa's farm. So peaceful."

Yeah, it was. The photo served as his escape hatch some days. At least the family hadn't sold the farm when Grandpa died but kept it in a family trust.

"I mean—well, Buck, I came down to ask you a little favor." Worry lines wrinkled her forehead. She wasn't the favor-asking type. His mom was the favor-doing type. "I mean, it might be a big favor. I need you to go somewhere with me tomorrow."

Tomorrow. Friday. Friday looked free. "Okay, Mom. No problem. Where?" He could maybe slip out for a family thing during lunch—lots of people did. Not Buck, but lots of other people, people with families, people with things to do.

"Tokyo."

Buck double blinked and shook his head.

"It's in Japan."

"I know where Tokyo is, Mom. What are you talking about?"

"Oh, I knew this was a mistake." Her big blue eyes glistened. She pulled a handkerchief from her purse and dabbed at them.

"No, Mom. Just tell me what's going on." Usually she was a pillar, a brick.

"I told your father we should just use a travel agent, but he said the Yoshidas had everything worked out. Plane tickets, sightseeing, accommodations. They want us to stay with them, you know. I'd never ask you if—"

"Back up, back up. What are you talking about?"

"You know how your father is, Buck." She rolled her eyes upward. "Hank Cooper. Head full of dreams."

His mom never spoke this candidly about his dad. She must

be really upset. Buck repositioned himself on his desk and folded his arms across his chest to listen.

"Did something go wrong with Nangrimax, Mom? The FDA didn't deny the application, did they?" Dad's latest invention could be the best wonder drug since penicillin. "I thought he had a deal in the works." With a guy in Japan. Ah, Tokyo.

"Oh, sweetheart. We're still waiting on that process." She heaved a sigh. "He does have a sweet deal possibility, but that's the thing. There's this Mr. Yoshida, a man with money and connections in Tokyo. Your father believes he could be key to getting the product off the ground there. It could mean the difference between glorious success or spectacular failure."

Buck tugged at his shirt. Failure. Not good.

"We're going to see Mr. Yoshida. And his family. And for some reason they insist on meeting our whole family, meaning you, too—even though it's during baseball playoffs, and I'll miss three games. I'd get your Aunt Nancy or your Aunt Phyllis to go, but no. It has to be the *three* of us. The Yoshidas have two sons, your dad says."

She got up and walked the five steps around the middle of his cubicle. "I don't know. We've invested so much . . . The point is, we're desperate to make a good impression, and it starts with all three of us showing up. Buck, I tried to tell them you have a job." A wince wrinkled her nose. "I'm so bad at these social things, and your father's worse."

And she thought Buck was better? Aunt Nancy or Aunt Phyllis or any of his dozen other aunts or umpteen uncles or bazillion cousins could make a good impression. Not Buck.

"Ma, I hadn't told you and Dad yet—but I've put in for a promotion. This might not be the best time—"

Her look of sheer despair brought him up short.

"But don't you think about that. I'll just run the trip past management."

"I'm afraid, Buck." His mom cast her eyes down at her shoes. "I'm afraid this is it. Your father only has one failure left in him."

Buck's throat caught. It sounded like he had no choice. "Tokyo. Tomorrow, then. I'm with you."

Relief spread across her face along with a happy smile. Buck glanced around and caught a glimpse of Alison's hair swinging along an inter-cubicle corridor. His heart skipped.

"Mom, I have an appointment to get to, but—tomorrow. Tokyo!" He shot a finger toward the ceiling, and the flab of his underarm wobbled. His sweet mom gave a little jump of delight and pulled a plane ticket from her purse and slung it onto Buck's desk.

"Oh, thank you. You'll help us so much. You *see* things. So. Six o'clock flight. Don't forget your passport. Oh, and don't bring that ugly duffel bag. The one with the stripes? It's just awful." She bustled away, purse swinging at her side.

Tokyo. Tomorrow. He'd have to find his passport. Oh, and pack boxes to move out. There was no way Mrs. Jenkins would object to his vacating the apartment two days early. Hey, maybe he could wrangle some frequent flyer miles out of this deal. Wasn't Japan about ten thousand miles round trip?

Holy nightmare, thousands of miles on a plane. In coach. He peeked at the ticket. Groan. He really didn't want to go to Japan. At least not *this* Friday. Sure, some other time, Japan would be great. Not tomorrow. The promotion was pending—but so were layoffs. Not that he should worry about those.

Still, his mom needed him; he might as well go and make the best of it. He owed them a lot more than simply taking a vacation with them. After all, it was ten days out of his life. What could happen in ten days?

He ran his fingers through his hair and huffed in exhaustion. Japan. And now, to Alison. Hot fear pooled in his gut.

Buck stopped by the men's room to freshen up. With a little

water on his fingers he smoothed aside some of that long blond hair. He pulled at his left eye. If he stood up straight, squared his shoulders, maybe—just maybe—he could pull it off, as long as he kept the goofiness out of his grin. He practiced a captivating smile, a casual smile, a winning smile. There. The right choice, the one he wore during his promotion interview. Yes. He got a vision of her hair shaking free behind her, and his heart kick-started again. Geez. He'd look like a beet in a dress shirt by the time he got out front.

As he passed his desk his phone rang. Stupid thing. Oh, but it could be Alison. In case it was, he should wait 'til the third ring— the perfect blend of *I'm busy, but not too busy for you, Alison.* How should he answer? *Hi, Alison. Oh, hi, Alison. Hi. Alison. You look nice today. Hi, Alison. You called?* No. He didn't want to sound like other guys, guys with lines. She'd probably heard a million lines.

Third ring. He gritted his teeth and picked up. "Hello?"

"Hi, Mr. Buck." Alison's angelic voice made Buck's upper lip quiver. "Hello? Yes, Mr. Buck. Sorry, I've been on the phone and then at break since I called you, in case you came by. Anyhow, it's about lunch."

Jackpot! He straightened his tie, and sat up tall.

"Lunch?"

"Yeah. Lunch. I'm *so* glad you understand. So many people around here are, you know."

"I understand." His breath came in ragged gasps. Idiot. He'd better calm down.

"Great! So great. So, you're available?"

Deep, cleansing breath. "Y-yeah." Whoa yeah. He was so very, very available.

"Good. Then is it all right if I forward the calls to your desk while I'm out, or would you rather come and sit up front and take them here? I mean, this is so great of you. Wow. The whole office, *everybody,* is going out to lunch and we totally needed someone—one of the better English speakers—to take the phones because we can't really just send every call to voice mail, you know. And, like, we're all going out to Charlie Unger's because, like, it's Trisha's birthday today and since she's the manager of our whole floor, we have to do something for her, and she loves Charlie's a ton, and we're just all so totally pumped that one of us is going to get the promotion and work directly with Trisha, because we all work out at the same gym, and it would be so fun to just spend even *more* time with such cool awesome people! So, we're making today a real celebration for everyone at lunch before we all head over to watch the Rangers game tonight together, since we're all such uber-fans. So, is around two hours going to be too long? You're not busy or anything, are you? I'll just program it to send the calls back to you. Great! You're the best, Mr. Buck."

His hand went limp, and the receiver slipped from his grip back onto its cradle. Within a few seconds, his phone began ringing—on four lines at once. He stared at the blinking lights.

What had he been thinking? A girl like that, and a guy his size? Every ring stung.

"Ar-har-har-har." Ranjit's laugh penetrated Buck's innards like a knife—one of those curly scary ones from India. "Heard the whole thing, Bucky boy. Ar-har-har." Ranjit stopped pushing his file cart. "That girl is made of Thai chilies she's so hot, and you? Look at you, pal. She'd never let you anywhere near her. What were you thinking? That she'd think you were a gentleman and treat her nice and fall all over you? Girls like that don't go for nice. They go for money. And abdominal muscles."

Stinging needles pricked the back of Buck's eyes. He clenched his fist. Why couldn't a universe exist where the fat guy could hope to get the girl?

"You should go analyze those drug trials, Ranjit."

But he didn't go away. He reached across Buck and whipped the plane ticket off his desk.

"What's *this*? You? Going to Japan? You?" Ranjit shuddered in his shiny, green silk shirt. "That country? You thought you were big for America. Cowabunga, baby." He stared closer at the ticket then waved it in Buck's face. "They got you flying *coach*. That ought to be a bad experience for everyone involved. Ar-har-har-har." He wiped a bit of spittle from his chin.

"But seriously, Bucky boy, Japan is the sweetness. It's like a sea of wonderful blackberries, ripe for the taking. Especially around four in the afternoon when all those high school girlies come mincing out in their tempting school uniforms. Long, sleek black hair, naughty blue plaid miniskirts. Feast for the eyes, Buck my boy."

Buck bit back a gag reflex. "That is so wrong, man."

"Wait until you see it for yourself, and then tell me it's wrong. Hey, there's enough of you to go around for six or seven of those innocent little berries. Splat! Have fun, Mr. Nice Guy." Ranjit the Horrible left. May the lecher never set foot in Asia again. Somebody needed to protect the women of the world from predators like that.

Ten days in Japan. At least it meant ten days away from this place.

Ignoring all the rings, he picked up his phone and got an inside line. He dialed Trisha the manager's number and got her voice mail.

"Yeah, this is Buck Cooper on the QC Team. I need to go out of town for the next ten days. Family business. If that's a problem can you give me a call?"

Trisha didn't call.

二

THE MOST BEAUTIFUL
SEPTEMBER. TOKYO

Buck wedged himself into the narrow chair of the stuffy JAL 747, his bulk spilling over into the seats on either side of him to the great dismay of the stern Japanese businessman on his left and the sour, pink-haired, teenage Goth chick on his right. The Coopers couldn't get seats together.

"Japan Airlines is here to serve you." A pert, pale-faced beauty with the sleek dark hair of Ranjit's daydreams offered Buck a hot washcloth.

He didn't know quite what to do with it. He blotted the rivulets of sweat coursing down his forehead and neck and then handed it back to the flight attendant. Her face didn't register any disgust. *That's what makes you a professional.*

After the plane took off he half-smiled at his row-mates, who scowled back.

The lunch offerings came around. The pink-haired girl muttered something like, "Go on a diet, dude," when he asked for the hot meal instead of the sandwich box. "What are ya, anyways? Some kind of wannabe sumo wrestler?"

Out the window brilliant stars shone. It must be late. For a long while he couldn't rest, even if his body, exhausted and sore from moving everything he owned into his parents' garage last night, tried to insist.

Once again they came to his rescue, those good folks, letting him stash his sofa in there. For now. Not a great achievement to move back in with his parents at age twenty-four, but under the circumstances, he had no choice. Still, it had loser written all over it. What did they call that, failure to launch? Buck cringed. No. It was only for a few days. As soon as he got back, a short ten days from now, he'd find a different place, somewhere with more space, maybe even somewhere where he could see the sky at night. Until then, he'd try and show his parents his gratitude for their generosity by being a good sport on this trip. And someday he would repay their kindness somehow. Yeah.

Sleep overtook him. Dreams crowded in, dreams of fighting off packs of wild ninjas, giving roundhouse kicks to the chin to stop attackers from robbing his mom and dad. *"Son, we always knew you would repay us."*

He woke up. Goth chick on the aisle was gone so he stretched his legs and walked around the cabin for a minute, but his parents were both asleep. With no one to talk to, he returned to his sardine can of a chair and dozed.

Worried dreams charged at him like wild kamikaze pilots, crashing and burning in his mind. Buck wandered aimlessly in ancient Japan. No one understood him, and he understood no one. Native people barely as tall as his waist pointed fingers in ridicule at his fat, at his height, and threw buckets of rice and fish at him as he spent ten days starving.

He awoke in a cold sweat and stared wild-eyed around the dim plane.

Come on, Buck. He slapped his cheek and dragged his hand down it. It wouldn't be that bad. It was only ten days. He'd been the butt of fat jokes all his life. So what if it happened in another hemisphere? On the other hand, maybe this trip would start his crash diet and he'd come home a new, improved Buck—leaner, meaner, and much closer to his after-photo weight.

If only.

Zoom, zoom, those kamikaze saboteurs dive-bombed him. The promotion. Alison. His dad and mom and their huge Nangrimax business deal. Eaglestone's impending layoffs and how much his workload might change. The outcome of his quality control study on the new cancer drug at work. His own health—or lack of it.

A future alone.

Hours later, Buck rode the buzzing escalator down toward the baggage claim. His parents, still groggy, didn't speak much. Buck let his eyes sweep across the open expanse of a sea of black heads, dark suits, black suitcases—quite a contrast to the light gray and polished metal of Narita Airport. Holy cats. He was the sorest of all possible sore thumbs. Six-foot-six in a five-foot-two world. Four hundred pounds in one-fifty land. Fee fi fo fum. He gripped the rubber railing.

Ten days. Just ten days until he would be back here, riding the escalator back up toward the gates. He could do anything for a week and a half.

An automated female voice at the bottom of the escalator chimed, *"Ki wo tsukete kudasai,"* which sounded like Rikki Tikki Tavi, that mongoose from *The Jungle Books*. Wrong continent—correction, subcontinent.

A taxi swept them from the airport, and Buck's dad called a steady stream of directions to the driver while consulting a map filled with hen scratches. Luckily, the driver ignored or didn't understand him.

Seventeen hours on a plane built for the Lollipop Guild Munchkins of Munchkin Land, and Buck slumped like a wet pile of ramen in the cab's back seat. Maybe the stewardess bludgeoned him in his sleep on the flight. Revenge for that sweat mop he handed her.

So far, downtown Tokyo looked like any other typical large city. Gray everything, with flashes of neon. A concrete blur. Maybe this was how Superman saw the world.

"Buck. We're almost there." Buck's dad clenched his son's arm. "We need this to work. I've talked with Yoshida over the phone, and I gather they're real formal people. Me, I'm an old Texan and don't know how to be formal. But your mother and I have a lot riding on this. A lot." His brow clouded.

"So, son, and Cissie my dear, let's all put on our best charm with the Yoshida family." He winced. "Without Mr. Yoshida's backing, the product will never go anywhere in Japan, and maybe nowhere else neither." He patted his wife's hand, over the white knuckles that held his arm in a death grip.

The taxi pulled up in front of a house, not big by Texas standards, but at least not an apartment building with laundry airing over balcony railings fifty stories up like the countless ones they'd just passed. The Yoshidas must have serious money for this kind of real estate.

"Is there anything specific I can do to help?" Buck should have asked this long before they got on the plane, not as they were exiting the taxi in front of the Yoshidas' house.

"Not unless you know how to get approval for the product through the Japanese bureaucracy." His dad smirked, and the door to the house flung open.

"*Ah, yokoso! Konnichiwa.*" Mr. Yoshida threw out wide arms in greeting but did not extend a hand to shake. After the arm throwing he made a simple bow instead. Behind him bobbed three other dark heads, Mrs. Yoshida and two sons, all with polite smiles. Buck glanced around to see if anyone else shook hands. No one did. Lots of bowing, however, and Buck decided to join the party. He bowed to Mr. Yoshida, Mrs. Yoshida, their older son, who looked about twenty, and their younger son, a teenager.

All of them mysteriously had the same name: Yoshida-*san*. Boy, that could make it easy on him as a visitor, but kind of complicated for them around home. It reminded him of that Dr. Seuss book where the woman had thirty-nine boys, and she named them all Dave.

"I'm Hank Cooper, and this is my wife Cissie." Buck's parents stuck out their hands, then withdrew them and tried awkward bows.

"*Hajimemashite.*" Mr. Yoshida bowed in return. "Ah, so. This must be Baku." He turned to Buck, and it took a second to realize why the man made a particular bow toward him. Baku. Buck. Got it. "*Wahhhh. Nan senchi desho ka naaah.* You are so *beri beri* tall." Mr. Yoshida sized him up, raising his arm skyward. Sure enough, Buck stood more than tall next to the Yoshidas. He was a Colossus.

"Pleased to meet you, Baku-*san*." Mrs. Yoshida inclined her head a bit. She wore too much bright red lipstick, but otherwise had a pleasant appearance. Her English, though heavy with accent, floated straight through his ears and into his brain. Suddenly, his years at Eaglestone, that hub of diversity and thick accents, came in handy. "So tall! And you looks so fat." She made "fat guy" gestures with her hands.

Buck didn't know how to respond. Thank you?

Then, the teenage son stepped forward and patted, full hand, on Buck's belly. "Do you sumo?"

At this, Buck's smile cracked into a genuine one. "Sumo? That's a good one."

"Does your son likes sumo?" Mr. Yoshida turned to Buck's dad, whose face flashed a moment of terror before shooting Buck a look that said, *Son, you better answer this right, or we are so cooked.*

"To tell you the truth, I don't know. I've never seen it."

The teenage Yoshida gasped. "You have never before seen sumo?" He clutched his heart. "No way!" Then he began speaking fast Japanese to his family, and Buck gave up following the meaning.

"Please, come inside my home." The mother waved them house-ward.

Buck followed his parents into a small cement entryway. A step up, about two feet higher, sat the flooring of what looked like the main house. Several pairs of shoes lined the lower cement floor and a few pairs of slippers sat on the straw mats of the higher house flooring.

Buck studied Mr. Yoshida as he entered backwards. In one smooth movement the man removed his shoes by using the lip of the step then let them drop, plunk plunk, in the entryway. Up top he donned the slippers and shuffled down the straw mat floor of the hall and into the house. Mrs. Yoshida did the same, as did the two Yoshida-*san* boys.

It took some effort to hoist himself doing that spinning, shoe-flipping thing, but Buck made it and put on the largest pair of waiting slippers. His heels hung over the back, but they could be comfortable. Sort of.

Unfortunately, his mother had been too engrossed in the home décor to notice the shoe operation.

"Why, look at this scroll. Isn't it magnificent? Buck, your Aunt Nan would just *love* something like this in her front entryway." Buck's mom wandered up the step and into the house. "I just love what you've done with this flower arrangement here. Is it some kind of *banzai*?"

"We say *bonsai*," Mrs. Yoshida replied, turning around to make her explanation. Then her eyes tilted toward the floor where Buck's mom stood.

Buck watched the whole incident before him unfold as if in

slow motion. Mrs. Yoshida went from happy-hostess to abject horror. Her eyes peeled open and her mouth formed a perfect O.

Buck's mom had stepped into the house-proper still wearing her street shoes.

Mrs. Yoshida flew toward her houseguest, all atwitter in Japanese, red lips sputtering, and guided her with a gentle arm back down the step onto the entryway.

"Oh, excuse me. Excuse me so much. In Japan, we leave shoes in the *genkan*."

His mom, poor thing, went red from tip to toes. In her life back home, Cissie Cooper stood as a paragon of manners. Buck saw her crumple and could imagine her reliving this moment for decades to come. Maybe it was a good thing Buck came along after all. They'd need to stick together to navigate strange waters.

Buck went to her and set her slippers in a convenient place to put them on. Then he gripped his father's shoulder and whispered, "Dad. Take off the shoes. Leave them here. Seriously."

His dad tuned in, "What? Oh, I get it. Slippers," and did as he was told. Buck breathed a sigh of relief.

Boy, he was going to have to pay close attention to how things were done around here. If a foreigner could turn a sweet Japanese woman horrified with nothing but a shoe, Buck needed to watch his every move. All of them did, or his father's deal could evaporate.

THAT NIGHT, BUCK SLEPT LIKE the dead. When he awoke, he emerged in a groggy haze to find himself alone in the house. No Yoshidas. No mom or dad. Just Buck. People were probably at work and school. Strange, it didn't bother him being alone in this place. Somehow something felt different inside him today.

Clocks read twelve-thirty, and Buck's stomach told him lunch called. For a minute, he considered rummaging through the refrigerator, but he didn't know protocol and decided against it. No sense taking a risk when there had to be a little eatery somewhere nearby.

But he needed to wash first. The straw mat flooring squeaked beneath him as he made his way toward what he recalled as the washroom, the mats slick under his feet, cool and dry despite the humidity of the late summer day. While he stared down at their bamboo grain, his head smacked into a low-hung beam that separated the two rooms. *Thunk!* No, he looked again. It wasn't a random beam—it was the doorframe itself. Ouch. Japanese construction obviously didn't take the possibility of people six-feet-six into consideration.

He lifted a hand to the painful spot. Great. A nice big welt on top of his head would look super cool. But glowing neon mark or not, he still needed to get something to eat. He would have to shelve his embarrassment and get out there.

In his regular life, Buck might not have gone sallying forth into an unknown world, but this morning a boldness filled him. Maybe the bump on the head caused it. Or something in the Tokyo air made him expand to larger than life. And not in the usual bad way.

Back in his room after bathing, he rummaged through his bag and pulled out a wad of yen he'd exchanged at the airport. That had better be enough for a meal. He dug out his travel dictionary where he had written down the Yoshidas' address so he could get home here again.

Outside, shoes back on, he first cast his eyes on daytime Japan. Tokyo loomed upwards all around him. Skyscrapers, trees, power lines all pressed upward and inward toward him. Nowhere in Dallas felt like this.

First off, he noticed the utter lack of space between the homes on the Yoshidas' street. Barely inches separated some of them. Then came the lack of space in the homes themselves. While the

Yoshida family lived in a broad home with nice landscaping of tiered topiaries and flowering bushes, three houses down sat another detached dwelling. Buck stretched his arms to estimate exactly how narrow this place was. No wider than Buck's arm span of six feet six inches. Man, who could live here?

Just as he asked himself this, a woman's face poked out the front door. It was as mottled and brown as a dried up apple, and sunken in at the teeth, but the eyes popped wide when they spied Buck. *"Sugoi!"* Then she gave her head a quick bob and pulled back inside the door. It shut with a click.

Buck continued grinning at the wide (and narrow) new world of Tokyo as he wandered along. Eventually, he emerged from the residential district into a little street of shops. Each gray stone or stucco building had a large front window with an awning. Wafting from the open front doors came various scents—incense, soy, fresh bread, raw fish. A sound system attached to one of the street lamps sent down strains of a pop song, a bubble gum beat with techno synthesized joy pulsating for the pleasure of the shoppers. Buck's chest did an instinctive jive.

That area then opened up into a wider shopping area. The world according to this street was sherbet-colored and bobbing with zillions of Mylar *Hello! Kitty* balloons. Scores of spiky haired teenagers sat on their haunches. Old women pulled wheeled carts. But no restaurants.

By this time, he needed a drink even more than he needed food. Maybe there was a vending machine. He scanned the area, and whoa. There appeared to be one every ten paces along the whole shopping street, almost between each pair of stores. He fished his pocket for some coins, but stopped short when he examined the contents of the first machine.

Farm fresh eggs.

Uh, weird. Not what he was expecting as a refreshing beverage.

He dropped his coins back in his pocket and moved on to the next machine a few yards away. No dice. These offered ten-pound bags of rice in eight different varieties. Beside them stood a selection of Rhinoceros Beetles. Real ones—alive and crawling. Unbelievable. He could love a place that sold beetles for coinage.

Eventually, after passing a dozen more boxes, featuring toilet paper, fishing hooks and bait, hot ramen, underwear, and *lots* of cigarettes, he found a drink vendor. At last!

"Ah, Nomimasuka?" A teenage kid walked up and raised an invisible can to his lips. *"Cow-piss. Oishii yo!"* and he bobbed his head with energy and shoved coins into the machine. He chose the one called Calpis, a clear bottle with blue polka dots on it and a milk-looking drink sloshing inside. The kid took a long guzzle and walked away. Buck turned back to the machine. His only other choice was something called Pocari Sweat.

Sweat or cow piss. *Two* refreshing choices.

Buck conjured up an image of one factory where workers who perspired on treadmills were scraped with a spatula in their efforts to collect big vats of sweat for the drink, and another factory where cows stood in line for urine collection. Come on. Who test-marketed these things? Buck shuddered. Then, on second thought, he might as well man up and give it a try.

The coins delivered his liquid sweat-refreshment in a tall blue can. It tasted kind of like energy drinks back in the U.S., and he downed it in a hurry, hoping not to savor the taste of sweat too much. Pretty good. He bought a second, as well as a Calpis for good measure.

"America! America! Sumo! Sumo!" Suddenly he found himself besieged by short people—children—yapping around him like puppies, shouting and laughing and pulling at his sleeve. They all wore matching navy blue uniforms and carried yellow umbrellas. But they weren't jeering. Instead, he saw in their faces joy.

Buck smiled at them all and gave them high fives. They squealed and jumped up and down. Several of them patted their own arms—insistently. Buck rubbed his chin in confusion. They patted harder and held out their forearms until, at last, Buck reached out and showed them his arm. As soon as he did, the children went wild. A dozen hands petted Buck's hairy arm. Buck smiled until one kid pulled at the individual hairs.

"Ouch. Hey." Buck yanked his arm away and smoothed the hairs back down. The kids laughed and catcalled before running away. Buck's stomach growled, a cross between a Cuisinart and a cement mixer. He had to have something soon. Preferably something without an exoskeleton. Impressing Alison Turner with his super sexy body or not, he couldn't just go cold turkey on eating. Buck needed food. Cold turkey. His head swam.

A street vendor stood on a busy corner beside a cart with steaming tins. Buck glanced in, looking for Polish sausages or pretzels. Wrong. In the vats of water lay—Buck couldn't say what—what smelled vaguely of fish sticks but looked more like giant macaroni shapes: long tubes, triangles, flat circles, all white but splotched with brown like a tortilla. Uh, no. Not today. Today, he needed something more reminiscent of actual food. He shrugged a smiling "sorry" at the vendor. The light at the busy crosswalk changed and signaled the crowd to walk.

Tires squealed half a block down. A car tore around the corner and screamed down the block toward them. The bulk of the pedestrians scrambled back onto the curb.

But not everyone. A silver-haired man in a business suit talking on a cell phone stepped off the curb and into the car's path. In an uncommon burst of speed, Buck lurched into action, shoving his way through the mass of bodies and leaped forward into the path of the renegade car. With both hands, he seized the back of the oblivious man's suit coat. It took both the force of all his strength and weight leaning backward to jerk the man out of the path, slamming himself next to the man onto the sidewalk and to safety just in time. The crowd parted for them amid shrieks. The idiot in the car tore past, horn honking all the way down the block followed by a police car, siren blaring.

Buck heaved a huge breath and turned to the guy, who lay stunned, stomach down, on the concrete. They both stared at each other, dazed. Buck popped up and helped the man to his feet. The crowd was still gasping.

The businessman slapped his head and checked himself all over. *"Sugoi! Doh-shita no."* Then he bowed to Buck. "Thank you very much! You are American, yes?"

Buck nodded, grateful to his very soul for fast reflexes. The man looked different from most of the other Japanese he'd seen, with longish silver hair parted down the middle and a bushy black mustache. Terror made his eyes bright.

"I cannot believe this. You saved my life. I have very important meeting today. If you are not here, maybe things would become very different. I am in your deep debt." The man bowed as deep as his debt.

Buck bowed in return. "No, please. It was nothing." He shrugged and grinned, his usual. "You would have done the same for me."

"Ah." The man gave Buck a once-over. "I think it is not possible for me."

Ah, the fat. Buck got it.

"Please. Let me pay you."

"Aw. You keep that there money, sir." Buck put up his hand to refuse it.

"So honorable. But I will do something for you, someday. I will not forget you. Here." He reached into his pocket and drew out a business card. Holding it in both hands, bowing, he extended it.

"If ever, ever you are in need of help of any kind while you are in Japan, do not pause. Ask me. I am your servant." He bowed again. Buck took the card with the same formality. The light changed and the man resumed crossing the street—safely this time—surrounded by a sea of other businessmen.

A soft, feminine voice sounded in Buck's ear. "Ah, excuse me?"

Buck turned around.

The sight electrified him. She was a foot and a half shorter than Buck, but she still looked statuesque in her swaying sundress. Long, obsidian hair tumbled over her shoulders in big, loose curls. Hazel eyes warmed him to his core. Were there flecks of gold in them?

"I saw what you did. It was heroic." Perfect, British-accented English came from a beautiful mouth. The tiny thing dipped her lashes in embarrassment when his eyes searched hers. A blush rose to her cheeks, which had the most fetching dimples *of all time.*

Then his own face grew hot, probably from the molten lava his heart just became.

She placed her fingers over her heart. "Such courage! Seeing you, I know now what I must do." She lifted those gold-flecked eyes to his and reached out to him. When her hand rested on his arm, an impossible thing happened—Buck felt weightless.

Before he could resurrect his voice, she whisked her way down the street, and left him standing there staring after her disappearing beauty.

三

ONE WONDERFUL SUNDAY
SEPTEMBER. TOKYO

Buck climbed out of the taxi back at the Yoshidas' place, his stomach finally full with those tortilla tubes—which ended up tasting like fish hot dogs, not half bad. The younger Yoshida-*san* kid bounced up and down on the outside stoop as Buck walked up.

"You are here! You are here! Coopah-*san*, we have to leave right now!"

"Where's the fire, Smokey?" Buck patted his shoulder to calm him down.

"We want to be there for the beginning." Youngest Yoshida-*san* bounced up and down and side to side. He wore a designer hoodie and a chain necklace. His hair spiked right at the part. Buck had that hairstyle when he was ten.

"Slow down, man." Buck grinned and patted the hopper on the shoulder. "What 'beginning' are you talking about?"

"Sumo! We have tickets for today's *basho* at the Kokugikan. Let's go!"

Normally, Buck would've had to mull it over before deciding to go to something called "the *basho* at the Kokugikan." Oh, well. Japan created the New Buck.

Buck turned on his heel and followed this kid down the sidewalk and out to a bigger street where Yoshida-*san* hailed a cab.

In the cab, the kid talked nonstop about sumo, dropping names and vocabulary Buck couldn't hope to follow. In the midst of it all, however, he gave Buck the most useful piece of information he'd had all day, "You can call me Hiro, by the way. I'm fifteen, and I'm going to be a sumo commentator someday."

"Good for you, Hiro. You go for that. You can call me Buck."

"Buck. I like it. Buck, Buck, Buck." Hiro looked up at Buck like he was some fascinating giant. "I like your long hair, too. So wavy. It could already go into *chonmage* so easily. No problem."

"What's that?" Buck had better start asking questions if he ever hoped to get a grip on the wild world around him.

"*Chonmage?* It's the sumo hairstyle—the topknot. You know?"

Buck dredged up an image of a sumo wrestler's hair. Ah, yeah. The ponytail thing on the crown of the head. He'd never seen a blond one. Maybe no one had.

"How come your English is so good, Hiro?"

"Aw, not that good, really." Hiro's head dipped a moment. "I did a home stay two years ago. I lived in Kansas City!"

That explained it. The kid could spew English faster than a lot of people back at Buck's high school, though that wasn't saying much.

The cab whizzed through Tokyo traffic at breakneck speed. The air, even in the car, smelled of fish and soy and exhaust. They raced past ten million bike riders, old men smoking cigarettes, a children's park with towering trees, and a huge metal dinosaur.

When the taxi stopped, Buck and Hiro piled out. A massive square building loomed from atop scores of steps.

"It's the Kokugikan!" Hiro shouted, grabbing Buck by the hand, tugging him toward the doors. The place reminded Buck of a convention center—Dallas was chock full of those. The only thing the two story box with the green metal roof lacked was a ridiculous parking lot sprawling a mile around the place.

Bodies, all shorter than Buck, topped by heads of straight, black hair, streamed up from the subway station and in through the double doors.

"Buck! Do you love it? You do! Look! The place is filling up. We have great seats. You will love it. You will!"

Inside, it reminded Buck of the basketball arena back at college, except the seating areas rose up in four sides, a square. In place of the basketball court down center stood a much smaller square stage about the size of a boxing ring but without the ropes. Above, on the metal scaffolding ceiling, hung rows of enormous tapestries of fat guys wearing nothing but towels at their waists—and no abs to merit the exposure. Buck instinctively ran his hands over where his own abs might be, buried deep down inside.

Suspended about fifteen feet above the boxing ring hung the bonus feature of the day: a little house. Or, at least the wooden roof of a little cottage, suspended by cables from the ceiling and floating directly over the stage. From the edges of its ridgepole extended some wooden swords. Purple curtains dangled around the base of the roof where walls ought to come down, and big, fringed tassels hung on each corner. All this might have blocked a fan's view, but the half-house hung far enough above the playing surface that anyone in the audience could still see the action.

Sweet. Buck loved the strangeness of it all. What if boxing rings had this? What if sumo wrestlers' mamas nationwide hollered, "If you're going to fight and wrestle, do it inside the house."

Hiro guided Buck through the crowd. They descended the stairway down, down, down toward the competition floor. Just how close to the stage would they be? Hundreds of people were already seated, talking, rattling programs. Through the din of the crowd he could distinguish a familiar word here and there, and much to his surprise, they were directed at him.

"*America!* Big! Big *America-jin* sumo guy!"

Buck turned his head and shot his usual strained smile toward the calls from the crowd. However, he got a surprising reaction—smiles in return, and shouts of approval.

What was going on? Thousands of people had come to cheer for—and not jeer at—big, fat guys.

Buck hadn't just gotten up on the other side of the earth. He'd stepped into an alternate universe where the general populace hung happy banners of worship for guys who looked like he did. Warmth thawed a perennial glacier inside him.

The faces on the tapestries stared down at him from above.

He directed his eyes back toward the steps beneath his fast-descending gait, glad for his good sense of balance.

"We sit there, Buck." Hiro pointed to a pair of empty chairs close to ringside. Buck wondered how much the Yoshidas shelled out for such good seats, considering the high price of everything he'd seen in this country. Looking down, he balked at the narrow platform of a chair and winced as he mashed himself into it. He glanced at his neighbor, expecting the usual scowl and saw that beside him sat a young Japanese man. The guy looked up at Buck, and his eyes widened. With wonder, not contempt.

"*Sugoi!*" The guy smacked his forehead beneath his slicked-back hair. There was that word again. "You are American?"

Buck nodded, and the guy's eyes lit up.

"I have a friend. My friend lives in New York City. Shimada is his name. Do you know him?"

"Uh, no?" Buck chuckled. A zillion people lived in New York. Imagine calculating the infinitesimally small probability that he, a guy who hardly set foot outside Texas his whole life, would know one random Japanese guy in a city two thousand miles from his home.

"Sorry." Buck shrugged. "But if I meet him someday, I'll tell him you said hi."

"Shh! Buck! The *taiko* drums will start!" Hiro sat forward. A dozen soul-penetrating drums pounded through the air. At the far side of the ring stood a troupe of bandana-headed men wielding thick wooden sticks and pounding on large kettledrums in rhythm. Their arms struck, hard and synchronous. The sound vibrated into his chest and arms and past his hair. The drummers pummeled the skins of the drums with such force it was almost like a battle.

The drumming lasted several minutes and got the crowd warmed up. Then all was silent. Something big was about to happen.

And it did.

From somewhere in the darker recesses of the crowd marched the sumo wrestlers. He speed-counted fifty-four giants, arms folded across their broad chests, blocking their man-boobs as they entered the arena to the roar of the screaming crowd. He wanted to avert his eyes at first. These tubbalards wore only bright colored lava-lava wraps hanging from their non-existent waists. The aprons looked like the upholstery from a Chinese restaurant turned into shiny bath towels. From his seat, Buck could see just how enormous these guys were. For the first time in his life, he didn't feel like the Jolly Blond Giant. By comparison, Buck was an average Joe.

Nonstop bowing ensued, followed by more yelling on the loud-speaker, some ceremonial walking around the painted ring on the platform, and then the wrestlers marched off again. Buck wondered if it was over already.

Hiro explained. "They will go and prepare for their matches, change into their fighting *mawashi,* the sash around their loins. Today is the sixth day of the *basho.*"

Mawashi. The diaper. Yeah.

"A seven-day tournament?"

"No. Fifteen days. They each wrestle one time per day. They

match up against another *rikishi* in their group once only. No rematches. There is a formula, but more or less it is this: if they beat someone higher ranked, they move up a ranking at the next *basho*."

Wait a minute. There were statistics involved? With formulas? Buck's interest shot up. He needed to know about the rankings. No, he needed to know about everything. Was it like baseball? Did someone keep the stats somewhere official? Did individual wrestlers have scoring histories? How did they win? Were there different moves? He barely knew where to start pumping Hiro for information.

"So, they compete against other wrestlers in their group. How many groups are there?"

"In the Grand Sumo there are ten levels. Lowest is *jonoku-chi*. Look, here's a chart." Hiro opened the paper program and pointed to a pyramid graph. Buck studied it like a menu at a new barbecue restaurant.

"There are a different number of competitors in each level. *Jonokuchi*, about sixty of them, compete against their own level, plus against a couple of the bottom ranked sumo wrestlers in the next group up, which is *jonidan*. There are usually about two hundred and fifty of those. As they climb the ranks it works the same way." Hiro's voice sparkled. He reached into his backpack and dug out a cellophane bag of peanuts. They smelled of soy sauce. "Best win-loss scores advance to the next higher level at the next tournament. Promotion! The worst win-loss records will bump down a level. Demotion!"

Buck pulled at his chin and considered this. Several levels, all competing mostly against other members of their own level, but trying to move up the ranks to fight for spots in the higher group. Got it. *Man, this stuff is great.* Who knew?

Hiro pointed to the level called *sandanme.* About two hundred men competed there, but it narrowed down to 120 for the *makush-ita* rank.

"These bottom four groups are all non-professional. Amateurs!" He held the paper up and rattled it. "They compete early in the day, and the farther up the pyramid you go, the better the competition. The real champions compete last." Hiro spoke with his mouth full of the peanuts, chomping, and eyes alive. He sounded like an American kid who knew his Baltimore Orioles or his Dallas Cowboys like catechism.

"The center section is called *juryo*. Twenty-eight of them. Always. They may be the lowest ranked pros, but they are still super great."

Buck loved to hear Hiro's Japanese accent when he said the words "super great." Hiro sounded super great.

"And the top tier?"

"Those, yes. Those are the supernova stars of sumo." Hiro looked skyward. "The top tier includes the top five levels. You saw them after the *taiko* drums."

Yes, all fifty-four monstrous whales of men. Buck tried to repeat Hiro's words in his mind, and he knew he was messing them up.

"*Taiko?*"

"Right," Hiro played air drums. "Loud drums. Only the best of the best gets into the top level. Very competitive. The best right now is this man." Hiro pointed to the tip of the pyramid and scowled. "Butaniku."

"I'm sorry?"

"That is the sumo name of the current grand champion, the *yokozuna*. Butaniku." Hiro spat the name. Apparently, Butaniku sat higher in the lists than he did in this fan's estimation.

"What's wrong with him?"

"Everything." Hiro pushed out his lower lip and refused to elaborate.

Buck sat back to bask in it. Fascinating. No, *awesome.* A little pool of happiness began to bubble up in his soul. Super great. "You have a favorite, I bet." Buck elbowed Hiro in the ribs.

"Oh, yeah. Torakiba." Hiro practically genuflected. The guy must be good.

Torakiba. It about twisted Buck's brain in a knot trying to remember it. To-ra-ki-ba. He would get this eventually. He would.

"They compete today?"

"At the end. Like I say, they save the best for last."

The last of the massive men marched up the diagonal path out of sight, and the crowd quieted down. Men, women, teenagers, old people, all with the black hair, all with similar faces. Buck's statistician's eye approximated fifteen thousand seats in this place, probably eighty percent packed, and only day six of a fifteen-day competition? The excitement in the arena was palpable. Buck's soul began to hum along with the electricity in the air.

"When does it start?" There seemed to be a lot of hurry up and wait.

"Not until after the comic sumo." At Buck's shrug of confusion, Hiro continued. "This part of sumo they do a short show. It is funny. Sometimes a big wrestler fights a skinny man, or sometimes they show how 'not' to sumo. Once I heard they called a fat woman from the audience and forced her to wrestle. It was not in Tokyo, though—Fukuoka, I think." Hiro scowled. "Women do not sumo." He spoke this as though a woman in sumo were a sacrilege.

Okay. Buck's western upbringing questioned that issue. A lot. He changed the subject.

"I don't get it. How do you win?" Buck reached into Hiro's proffered peanut bag. Not peanuts—they were some kind of peanut-shaped rice cracker, shiny, tasted like soy and sushi. They could grow on him.

"It is simple." Hiro sat up straighter. "There is the ring." He pointed to the stage area. It was about three feet high and about fifteen feet square. On it was painted a ring with two parallel lines of paint inside, a few feet apart. From above, the ring looked like a giant electrical outlet.

"Each man tries to push his opponent out of the ring, or make him touch the ground with any part of his body other than the bottom of his foot."

Okay. Simple.

"So, the big guys face the big guys, and the medium guys face the medium guys?" Buck asked this and remembered there wasn't a single medium guy in the pack.

"No weight classes. Every wrestler competes against every other wrestler in his level, no matter their weight. Yes, the heavier men have advantage, even when they are strong to start with. That is why they eat so much *chanko nabe*."

"What's that?" It sounded like Campbell's Chunky Soup. Or blowing chunks.

"Thick soup with meat and cabbage and eggs and bean sprouts. Very filling. Special sumo food."

The truth lay somewhere in the middle.

"Is it good?" Buck's stomach growled when he heard about the soup. It had been a while since the fish hot dogs.

A man of incredible energy started shouting through the loud-speaker. Hiro translated.

"The comic sumo is starting. It sounds like...they will do three skits. The first two are traditional, like I explained. The third will have a surprise guest star." Hiro sounded dismayed. "They will be selecting a member of the audience." He frowned and huffed in irritation. "If it is a woman, I am sorry, Buck. I will have to leave."

Hiro, defender of tradition. Buck couldn't afford to be a purist. He was just wrapping his head around it all.

It began.

The slapstick skit needed no words. The small man approached the massive sumo wrestler with a cocky attitude and got trounced. In the second play, two ancient sumo wrestlers went at each other with decrepit vigor and then simultaneously fell backwards onto the floor into deep sleep.

Buck laughed along with the audience. The guys' wrinkles-a-flapping made Buck chuckle. Hiro looked up at him and gave a broad smile. Buck liked this kid.

"Someday, Buck, I want to be a sumo commentator. Did I tell you this already? It's my life-dream!"

The lights suddenly snapped off, leaving Buck in inky darkness, wondering whether he had his own "life-dream." The loudspeaker's voice rumbled, with a drum roll of Japanese ilk bumping behind it. Buck had no understanding of the words, but he knew they were introducing the guest wrestler. Who could it be? Some international star even Buck would recognize? He let his mind wander through possible celebrities as his eyes followed the moving spotlight from one section to another in the arena.

When the spotlight came to a stop, it was shining directly into Buck's eyes. His hand flew to shade them.

"It's you, Buck!"

"It's me? What's me?" A rush of hot fear sloshed up from his gut and colored his neck and head red.

"You're on the TV screen up there—quick, smile!"

Buck squinted, smiling in confusion, but then he realized almost fifteen thousand people were staring at him and screaming. Horror. He strained out his best grin, looking back and forth to no avail. The spotlight blinded him. What was going on? How long would they torture him with this fierce glare? Move it along, already. Yeah, fat guy in the audience here—fat enough to be a blond sumo wrestler. Fine. Pick on someone else now.

But the light didn't dissipate, and the audience started chanting and clapping. Then the clapping got rhythmical, and soon Hiro joined it, too. All the air sucked out of Buck's lungs, like someone just opened an airplane door. Where was that dangly air mask when he needed it?

"You need to stand up, Buck. Go toward the ring."

Go toward the light was more like it.

四

THE SEA IS WATCHING
SEPTEMBER. TOKYO

"You're kidding. You're kidding, right?" Buck stared around at the crowd in confusion.

"Go on!" Hiro kept up the clapping. Buck wanted to melt away and die. Here and now. Why was this happening to him? Recognition, being the center of attention, the subject of chanting. Nothing in his life had been like this before—at least not in a positive way. He might throw up.

He looked up and saw on the video screen an even more gigantic version of himself—his Crest toothpaste perma-grin looking stupid and his thick wavy blond hair blazing gold. He couldn't be more of a contrast to the sea of composed happy faces surrounding him.

The chanting overwhelmed both his inertia and his desire to run away shouting. With a curdled smile of fear, he tripped his way over the feet of the people on his row, stumbling down the final stairs toward the stage. Terror gripped him. Meanwhile, the big screen projected his face in a grotesque close-up. Sick. His pores looked like manholes up there.

When he got into the ring, he was greeted by a giant. A Goliath incarnate, but probably less hairy—and less clothed. The sumo blew hot, heavy breath in Buck's face and bowed to him with a scowl.

Buck knew this was for show, but it scared the living daylights out of him. How could these strangers put him on the spot like this? *Just run with it,* his mind told him. *I can't disappoint them, not Hiro. Mr. Yoshida will hear about this, and Dad's deal is on the line. Keep it together. Be a sport.*

Buck returned the bow of the big, sweaty, bronze-skinned man across the circle from him. *I can't believe I am doing this while I'm awake.*

A gong vibrated. The sumo warrior stomped his feet, marching in place, his knees up and out to the sides like he was bowlegged. Buck mimicked him, and the audience roared.

With a grimace, Buck glanced out toward where he thought Hiro sat, but the bright lights were blinding. Buck stood alone. The lights now isolated him and became a strange kind of blessing—they made him less intimidated by the crowd, which he could now only hear and not see.

Across the circle from Buck, the serious sumo wrestler grabbed a fistful of white granules from a bowl on a pillar and scattered them across the circle. Buck glanced over and saw a similar bowlful of the granules on his own side of the ring. Salt—sea salt in big crystals. For whatever reason, he tossed a handful of it on the ground. The crowd roared. Buck figured whatever he had done, they liked it. Either that, or he'd committed some egregious offense. He waved a little bit to a ringside person whose face he could vaguely distinguish. The person waved back just as another gong sounded.

Suddenly, the sumo warrior came at Buck with shocking speed. How could someone that large move so fast? Buck jumped out of the way, but the sumo guy turned and grabbed him by both shoulders. Buck's instincts kicked in and he grabbed the guy's shoulders right back. In an instant they were locked and pushing each other.

Hiro's explanation ran through Buck's mind: *Each man tries to either push his opponent out of the ring or else make him touch the ground with any part of his body other than the bottom of his foot.* Simple, right? No. Not that simple. This guy weighed as much as a John Deere tractor. Suddenly, Buck recalled the bad three weeks he had spent on his high school football team as a linebacker, before he went back to being friends with the foreign exchange students and running the tech crew for the drama club.

Buck shoved, snorted, sweated, and the guy didn't budge. The audience loved it.

After about thirty seconds of ridiculous, vain efforts, Buck let up shoving. In a nanosecond, the real sumo wrestler gave Buck a soft nudge. Buck glanced down and saw his sneaker cross over the line and plant itself outside the ring. *Aaaaw.* In good-sport defeat, he slapped his hand to his head and reached out to give the victor a handshake. The victor bowed, and Buck shrugged and bowed back. Then he smiled, waved to the crowd, and someone official-looking came and guided him back to his seat.

Hiro slapped him hard on the back.

"Buck! You are the bomb!"

"Naw." Buck blushed.

"Yes! You rock!" Hiro snatched his cell phone out of his pocket, elbowed the fellow beside him and requested a picture of both of them together. Hiro made the peace sign with his fingers. Buck's fingers went into a V for victory.

"I can't believe it! You! Buck! You executed a near perfect *uwatenage!*"

"A what?"

"Well, it wasn't exactly perfect because it, uh, didn't work, but still! Your skill at the classic technique of *uwatenage* is blowing my mind!" With both hands up, Hiro gave Buck a double peace sign and shook them spiritedly.

Buck still didn't have any idea what that term meant. Public humiliation, probably.

"*Uwatenage*, Buck. After establishing outside grip, the attacker throws his opponent by heaving him down at a sharp angle as he turns away." Hiro rubbed his chin. Buck assumed the kid was either joking or giving him some kind of false flattery. He couldn't be serious. Nevertheless, Buck sat back with an unexpected sense of satisfaction as he soaked in the rest of the—what did Hiro call it—the *basho*? He whispered the word. *Basho*.

Further explanations had to wait because of the noise of the crowd. The drums beat again and the matches began. The whole evening flew past. A thousand questions roiled in him.

After six or seven hours of competition, and a mighty sore backside from the wooden seat, Buck and Hiro stood to leave. Buck stretched a moment, but in a flash dozens of smiling members of the crowd thronged him and patted his shoulder, bowed, and spoke in staccato blasts, what must have been praises for his showing. He grinned and bowed. Whenever someone acted like they required an answer, he shrugged and shook his head. This went on for nearly an hour until Buck and Hiro found a taxi, where Hiro promptly zonked out. Buck's questions would have to keep for tomorrow.

Stupid jet lag. He lay in bed staring at the beamed low ceiling later that night, the glow of streetlights mellowing his room.

Man, what if this were his real life? It made Eaglestone seem like a medically induced coma. This day was vibrancy. He, Buck Cooper, was alive! And awesome.

Too bad he had to go home in nine days.

THE NEXT MORNING, BUCK HEARD disco music playing in his mind—the kind that made him want to groove. He snapped his fingers along to his head song and shimmied down the hallway to breakfast, ducking in time to miss the low doorframe.

Hiro and Mrs. Yoshida sipped from small lacquer bowls at the table. Mrs. Yoshida placed a bowl of steaming broth in front of Buck, and he was surprised to see tiny slices of green onion floating beside what looked like solid mini-marshmallows. Following the hosts' example, he picked up the bowl and sipped. Not bad.

Also, not marshmallows.

"This is *miso shiru*." Mrs. Yoshida held out her bowl and tipped it toward him. "*Miso* soup. We Japanese like to eat miso soup for breakfast. It has soybeans and onions and tofu. I hope you like. You like very much."

Tofu. Bean curd. Sounded like a swear word, as did so many other low calorie foods. Fatty foods came adorned with names like succotash and streusel, Viennetta and Fudgesicle—sensual words—words that made Buck's eyes flutter and roll upward as he inhaled their delicious images. Not tofu. But the inner-disco drowned out the scare of diet food.

First he endured it, then the soup grew on him. A lot. If only there were a gallon of it hiding somewhere so he could actually fill his empty gullet. Not likely.

"It's delicious," he said. Another day, another giant step toward his "after" picture. This trip was torture for his stomach, but it would be good for it in the long run. *Just keep telling yourself that.*

Earth, Wind and Fire sang something about September behind his eardrums. Never a cloudy day. He grooved as he sipped the final dregs, only stopping when Mrs. Yoshida glanced at him.

"We saw Baku-*san* on television, Hiro. I only wish his parents stay awake to see him. They will sorry they missed."

Huh? A drop of soup flew from the back of his throat up through his nose. What? The music in his head screeched to a halt.

"Buck is the bomb!" Hiro gulped the last of his soup and then made a beeline for the TV in the nearby living room.

"Oh. Sumo is on television?" Buck tried to mask his gasp.

"Of course. It is national sport of Japan. Great interest in who win the Emperor's Cup at Tokyo tournaments. Not everyone watch from beginning to end, but most Japanese people watch part with comic sumo and highlights of matches with some grand champions." Mrs. Yoshida dropped her eyes to her teacup then looked back up at Buck. "You very entertaining, Baku-*san*. All news stations showed 'short clips' of Baku-*san* after those matches are finish."

Short clips. She pronounced it more like "shoat kuripsu," but he knew what she meant—Buck's humiliation had gone viral.

Buck's heart thudded in his chest harder than it had when he took the stairs to get his coffee on the fifth floor last week. Geez. And he had promised his parents not to do anything to endanger his dad's deal and the future of Nangrimax. Now, this. Could he have been more conspicuous than national television and "shoat kuripsu?"

His face flushed bright red, and he gritted his teeth behind his grin. Shooty, shoot, shoot. Alison was probably surfing the web back at her desk at Eaglestone. There was a ninety-nine point nine nine nine percent chance a clip of him was already circulating on youtube. She might be watching it right now. Maybe over Ranjit's shoulder. He could almost hear Ranjit's grating *ah-har-har-har-har* from here. His worst nightmare: becoming a celebrity for all the wrong reasons.

Then again, who in America paid attention to sumo? He certainly never had, and he was a sports aficionado. There was still a two-point-three percent chance he was safe.

"If now you look at *telebee*, you may see little bit." Mrs. Yoshida took her bowl to the sink. The red lipstick glowed once again, but it looked better today. She looked happy, not horrified at Buck's public display. She rinsed and washed the bowl, then turned to him and smiled. "I think everyone in all of Japan see you by now. You big famous. In Japan we all everyone watch sumo. You go out? Everyone know you. Be careful. Many girls will like you blue eyes."

Hiro turned up the TV set on some kind of sports channel. Buck knew he should look away, but his eyes were drawn to it, as to one of those autopsy crime dramas with graphic gore.

Sure enough, two well-dressed male commentators narrated a scene of Buck versus the volcano.

"Kono Amerika-jin wa, ne, sono itsu mo niko niko shite, izen no ozeki-san wo pushu shite..."

Buck understood none of it, and yet all of it, due to the pictures moving on the set. There he was, blond hair blazing in the light, white teeth glaring out from a ridiculous grin, his Dave Matthews Band concert T-shirt looking more rumpled on TV than it did on his body now, fourteen hours later. He could die right here.

Buck's parents entered just as the clip ended. They looked dressed for sightseeing.

"Mr. Yoshida has arranged for us to have a tour of the sights of Tokyo. We'd like you to come with us, son." It wasn't a request.

"Time to meet your adoring public, Buck." Hiro gave him a guy-nod.

Buck's dad frowned. "What is that supposed to mean?"

"YOUR FIRST STOP IS UENO Koen," Mr. Yoshida announced before dropping them off. "It is one of the biggest parks in Tokyo. Much like Central Park in New York City, but much many more cherry blossoms in springtime."

Ten minutes later, Buck wandered the park, following his parents, while his dad, all flustered and noisy, interpreted the map looking for the zoo Mr. Yoshida promised was there.

Out of nowhere, strangers began to approach Buck. Lots of them. He was Gulliver in Lilliput, wondering if the smaller folk planned to throw a net over him and take him to their leader. They circled him at a distance and he imagined a mild aura of menace on their faces, but he shook that off.

Pointing and whispers followed wherever they went. Paranoia came in waves and receded. It weirded him out, and his parents started to notice, too. Everyone walked a little faster. Even when bullies taunted and persecuted him on his way home from school as a kid, Buck had never felt so Children-of-the-Corn.

It took a while, but they did find the zoo. Mr. Yoshida had been right—this park sprawled. The walking was taking a percentage of his weight off for sure. Yes. Another mile, another pound, which meant less of him to be seen by gawkers.

"Sumo! Sumo!" A child of about five came running up to Buck and held onto his leg. His mother chased up and pulled him off, scolding him. Then she glanced up at Buck and, blushing, apologized.

"So sorry." She dipped her head again before speaking in halting English. "We watch you last night. My son now wants to sumo." Then she scurried off, scolding the boy all the way.

Near the monkey display, a group of elderly men heckled Buck briefly, shaking hats or canes in his direction and speaking in gravelly Japanese. Buck understood none of it. In defense he smiled and shrugged before waving. This created a roar of approval as he and his parents walked away.

"I can see a zoo in any city in America, son, but I can only be an exhibit in a zoo in Tokyo." Buck's dad waved his arm up and down and all around. "What are all these people thinking we will do? Juggle? Stand on our heads? Fly?"

"I know we look different, sweetheart," his mom said, "but not *that* different. Maybe it's your blue eyes they like."

Over the next hour they were approached by no fewer than fifty people. Eventually, Buck's dad stomped off for an evasive pit stop into a restroom, and Buck's mother used the opportunity to take Buck by the arm and question him.

"When are you going to tell us what is going on, Buck? It might have started out as fascination with us for being tourists from another land, but this is getting a little extreme. Did something happen I should know about?"

Buck showed his palms. "When I went to the sumo match with Hiro last night I might have spent a little time on camera. I guess sumo is pretty popular. Lots of viewers."

"And they all saw you? All these people?"

There was no way to make her understand the sweetness of it, but he directed her to a stone bench and gave it a go. They were interrupted three times by passersby. His mom grabbed Buck's forearm.

"You're telling me all these people—from little children to the elderly—saw you on TV last night when they were tuned in to watch big, naked, sweaty men shoving each other around?" She blinked her eyes a dozen times fast then gave a shudder. "It's a little gross, you know, as a sport."

Buck's dad came out of the restroom but got absorbed in reading about lion habitat and didn't join the conversation.

"They weren't exactly naked, Mom. They had on—" Oh, what were those things called? His mind groped for the word. "They had on *mawashi*, those diaper things. It wasn't lewd, I promise." In fact it was graceful in a way, but she probably couldn't grasp that without ever seeing it.

The Cooper family left the zoo and re-entered the park proper. Long arbors of hundreds—maybe thousands—of trees lined the walks. Buck wondered if they were cherry blossom trees. Wrong season. Too bad.

Buck's dad gripped his map of the park and mumbled something about a taxi stand and, "some real food." Apparently the *miso* soup didn't do it for him this morning.

"Excuse me." Seven or so people popped up out of nowhere and surrounded Buck and his parents. Several held cameras, including a couple of TV cameras hoisted onto shoulders. Fear shot through Buck.

"Excuse me? Are you the American who was seen at the Kokugikan last night?"

Buck's father stepped in front of his family, shoulders squared. "What in tarnation is a Cuckoogeekan?"

"Dad," Buck whispered, "it's the national sumo arena. It's where Mr. Yoshida's son took me last night. I . . . was featured. Briefly." If only his dad had listened when Buck explained things to his mom, because now he suddenly wore a dozen questions on his face.

"I'll take it, Dad." Buck stepped to the front, an action as foreign as Japan.

"Yes. I'm the American from last night."

Umpteen questions hurtled at him.

"How long you have been training?"

"When does you make your sumo debut? At next basho?"

"How you feeling as first blond sumo wrestler Japan has ever seen?"

"Which stable do you belong to?"

"What did you eats for breakfast?"

Something he could answer, at last. He held up his hand to turn back the volley.

"Hi, uh. I'm Buck Cooper. I'm just here on vacation. Yesterday was my first time seeing sumo, and it was the most fun I've had in years. Maybe ever." At this, the gathering crowd applauded. He heard whispers of translation and a few *a-ha-has*. "And we had *miso* soup for breakfast."

Approving "ah"s rippled through the crowd.

Before more questions could launch, Buck's mom grabbed him by the arm and looked up at him with pleading blue eyes that matched his own, "And we are going home to the great state of Texas next week. Buck won't be staying to start a career as a sumo wrestler, thank you." She offered a little nervous laugh, but Buck knew she didn't find the situation remotely funny. Annoyance steamed from her skin.

The reporters didn't question her but looked to Buck for answers. Soon Buck put his arm around her and gave her a side hug.

"I'm just here on vacation. Thanks." Saying it gave him an unexpected pang.

Buck and his mom then followed as his dad led them toward a taxi stand he'd located on his map.

"But, Cooper-*san!*" One reporter called after him. "What about the Kawaguchi brothers?"

Kawaguchi brothers? Never heard of them. He shook his head at the scrawny microphone-wielder.

"The Kawaguchi brothers say they are in negotiations to sign a deal with you to join their father and study with most respected sumo trainer in Japan. That would be a great honor, to be tied to such a family. Will you accept the offer, Cooper-*san?*"

His head swam. Rumors, the sudden fame, the weird names, the crush of reporters chasing him. Too confusing. He'd never been notified of any signing offer. Wouldn't that be funny.

"Sorry, I can't comment."

When they were safe in the taxi, Buck's dad turned on him.

"What was all that 'no comment' malarkey? Are you suddenly the Chairman of the Fed? You're guarding some big secret?" This was more than just jet lag spoiling their mood. Buck didn't know what all hung in the balance. He never meant to mess things up.

Buck's dad stared out the window as Tokyo's noontime crawled past at a snail's pace.

Buck knew his *no comment* comment sounded lame, like he was trying to be someone important when he said that, but it was what jumped into his head. And it wasn't untrue. He'd never heard of any of the people the reporters mentioned, and he had no clue what rumor they'd heard. Cow-a-Gucci Brothers? Mind boggling.

"Dad, it wasn't intentional. I guess I was kind of just part of the halftime show. Only, it was at the beginning . . ." He trailed off. It wasn't helping.

"Buck. I thought we agreed." Buck's dad looked at him now. "Now you went and drew so much attention to us. I'm no expert, but in this country, my *Business in Japan* guidebook says decorum is paramount for respectability, and respectability is paramount for any kind of business." He gripped Buck's forearm. "Jumping on a stage? Not showing a lot of decorum."

His dad was right. He should have thought it through. But there was no way out of climbing on that stage last night. The spotlight and chanting crowd gave him no choice.

He hated having his dad mad at him. He took a moment and re-explained the events of the night before to his dad, hoping he'd take some pity. "I'm real sorry, Dad, Mom. I don't know how I could have avoided it. Things happened faster than I could process it all. It's a done deal, now, and I guess we just have to make the best of a bizarre, foreign situation. I'll try to make it up to you somehow."

Mr. Cooper stared out the window for six blocks then slapped his knees and turned back to Buck, softening to his normal tone.

"Fine, Buck." He sighed. "I understand you got caught up in a pressure-filled moment. It's just, a lot is at stake here. Everything your mother and I have worked for over the past three decades—it all hangs in the balance. It all hinges on this one deal. On Nangrimax, Buck."

"What do you mean?" Please say they hadn't mortgaged the house for this. His mom and dad shot a look between themselves before his dad spoke again.

"Son, I can see all this flash of fame is affecting you. And I don't begrudge you it. That flash can be blinding. I'm just asking you, please. Don't let it get to you just now. We all need to focus."

Buck nodded. His dad didn't need to go on. His mother looked on the verge of tears or heart palpitations, and Buck knew he'd fight off bands of marauding ninjas to keep them safe.

THAT AFTERNOON, HIRO AND BUCK sprawled in front of the Yoshidas' TV to watch the day's installment of the sumo tournament. Even though he squeezed his eyes shut every time a replay of his big self appeared from yesterday's tournament, Buck tried to absorb every detail. He asked Hiro dozens of questions.

"What's that the guy is drinking right before the match?"

"That's *chikara-mizu.* Power water!" Hiro pointed to the wrestler administering the drink with a ladle. "That guy is the last one from the contender's side to win, and he is transferring the luck."

"So, what's that weird paper?"

"*Chikara-kami.* Power paper!"

"Right. And it's good for—?"

"Masking the wrestler's mouth while he spits out the power water."

Gotcha.

For a while he sat on the edge of his seat, leaning toward the TV, as though he could leap into the action. Later, Buck settled back onto the sofa. He propped his stocking feet up and nestled into the entertainment.

Other ceremonial details fascinated him. It turned out the salt Buck scattered was meant for the Shinto gods, to appease them, and all that stomping Buck's opponent did was to scare evil spirits out of the ring. No demons allowed in sumo. With the size of those guys, it had to work.

Each match-up lasted less than a minute, and quite a bit of fanfare and waiting occurred between contests. On cue, when a new wrestler, *rikishi*, appeared in the ring, Hiro peppered Buck with facts: tales of the wrestler's rise through the lower tiers, his current ranking, plus the signature techniques he used to beat his opponents in the past. Each of the better *rikishi* had three or four skills in his arsenal, and sometimes the opponent could play on this knowledge.

Buck basked in it as he guzzled glasses of mystery iced tea and shoved handfuls of shrimp-flavored chips into his mouth. Nice, salty brain fuel.

"So, wait. A person could calculate odds of winning?" Statistics! He conjured up the start of a formula using the fifty-four professional slots on a mental rankings sheet. If nothing else, Buck could see himself as a sumo bookie.

"Sure, sure, but don't even think about betting on sumo. The JSA forbids betting. Japanese mafia, called *yakuza,* always trying to gamble on sumo in secret, but the JSA can overpower even *yakuza.* JSA is very powerful."

"Japan Sumo Association?" Buck took a stab at the acronym.

"Yes. Nobody messes with them. They will eliminate you."

All too soon, the *rikishi* for the final bout of day seven stomped in the ring. They were huge, but their grace and body control filled each move with helium.

"They saved the best fight for last!" Hiro's eyes shone. "These are the number one- and number five-ranked *rikishi* in all sumo. Number one, the one with the flattened nose, that's Butaniku. The *yokozuna.*" He frowned.

Buck remembered the tiptop section of the pyramid and this

guy's face—nasty looking, like a fierce warthog. And something else was different. "Is Butaniku Japanese?"

"Nnnno. Korean." Hiro sneered. Back at Eaglestone there was water-cooler World Cup soccer talk of a rivalry between Japan and Korea. Maybe that fight spread beyond soccer. "He is a shame. I want to obliterate him."

The two champs began circling each other on the stage.

"The only guy I hate more than Butaniku is Sobakubi. That loser! Sobakubi might be Japanese, but he doesn't deserve to be. So spoiled! Just because his father is high up in government—" Hiro muttered something.

"Wait. You said Korean. Foreigners are allowed to become sumo wrestlers?" Buck's heart sped up.

"Sure. Sumo has a long history, and very few *gaijin* have ever been good enough to rank. In the 1980s, Konishiki and Akebono came from Hawaii. They dominated sumo for a decade. Now sumo is international. More and more *gaijin* join sumo all the time."

Buck didn't want to keep asking the meaning of every word. Context hinted *gaijin* meant *foreigner*.

"So this Butaniku guy. Is he everyone's favorite?" Buck baited Hiro, who groaned and stared at the sky.

"No!"

"Don't hold back, man. Tell me what you really think." Buck crunched more shrimp chips.

"Butaniku is an embarrassment!" Hiro tossed a shrimp chip at the television. "Everyone who cares about sumo believes Butaniku brings shame and sorrow only. He is a pig."

"Wow. Shame, sorrow, and pig—harsh words about a champ, Hiro."

"He deserves them. He drinks too much. He brags too much. He fights in bars with other wrestlers. In fact, he was suspended from the last tournament for punching another *rikishi* in the dressing room." Hiro's voice lowered to a whisper. "He went to an Osaka *jail*." Hiro's eyes were huge and disapproving.

Jail—what was the big deal about jail and athletes? Butaniku sounded pretty much like the classic American pro player.

"The other guy looks pretty good."

"That's Torakiba." All sneering evaporated, and Hiro got a dreamy tone. "Ranked number five—for now. He will rise. He is a serious contender. *And* he's been racking up the wins lately." Pride oozed from him, almost like his fan energy had helped the guy win.

Torakiba looked even more fierce that Butaniku, which seemed impossible. A long set of canines, practically fangs, jutted from his top row of teeth. Whoa. And check out the fingers—the claws came as a matched set with the fangs. Maybe it was only because of how he was holding his hands. Still, that guy could use a muzzle. A cage. Probably a manicure. Everything about him zinged with razor sharpness.

"I'm Torakiba's number one fan." Hiro glowed. "Ever since he got into the professional ranks I've seen all his matches because Torakiba is a champion in and out of the ring."

"Yeah?" Buck shook off his revulsion. If Hiro considered Torakiba worthy, Buck should at least give the guy a chance. After all, from what he'd heard, dentistry abroad paled compared to America's orthodontic miracles. The guy probably couldn't help it and was making the most of his lot in life.

"Yeah. All his winnings? I read that he sends them back to Nagoya to his mother who is sick in a nursing home. Good man."

The match began. Warthog battled hard for domination. Torakiba Tiger Fang grabbed for the warthog's leg and looked like he would try to throw him—or bite the leg off in a single snap of the teeth. Warthog moved too fast, keeping his leg planted before going for the fanged one's diaper-sash-thing. He grabbed at it and pushed Tiger Fang around the ring. Ouch. Torakiba felt that for sure, but he stayed inside the line.

"Isn't that an illegal move?" Buck asked Hiro. If it wasn't, it should be.

"No. Pulling the *chonmage*, the topknot hairstyle, is illegal because the *chonmage* is the symbol of the sumo wrestler. He receives it when he becomes a *rikishi*. If he ever cuts it, he is no longer *rikishi*. Ever again!" Hiro sat on the edge of his seat to convey the drama of the hairstyle. Then he sat back and crossed his arms over his chest. "However, grabbing the *mawashi* is legal. In fact, it is expected. It is a strong move."

Wow. Mega wedgie in front of thousands of screaming fans.

The battle got more intense. Butaniku power-clenched Torakiba, twisting his upper body and shoving over and downward. Suddenly, Torakiba made a move that Butaniku didn't expect. From the confines of the hug of death, Tiger Fang hooked his heel behind the warthog's and shoved his knee into Butaniku's inner thigh. Then he pulled him by the arm and threw him sideways to the ground. *Crash!*

The champ hit the floor. The repercussions rippled clear across town to the Yoshidas' living room.

"Yes! I love to see Torakiba's signature move, the *chongake!* It is the pulling-heel-hook! Nobody does it better!"

Butaniku laid there a moment, stunned, but shook his warthog head and stood up, bowed, and the two left the ring amid audience screams.

"That is why Torakiba wins!" Hiro clapped along with everyone in the crowd on TV then flopped on the sofa in happiness. "It is my prediction Torakiba will win this *basho*. He deserves it. He is everything true fans want in a champion. He will be *ozeki* after this. Champion! We need a strong, dignified gentleman as *yokozuna.* Not Butaniku. But Torakiba is so polite, never bragging. Honorable. After today's win, he will get the *kachikoshi* and win the Emperor's Cup for this tournament!"

Emperor's Cup? Buck imagined a nice trophy for the winner. Maybe something gold on a wooden base. It probably came with a cash prize, a thousand dollars maybe. Something to keep the wrestlers in diapers and hair gel.

"Butaniku, Torakiba—are those their real names? They're Japanese words, I take it." There was an impossibly low statistical likelihood that a Korean family gave their newborn son a Japanese name in random hopes he would one day grow up to be a sumo champion in Tokyo.

"Yes. Every new *rikishi* gets a sumo name. Often his trainer chooses it, and maybe it is very poetic meaning. Torakiba's sumo name means fang of a tiger."

"Like *Tora Tora Tora.*"

"You're getting it, Buck." Hiro flashed Buck that good old peace sign.

"BUCK! YOU GOTTA GET READY. The *Fukuro Matsuri* starts in an hour, and we have an hour ride on the slam train to get there. Families—already gone. Quick! Put this on." Hiro was hyperventilating as he shoved a thin cloth thing at Buck, who'd just gotten out of the bath.

Buck stared stupidly at the blue bathrobe. Hoo doggie. He wasn't going anywhere in that thing. No way, no how. Not to a Frooko Nothing nowhere. And especially not this early in the morning.

"We got to leave right away. Strip down. Wear this. Come on!" Hiro did his back and forth foot-hopping thing again, and looked so desperate that Buck finally complied.

"Could Ritalin be your answer, Hiro?" Why, oh why, did he let himself get weaseled into doing stuff like this? It was like how he got hit up for twenty bucks every time he turned around. Just couldn't say no.

Well, to be fair, this didn't rank as quite that bad. Here was a nice kid who simply wanted Buck to wear some weird bathrobe and go outside to some—what was it called?

"What are we going to again?" Buck emerged from the bathroom wearing the blue and white patterned robe. It tied where his waist would be if he'd had one.

"*Fukuro Matsuri*. It's an annual festival, and there will be a parade of portable shrines carried through the streets, plus traditional dances, loud *taiko* drums."

Buck liked drums. But why the bathrobe? He shook his sleeves at Hiro.

"Very fancy clothes, shoes. Everyone must wear some traditional Japanese kimono or *yukata*. That—your clothes—it is *yukata*. You like!" Hiro commanded.

"What am I supposed to wear under this thing?" Breezes wafted in places they shouldn't.

"Nothing. You like!"

No, he would not like, and he was going to pull on his boxers whether Hiro approved or not. He made a quick grab for a shirt to wear as an undershirt.

"No shirts over *yukata*." Hiro pulled at his own robe. His had flowers, too.

They went toward the *genkan* where all the shoes stood in neat rows in the cement entryway. Buck went for his size fifteen Nikes, but Hiro pulled him back.

"No *gaijin* shoes today, Buck. Today you wear *geta*." And he handed Buck a pair of wooden flip-flops. Beach shoes made out of wood. Buck turned them over to find two parallel inch-high square dowels under each *geta*, one at the ball of the foot and one halfway down. Well, those didn't look like they'd get Buck to hurry *anywhere.*

"Come on. Your parents, my parents, they are waiting!"

Buck hustled after Hiro, doing a clopping Oompa Loompa walk down the street two or three blocks to where a subway station entrance gaped. Hundreds of people crowded toward the escalator going down. Buck got caught in the flow, like being flushed down a toilet. At the bottom of the stairway, he nearly stumbled at the sight—beneath the bustle of street-level Tokyo, a whole other Tokyo existed—shops, newspaper stands, food vendors.

Trains whooshed in and out of the station. Because of his height advantage, Buck saw clearly what these trains contained: way too many people. Wasn't there some kind of fire code violation here? Faces pressed up against windows. No one reposed in soft seats. How did they all fit inside?

A new train pulled into the station. A few bodies boinged out, and sixty waited at each door to enter. Nine entered without too much problem, but the remaining fifty or so pressed inward anyway. When they could go no further, they got help—a security official in a blue uniform wearing white gloves began pushing on their backs, shoving them into the train. It happened fast, and everyone acted like it was as normal as could be.

Buck felt queasy.

"This is slam train, Buck! Very full train! You like!"

Buck looked down at his scant clothing. He thought about close proximities to countless other bodies. He thought about Chinese water torture. Maybe this was Japanese clothing torture. Death by indignity. And smashing.

"Yee-haw." Their train pulled in and Buck lined up to get on. When it looked like no more could possibly ride, the hands hit his back. Into the sardine can he wedged, barely able to breathe, and grabbed a high bar. A little old lady's head impaled itself in his armpit. Poor woman. He couldn't expand his lungs fully. An umbrella jabbed his ribs, and an elbow gouged his spine. He looked up. Ads plastered the ceiling. At least he was tall enough, towering over everyone else, to not have to breathe everyone else's breath. Wait. Hot air rises. He closed his eyes, gripped the bar, and thought of the wide-open fields of his grandpa's farm back in Texas.

Just when Buck couldn't suppress the images of the Star Wars trash compactor scene any longer, Hiro said, "This is our station. Called Ikebukuro."

Not that Buck could repeat the name, but he shook his muscles free in relief as they rode up the escalator from the teeming station. Above ground, grey granite rose all around him, scraping the grey sky. Splashes of fall colors nearer the ground gave the place vibrancy.

In an instant, he was swarmed.

"Look! It's true. He is sumo! *Rikishi* always appear in public wearing *yukata* robe!"

Buck towered over a small mob as Hiro disappeared into the crowd. Groupies held up their cell phone cameras, snapping shots of him from all angles. Most of them got him from "not his best side," the angle where his double chins got the greatest prominence, making him look like a puffer fish. But he smiled for them. A young girl screamed, another sighed. The crowd pressed in on him. This was the third day in a row without his invisibility cloak. If only he could pull his head into the folds of the *yukata* like a tortoise.

One brave mobber with spiky green hair got close enough to poke him in the arm with one of those spikes.

"So, this is your sumo clothing, then?"

"Mine? No. No-ho-ho-ho."

"Like Santa Claus. Ho ho ho!" Another teen girl gingerly patted his stomach and repeated the ho-ho-ho about six times until his grin turned to steel. Other questions came firing at him, all in broken English.

"We heard on NHK you will be in the lists for the Tokyo *basho*. Is that true?"

"What stable are you training with?"

"What will your sumo name be?"

"You are so fat, Baku-*san*. You will be very good sumo." A girl in one of those schoolgirl uniforms Ranjit had so accurately prophesied of beamed up at him. It distracted him. A lot. Especially when she nuzzled up to him and batted her eyelashes.

He gathered his wits with great effort.

"I'm not really planning to do sumo. Not for sure." His lungs contracted as he gazed down at those eyelashes.

"Have you signed any contracts?"

"Brother," he muttered under his breath. She was a sweet little eyelash batter.

"Brother. The Kawaguchi brothers! On the television they said it was a secret and you had signed no deals, but I thought so." The green spiked speaker announced, "Hey, everyone. He signed with the Kawaguchi brothers. I knew it! I knew it!"

Before Buck could make a retort, Hiro grabbed Buck's arm. "Your parents are over there. We need to go if you will carry the *mikoshi* my father paid for."

Buck waved goodbye to them, grinning broadly, grateful for whatever a *mikoshi* was. He lumbered away through the streets and away from celebrity. Hiro tugged at his arm all the way. Smells of chicken ramen wafted from an open shop door. Music played, heavy drums like the ones at the sumo match.

Taiko drums. They pulsated, fierce, but they matched his heartbeat. Skyscrapers stretched up forever, and even Buck felt small in Ikebukuro. The mob at the taxi had caught him unawares. All this unexpected attention confused him, made him nervous, but he couldn't say he hated it.

Weird. He hadn't given the guy an absolute no about sumo. Of course he meant an absolute no. So, why couldn't he just say it?

"We're here. You get to help carry the *mikoshi*. It's a shrine on posts. Very beautiful. Gold leaf. My father arranged it for both you and me. You smile, Buck. And keep up." Hiro patted Buck as they rounded a corner to where a dozen guys all in their *yukata* waited near an ornate red and gold box with tassels on their corners. It was about the size of a golf cart, but hoisted up on posts to be carried like a coffin.

Please let no running be involved.

Around them, in the covered shopping street, light filtered, all pink and green and golden. Balloons and banners bounced as the parade lineup began.

And then, he saw her.

All aglow, she stood in ethereal beauty, a column of butterflies awash in a slanting ray of sun coming through a skylight in the pavilion cover. Dust particles shimmered in the light, dancing with happiness just to be near her.

Buck rocked back on his heels. He had never seen anything as stunning in his entire life. Time stood still. Her kimono's deep blue silk made him think of the ocean, and she wore it perfectly. Her eyes searched around, a hint of smile behind them.

And then—she looked at Buck and smiled. Buck's breath caught in his throat.

The *dimples*. They were the same dimples. That same electric current surged through him, paralyzing him. This must be what it felt like to be tasered—but with joy, not pain. The Taser of Joy.

Everything around the angelic girl faded to black and she stood awash in a sea of soft blue light. The woman was poetry in blue. Magnetic forces uncontrollable pulled him toward her.

Then he stopped short.

A glance down jarred his memory—here he stood in the human incarnation of a white whale. His own contrast to her exquisite perfection—his folds of flesh so pasty and fuzzy—how could he even think she could find him attractive?

He was a fool.

"Buck! Our *mikoshi* is ready." Hiro tugged Buck toward two tall wooden doors. "My father will not be happy if we are late. Your parents are watching. See? They are over there in the crowd."

Buck tore his eyes away from the girl for an instant. His parents waved. But the girl! He couldn't lose her now. That girl—she struck him like a tuning fork and made his blood resonate and sing. Fate had brought him back to where she was, and he couldn't squander this chance. A steeling breath, and he moved toward her. Nothing could stop him. Not that golf cart box on posts, not this ridiculous dress he was wearing, not even the risk of his parents' shame. Nothing—

"Excuse me. Baku Cooper-*san*?" A pair of young Japanese men in business suits blockaded him. Hiro glanced over his shoulder with a helpless look and went through the double doors. Buck stared after his dream goddess as she melted into the shifting crowds.

Gone. And the thrill of her energy dissipated into nothingness. He felt his soul stretching out to search for her, but he was stuck here with these men.

The blockade spoke.

"I am Kawaguchi Moto, and this is my brother." He bowed deeply. Buck, eyes darting around in a desperate search for the girl, returned the bow.

"Kawaguchi Taro *desu*." The second man bowed.

Buck returned the pleasantries, but impatience rattled him, a grin pasted on his face to be polite. The men looked even more similar to each other than most of the native people he had met so far on this trip. They had to be brothers. Then, it clicked—from ear canal to brain: Cow-a-Gucci. The brothers.

His saliva turned to Texas dust. A bead of sweat formed along the back of his neck trickling down his spine.

"We would like to discuss your future."

"My future?" Buck took a step back. "My future in Dallas, Texas, as a quality control researcher and a poster boy for diabetes prevention? That future?"

"We see a very different future for you, Baku Cooper-*san*." The first brother raised a single eyebrow and glanced at the second, who gave a slight nod but didn't smile. They both took a step toward him. "We are prepared to offer you a position in our father's stable where he is the honorable trainer Kawaguchi Oyakata."

Buck stared at them, his smile wilted slightly. They were serious—to their cores. Boy, people around here took this sumo thing to heart. His head swirled.

"Look, I have no idea how you found me. I'm only a tourist. My father is here on business. I didn't even plan to go to the sumo match. It just happened. Sure, yeah, I loved it. It was a great time, best time of my life, maybe. But me? A professional athlete? Ha! Now who would ever believe that?"

The Kawaguchi brothers didn't even crack a smile.

The first brother spoke again. "Baku Cooper-*san*. You have a gift. In all our years of evaluating potential sumo *rikishi*, we have never seen such natural skill. Your size and strength are one thing—though your advanced age might be a concern." He bit his lip.

Twenty-four is advanced age? Still, the compliment warmed him.

"Cooper-*san*, your intuitive technique shocked every scout

in the sport. We came to you immediately. You are very lucky—because we found you first. Our father is indisputably the best. Once again, Kawaguchi Oyakata is his name. He will take all your natural talent and turn it into skill."

The Kawaguchis stepped closer to Buck and the talkative one spoke. "You will become a champion."

At this, Buck stopped sponging up the flattery. This sent reality hurtling out into space. He threw his head back and guffawed.

"I get it. I'm being punked. No. This is one of those high-pressure deals like you hear about on news exposés. Innocent kid gets lured in and then gets taken to the cleaners by sharks." His gut bounced as he chuckled. "Oh, not that you two even remotely resemble sharks. But, hey. Super nice of y'all to think of me for your scheme, but I've got a life back home. A job and things." A job he was great at—but could never love, if he were at all honest about it. Just because a person is good at one thing doesn't mean he should do it professionally.

He felt a soft presence at his side. His mom snuck up on him while he was busy focusing on vain flattery. She solidified his trip back onto the reality bus. Down there in her Japanese garb she looked kind of cute. However, something about the look in her eyes, wild and worried, made his stomach clench.

"Buck, honey?" Her voice had a tremor. "Who are these men?" She shot them a brief, suspicious glance. His mom held her cell phone out to him. "I have a telephone call for you. She said her name is Alison Turner."

The rabbit's feet of his racing heart lurched to a halt.

Alison Turner was calling him.

No. Way.

He snatched the phone from his mother's hands.

"I have to take this. Excuse me." He stumbled away, clutching the phone.

Buck's mind raced through everything that a call from her could mean. First off, it meant she noticed him, and more than just a desk fill-in during lunch. Oh, yeah. Nice guy gets girl. Well, at least it meant she knew he was alive. But, wait. It was after hours there. It meant she had to be calling with a purpose. Social call? Maybe?

No.

The promotion.

He knew it.

Yeah, oh, yeah. That promotion was *so* his. When he applied, there was no question he was the most qualified candidate. For sure the higher-ups had to notice his hard work. And they'd asked Alison Turner to deliver the great news herself. In fact, she'd probably asked for the privilege.

Everything was falling together.

Girl, check. Job, check. Awesome secret-life-as-sumo-wrestler job offer, check. Too bad he was going to have to turn down these very stern bozos. Like he said, he had a life.

He took a deep breath. "Hello?"

"Mr. Buck? So glad I finally tracked you down."

"Me, too, Alison."

"Phew! So glad you speak English so well. Anyhoo, reason I'm calling you in the freaking middle of the night—sorries a bunch—is that the promotion was finally finalized—"

"Yeah?" Buck bated his breath. Go on.

"Like, Trish totally gave it to me. Can you, like, believe it?"

No, he couldn't. His tongue swelled at the back of his throat. He was gagging.

Alison? The front desk girl? But she had never done any quality control research at all. Confusion staggered him, and his jaw hung slack.

"So, totally the biggest bummer of this, *however*, is that my absolutely first duty in the new jobber was that I got assigned to call every single person who got laid off in the newest round of layoffs, no matter where they were, on vacation in New Mexico or not, and they told me I couldn't *rest* until I got the word out to all the poor unfortunates. So, like wow. You're the *very last final* person I have to call. It's been *so hard* and I'm exhausted, you know. But so, I guess that's it. I'm calling to tell you you got laid off today and the company extends its *deepest condolences* and wishes you the best in finding future employment. Since you're out of town on a vaycay, we're going to just keep your final check and all the stuff from your desk. We cleaned it out for ya and put it in a box here at Eaglestone for you to come pick up whenever, but because it's a layoff there's no severance, just a few weeks' pay instead. So don't, like, look for that check this time, okay?"

This time? Some of this information sank in. He let the rest bounce off. The "vaycay" part he let roll away on the cement sidewalk, possibly falling through a grate into a storm drain somewhere. His arm fell slack at his side.

He just got fired. By that dimwit. The huge, cursive letters of her name, perpetually written in the clouds of his mind by his heart's own skywriter, blew away in a gale force wind. Gone. Every last ounce of Alison from his soul.

He had no job to go home to. No income. No benefits. No salary. No desk. No projects. No coworkers. No partially obscured view of the city. And to top it all off, no apartment.

His legs turned to water. It was as if someone had come and taken a great big "life eraser" and rubbed out everything he'd been a week ago.

Blank.

WHEN THE RINGING IN HIS ears subsided, he became aware of his mother's breathing beside him. He glanced around for the

Kawaguchi brothers, but they had receded to make their own phone calls.

Buck looked down into her eyes, a plea pulsating there. She whispered sternly, but still in her soft, southern way.

"Son, I know something incredibly unusual is happening to you right now." She rested her hand on his arm. "And I love you. You are my whole world. But you have got to get your head on straight."

This strong version of Cissie Cooper appeared only in emergencies—the version that could organize a block party, or calm an extended family argument, or head up the details for a funeral.

"Now, I've heard rumors. Mrs. Yoshida explained them. And the reporters? My gosh, son. All of this mayhem points toward a completely unacceptable lifestyle for a good Baptist boy like you." She cleared her throat. "That is all beside the point. Think about it, son. You *know* those people would never accept you for who you are. There are *things* that go on in sports, behind-the-scenes things. Things I don't even want to *think* about happening to my sweet son, even though you're a grown man now." She gripped his arm, worry filling her face.

Buck understood her—hazing, hate crimes, brutality against the guy who was different or new. Throughout his life Buck had faced the pummeling fists and taunting words of bullies time and time again. Words, he could take. A punch in the face—that, he really hated. Before he got his vertical growth spurt at age fifteen, Buck had been the short, fat kid, and every walk home from school was a minefield of potential beatings. He tried to hide them from his folks, but he knew they knew, even though no one said anything. His mom hadn't forgotten those times.

"And it's not just that, Buck. What about football? Remember football?"

Buck remembered football, all three weeks of it. A frown

wrinkled his mom's brow. He couldn't tell if it meant worry or shame. A man doesn't quit his high school football team in Texas without serious ramifications to his and his family's honor.

"I realize you can make your own decisions, and I don't have the kind of influence I once had over you. I didn't raise you to be afraid, but I didn't mean for you to become a reckless and thoughtless man, either. Think of your safety. And oh, please, please, don't mess up your father's deal. All this? It's just a moment of time. The Nangrimax deal of your father's? That deal could mean *his* whole *life*. Please, Buck. Consider."

The Kawaguchis started closing in on him again. They didn't look patient. Meanwhile, the intensity of his mother's stare practically melted Buck's face. He looked away, but her words sounded in his head: *This deal could mean your father's whole life.* That's why he was here. To support the Nangrimax deal, show family solidarity. His dad's deal, his dad's life.

Buck stopped. What about his own whole life? Did he *have* one? Did he *want* one? All the years in college, at Eaglestone, working as a statistician, why? Because he *should?* Because his dad loved medical research? Because it seemed like the thing for Buck to do at the time?

He looked back down at her. He loved his parents, and wanted their deal to sail through; he would give almost anything to ensure that. Almost.

The Kawaguchi brothers edged into his space again. Their aura almost glowed. Looking at them, Buck saw a shining path opening up, one where he had a purpose, maybe for the first time ever. This moment—the pleading of his mom's face, the swirling of the fall leaves in the September breeze, the neon lure of a new world—would be branded on the insides of his eyelids forever. He stared at his mom, and at his dad across the street, recognizing their wishes, and hating with all his heart to disappoint them.

He begged a thousand silent apologies before he gritted his teeth, took a glance at the sky, and then said it.

"I would be honored to accept your offer, Mr. and Mr. Kawaguchi."

五

THE IDIOT
SEPTEMBER. TOKYO

The Kawaguchis' black Mercedes pulled away from the front of the Yoshidas' house. Buck sank down into the leather seats, fingered the fancy electronic buttons. It must be a sport for the very rich, running a sumo training club.

Buck craned his neck to stare out the back window to see as Hiro jumped up and down, giddy with excitement, waving goodbye and flashing the peace sign over and over. Mr. and Mrs. Yoshida nodded approvingly, arms crossed with pride, and the older brother yelled, *"Yatta!"* and grinned in triumph.

Buck willed his parents to come out the door, to give him one last look, to forgive him with their acknowledgment as he disappeared. Nothing could erase the image of their disappointed faces when he told them.

Come out. Look through a window. Anything. Please!

Nothing.

He kicked the duffel bag at his feet, which he brought even though Hiro had insisted he wouldn't need it.

"*Rikishi* live a very simple life. You won't even need these few things." Hiro then regaled him with predictions about Buck's boundless future successes, which the fates guaranteed, in Hiro's enthusiastic opinion.

Buck wondered.

Tokyo bumped past. Traffic choked narrow streets with black sedans, white sedans, pink and green SmartCars and mini-trucks as far as he could see. Bicycles careened through sidewalks already teeming with pedestrians. Dallas never swarmed like this, not even at Six Flags Over Texas on public school spring break. At least he wasn't on a slam train.

After a bit, things opened up and the Kawaguchis' car hit speeds that would pull the skin on Buck's face taut if the windows were down. He tried picking out words from the brothers' conversation, but only caught *hai,* or *sumo,* or his own name. If he planned to survive, he'd have to pick up more of the language. It was like being functionally deaf.

His worries wafted away from his parents toward what lay ahead. Hiro acted like the wrestlers made good money, and Buck wondered how much money was good money. Maybe there would be a set sumo stipend for working, or maybe his income depended on his winning a certain number of bouts, or a mixture of both. Truth was, a single yen was better than the zero yen he'd be earning back home jobless. At least the people in charge here had a stake in not letting him starve to death.

He banked on having enough food to eat. The tastiness of it, not so much.

Either way, he was in a car, riding toward his new life as a *professional athlete.* An excited huzzah rumbled at the back of his throat. A few months back he watched an ESPN special on lifestyles of the pros—bedding made out of real mink fur, solid gold toothbrushes, a different wristwatch for every day of the year. Excessive, yes. But he did like the idea of a personal chef. Even in Japan he knew it wouldn't be hard to find a chef who could whip up a pot of chili beans or a rack of true southern barbecue now and again to beat the homesickness.

"We are here." The taxi stopped at a cramped old building. "This is the Kawaguchi stable." The Kawaguchis opened a faded grey door to a place where they kept the company's animals. Weird, but he chalked it up to another Japanese cultural thing. He glanced around the bare room. Only straw mats covered the floor. The walls were dirty, and the place smelled like his eighth grade gym class, but with more dead fish and stale beer odor tossed in for bad measure.

"This will be your—how do you say—accommodations."

Buck spun around faster than a Texas tornado. "Excuse me?" Wait. Stable equals animals, right? This had to be a practical joke. Other than the straw and dirt, it didn't look like a stable. It looked like an abandoned warehouse on the wrong side of the tracks in Detroit.

"This is where you will sleep."

"Where, exactly?" It was a far cry from the Marriott. Or Motel Six. Or even the Spur Shack, which offered weekly rates starting at thirty-five dollars downtown by Eaglestone.

One Kawaguchi pointed at the corner. There was a bare spot, on which lay a stack of ratty looking long pillows—futons. He would be sleeping on the floor! His western-style bed in the Yoshidas' home had spoiled him. People still slept like this in Japan?

In the corner he noticed what looked like a footbath for only one foot, a ceramic hole with a flush handle at one end—a Japanese squat toilet. Holy crap. He'd taken the Yoshidas' western-style toilet for granted, too. A squatter. How on earth was a four hundred pound man supposed to navigate that thing?

Buck's dismayed whistle echoed off the cement and old plaster.

"This is Kawaguchi stable, the most honorable stable in all sumo," the talkative brother said, his voice tight with pride. "The life of a sumo *rikishi* is very simple, Baku-*san*."

Simple. In other words, "luxury-free." Buck dropped his

suitcase in the corner. The ugly duffel with the stripes looked ridiculous in this strange, medieval space. Nothing he brought with him from America was useful to him now. Not his books, not his clothes, not his language, not his sense of humor, not his physical un-fitness.

The stack of futons made him nervous. Was he expected to climb atop it like some princess in a fairy tale? He eyed the dirty edges of the futons. It hit him that a large number of big, smelly roommates must share this condominimum.

They led Buck out of the room and down a grungy hallway, walls encrusted with a dozen coats of paint, Japanese characters scratched down to the white plaster, greasy handprints and black streaks of filth. Animal quarters would be more accurate.

"Everyone is working hard now. Tonight will be the *koen-kai*, a sponsor party. The companies who underwrite the Kawaguchi stable will treat the *rikishi* tonight. You will not attend. You will sleep. Life as a *rikishi* begins early."

"How early?"

"Before dawn."

"Before or after breakfast?" Buck thought about miso soup at the Yoshidas, and wondered if that was the national standard morning fare. He could use a stack of blueberry pancakes right about now, smothered in syrup.

"Sumo *rikishi* do not eat the breakfast."

Buck gasped. No breakfast? How could a growing boy keep his weight and energy up without even a bowl of Frosted Flakes to start the day?

Kawaguchi must have seen Buck's terror. "Lunch. You will have the big lunch. Very big."

He stood still in his getup from earlier, the light kimono with almost nothing else on. They'd given him no time to change once he said yes. He slid his hands into opposite sleeves and folded his arms to keep his fingers warm against the September night's sudden chill.

His eyes darted around. No heat vents. Nothing but the warm breath of a dozen obese men to heat the room at night—nasty.

"A few words of advice, Baku Cooper-*san*." Talking Kawaguchi didn't turn back to look at Buck as they navigated the hallways. "First, from this moment, your trainer is your supreme being, the god you obey. Kawaguchi Oyakata speaks, and you respond. No questions."

Inside, his Southern Christian sensibilities recoiled. But Buck nodded.

"Next, there is a 'pecking order' in sumo. It will not be difficult to discover. Do what the senior *rikishi* require, or suffer. In case you did not know, you, Baku Cooper-*san*, are at the bottom of the pecking order."

Buck looked at the guy to see if this was another potential joke. It wasn't.

"Come. We will see training *dohyo.*"

"Hup! Hup!" The sounds of athleticism tapped in staccato bursts. Buck followed the Kawaguchis into a room about the size of his parents' garage. Dirt covered the ground. A training ring was made out of short straw bales, about fifteen feet in diameter and four inches high; its top was rounded like a huge boa constrictor. A tumult of activity went on around the room. A dozen or so men in white *mawashi*, the loincloths, sparred. Several stood outside the ring performing a stomp-squat-kick-to-the-side move, over and over again. Others did a form of pushups.

One *rikishi*, white-clad, stood in the ring listening to a fellow *rikishi* in a black *mawashi*, barking *hup, hup*. On cue, the white-clad *rikishi*—clearly a trainee—barreled toward the hup-caller's chest, missed his target and fell to the ground; his trainer had evaded his advance, pushing him by the back of the head into a painful looking somersault on the dirt.

After the tumble, the rolling wrestler sprang to his feet and stepped aside for the next guy. Hup, hup, charge, roll. Their backs got covered with layers of red clay dust. The topknots in their hair flopped in various states of disarray. No one smiled much. They all looked exhausted.

The last *rikishi* in the ring made his lunge for the hupper and missed badly. The guy in black shoved him hard to the dirt, pounded him while he was down, and then grabbed him by the hair and began dragging him around the ring by his topknot.

Ouch. Buck winced. *Hey, wait a minute.* He tapped Kawaguchi on the arm.

"Stop the presses there, boys. Isn't pulling the topknot off-limits?" Buck remembered clearly: Hiro told him this, and Hiro didn't lie.

"Only in competition. It is necessary in training ring. The learner must experience humility. He must learn not to make the mistake. Our honorable father, Kawaguchi Oyakata, teach him this." The less-talkative Kawaguchi beamed with pride as he looked on the trainer. The father turned toward the son and gave a twitch of a nod, and the boys both bent in half in bowing response. Buck reacted fast and bowed, too, as it hit him—the hupper was Buck's trainer. His future. And he'd signed up to submit to whatever pain Kawaguchi Oyakata inflicted.

A headache sizzled on the edge of his brain. A couple of squat-kickers glanced Buck's direction, but they gave no sign of acknowledgement. Walls went up. Nobody looked the least bit friendly. Buck grinned his usual grin, but this only made everyone glance away. Ouch.

Their practice ended, and he didn't know where the other

men went, parties, baths, somewhere—but Buck returned to his room. Alone.

This morning he'd had a job and a plane ticket home and parents who loved and respected him. And pants. *What a difference a day makes.*

Dusting off the top futon, Buck flung it out and laid down to rest. His stomach growled in empty anger. For a long while he stared at the black space above him. Images of the stomping and squats replayed in his mind. Tomorrow morning, that would be his life. Heat burned his face. What had he done? Those guys out there—they took a physical pounding a hundred times worse than Coach Brill ever demanded of the Bearcats football team back in the day when Buck spent just three weeks of summer heat on the gridiron. A pulsing fear matched the pulsing of the artery at the side of his neck. He squeezed his eyes shut.

The next thing he knew, someone was kicking him awake.

六

I LIVE IN FEAR
SEPTEMBER. TOKYO

"*Ore! Oki nasai!*" a voice snarled. Buck twisted away from the increasingly fierce kicks and bounced to his feet as fast as he could, not taking time to rub the sleep from his eyes.

"Whoa there, boy. I'm up, I'm up." Buck fended off the advancing attacks, waving away the yelling, which he couldn't understand, but got the gist all the same.

"*Oide.*" A signal to follow accompanied the command, and Buck trailed after the kicking menace down a dark hallway to the kitchen. The kicker, a short, angry man in the standard-issue topknot, pointed to a massive pile of vegetables and pulled a knife out of a belt around his *rikishi* kimono. He thrust it at Buck.

"Cut these?" Buck picked up the blade. His innocence wasn't received well. A barrage of insults flew at Buck in the foreign tongue, and Buck decided to shut up and chop. So much for the personal chef fantasy.

Several dozen carrots later, the kicker reappeared, this time with a butcher knife.

"Yellow head!" The butcher knife waved in Buck's face, then pointed at his heart.

"Ho, now. Watch where you're pointing that thing, buddy." Buck batted it away. The assailant, not amused, brought the knife forward again. Buck tried to wave it off a second time, but the knife struck at Buck's hand, slashing a cut straight across the center of his palm.

Buck stared in horror as the blood oozed out of his stinging palm. A drop fell onto the pile of chopped carrots. Then another. Then another. The blood drained from his face, through his neck, stomach, legs. His knees buckled, and he fell with a thud onto his side. Everything went black.

The ringing in his ears wouldn't stop. It sounded like his alarm clock. Buck reached out to shut off the stupid thing, but he found nothing on his bedside. He pried his eyes open. Carrots surrounded him, and his hand throbbed with pain. He grabbed it and felt the sticky warm sludge of congealing blood. He knew better than to glance at it. Now he remembered—that was how he got down here in the first place.

He forced himself to sit vertically. It took a minute, but the ringing subsided, and the blackness at his peripheral vision lifted. Somebody had already slashed his flesh, and Buck hadn't even been on site twelve hours yet. And the kicker-cum-slasher left him bleeding on the floor. What kind of a place was this, anyway?

With difficulty he stumped his way over to the sink to wash the wound.

Maybe his mother was clairvoyant bringing up his short football career. The urge to walk away before he was murdered swelled inside him. However, he couldn't bear to prove his parents right—that this life wasn't for him. Not after their strong disapproval and non-farewell. He wasn't a quitter. Not yet.

HE SPENT MOST OF THE morning hours in the kitchen. Even after the slashing he didn't get any slack. Buck put on the speed—bandage and all—and the rest of the vegetables met their match. The stable cook, a different young *rikishi*, slung them into his stew just as Buck was summoned to the training *dohyo*.

"Cooper-*san*."

Before Buck stood one of the most imposing men he'd ever seen. Buck towered over his five foot ten, but it didn't matter. The trainer had presence. It had to be the voice—it resonated like the *taiko* drums. By instinct, Buck bowed as deeply as his wretched body would permit.

"I am Kawaguchi Oyakata. You have come to my stable because my sons saw your feats in the *dohyo*." The only thing Darth Vader lacked was the scary mask-breathing. "I do not know if I agree with their decision."

Buck glanced up. Hadn't the father sent the sons to collect him? Wasn't he a desired commodity? His ego popped like a balloon in a cactus garden.

"Very tall—195 centimeters, *desho*." The trainer looked him up and down. "Over 170 kilos for certain. Humph." He wagged his large, square head. "Too big."

Too big? For a sumo wrestler?

Kawaguchi Oyakata grumbled like a diesel engine. "Beginning now, you will prove yourself worthy to be here, if you desire to stay. Every minute you spend in this stable will be watched. You *will* meet the high standard of the Kawaguchi-*beya*, or you will be made to meet it." A look of menace crossed the stern face. A nod dismissed Buck.

Buck didn't speak. Instinct told him to shut up. His stomach, however, didn't get the memo. It gurgled like a garbage disposal.

"What was that?" Kawaguchi thundered and lifted a hand to strike.

"No, sir," Buck stuttered. "My stomach—it's used to eating breakfast."

"Breakfast!" Kawaguchi Oyakata roared and lurched upward,

an inch from Buck's face. Buck could smell the foul breath of the breakfast skipper. "Breakfast! I told my sons you looked soft. *Soft!*"

A balled fist landed with power in the center of Buck's gut. He stumbled backward slightly but righted himself fast, planting his feet. He set his jaw against the pain. The stablemaster leaned in.

"Soft, weak." Kawaguchi's eyes narrowed. "Too old. Much too old." He sized Buck up again. "However, you have good balance." Satisfaction flitted across the trainer's face. "Balance is the key to sumo."

Balance he could do. A sigh of relief escaped Buck's lungs.

Kawaguchi's chest rumbled, "Balance will not be enough."

The trainer led him from the kitchen to the *rikishi* preparation rooms. First, Buck took an ego-pounding on the stable scales. Teeth tisked, just like every doctor visit he'd been to—but that was nothing compared to the stripping down for the *mawashi*-fitting: every pore and hair exposed to the eyes of sumo stable staff, who chucked loin cloths at him and yanked fabric to places where the sun didn't shine. One angry guy whipped the coarse canvas around Buck's middle, giving him a midriff welt. And he thought the *yukata* was the worst thing he'd ever worn in public.

Next came the *tokoyama*—the hairstylist.

"You get *chonmage* today. It is your gift and your symbol. Treat with respect." The man slathered him with advice and chamomile oil, then he slicked Buck's hair up so tight it pulled the corners of his eyes taut.

Finally, Buck stood at the training ring, wearing only the amateur's white *mawashi*. A chilly breeze made his arm-hairs stand on end. Never in his life had Buck felt so publicly exposed. Even his head felt naked.

No one acknowledged Buck.Naked and alone. Barraged by insults. Surrounded by strangers—hostile ones—gunning for the demise of the whitest guy in the room.The training room in the heart of the stable held all of them, but barely. It was shabby—a dirty shame of a sink and a squatter toilet in one corner. Towels hung from a bar along one edge in various states of sweaty grime. The pen smelled like sardines, body odor, and urine.

Only three of the men wore the black *mawashi*, including Kawaguchi Oyakata and one other man who looked sort of familiar. The rest wore white, like Buck.

One amateur kicked at clods of dirt with his toe. Something was wrong with his skin. Scores of small black spots festered all up and down his back, about the size of a dime, ringed by red scabs. Where did something like that come from? *Poor fella. Please, don't let that be catching.*

Yelling began. Buck did his best to follow the move of the moment. First they slammed onto their stomachs for modified push-ups. One, two, five, twelve. His biceps strained. He tried to keep up, but the shouting required more and more push-ups—close to a hundred. He struggled to hoist his weight off the ground.

"Lazy American!" A lash cracked across his bare back. "Push up! Push up!" Ribbons of pain sliced through him.

Buck's arms burned like Vesuvius, but he pushed, and pushed, and pushed up. At forty-five he collapsed. The sound of the lash whooshing through the air toward his back came again, but halted at Kawaguchi's shout.

"Dohyo ni haire! Ima!" The trainer stomped and pointed at the ring. All the *rikishi* raced to the edge of the circle and stood at attention.

An old man dressed in an ornate kimono and fancy hat padded up. With a wooden paddle in one hand and a clutch of tree branches in the other, the man chanted, waved the branches, then the paddle. Next he sprinkled generous handfuls of that rock salt onto the circle. More chanting followed. All the *rikishi* knelt and did some bowing. Buck copied them, and then the old man left. A purification ritual.

Then the real torture began.

Autumn sun warmed the day. Sweat beaded up and poured down their backs. Humidity thickened the air. First, a small man, barely two hundred pounds, stepped into the circle at the trainer's shout. On command, he took a pass at the trainer, head down, aiming for the chest. The coach made a deft step to the side, and with a swift hand shoved downward onto the little guy's head. This sent him into a painful looking somersault, the same chore-ography as yesterday. The kid rebounded fast, though his back and the back of his neck and legs now silted with reddish sand.

The kid gave a nod of a bow, and then went again at the coach. Boom! Another roll in the dirt. And another. And another. Buck began to wonder if he was even trying. A purple bruise began to spread on the uppermost vertebra of the man's spine.

A different trainee stepped forward for his turn. Buck watched the same thing happen to him, but with a little more success. He inched the trainer back, and didn't have to do a head-plant. Meanwhile, Buck and the rest of his fellow trainees stomped the squat kick-outs until Buck's thighs seared in pain. It almost made him wish he could start his somersault torture regimen to give his thighs a rest.

"Asagohan!" The trainer shouted in Buck's direction. "Asagohan!"

Buck didn't know what the word meant, but no doubt the trainer summoned him.

He bowed, entered the ring, and then on cue, barreled for-ward, head down, aiming for the chest of Kawaguchi Oyakata at full Buck-speed.

The next thing he knew, his forehead hit the clay.

"Roll, Asagohan. You must roll." The coach shouted a word

that sounded like "ro-ru" into the side of Buck's face, which was now disintegrating. Or maybe those were the grains of sand falling from the point of impact.

An age passed before Buck could right himself. He sprang to his feet. It came out wobblier than he intended. Stifled snickers came from the sidelines. He swallowed a scream, forced a smile. Woozy, he started the routine again.

On cue Buck thundered forward, this time making contact with Kawaguchi Oyakata's chest before the trainer could dodge entirely. Still, Buck went down again.

This time, though, he figured out how to roll. Somewhat. After the initial tuck and flip, his feet splatted hard against the clay and he sprawled on his back. Before he could shake the stars from his eyes, a firm yank gripped his hair, and dragged the full bulk of Buck's weight bumping across the lumpy dirt. Buck's scalp stung as tears sprang from his tear ducts. The skin on his skull was going to detach, his neck would give out, severed from his heavy torso.

The ugly ceiling roiled above Buck's eyes—brown water stains. Or blood? Ugh! He might cash in his chips right here and now. These could be his final moments before his decapitation on day one as a sumo wrestler.At last, the merciless tugging relented and Buck's body came to a thudding halt.

AFTER AN ETERNITY, LUNCH ARRIVED. Buck brushed sand from crevices on his body he rarely noticed, then washed his injured hand painstakingly. The stew he'd shed blood for this morning smelled appetizing enough to incite insanity. His empty stomach cramped at the scent and his mouth watered as he stood in the long line. This was the longest he'd gone without food in years.

The other guys waiting squared off in heated battles of rock-paper-scissors. With each throw of the sign, they chanted, *"Jan ken po!*" Some of them got into it. That had to be the weirdest thing he'd seen so far in Japan, but at least they had something to do.

The other *rikishi* with the black *mawashi*—the familiar-looking one—strutted past the chow line. Now, with fewer distractions of bodily harm, Buck finally recognized him—Hiro Yoshida's hero: Tiger Fang.

Up close it seemed the champion's gleaming teeth had sucked back into his head. Or maybe he only shined them up for competitions. The famous mountain of a man grunted and made gestures toward various pots of food, then stalked out of the kitchen into a side room where he plopped down at a low table.

The gentleman sumo wrestler.

The teeth zipped out again when the requested food was served to him. He gnawed on a chicken bone borne to him on platters by white *mawashi*-wearing servants.

Buck knew from day one he'd be sharing a stable with Tiger Fang. In fact, Hiro had practically gone apoplectic with joy when Buck agreed to go with the Kawaguchis. Still, Buck somehow never expected to see him up close. Now he stood within a stone's throw of Hiro's favorite wrestler. The kid would go berserk.

The line inched forward, giving Buck a clear sightline to Torakiba. This guy could be the next grand champion. Maybe Buck could take a lesson, watch the champ, emulate the gentleman's manners. Except the frown, of course. Buck could never paste a frown so unfriendly on his own face without breaking into laughter and feeling like an idiot. Frowns didn't equate to good manners in the Texan world Buck grew up in. There, a gentleman wore a pleasant expression.

Torakiba's frown looked like an upside down polish sausage. From it issued barked orders. Maybe shouting was gentleman-like in Japan. Buck glanced around, expecting to see admiration or loyalty on the faces of the *rikishi* around him. Instead, he saw fear and contempt.

A pair of lower-ranked *rikishi* bustled into Tiger Fang's room. They bowed low and presented the champion with three more trays heaped with food and tea and bottles of Kirin beer. Torakiba snapped angry words at them. Never turning their backs on him, never lifting their heads, they inched back from him, pausing at the door.

Torakiba sucked down bowls of soup, shoveled in mouthfuls of meats and rice. He swallowed without chewing, snarling at his servants. With those long claws, he picked up a slab of meat and tore at it with the extra long canines.

Buck gawked. This guy exemplified a gentleman's manners? Hiro couldn't possibly know about this.

Tiger Fang tasted another dish. The upside down sausage let out a howl and spat the food back into the bowl. He hefted the bowl and hurled it at a servant's head. The servant saw the bowl coming at him, a look of resigned doom in his eyes. But the poor bloke didn't duck; he just took it right on the cheekbone. *Thud!* Instead of charging forward and punching the guy, like instinct would have dictated, the victim gave a simple bow of resignation. Torakiba followed up with a litany of curses.

Buck turned away. Gentleman sumo wrestler, my foot!

His hand began to throb again, and the line inched forward. Thank goodness. As far as Buck was concerned, Tiger Fang was like a nest of vipers—once you establish its location, it's best to leave it completely alone.

Ten minutes later, Buck sipped his soup from a huge china bowl, lifting the chunky parts to his mouth using a large, oval, flat-bottomed spoon. Gratitude flooded him. Food! He'd never order it in a restaurant, but hunger made it the best food on the planet. He gulped down the broth, dug around for all the good meaty parts, and guzzled his drink. Now, if he could drift into oblivion for a long nap, it would be perfect. The morning's workout left him bruised and achy. The hand stung. It could use stitches, no doubt, but in his weariness he knew he couldn't even muster the strength to get it taken care of.

He cleared tables with the kitchen staff, dead on his feet, and then looked around for the hallway back to his ratty futon, so weary he might collapse against the wall. His body couldn't possibly take this daily pounding. Maybe this was hazing, giving the new guy the worst at the beginning. His gut said no.

Was it too late to tell the Kawaguchi brothers he'd made a mistake? That he was just kidding when he said yes, he'd join up? Probably ninety percent of boot camp enrollees felt like Buck after their first day—run over by a truck. A big one. With studded tires. And flames painted on the side. And a deer catcher grille.

"Asagohan!" Kawaguchi Oyakata's thundering voice woke him. "I think you is fatter. That is no not good." His low murmur rumbled disapproval. "You is new *rikishi*. Every new *rikishi* is *kohai*. Do you know *kohai*?"

Buck shook his head. He did not know *kohai*. And he probably didn't need to know *kohai*, seeing as how this day was probably both his first and his last. Where was a phone so he could call a cab back to the Yoshidas'?

Except he couldn't bear to face his parents. As much as they didn't want him to begin, he was pretty sure they wanted him to quit even less.

"*Kohai* is junior. *Senpai* is senior. You, Asagohan, will be junior." He motioned for Buck to follow. "Great honor comes to you."

This confused Buck as he trundled down the corridor behind his trainer. Being junior didn't sound like a great honor. It sounded fishy. Memories of the obsequious, bowing food-presenters at lunchtime popped into his head. They looked junior, and not too honored.

The trainer led Buck into a room that looked like private

sleeping quarters. Wait. Buck couldn't have earned his own room already. Naw.

"Each new *rikishi* is given a *senpai*. Kawaguchi stable's most honored *rikishi* requests you as *kohai*. Congratulations. Your *senpai* is *ozeki*—champion. He sleeps in these quarters. You begin today as personal *tsukebito,* special sumo servant to Tor-akiba."

Tiger Fang.

七

ALLEY CAT
SEPTEMBER–OCTOBER. TOKYO

"*Kutsushita! Motto kure!*" Torakiba's upside-down-sausage frown barked. He pointed at the split toe white socks and commanded Buck to place them on his feet, feet with tops so rounded only the sumo-style cloth shoes could cover them. The upper ranked *rikishi* got the perk of wearing shoes *not* made of wood.

Nine long days into his life as a slave, Buck knew the drill. When his *senpai* said jump, no "how high" mattered. What mattered was speed and accuracy. A lack of either would produce yelling, projectile objects, and more intense lashings. Punches in the kidney. A whacking with a bamboo rod that squeezed tears from the edges of his eyes.

The system tolerated zero retaliation by the *kohai.* Insults flew at him as fierce as the physical punishment.

"Tigers' teeth are sharp. Your skin is thin," came through bared teeth.

There's nothing thin about me, pal.

Buck cringed through the task of shoving socks and cloth shoes onto Tiger Fang's fat foot—and ached for his own cloth shoes. These wooden *geta* killed. Only higher-ranking feet deserved comfort. Or, less discomfort. At least the feet were clean. Buck made sure of it—he washed them himself.

Torakiba hoisted himself onto those fat-socked feet and tottered out of his private room and into his private dining nook where he plunked down on a square silk cushion and stretched his legs under the short table. Buck arranged dishes of food from the side table carefully on a square lacquer tray. Smells of fried meats and vegetables wafted through the air. Buck kept his head down.

Then he saw it. Watermelon.

At the end of the buffet meant only for the champ, sat a pile of elaborately sculpted watermelon slices: shapes of flowers, mushrooms, perfect spheres. It looked like a Baptist Ladies Luncheon on steroids. He closed his eyes, and the freshness filled his head with the scent of springtime and newly mown hay, making him feel like he was still on the same green earth as his own. There was more watermelon in that stack than even Buck could down on a hot July day, but it all had Torakiba's name stamped on it. Buck lingered in front of it, inhaling, until Torakiba noticed him and raised a jagged eyebrow.

"*Baka!* Bring me *suika!*"

Suika. What dish was *suika*? Buck's eyes scrambled over all the possible dishes.

"It's the watermelon," the other body servant whispered.

Talk about pearls before swine. His forearms trembled as he balanced the tempting tray and placed it gingerly before his *senpai.* Remaining in bowing position, he retreated to the edge of the room.

Buck's mouth watered mercilessly. Torakiba plunged a meaty fist into the delicate fruit, shoving handfuls of it into the pouch of his cheek. Then Torakiba's face fell into a sour frown and he stopped chewing.

"*Baka!*" he snarled, his mouth full of watermelon, nodding for Buck to approach. Buck scrambled forward to the foot of the table and knelt, awaiting orders.

"*Mazui!*" Torakiba thrust out his arm and swept the tray of fruit from the table, sending it halfway across the room where it splatted on the floor. Perfect fruits lay smashed in a heap, their juices trickling down between the weave of the straw. Part of Buck's soul seeped down there along with it. He lifted his eyes to scowl at Torakiba. Torakiba's own scowl reflected at him. He leaned forward to where Buck knelt, disgusted. The champion's cheeks compressed, and he spat hot, masticated fruit onto Buck's face. Wet, warm mash dripped down his skin and off his chin onto the bare part of his chest where the *yukata* formed a V.

Buck clenched his teeth. Lifting a hand to wipe himself dry would incite a beating more ferocious than usual—he could see it in the monster's eyes. They stayed locked on Buck's, challenging him. Humiliation burned in him at the dog who would destroy a thing of beauty so wantonly. Buck fought to keep his breathing steady. He refused to look away.

Torakiba muttered something that sounded like, "Come on, punk," through pinched mouth. More juice dripped from Buck's jaw to his chest. He kept his eyes fierce.Only a rattle from a tray on the side table diverted their eyes. The other body servant glanced up in fear then went back to work.

A tie. Their staredown ended in a tie. Buck jumped to his feet and went to the side table. Torakiba horked down a hunk of fish, hacked up a loogey, and lurched to his feet. He grabbed a full beer bottle and lumbered out of the room.

Buck choked back his bile, and finally wiped the filth from his face.

BUCK HAD HAD ENOUGH. A guy had to be able to get a bath around here. That foul spit. He could still feel its ooze, smell its sulphur—he had to get it off him. And these sink baths he'd been taking for the past nine days would not cut it anymore. Days' worth of red dirt encrusted his every crevice. Weren't the Japanese supposed to be super clean?

Not even a tub. This was pure injustice. He made yet another desperate search for showers, big metal barrels, anything. An unfamiliar sumo wrestler shuffled past, humming to himself. Buck was going to have to swallow his pride and ask. Desperation demanded it.

"Excuse me." Buck called to him over iPod earbuds. "Where can a guy get a bath around here?"

"Not *around here*." Buck was in luck. The shuffling *rikishi* understood him.

No. This is unacceptable. Everything in Buck revolted against this answer, his breath coming fast. No breakfast? Fine. No actual beds—okay, whatever. But no bathing? Seriously? What happened to that good old Japanese-clean-freak stereotype? *Come on.*

The guy followed up with a quick explanation. "Not around *here*. Out *there*." He pointed toward the exit to the street. "Public bath house. Good time. You like. Very nice."

Great. As if public near-nudity weren't enough for these people, now he had to participate in a public full-nudity at a bathhouse!

"This way. I show." The guy grabbed Buck by the arm and led him down the hall, out the door, down the street a few steps, and into a well-tiled, extra humid room. Buck stared. Fluffy white towels covered the most naked parts of a dozen seated men, and several half walls separated them into cubicles. At each man's side sat a miniature (by comparison) Japanese woman of middle age, who held various scrubbing instruments, a bucket of water, and some kind of soap.

"See? Soap lady. She wash. Then you bath."

Buck didn't listen. Across the room lay three large rectangular, blue-tiled pools. Steam rose from the calm surfaces. Dozens more men soaked, heads leaning back, eyes closed.

The water, the repose, looked so inviting after putting his body through such a traumatic day—nine days to be exact. Buck went straight for the water, not caring to remove his clothing. All he wanted was a good wash in one single dunk—he intended to get up right after.

"Ja! Matte, matte, matte!" His guide grabbed Buck's arm. "Soap lady first. Then bath."

Buck snapped out of his reverie. "Soap first?" His senses reignited.

"Hai. Yes."

Buck looked around again. Then he figured things out. The washing came before the dunk. It was a public tub after all. Made sense.

"Soap lady?" Did he really have to submit his personal hygiene to a stranger? "I don't want—"

The shuffling Sherpa who brought him here interrupted, "Very nice. You like."

"Possibly, but I'm good with washing myself. No soap lady." Buck stood his ground on this point. No strange women. No way, no how, no nothing.

It took a minute, but the pressure relented. Buck grabbed a bathrobe hanging nearby, covered himself as well as he could, and washed up. Then he realized that in order for him to get from the semi-private washing cubicle to the water, he was going to have to make a nude walk of blubber shame. The song his mom used to sing when she and dad drove to Galveston Island—about the yellow polka-dot bikini, where the girl tried to hide all the way from the locker to the blanket to the water, because she wore the wrong swimsuit—popped into his mind.

He stood near the edge of the cubicle, a towel around his belly, dreading what must come next. The water beckoned. Modesty inhibited. He glanced down at his body, all splotchy pink and hairy in all the wrong places. He needed to get under the surface of the water fast.

"Go," the nearby soap lady urged.

Buck's eyes darted around. Like always, being the odd-one-out in a country of uniform appearance, he got the stare of every eye. The cloak of invisibility he used to take for granted, where was it when he needed it?

"Go." She urged him again. Everyone watched. Buck clenched his teeth and moved swiftly with one hand grasping the towel. His legs bounded toward the water. In the space of a split second he leaped over the heads of the sitting bathers and cannonballed into the middle of the pool.

Bath water at last.

He sank into the tub, leaned his head back and closed his eyes. Each of his one zillion muscles relaxed in the hot water as his body molded itself against the tile. Even his toes released stress.

That Torakiba, with his foul attitude and spit, had to go down. But Buck didn't want to be the one to take the guy on. In fact, ten days into this joke of a life, he was ready to turn in his stupid *yukata* and board a plane for home.

Except for two things.

First, he didn't have much to go home to. Sure, his parents would probably weep with relief, but then what? With no job, no apartment, no nothing, he'd be stuck in their garage for who knew how long. Their joy at seeing him the first day would seriously wane by the thirty-first day.

Second, he couldn't shake the image of those dimples. That girl—every time he considered hitting the pavement, he'd see those dimples and the soft smile; he would hear her telling him again that he'd given her courage. *Courage.* He was someone else's courage. He couldn't live knowing he'd been a coward when the girl of his dreams saw him as brave.

Notwithstanding a chewed watermelon face-bath, Buck had to stay for the long haul. That's all there was to it. Even if he never made a single friend and had to power through it all alone. Even if it meant getting his face kicked in day after day.

CLEAN, BUT EXHAUSTED, BUCK SPREAD out his futon, snagged his Japanese vocabulary book from inside his pillow and flopped down on his mattress. He lay on his side and went over the words: *Kiiro.* Yellow. *Ao.* Blue.

"Dude!" A voice jarred him—a surfer's voice. "What's that smell?"

人

RED BEARD
OCTOBER. TOKYO

"Seriously, man. Don't tell me you found somewhere in Tokyo where you can buy Icy Hot." A man's voice cut the afternoon air—in English.

"Sorry?" Buck sat up straight on his futon and shoved his vocabulary book under his pillow. A silhouette of a *rikishi* filled the doorway. "Had to go to the basics and get wintergreen oil. It's not the real thing, but it does the same job. Seems to, anyhow." Buck pulled out the bottle of substitute muscle salve and tossed it to the man in the doorway.

"Love that stuff. I heard there was a new, huge American *rikishi,* but shazowie. Look at you. You're a lumberjack. Where's your Blue Ox Babe?" The guy stepped out of the shadow and into the room: Japanese face, sumo body, and the most slacked posture Buck had seen on this island.

"It's home in the barn, but don't call me babe in public. What will the guys all think?"

"I'm Wally Wada, by the way. From Honolulu. Around these parts everyone calls me Akabaka, but I prefer 'dude.'" He protracted the syllable, surfer style then came in the door and tossed back the fake Icy Hot.

"Dude." Buck parroted him. "I'm Buck. You a *rikishi*?" Buck asked, although he already knew the answer. Wally Wada from Honolulu wore the *chonmage* ponytail and was wandering around the stable with a *yukata* on. Who else would do that on purpose?

"Sort of. I mean, yeah. For now. But not this stable."

"For now?"

"My mom's Japanese. So's my dad. They moved to Hawaii before I was born, but Mom's family is a sumo legacy family—you know, like the Ginza family, just not as big money."

Buck didn't know about the Ginza family, though kitchen knives rang a bell. Or was that Ginsu knives? The voice of someone speaking quasi-normal English sounded like a dinner bell to his soul. Dude's talking made the tension in his battered muscles relax more than any dosage of Icy Hot.

"You're not in this stable?" Buck would have remembered the swirly tattoos that covered Dude's shoulders and back. They looked very Polynesian.

"Dude." Wada drew out the syllable again. "The parents thought I needed some manners so I got sent over here to crazyville. I mean, yeah. My mom and dad were pretty T-O'ed that I didn't apply for college in time. What can I say? I got lazy. I was a senior. I was to-tally irresponsible. So is that a good reason to send you off to quasi-military training grounds in a foreign country? Geez, dude. Just because Hakabata Oyakata is my uncle doesn't mean he whacked me any less than those other guys. Check it out, dude." Dude extended a well-scarred arm for proof. "Family affection. Japanese style."

The scars looked terrible, and multi-layered. Buck wondered if Dude's parents knew about the beatings. Probably, if they were a sumo legacy family as the guy said. Imagine knowingly sending a son into this. It blew his mind. If Buck's mom had any idea what all went on here she'd kill him herself before letting him join up.

"At least it's not cigarette burns. Some guys have them up

and down their backs. Black scabs ringed with red. Killer." Dude winced. "I'm over in Hakabata stable with the *uncle*-man. All the other *rikishi* over there are a bunch of punks, all Japanese, and they think foreigners pollute the sport."

"But you're not a foreigner." Full-blooded Japanese wasn't foreign.

"Yeah, but I am. I mean, anybody not full-blooded and born and raised here is foreign. I mean, it's the attitude. Bugs me, you know? This whole superiority complex. I mean, get over it already. Yeah, Japan is super special. So are a lot of other places. Sheesh. Look at whatshisname in my stable. He's half-Japanese and they refer to him as *hanjin.* Half-person. No, seriously. Half a person."

Buck couldn't believe he was having an actual conversation with someone—about the things that troubled his subconscious so much, and with someone who seemed to completely get it. This was his first un-alone moment since arriving in the sport.

"My plan is to survive here, and buddy, I am going to find me some good golf. Somewhere. Even if I have to sneak onto a golf course. Pow! They nabbed me doing that once. Got off with a warning. So, you got a sumo name yet? A *shikona*?"

"I don't know. What's yours again?"

"Akabaka. Love it, right? The Red Idiot. Very flattering. My beard comes in red, so they think it's funny." Dude leaned over and punched Buck in the shoulder. "And what do you mean you don't know if you have a name?"

"Kawaguchi Oyakata—"

"Call him The Gooch, dude. Everybody does."

Really? Whoa-kay. "The Gooch keeps saying something like Asagohan. I don't know why, and I don't know what it means."

"Huh. Unless it has a different kanji I don't know about—my poetic Japanese is rusty on a real good day—it sounds like the word *breakfast.* Why would he call you breakfast?"

"I don't know." Buck gave a slight shrug.

But he did know.

He stared at his feet. What a humiliating, stupid name. It sent him hurtling back to junior high again, with bullies and cruel nicknames all over the place. Years passed, and yet he landed smack dab in the middle of it again.

Breakfast. Ugh. A *professional moniker*. Was "Breakfast" any better than his junior high taunt-name, Buttcheese? Not much.

"So, the Icy Hot working? The workouts kill, right? Hard on the old muscles." He pronounced it *musk-ulls.* Surfer English. Surprisingly soothing.

"Seriously. Yeah, but the Icy Hot is less for workouts and more for the forty pound brick my *senpai* made me hold for three hours yesterday. Oh, and for the lower back from when all fifteen *rikishi* put me at the bottom of the dog pile this morning."

"Right. No broken beer bottles, though, I hope." Dude took the hazing reports in stride.

"Not yet." *Broken beer bottles? What the—*

"I like you, kid. Who's your *senpai*?"

Just as Dude asked this, a looming presence appeared at the door of the sleeping area. Buck figured some of the others would be finishing their lunch and beer and coming in for a sleep soon. He glanced up. Like the devil, someone had only to speak of him and he appeared.

Dude's face spoke volumes: *No! Not that guy.*

"Asagohan!" Torakiba pointed at his own feet, *"Ima! Ashi wo naosere."*

Footrub hour. Dude backed away in silence but sent a look— *Dude, your life sucks*—in Buck's direction before sneaking out.

Buck sucked a quick cleansing breath for strength, and obeyed, but not quickly enough. Torakiba bared his vicious teeth and spat curses through the whole rubdown. Buck kept his face a stone, his breathing even. When it was over, Torakiba thanked him with a fist to Buck's kidneys before exiting.

Buck clutched his side in pain. There had to be an upside. Later, Buck lay on his futon smelling the Icy Hot on his ribcage. At least it wasn't cigarette burns or broken beer bottles.

"DUDE! DO US A SOLID—GET off your butt and help!" Dude's voice echoed against the shiny tiles of the train station as he came thundering toward Buck at full running speed. Buck hadn't seen him in three weeks, and now he was shouting for help in the subway station. Buck dropped his newspaper and lurched to his feet in the fluorescent glare of underground lighting.

Dude went blazing past, followed closely on his heels by another guy—huge enough to be a mobile Easter Island statue, but wearing a sumo robe and platform wooden shoes.

Buck chugged to catch up. "Why are we running?" A platform and seats whizzed past them as they wove through the quitting-time crowd. Tons of drunken businessmen and a few million kids in yellow rain slickers blocked their path, but they dodged well.

"Getting my friend Reggie away from that psycho chick, dude," Dude drawled, huffing hard. Buck shot a look over his shoulder and saw the wild intent in the girl, even through the cake of white makeup and beneath the black wig. A geisha!

Reggie, the hulking mass with a forehead of epic proportions, raced toward the open doors of an already full train.

"Distract her!" Dude dashed after Reggie.

"How?" Indecision clutched Buck. Distract her?

"Use your charm, dude."

Buck thought fast and stuck out a foot. He tripped the poor girl—but he caught her on her way down. "Sorry, miss." He righted her and set her on a bench, discombobulated, just as the train doors began to close.

Dude and Reggie were wedged in the door, and an official in blue uniform shoved against them with his white-gloved hands. Buck made a break for it and dove into the final push of the train jammer's hands. The doors shut, snagging a corner of his *yukata.* His body crushed against everyone in that metal tube. Like a canned ham that smelled vaguely of seaweed.

All he could move were his eyes. His face smashed up against the glass of the door, and he managed to glance at the geisha's face. She stared longingly after Reggie. Wistful. She waved a handkerchief in his direction.

When the train pulled into the darkness of the tunnel, Reggie exhaled a puff of hot breath onto Buck's neck.

"That was a close one. I gots to say, *muchas gracias*. You's an *amigo* back there."

"You're not Japanese," Buck squeaked. The elbow of an American businessman jutted into his ribs. The train hummed along.

"Nope. Reggie's a Filipino," Dude answered. "And a lucky one. That girl almost caught him this time. Good job, Buck. I knew we could count on you."

Buck frowned. "What's the matter with her? She looked fine to me." *Real fine.*

"Miss One Thousand Autumn Leaves has a thing for Reggie." Dude chortled.

"She won't leave me alone, *esse*. My Japanese—it's not so good. Got me in trouble a time or two."

"Like with the geisha?" Buck raised an eyebrow, albeit toward the black of the tunnel. The train hit a corner and jostled. The elbow moved out of Buck's ribs and he could breathe a little better.

"It's pretty bad, but I can't help it, you know?" He pronounced his "you" like "ju," which sounded as familiar as a Baptist Sunday School song to his Texas ear. "This girl, she just doesn't get it. She thinks I am her true love. And I have to keep on telling her, no way, you know?"

"What's wrong? Don't you like her?" Maybe she wasn't pretty under all that white makeup. But sumo wrestlers and other guys Buck's size couldn't be choosy. If the girl showed an interest, the guy should pay attention.

"Seriously, man. She's *muy bonita.*" He made a kiss-smack sound. "And she can really hang a kimono, if you knows what I mean." Buck had seen the green silk kimono, if only briefly. Reggie was right. "But I'm just kind of busy. Don't have time for all that drama, you know?"

"And now she won't leave you alone."

"Believe me, man. You do *not* want to get yourself stalked by a geisha. They have ways. They have connections. They know everybody. You cannot hide from those girls, man."

Dude wrangled himself nearer and said, "Reggie got here a month before you."

"So, you're enjoying the fun of being a *kohai,* too, I take it?" Buck asked.

"Yeah. We're enjoying tough *kohai* times, and not enjoying them very much." Reggie chortled.

A joke? Buck let the first joke he'd heard in months waft through the air, like the smell of hot, fresh bread. *Amigo* for sure.

"Who's your *senpai?*"

"Sobakubi." Reggie snorted. Buck remembered that name—the man Hiro hated with a passion. "They nailed me to the worst guy in the stable. Sobakubi, his eyes so fat and round, like bull's-eye targets. I'd like to take my shot. Spoiled son of a cabinet minister, thinks no rules apply to him and does whatever he wants. Once he made me eat food he had already chewed. Man, that was not cool. If I get some kind of rash or parasite from his saliva's germs I'll never get any good endorsement contracts."

"And you'll never have enough money to marry that girl," Buck chuckled. Bummer for Reggie. But there were enough bummers to go around. His own Torakiba, for instance. The train pulled into the next station.

"We can go up and walk back from here. It's only a half a mile. She won't find me now." The doors opened, and Buck had no choice but to pile out. He was like one of those spring-loaded snakes in cans magicians use. Reggie and Dude followed. "You showed courage back there, Buck. You wanna go get something to eat with us? There's a good ramen shop around the corner here."

There was. And he did.

Just when the steaming bowls of noodles arrived with the wooden chopsticks, and Buck was about to lift a bite to his mouth, Dude asked, "So, dudes. Are you ready for your first exhibition match? We leave tomorrow morning for Chiba."

Fear clutched Buck. Tomorrow he had to prove himself in the ring.

九

HIDDEN FORTRESS: THE LAST PRINCESS
OCTOBER. CHIBA

The chartered bus pulled up in front of the Chiba Prefecture Grand Recreation Center—an ominous name for a boring looking building, a building where today Buck had something to prove.

It seemed a zillion years ago when he stood on the clay in Tokyo, the audience cheering for him during comic sumo. On that day, Japan embraced him because he came as a pleasant surprise—blond, fat American who smiled, and had a little bit of fight in him.

Now, however, Buck knew group mentality worked against him. Unless he proved himself worthy of the sport, the masses would reject him as a one hit wonder.

Buck winced as the *tokoyama* hairstylist pulled his hair into the topknot so tight it stretched the corners of his eyes back into an Asian slant. Slathered oil dripped at the edges of his hairline, smelling like chamomile. He swatted at a stray bead of oil as it made its way down his temple.

Buck's stomach clenched. His match would be early—new debuts always were. He could really botch all the ceremonial gobbledygook. It was one thing to act amateur during comic sumo while a tourist, but another thing to blow it as an actual member of a stable. It would really embarrass The Gooch big time. For that, he knew he'd pay. But he didn't want to pay—he was so tired of paying.

Wearing just his *mawashi,* without the protection of even one of those stupid thin robes, Buck marched into the hallway to figure out the schedule.

"Look! Look!" A *rikishi* from Buck's stable waved a program in his face. "See, Asagohan? You go first match!" He pointed at the list.

Nothing but hen-scratches. Illiteracy sucked.

"Asagohan fights Oishiringo. Go, Asagohan!"

The drums beat, echoing in his chest cavity. Higher ranked wrestlers marched into the arena, their embroidered silk aprons flapping. Torakiba's fans roared. The wrestlers circled the *yobi-dashi*—the caller. Buck seethed. Someday that would be him. He'd be marching in that ceremony, not standing here with scabs on his spine from getting dragged around by his hair.

The giants slugged past him, cocksure and fierce, on their way back to the dressing room. Buck's ears thrummed. The *taiko* drums stopped dead silent, only to make way for the announcer's voice calling out two names: Asagohan and Oishiringo.

Buck's mouth went dry, and his palms got wet. He couldn't do it. He was toast.

He approached the *dohyo* strutting on the outside, stumbling on the inside. He kept his eyes off the crowd. *Focus. Focus.* He bowed before stepping up onto the clay platform, grabbed a handful of the coarse white salt crystals and sowed them liberally across the ring. Then he bowed again. The ringside staff offered him the power water. That stuff tasted like bile. When the official offered him the power paper, Buck gladly spat it onto the ground behind the paper shield.

The *yobidashi* waved his paddle and made tight, choreographed moves all around the ring in his elaborate kimono and mortarboard cap with a chinstrap. It ended too fast.

Buck squatted at the line in the sand across from a Mongolian behemoth with a round face and a cherry red spot on each cheek: Oishiringo.

The Mongolian sniffed, a haughty sneer, which sent ire boiling in Buck's gut. The cavalier angle of the Mongolian's eyebrow said a lot—the man wasn't taking this exhibition bout seriously. Forget toasted breakfast. Oishiringo was going to get a surprise.

The *yobidashi* waved his clapper and leapt backward.

Buck sent his body hurtling in the direction of the apple-faced man, head down, aiming for the center-right of his chest. Before Oishiringo could even get in a face and chest slap, Buck had him by the *mawashi*. And he kept moving. The Mongolian's feet began to slide backward. Oishiringo, looking shocked, squirmed out of the hold, and Buck let go of the *mawashi*. He grabbed for the biceps, all the while moving forward, driving and driving Oishiringo back. Adrenaline coursed through his veins. He gave a final shove—Oishiringo tripped over the edge of the ring.

The crowd went crazy.

"*Kachikoshi*, Asagohan," the announcer called. The winner, Asagohan.

Buck had won his debut match!

He exhaled at last, and a smile roiled to the surface of his face. He waved to the crowd, bowed once, and then practically skipped up the gangway. Back in the dressing room, he collapsed on the bench in a post-adrenaline heap. Exhibition or not, he won! Yeah, baby! Nothing could bring him down—

Tiger Fang growled. "*Cowboy!* Straighten my *mawashi!*"

Buck's smile melted off. He got to his feet and obeyed the barked command, making sure each of the white rickrack-looking zigzags dangling from the champ's belt hung straight. The humiliation of the task burned.

"Asagohan. Oil my back."

Buck barely contained his seething. He followed the champion down the passageway from the dressing rooms toward the ring. The crowd craned their necks to catch a glimpse of Tiger Fang, the *ozeki*. Buck caught gasps and whispers of Torakiba's name on hundreds of lips. He glanced up. Torakiba's mouth pulled into a fiendish grin, revealing his razor-like teeth. Maybe there was a second concentric set, like a shark's. Torakiba gave a gracious bow to his fans, who went wild—screams, applause, fist pumps and all.

It sickened Buck. If only they knew what a complete and total beast their hero really was, they wouldn't have worshipped him like that.

Suddenly, the *senpai* stopped short. Buck bumbled into Torakiba's back, but the champ didn't notice or yell or pound him or anything. A new figure loomed before them, and a voice resonant with sub-woofers spoke.

"Ah, Torakiba. You are here with your *tsukebito,* I see."

Buck peered hard at the person who could shut Torakiba up. Whoever he was, the guy had a presence, even among giants. No wonder Torakiba stopped. Anybody would stop for a voice like James Earl Jones's.

For the first time ever, Buck saw Torakiba's face exhibit fear and respect. The champ bowed to the older man in the black kimono with the silver embroidery. An official. He sizzled with importance. Buck followed the example of his *senpai*, bowed, and said nothing.

"Asagohan, I believe?" The official turned to address Buck.

Buck bowed again to the man, feeling the thrum of that voice in his chest. The official's shaven head sported grey stubble above the ears, and wrinkles ran deep in the folds of his face, almost like a human Tiki necklace.

"You are very, very lucky to have this Torakiba as your *senpai*. And not just because it is such an honor for you." A snide twist curled his lip. "The luckiness is because you will not have to fight him in the *dohyo* as you are his *kohai*. You could never defeat his *mitokorozeme*. Could he, Torakiba?"

Torakiba snorted.

"You have been working on your *mitokorozeme*, I am sure."

"Hai, Ginza-*sama*." Torakiba bowed, almost bent in half, toward the official. Ginza. Buck had heard that name before.

"I must go. You may like to hear my announcement today, Torakiba. Please listen for it. It is a large part of how I plan to keep sumo pure." He nodded in the direction of the champion, then turned to Buck. "Asagohan, *ganbare.*"

Buck knew this phrase to loosely mean, "Hang in there," or "Keep up the good work." And what was that "keep sumo pure" comment about?

The announcer called Torakiba's name, and Buck stood back, melting into the mouth of the staging area as the *ozeki* marched out to the roar of thousands of fans. Reggie appeared at Buck's side along with Dude, eyes gleaming and bursting to speak.

"Dude, Asagohan, I can't believe you were just talking to Ginza-*sama*. Great honk!" The three stood shoulder to shoulder, watching the sharp-fanged champ face another top-ranked *rikishi*. This match-up against stars of sumo was what the people paid money to see.

"Wait, first tell me what *mitokorozeme* is, then you can tell me who is this Ginza-*sama*, and who cares." Buck watched as Torakiba's sweat speckled the referee's kimono.

"Where did you hear that word?"

"Just tell me what it is. Quick, before I forget the word and why I wanted to know it."

"*Mitokorozeme*. It's a sumo technique." Reggie jumped in. "Nobody hardly ever does it no more because it's, like, three moves going on at the same time. Very tricky for even the best of the top guys."

"Three moves?"

Dude jumped in. "My uncle is a trainer, dudes, and he can't even do it. Where'd you hear about it, Buck? Spill it."

Buck pressed half moons of pain into his palm as he thought of Torakiba and his secret skill. "What three moves?"

Reggie scratched his head. "All at the same time the attacker has to do an inside leg trip with one leg, *and* grab the guy's other leg behind the thigh and pull it out from under him, all while ramming his head into the opponent's chest to knock him over backward. Get it?"

"Yeah, dude. The only thing harder than *executing* the move is *defending* against it. Forget it, Buck." Dude snapped and pointed finger guns at his head.

"That's why nobody does it no more. We don't even learn it in the stables. It's from old times. Forget about it, Buck. Quit wasting your time. Nobody's doing nothing like that. Do something smart. Find out about Ginza. And his sexy daughter." Reggie shoved Buck's shoulder just as Torakiba shoved his challenger's shoulder and grabbed him by the back of the knee. That guy had skills.

Buck tried imagining the move. Hard to even picture, let alone execute. A curse floated through his mind.

"Fine, fine. Who's Ginza, anyway? You told me about him before, Dude," Buck said, half-listening to the audience's screams for Torakiba's *mawashi* grab.

"Ginza, dudes. That guy is only the *dynastic head* of the most *revered* sumo-legacy family of *all time.*" The lilt of Dude's Hawaiian accent emphasized the important points of his explanation. "He's, like, a king. One of the head honchos at the JSA—big time sumo official. He rules it with an iron fist, keeping sumo pure, that's the king's big crusade. And he's got a daughter—the princess. Called Chocho. Seriously, man, she's *gorgeous*—eyes like inky pools of heavenly love, a smile that makes your little heart go pitter pat. Plus, curves from here to Guam. Totally ace. No man alive who ever saw Chocho Ginza could honestly say he wasn't at least a little in love with her."

As Torakiba's match commenced, Dude went on about the daughter. She smelled Downy-fresh. She walked on water. She was the triple threat—smoking hot, way smart, super rich.

Whatever. Chocho Ginza—probably a very nice girl, but Buck's heart only admitted one woman at a time. Right now the girl with the dimples took up all the space inside it.

He glanced out at the crowd. Dimple Girl just might be here tonight. A guy could only hope—that maybe she had come to Chiba to see his debut. After all, she did say he gave her courage, right?

At that moment, the crowd all leapt to their feet. Torakiba tossed his opponent off the *dohyo* and into the third row of the crowd, farther than a lot of people could toss a can of soup. It looked like Torakiba took the exhibition seriously today, too. Maybe the talk with Ginza had fired him up.

Mitokorozeme. Torakiba was learning it. An old-fangled move nobody would expect or learn to defend against. Well, High and Mighty Ginza should bet his boots—those stupid toe-shoes—that Buck would be ready to go up against Torakiba's fancy move. Whether the day ever came or not.

Buck didn't want to watch anymore. He would do something more productive, like look for Dimple Girl again while Torakiba received his applause and left the stage. Before he could search long, Dude grabbed Buck's arm and hissed.

"Dude, look who's up at the microphone now. Your new best friend Ginza."

Reggie elbowed Dude in the ribs. "Translate for us, mighty Japanese speaker."

"Uh, okay." Dude listened a moment. "His family is honored to be servants of the great sport of sumo for many decades. In a little less than two years a huge milestone will arrive—one hundred year anniversary of Ginza and sumo, a partnership—an alliance. He wants to celebrate by giving the gods of sumo an offering they will enjoy."

"An offering to the gods. Not seriously." Buck chuffed. "Excellent. Crazies on every continent and isle of the sea." It sounded more like a remote island of Polynesia where they still burned stuff in front of big stone idols, instead of the island of Japan, origin of robot toy dogs and Nintendo Wii.

Dude rubbed his chin. "Seriously wacked. I never expected anything this rad to happen at this Chiba *jungyo*. So glad I came. Now he's saying something about being the father of no sons. Yeah, I heard that before. He's been notoriously and publicly morose about having no heir. No sons. No grandsons. I guess that'd be kind of a big deal with a fortune that size."

"I thought you said he had a daughter. Inky pools of molten love," Buck said.

"A daughter, sure. A stunning daughter. Not a triple bogey like that chick over there." He motioned toward a homely woman on the front row. "Or a par like that one." He pointed to her friend, who looked pretty normal. "No. Ginza's is double eagle all the way. A fall-off-your-surfboard-and-do-a-head-plant-into-the-curl gorgeous daughter. They call her Chocho. Yowza."

Dude slapped himself and let his hand drag down his cheek.

"But she's not a son, so this *baka* doesn't care."

"Did he say what the offering is to the sumo gods? Is it a vat of *chanko nabe* the size of a Toyota?" Buck was ready to put this Ginza crackpot into the "ignore it and it won't bother you" category, but he played along for the moment.

"Who knows? He's being all mysterioso about it. Says he will announce more details in coming months as the anniversary gets closer. Meanwhile, let's just check out the babe-a-licious daughter. Seriously hot. Not anorexic like all the weight-obsessed skinny Japanese girls. Got a nice—*you know*—bikini body."

"That's too weird, *amigos*." Reggie saluted a fan, and the three of them turned to go back up the *hanamichi* gangway toward the dressing room. "Like, does this guy thinks the gods of sumo care enough to somehow magically send him a manchild, drop it in his little family *butsudan*? And then what?" Reggie grunted. "The child will bring balance to the force of all Ginza enterprises? That *hombre* is messed up."

Poor, beautiful daughter Chocho, whoever she was. A dad that weird. Had to be tough.

They'd gone only a pace or two when Dude thrust out an arm and made them stop and turn back. "Wait. They just said he's inviting the daughter forward now." He pointed toward the ring. "That, boys, is Miss Chocho. Watch the sway of those luscious hips." Dude sighed at the sight of her, and Buck turned to see as she joined her father on the stage. Silence fell over the crowd.

Buck squinted. He couldn't quite see the face of the girl in the royal blue silk kimono, the poor waif. Ah, she turned his way at last.

Wow. Pretty. Very pretty. Of course, dressed in the traditional style she would look beautiful no matter what. All the Japanese girls did. Royal blue silk—that was like the girl with the dimples when she stood in that shaft of sunlight under the autumn leaves. That face stayed etched in his mind and in the fleshy tables of his heart.

Ginza reached out and took his daughter's arm to guide her in a circle around the ring, like a prize sheep at the county fair. Buck stared at her smile.

And then, he saw the *dimples.* Chocho Ginza. He'd found Dimple Girl!

Buck had to plant his feet on the ground just to stop the room from spinning and pulling him to his knees. *Steady, boy. She's in this room!* Hot fear and happiness and torment surged in him. After all this time, seeing her again almost floored him. He always wished—but never dared expect—to find her, and now! Just like what he'd expected all along—she had to be some kind of royalty, and being the daughter of Ginza-*sama* qualified her as princess of sumo. Of course. And she wore it with grace and elegance.

Buck had to force himself to close his jaw, which had now dropped to his chest. A sigh of longing escaped his lungs.

There she stood, in another shaft of light, with tens of thousands of eyes admiring her. She was a thing of beauty all the world recognized, one every man in this room would probably like to own.

Buck didn't stand a chance.

AFTER THE RAIN
NOVEMBER-DECEMBER. FUKUOKA

November came at last, and with it came the Fukuoka tournament on the island of Kyushu in the far south of Japan, almost to Okinawa. Training and *senpai*-torture continued, but Buck now had a focus—a concrete reason to endure it all: Chocho. He'd found her again. Hopeless crushes were his specialty, but this time, something diverged from his usual pining for the unreachable star—when she spoke to him in the street, his soul had *felt* hers.

In his spot at the lowest rank on the totem pole of sumo life, Buck only competed every other day. During days one through fourteen, he faced Mongolian Oishiringo again—the guy he crushed into applesauce in Chiba—plus five others of his same tier of bottom feeders, and he dominated.

Beginner's luck, perhaps, but the crowd adored him, calling *Breakfast, Breakfast,* wherever he went. A dumb thing to chant, but still, Buck's confidence soared, a balloon on the world's longest string.

Then day fifteen hit.

Buck made his way through the tangy fall air to the Fukuoka arena from their makeshift stable a few blocks away. Windy gusts cut through his stupid excuse for clothing. Buck shivered and walked faster.

Out of the nook in an alleyway, a guy in a suit sprang.

"Asagohan! Asagohan!" A reporter. A young one. A long shock of black hair covered half his face. "I am Tanaka is my name. My is English so bad, but I ask you." He flicked his head to the left and the shock of hair moved out of his eyes. Buck watched the repetitive action and realized he'd suffered many days of it himself, before the *chonmage* topknot freed him. A little soft spot formed in his heart for Tanaka.

"This is your first appearance in real tournament as *rikishi*. Do you have butterflies?"

Butterflies? His mind swept to Chocho in the shaft of light, dust particles like butterflies surrounded her. His face felt warm and he shook off the image.

"Then you are not nervous at all?"

Ah, nervous butterflies. Honestly, sometimes these people memorized the most random phrases in their English classes. "Yes, I mean. Butterflies are in a war in my stomach." Might as well humor him.

"A war." Tanaka scribbled something on a notepad. "I like you, Asagohan. You is big nice *gaijin*."

Buck chuckled and patted Tanaka on the shoulder. "I like you, too, Tanaka."

Tanaka flipped his hair out of his eyes again and got serious. "Today, Asagohan, you will face Sakanakao. It means Fish Face! He is the tallest *rikishi* in your rank. Are you happy to fight against someone taller than you?"

Buck hadn't known. He hiccupped. Up to now Buck had relied a lot on his height for his wins. But to face someone taller? Buck's confidence flew away as if someone had just snipped the string that had held his balloon.

ACROSS THE *DOHYO*, SAKANAKAO, HAYSEED yokel from Bulgaria

rolled his googly eyes. He was tall—really tall. It freaked Buck out. In an instant, the guy had Buck by the neck with one arm and by the *mawashi* with the other.

It happened so fast. Buck had to fight back. He wrested himself out of the neck-hold and spun around, only to get a faceful of fish again. His eyes flitted to the audience.

Chocho!

Ringside, she held her hand over her mouth. Her eyes were intent on Buck, almost pleading with him. Every ounce of Buck's remaining focus melted into goo. A lifetime ago he'd looked into her gold-flecked eyes, felt the pressure of her arm on his while he became lighter than air. And now here she sat. His mouth went slack as he stared at her—*guh*. Now who was the fishface? Man, oh, man. He was such a dork. He heard that *Star Wars* conversation in his head: *Say, what do you think? A princess and a guy like me?* And his inner-Luke-Skywalker responded with an immediate *No*.

Less than a second later, Buck tasted a mouthful of sacred, purified dirt. Humiliation burned in him. In a blaze of crimson, he hobbled off the stage. It smoldered as he made his way up the ramp to the dressing room area. He couldn't look back at her now, especially when she had just witnessed his major defeat. To a lurch named Fishface. For the rest of the *basho* he wandered the hallways trying to shake off his self-loathing. He was going to skip the award ceremonies. He didn't care who won or lost in his own tier, or any other.

"Hey, Buck. What's the matter? You look like you just got your first taste of *nat-to*," Reggie called.

"Stupid bout. Geez, Reggie. I hate wallowing here in the lowest ranks like a hog in the mire. It's killing me." Buck forgot he was talking to a fellow hog-wallow dweller.

Loss, dimples, loss, dimples. He was obsessing. She had leaned on him for courage. But the pitiful thing was that the first time she saw him try to take himself seriously, he failed her. Some courage.

"You still ripped it up out there, Buck-man. You don't got nothing to be ashamed of. Probably went up a rank. Unlike me. I lost to the Mongolian." Reggie gave the thumbs-down.

"Oishiringo had his last good night against you. He's going down next time, Reg."

Dude strutted up to them and leaned a hand against the brick wall. "At least Reggie got a nice dozen roses out of it." He pulled out a cigarette and lit it.

Buck waved away the smoke. "Flowers?"

"Not real flowers." Reggie punched the wall and immediately put his hand up to his mouth.

"No-oh-oh. Not real flowers. But real green." Dude slapped Reggie on the back. "His girlfriend-o sent him a dozen origami roses she folded all by her geisha self, all for him, out of *sen* yen notes."

Reggie grimaced and kissed his knuckles. "Them geisha stalker girls. They is very dangerous."

They rounded a corner that opened up into the gangway.

"They're calling our rank's awards. We need to get our fat lards out there." Dude pulled them toward the arena.

Buck dug his heels in. He wasn't going down there. It had nothing to do with him.

"Come on, Buck. Move it, already." Reggie and Dude overpowered his resistance. They jostled him down toward the stage area. An interminable line of sweaty, *mawashi*-clad *jonokuchi* rank wrestlers stood at attention for the ceremony. Buck and his cohorts joined them. Buck's heart clunked.

Ginza-*sama* was presenting the award for Buck's rank. Chocho's intimidating dad's eyebrows waggled. Those things might spring to life and crawl off his face.

Softly at first, but then growing louder, chanting began in the far west balcony of the arena. *"A-sa-go-han, A-sa-go-han."* Buck looked toward the sound. It grew and began to catch on in other sections of the crowd. *"A-sa-go-han, A-sa-go-han."*

His heart sped up to meet the rhythm. He waved to the fans—nice useless folks who could do nothing to repair his disaster. He'd done them wrong today, and he returned a weak, apologetic smile.

The inevitable words, *"Kachikoshi Sakanokao,"* which meant "Win, Fishface," should rumble out of Ginza's mouth soon. The googly-eyed one was going to walk up and get the win envelope, and Buck was going to be stuck here, with only this horrible realization—after tonight he might never lay eyes on Chocho again. A defeat like this while still ranked so low could mean the end of him.

Reggie's elbow wedged hard in Buck's ribs, and he shoved him in the general direction of the daunting Ginza.

"Asagohan—*ike!*" Weeks of Torakiba taught him the command, "Go!"

"What? What is it?" he called over his shoulder as he trundled down the gangway.

"You won!"

Won? No, not after his humiliating loss to Fishface. Buck's eyes shot around the arena. All eyes focused on him. The crowd's chant of, *"A-sa-go-han, A-sa-go-han,"* had now broken into happy screams. Buck stumbled toward the *dohyo* and the frowning Ginza, who didn't share the crowd's enthusiasm. Contempt muddied his face.

Buck bowed and accepted the proffered envelope with both hands.

Ginza leaned in and hissed, "As if it weren't bad enough having sumo defiled by foreign men who at least look like men—now we have *you,* this yellow head in the whited skin of a dead eel dirtying our sacred sport."

Buck double-blinked. Nice way of congratulating the new guy on his first success—with blatant racism and insults. Buck shot Ginza a look of disbelief. Totally psycho. Who was this guy? The Japanese Archie Bunker?

Buck pulled his lips into a grin and gave his now-signature wave to the chanting crowd, and the audience went wild. Amazing. The screams were for *him*. He searched for Chocho—what would she think of him now?

There. Her pearlescent skin and dewy eyes shone back at him. His heart leaped when their eyes met for a split second, but plummeted when he got scooted from the stage.

Back in the safety of the dressing room and clutching his winner's envelope, Buck winced when Dude punched him hard in the upper arm.

"Nice job. Looked like Ginza, The Big Kahuna of sumo, gave our boy what-fer. Way to go, Buck-man. You've arrived."

Whited eel skin? Buck examined the skin of his arm. Maybe he didn't know enough about eels to judge.

Dude took a bite of a huge apple. "Too bad your *senpai* got his butt kicked by the grand champ. That'll stink like my aunt's ancient poodle for you. Torakiba hates that Korean."

A guy from Buck's stable bustled in. "*Ossu*. Asagohan. Letter for you." The messenger waved a note his way. "It smells real nice." He sniffed it and rolled his eyes heavenward. "Like a sexy woman wants you."

Buck snatched the envelope out of his hands. "Hey." He shot the messenger a warning look. "Watch how you talk about a lady."

Buck thought he smelled flowers as he felt the white linen paper and ran his finger under the flap. He turned his back to the other guys and read the short sentence.

Congratulations on your kachikoshi.

A drawing of a small butterfly perched at the bottom of the translucent rice paper.

"Hey," Buck asked the others. "How do you say butterfly in Japanese?"

"Chocho." Delivery guy had turned to leave, but when he gave this response he pulled up short. "Wait, no. I cannot *believe* it. You did *not* just receive a special letter from the *beri beri* beautiful Miss Chocho Ginza-*san!* That girl is like electric sexy woman."

Buck made a fist and brandished it. "That's a lady you're referring to, pal."

"Fine, fine. Cool down, Asagohan." He slunk away, and Buck put his indignation on the back burner.

Chocho. It meant butterfly. His fingers tingled.

A bunch of guys shoved up near him to inspect the note, but he clasped it to his chest and pushed them back with an outstretched hand. His face went hot with bliss.

Wait. He'd better double check. "Does she send congratulations cards to all the winners?" he asked.

"No. Never. And *never, never* to *jonokuchi* bottom rank."

Never? Buck clutched the letter even closer. Her face *did* tell him something tonight!

Dude sidled up to Buck. "Okay, spill it. You've talked to her?"

"Once. A little. A long time ago." Only two months, but a lifetime gone.

Every man in the room turned to stare at Buck. "You've seen her in person?" "Wow." "Chocho Ginza-*san* is the girl of my dreams. Every kind of them." "You suck, man. How do *you* get a girl like that?" "She's the hottest thing this side of the sun." "I'd like to get me some of that."

"Watch it, men." Buck turned on them. Fierce protectiveness bubbled just under the surface of his skin. He was a grizzly bear, and they'd better shut up, or else.

He pushed his way out of the cloister and strode out the door before he punched somebody. Shoving the note into the folds of his *yukata's* sleeve, he bustled down the hallway to get some solitude, and savored the moment.

But he couldn't have that. In an instant, Tiger Fang loomed up.

Day fifteen hadn't been a gold star for Tiger Fang here in Fukuoka, either. The loss had kept the Emperor's Cup for this *basho* firmly in Butaniku's warty warthog hands. Torakiba's whole body filled the passageway, anger burning in his eyes.

"Asagohan!" Torakiba slapped Buck with an echoing crack across his cheek. Buck didn't dare lift his hand to the spreading pain in his eye. *"Ima! Oide!"*

Buck followed, but not willingly, down the dark corridor and out to the alleyway behind the arena. His eye started to swell—he touched it while Tiger Fang's back was to him.

Buck trailed the champ, expecting insults hurtling at him about his "big" win in the lowest ranks, followed by a little roughing up. The usual. But the usual beating could have happened inside the emptying arena. Buck's palms began to sweat.

Torakiba led Buck to a deserted doorway in the Fukuoka alley. Buck glanced around. No humanity came into view. He could use the thousands of fans thronging the alley right about now. Stupid wish for solitude. *Be careful what you wish for, idiot.*

Murder gleamed in Torakiba's eye as it fell on Buck in the wintry moonlight. Something dark and ugly lurked here.

The first blow struck Buck's jaw like a wrecking ball. The second connected with a place buried so deep beneath the fat layers Buck never imagined reaching it was even possible. Torakiba's fist bruised that unidentified internal organ.

A moment dragged in pain before Buck's mind could register the attack. By then a third blow came flying at Buck's cheekbone, knocking his head hard against the bricks of the alleyway. However, Buck didn't stumble backward. He planted his feet on the cobbled street. With precision, he lifted his hand to block the impending blow, sending Torakiba a-wobble with the counterforce.

Torakiba snorted in anger and resumed his attack with greater ferocity, the fists flying almost like a wheel of punches to Buck's face. Buck blocked them as well as he could, but the *ozeki* had power, and each blow seared through Buck's muscles. He landed a doozie on Buck's right side, knocking him breathless. His ribs crunched as they broke, right before Buck slumped to the ground in a heap of pain against the wall.

How was it that the *kohai* had to take the brutality for his *senpai's* loss? Buck bounced from side to side with each falling fist, powerless to right himself, gasping for breath. One loss and the *senpai* put him through the wood chipper.

It just. Wasn't. Right.

His skull smacked against the wall, jarring his brain. Bolts of agony shot down his neck, making him twinge all the way to his fingertips. Worst of all, he couldn't strike back. Stupid, stupid, stupid rules!

Hunched in pain, he squeezed his eyes shut and tried to send his mind somewhere else. The farmland and the sky—they existed a long time ago in a galaxy far, far away. Blows fell one after another, a meteor shower of punches, exhausting him. Buck cursed and cursed the rules that had forced him to stand here and take the punishment, or be history. He hated the rule-makers and the rule-enforcers and the rule-taker-advantagers. All of them. Every urge in him said fight back. Only his rational mind kept his fists down. And only barely.

At last, it subsided. Torakiba let up, wiping his palms on his *yukata.* Buck exhaled, clutching his aching side, trying not to whimper.

Torakiba gave Buck a final kick in the cracked ribs before turning to leave. Over his shoulder he shot a last glance of disgust at him and guffawed as he left. "You mess with a tiger, you will feel the teeth."

Buck lay in a heap and inhaled in tiny increments, wincing in pain with every breath he took.

Halfway down the alley, the beast turned back and coughed, "Never look at her again, *Cowboy*. You defile her with your eyes!"

$$+$$

THE SEVEN SAMURAI
DECEMBER. TOKYO

A month passed. The swelling had gone down, and Buck ventured out in public with the guys. He really ought to find a Christmas gift to send home, but it was hard, since all they'd likely want was for him to quit this life.

"Something about the Christmas spirit, right? It's better to give than receive." Buck shivered in his *yukata,* but it was nice to be out in the fresh air.

"Especially if it's a punch in the head." Dude smacked a fist into his palm.

"Right." Buck caught a glace of his reflection in a store window. The shiners weren't even purple anymore.

Dude, Reggie, and Buck strolled down the sidewalk of a shopping district, Reggie's hands dangling bags of gifts and groceries. "I'd like to give Sobakubi a whole lot of gifts for Christmas. But not these kinds." He lifted and shook his packages.

"Yeah, your *senpai* sucks, dude. No question. He's even worse than Buck's because he's not even a very good sumo wrestler. He's got no game." Dude flipped a stray strand of hair out of his eyes.

"What's he even doing in the sport?" Buck took a big bite of his fish hot dog from the street vendor. The tortilla tube thing had really grown on him lately. Anything for a little variety—it beat *chanko nabe* for every meal.

"His daddy makes him do it. And he likes the money and the girls." Reggie kicked a rock; it skipped down the sidewalk into a storm drain. Buck wished again sumo wrestlers were allowed to wear coats over their *yukatas*. It just seemed cruel to make a guy freeze like this. His belly jiggled in a shiver.

Buck stopped short. He craned his neck to look at a girl in a purse shop, thinking she might be Chocho.

"You're obsessed, dude." Dude chomped a pile of *mochi*, a rice-based pseudo ice cream. "You think you see her everywhere, and it ain't so."

"Whatever. It might be her—sometime. Wait just a sec." Buck halted at the base of a steep granite stairway that rose between a couple of shops leading up a hill to more apartment buildings. Moss on the edges of the stone steps looked slick after weeks of rain. "I'll be right back."

"Where you going?" Dude hollered. "Remember. I gotta get back before my uncle starts missing me. Come on. You got enough chocolate covered macadamia nuts to choke a horse."

Buck called over his shoulder, "The guy gave me too much change. I'll be back before your *mochi* can melt."

Buck bounded down the sidewalk, dodging shoppers like he was in a pole-position video game, until he arrived out of breath at the shop where he'd bought the chocolate. The clerk bowed more than a dozen times and thanked Buck five dozen times, including Buck's favorite, *"San-kyu, san-kyu, beri-beri-machi,"* phrase. *"You is beri honest-o."*

When Buck got back, completely out of breath but lighter for it, they continued walking down the narrow street. Dude jostled his arm. "What was it, a few yen? Why'd you bother?"

"Because it wasn't mine, man. I couldn't keep it."

"Sometimes you're a saint. Saint Breakfast." Dude bent down and picked a rock out of his sandal. He flicked it in the bushes.

"I bet Chocho would get all fluttery about it if she could see you." Reggie snorted. The teasing never stopped. "Not that I blames you for being obsessed. The woman makes my eyes pops out." He popped a handful of chocolate koala cookies in his mouth and followed them with a chaser of *senbe* savory rice crackers.

"Keep them in your head, dude. Buck here doesn't like nobody looking at his woman." Dude gave Reggie a swift punch in the arm. "Right, Buck? Not that lowlifes like us would even have a chance with Chocho Ginza, girl with the body that won't quit. Girls like that only know champs exist."

Buck shot them both a sideways glance and suppressed a growl. Territorial instincts surged in him. Nobody could talk that way about Chocho around him. Nobody. However, Buck would have to beat *himself* to a pulp if he acknowledged any of his own deeper thoughts. *She was so fine.* A chilly December gust made him shiver.

Dude tossed his *mochi* wrapper in a trashcan. "Sorry. Listen, it's only a matter of time for you, Buck. The way you're ripping it up, you'll be up there in the *kessho-mawashi* parade in no time, marching into the ring in your fancy pink apron, stomping with the sumo champs. I mean, look at your lineup for January. You'll go up against Hamigaki, the Giant of the Gobi Desert. Before you know it you'll be battling Jinbeizame. When you beat Jinbeizame, everybody will notice."

"Why? Who's Jinbeizame?" Buck asked, chomping on the final Pocky chocolate covered pretzel from his box.

"Who's Jinbeizame! Give me a break. Mr. Whale Shark is only the Jack Nicklaus of sumo."

"Who's Jack Nicklaus?"

"Come on, man. The golfer? Seriously?"

Buck pulled a frown of ignorance. Golf wasn't a spectator sport, not like baseball and basketball and football, or even hockey.

"No. Fine then, he's the Ben Hogan of sumo." Dude paused for the recognition, but got nothing. "Ben Hogan? Best golfer Texas ever produced? Geez. You guys disgust me. Fine. Jinbeizame. He's on his way down the ranks, but he had a stellar sumo career in his day." Dude huffed and marched ahead of them muttering, "Who's Ben Hogan—are you kidding me?"

Reggie and Buck stopped to grab a *mochi* ball from the vendor. Lots of people were out, and the neighborhood teemed with life. A few fans tugged on Buck's sleeves; he smiled at them. He even saw a couple of familiar faces here and there, which gave him an inexplicable feeling of *home* in this Ryugoku neighborhood.

A noise clattered from an alley between this store and the next one. A tumbling metal grocery cart and its elderly owner sat in a heap. At the same moment, a young man approached Buck with a camera.

"Sorry." Buck held up a finger. The fan would have to wait. He tugged Reggie toward the woman.

"Are you all right, ma'am?" Buck helped the old woman to her feet at the bottom of a stairway to an upstairs apartment. She was only about half of Buck's height, bent with age, and as wrinkled as a walnut. "How far are you planning to pull this cart? It's too full for a long walk. You going up?" He stooped to pick up spilled groceries. She waved a hand violently at him.

He tried again in broken Japanese, *"Kono nimotsu wo motte, doko ni ikimasuka?*

She pointed to the steps and said about a thousand words. Buck turned to Reggie for help.

"She's going up there." Reggie coughed. "I'm heading home, man. First the money back, and now this? You go do your good deeds. I gotta get back to practice or I'm dead meat."

"Thanks. Fine, just cover for me, will you?" Buck finished

scooping up the turnips and greens and the huge bag of cat food, and placed it all back in her cart.

"Let's go, ma'am." He hoisted the cart into one arm, giving the woman his other arm. Together they ascended the steps.But was glad for the first time outside the ring that he'd done all those squat kicks. He deposited her and her cart safely at the top near a door. The lady retreated inside, bowing repeatedly.

Buck skipped down the stairs, feeling lighter than he'd felt in years. At the bottom, a camera bulb flashed in his face.

"I gots it." It was Tanaka. The reporter. Buck hadn't recognized him a minute ago. His gut wrenched. "Great story for my sports editor. He like so very much." Tanaka grinned.

"Tanaka. No, man. You shouldn't—" Buck dreaded the backlash. Torakiba was the gentleman wrestler, a fact everyone knew. And Buck horning in on his territory—that probably wouldn't sit well. "Don't print that, pal. Can't we just keep this private?"

It was too late. Tanaka had raced down the street. Sumo feats, fine—publish those. But this kind of stuff? It could be disastrous. He could almost feel the butt of Torakiba's palm against his jaw already. He should've chased down Tanaka and taken care of the camera. Couldn't the guy just let a good deed go unpunished?

"MERRY CHRISTMAS." BUCK HELD THE big, green telephone receiver to his ear as he stood in the lobby of the stable. Never had these words come with so much trepidation. For the first time since he got into the Kawaguchi brothers' cab three months ago, Buck called home. It was Christmas, and he was expecting his parents' hearts to be much softer.

"Buck? Is that you?" A quarter-second delay from his mother's voice threw him. She'd hesitated. "Your voice sounds muffled."

JENNIFER GRIFFITH

He was still suffering from a swollen jaw from the fallout of the newspaper article—Tiger Fang wasn't amused.

"Hi, Mom. Yeah, it's me. I'm still here in Tokyo. Look, before you say anything, I want to tell you I'm real sorry about how we left things back in September," Buck said.

Another delay.

"Oh, Buck. Don't give it another thought. Your dad and I would have called and gushed over you a thousand times since then if we'd had your number." His mother sounded breezy. "You missed a real nice turkey dinner here with all your aunts and uncles and cousins. Are you eating okay? Are they treating you right?"

Buck glanced down at the body belt encasing his cracked ribs. The doctors were treating him right, and often. That—plus a hundred other details—his mom did *not* need to know.

"It's a completely different life here, Mom. Nothing like I expected. But I've made a few friends, and I did all right in my first tournament. You and Dad would have been surprised." He might as well tell her. "I won the prize for my division."

"Well, now. That's real nice. I'm glad you're having such a good time!" His mom's love for him came through loud and clear. Waves of relief washed over him. "I sure wish you were here, son."

"Me, too, Mom."

"Uh, do you have any idea when you're coming home?" Her voice quavered. It tugged at Buck's heart.

"Not yet." He bit his lip. "I want to see you and Dad, but I have a few things I need to accomplish here." Quite a few.

There was a pause, but she brightened. "Oh, now. Here, tell me about your Christmas. Have you been to any parties or had a decent Christmas meal?"

Buck snorted. As if. "Yeah, no. Christmas isn't really like Christmas here in Japan. It's kind of more like how we celebrate New Year's, which is their big religious holiday, I hear."

He answered all his mother's questions with a degree of vagary, bordering on lies, before asking, "Hey, is Dad there?"

"Hello, son." His dad joined the call on the other line. Buck tensed.

"Hey, Dad. So, um, how's your Nangrimax deal going with Mr. Yoshida?"

"We just don't know, son." There was tightness in his voice. "There's an approval process, and the Japanese Ministry of Health has to clear it for the use we are looking at. Yoshida is hopeful, but I have a history with bureaucracies that makes me a little less optimistic." He sounded weary.

"We're praying so much our knees are getting calluses." his mom interjected with an intensity that alarmed him. "I'm pulling out my hair, going grey over the house and even your —"

"Now, Cissie," Dad cleared his throat. "Let's not worry Buck with the details."

"What is it, Mom? Tell me. Is it Grandma and Grandpa's farm?"

"How did you know?" His mom sounded shocked. "It's just that your Uncle Joe is having a hard time keeping up with all that land and running his landscaping business. It's more difficult than he expected and ..."

Buck's gut lurched. "I—I could come home. I could run the tractors if you need me to. Do the irrigating. Take care of the horses," his voice trailed off. Buck couldn't go. He couldn't take care of Rosie and Ninety-Nine, as much as his heart longed to. The last time he'd been able to ride Rosie he was twelve. Buck's face burned with self-loathing at his size again.

"No, no. Let's not go into all that now. Much as we'd like to have you home, running the farm isn't a practical idea." His father changed the subject. "I haven't heard anything about your life over there. You've got a tough row to hoe, I'll wager."

You have no idea. "It's not all Snickers bars and Hot Cheetos, that's for sure."

"Well, like Winston Churchill said, 'If you're going through hell, keep going,' Or was that Rodney Atkins?"

An operator's voice chimed in his ear. It sounded like it was telling him to insert more money, but he couldn't be sure. He fumbled through the pile of coins on the telephone table, but now that he looked, they were all one-yen coins, tiny plastic-tin play money. Frantic fingers shoved them into the phone anyway, but they came rolling out the coin return slot in the front of the green phone. No!

"Mom, Dad. I love you. Phone money running out. I'll call you—"

Click.

Soon. I'll call you soon.

十
二

DREAMS
JANUARY–JULY. TOKYO-OSAKA-NAGOYA

"Happy New Year!" Glasses clinked as the clock struck midnight and the Kawaguchi stable brought in the new year together at a crowded bar in downtown Tokyo. A live band played, interspersed with some bad karaoke. The Gooch did his own impression of "Let it Be," and it would take years before Buck could scrub that one from his mind and ears. Alcohol could be a frightening social lubricant.

Six or seven other stables joined Kawaguchi's—Dude had gone home for the holiday, and Buck hadn't seen Reggie since before Christmas. He was flying social solo. His hawk eye searched for Chocho to no avail. Of course, a girl that gorgeous would've had a New Year's Eve date lined up for months. She wouldn't be at a bar full of sweaty fat guys drinking themselves blind.

Buck ordered a bowl of ramen, because nothing said happy new year like noodles, and settled near the bar. He should have looked before he sat.

"Asagohan!" The warty warthog face of the *yokozuna* leered in beside him. "You big American, yeah. Americans stupid. Butaniku hate."

Nice. Hate as a New Year greeting. Buck smiled and tipped his glass at Butaniku. Then the moment got worse.

"Ah, Asagohan, darling of the front page of the newspaper." A tubby piglet bellied up to the bar next to Buck in the form of Sobakubi. The round pig eyes of Reggie's *senpai* made Buck's skin crawl. Sobakubi wore a satin *yukata* and a lot of gold jewelry. It looked like it might get caught in his chest hair and pinch. "You little do-gooder. Who are you trying to impress?"

Buck had seen the photo in the paper. He couldn't read the article, of course, but the picture said it all. Dude and Reggie would have given him grief about it, and Buck didn't need everyone to think he was some kind of vigilante. Maybe the news would go away. Maybe Sobakubi would go away. Buck decided to ignore the piglet. Talk about a bad decision.

Sobakubi shoved Buck's shoulder and spun his barstool around to face him. He blew a long breath of cigarette smoke in Buck's face. It stung Buck's nose and made his eyes water. He choked back a cough.

"It might be all-American Boy Scout of you to be doing helpful good deeds on old ladies, but you are *kohai.*" The word hissed like a curse. "*Kohai* must stay invisible." He leaned in close, within a centimeter of Buck's face, and blew more smoke. With one hand he grabbed Buck's shoulder, and with the other dug powerful fingernails into Buck's thigh. They seared as his skin broke in four little half-moon wounds. "Got that?"

Buck wrested himself from the grip of death and got to his feet. He pushed past Sobakubi and moved toward the karaoke singers. A girl was singing "Sweet Home Alabama." It just didn't sound right. He ought to go home. Butaniku and his foul toady Sobakubi completely ruined the festive mood for him. Even the sushi didn't look good anymore.

"Asagohan!" Tiger Fang yelled. The champ came stumbling up to Buck and draped a limp arm over Buck's shoulders. Great, now he was going to ask Buck to give him a thousand yen or a head massage, or something demeaning. "You helped the old lady up stairs." Tiger Fang sneered, the stench of alcohol and fish escaping his mouth. "What makes you think you are some knight on a white horse? You thinks you are the Christmas angel on top of the tree, looking down on all the rest of us. No! You are just a cowboy." He slammed a fist on the table. "Stay with the cows!" The snarl dripped from his lips.

"Happy New Year to you, too, Torakiba. May you have all the good year you deserve." Buck wriggled free, and Torakiba collapsed onto a barstool. Across the room Buck saw an open booth near the band. He headed that direction to get away, but he wasn't fast enough.

"I said, *stay with the cows!*" Torakiba came barreling after Buck, and sloshed a hot cup of tea in Buck's face. It burned his eyelids and upper lip, then his neck. The band stopped, and everyone turned to see what he'd do. If this were his high school, some wimpy kid would initiate the chant, "Fight, fight, fight!" Japanese held their breath.

Buck stared Torakiba down. His ire ignited, and he balled his hand into a fist. He had never needed to strike a drunken person before, but the temptation to do so was growing in him. Actually, it might not be a bad idea—Torakiba wouldn't remember it in the morning. There might not even be consequences to face.

Buck seethed a moment, breathing deep and thinking it over. "What is *with* you and putting things in my face?" *To pound or not to pound?* "No, you're not worth it." He lifted a sleeve and wiped off the hot tea. "Some gentleman," he muttered and stalked away from the reeling drunk.

A collective exhale released into the bar's air, and the music started up again.

Some happy new year. It was starting out just grand.

THE JANUARY *BASHO* BLEW IN on an icy gale. Buck had never been so cold, so consistently, for so long. The only reprieve came at the bathhouse, where he could sink into the hot water and finally stop shivering. Tokyo was an icebox on steroids.

On the other hand, in the *dohyo,* Buck was on fire. In the second from the bottom rank now, he sizzled past his first opponents, including Hamigaki, the Giant of the Gobi Desert. That guy was a brick wall. The JSA bumped Buck up yet another rank.

Then in Osaka in March, he had a bad streak. He smoked out against Oshaberi, who never stopped talking the whole time he wrestled. And his win-loss record didn't shine going into the final day. He had to redeem himself big time—and he was pitted against the Ben Hogan of sumo, Jinbeizame. It was the only way Buck could get a toehold on the next rung of the sumo ladder. And he needed to. He had to get out of the amateurs. They were sucking the life out of him, one beating at a time.

"So, you against Jinbeizame, eh?" Dude jostled Buck's arm and took a bite of a round pear. "He's huuuuuge. You're not going to believe it when you see him up close. He's like a whale shark. He's like the Loch Ness Monster."

"I thought you said he was like Ben Hogan." Buck kept doing his pushups in the dressing room. "I was looking forward to seeing some plaid pastel pants and a tacky polyester shirt. Maybe a visor."

"Dude. I wish I could wear a visor out there. Those lights melt my hair sometimes. Did you see all the sweat? I practically soaked the ref in my last match-up against what's-his-head. Not sanitary, I'm telling you." Dude drifted off, and Buck steeled himself for the match. Every match mattered. Every point counted. So many gallons of sweat he'd swabbed from Torakiba's back and wrung onto the dirty ground—he could drown in the nastiness of it. Without this win against the has-been, Buck could just add another two months to his sentence.

Jinbeizame's heyday was going to slide even farther into the past.

They called Buck, and he climbed onto the stage. The whale shark snuffed and puffed. There was definitely something of the leviathan about him—but no plaid pants existed in that size.

The signal came, and they sprang at each other. Jinbeizame showed technique Buck had only seen in the upper ranks, and Buck got the most vicious face and chest and arm slapping he'd ever received. His skin stung. One slap tweaked his nose, and instinct made him slap right back. Buck whacked the old timer across his cheek, which made the opponent furious, and a snarl came hurtling at Buck's face along with spittle and fumes.

Buck lowered his head and made a run for the Jinbeizame's chest. The impact echoed like an empty barrel. He snatched at Jinbeizame's arms, pinned them to his sides, and began shoving for all he was worth.

The audience didn't care that the former champ was on his way out of the ranks—every time Buck made a strong move, silence deafened from the stands.

Jinbeizame fought back against Buck's push. He planted his feet hard. Buck couldn't budge him more than half a meter or so. And then the big man retaliated. Buck let go of his opponent's arms and grabbed him around the waist, yanking at the *mawashi*. Jinbeizame pressed against him like a Mack truck. Buck planted his own feet to stop the force.

Buck puffed like a steam train. He had to heat up and resist with pure power. He stoked the fire inside himself.

Luck favored Buck. Jinbeizame's knee gave way. It buckled, and Buck's own reflexes snapped on. Seizing opportunity, he wrested the whale shark the rest of the way to the ground.

"*Kachikoshi,* Asagohan."

Victory. The crowd booed, but inside, Buck cheered, knowing he was one step closer to getting away from Torakiba.

"THAT WAS AMAZING, BUCK!" HIRO'S voice crackled over the Kermit-the-Frog green phone in the hallway of the stable. "I saw the replay of your March *basho* matches online. I'm still watching it every day in our cherry blossom springtime. You and Jinbeizame. *Yosh!*"

"Thanks, Hiro." Buck was glad to hear the kid's voice.

"If I reported it, I would say it this ways: 'Newcomer Asagohan ate ten of his opponents for breakfast in the last three *bashos*, with techniques that come as naturally to him as breathing the air. He pummeled men with twice the training during the Osaka *basho* in March. This blond American is the one to watch at Nagoya's *basho* next week, folks.'

"Do you like it? Do you? You do! You like sumo! I knew you would be a champ! It's only a matter of time. In one year or so, you are going to be in the ring fighting for the Emperor's Cup. You will make it to the top even faster than my hero Torakiba."

Buck had no response to that, but it was cool to know Hiro followed his career. He liked that kid. "You're going to be a great sumo reporter someday," Buck said.

"I can't believe how fast you are climbing the ranks, Buck. Only just one more rank to go and you will be in *makushita.* Then you can almost go to *juryo. Juryo* is where you become a *senpai.* You deserve it. But it will be so very sad, too."

"Why's that?" Buck spluttered.

"Because then you won't get to be around the great Torakiba every hour of every day. What I would give to get to be the guy to wipe his shoulders after a match. You're so lucky."

Yeah, real lucky. Buck snorted. "I'll wave to you from the *dohyo* in Nagoya next week. You watch for it, Hiro."

"Really? Thanks, Buck." Hiro's voice crackled over the phone. "And Buck? Thanks for becoming sumo wrestler. You are awesome."

Buck signed off and went back to practice. The summer heat stifled him, humidity a hundred percent, and heaven knew how hot it was on the thermometer. Geez. Hot enough, for sure. Gullies of sweat poured from under his arms and soaked his *mawashi* belt. Months of constant workouts did do one big thing for him, though. His thighs didn't chafe against each other anymore, and for the first time in his life he couldn't feel pools of perspiration between rolls of fat on his gut or his back. He was still big, but he didn't think all his bigness could be pure blubber anymore. It was now more solid. And cellulite didn't dimple his thighs. Now his skin was sleek and smooth like the other guys'. But his weighing less didn't make it any cooler in here, sadly.

Back in his room after a bath, Buck plunked down on his futon and smelled the stench of a dozen other men who shared this dorm. Stupid amateur levels. He had to get out. *Juryo* blinked in neon beckoning just one rank above him. One rank, and he was a pro. A pro—and Chocho would notice him, take him seriously.

In the lower amateur ranks, a guy lived like a slave. In *juryo* he became a king. One leap of ranks meant getting paid to compete, getting out of kitchen duty, waking up later in the morning and going straight to practice instead of chores. It meant emancipation from being that bloodthirsty ogre's foot licker. It meant more comfortable shoes. He didn't care if the skill of the wrestlers thickened in *juryo*. If he had to claw his way to the top, he would.

"You going to the *koen-kai* tonight?" Dude stood in the dorm doorway, eating a foot-tall ice cream cone in the summer heat.

"Where in the Smurf did you get *that*?" Buck rose on his elbows.

"AM/PM Market. I eat one every day—trainer said I could in place of beer. I hate beer." He took a long slurp.

"Wally Wada, I need me one of those," Buck said. It had been forever since he'd had good ice cream. He looked down at himself, a hundred pounds lighter. Life without barbecued brisket and a little Rudy's sauce did that. Life without deliciousness did that. But that ice cream. If only it could perch on top of a nice warm pile of peach cobbler with a hint of cinnamon . . .

They walked along alleys pasted up with political posters featuring faces of various stoic-faced Japanese men. Buck couldn't read them other than the date—the nine and the moon in kanji—which he figured must be September. He patted himself on the back.

Only one poster featured a smiling face. It looked vaguely familiar. Or maybe he just looked to Buck like—who was it?—Lou Diamond Phillips, only with silver hair and a dark mustache. Buck would vote for the smiling guy, given the choice.

"Sweet day out here, dude." Dude shoved the rest of the cone in his mouth. "Got so excited when I saw the weather this morning I got all Hawaiian on myself. Grabbed my clubs and surfboard, skipped training and headed over to Tokyo Bay on this dump of a bus, and do you know, not a single surfable wave. Come on. The whole beach was filled with e-nor-mous concrete jacks. You know—the kid toy? Only enormous. And concrete. Wouldn't want to wipeout on that. No way. Concussion city. Might not come back up for air, you know. I had to go back into Chiba to the country club and mooch off a guy to get him to pay my green fees. Made par on the front nine. Totally sliced the back nine." He tsked. "But anyways, Buckster-man. Like I asked, you going to the *koen-kai* tonight?"

Dude turned down the narrow Tokyo street to where the AM/PM sat at the edge of the sidewalk, so different from Texas—huge parking lots, gas stations at every 7-Eleven.

"Not unless forced."

"I bet you'll change your mind."

"Statistical likelihood near zero." Buck hated those parties put on by the sponsors. Tonight, a company Buck had never heard of was hosting both Kawaguchi stable and Dude's uncle's stable. His poor Japanese made socializing a drag, and the food always consisted of frightening, low-calorie Japanese delicacies, and Buck was with Dude—drinking wasn't really his thing. So, *koen-kai* parties didn't appeal.

"I think you'll change your mind."

"I think I won't."

The ice cream case teemed with options. *Oh, my. So many to not choose from.* Green tea, rose, squid, ox tongue, sweet potato, corn, pit viper, Indian curry, wasabi, goat. Please say that meant goat's milk.

"Can you order me a vanilla?" Dude forked over a *sen*-yen note—about ten bucks—for Buck's vanilla and his own sweet potato cone. Soon his throat cooled with creamy deliciousness. They went back outside into the hot sun.

"Wacky training you were doing this morning when I showed up. What was that? Some kind of ninja warrior defense?" Dude made a kung fu hand, karate-chopping the air. "There's nobody in my uncle's stable or anywhere else working on anything that awkward, dude."

"Thanks." Buck slugged Dude in the arm and jostled the sweet potato cone. "Just messing around, I guess." Buck knew trying to work up a defense to Tiger Fang's obscure triple-pronged technique, the *mitokorozeme*, felt awkward. It must've looked completely stupid. Still, his neck hurt from the attempt, but he didn't care. He didn't care if years went by before the need for this defense came up, he'd be ready. He almost crushed the base of his cone just thinking about it.

Dude wiped his lips with his *yukata* sleeve. "I still say you're going tonight. And you wanna know why? Because Chocho Ginza will be there."

Buck choked. "Why do you say that?" *Stay cool, man. Cool.* Buck's arm trembled and his cone dropped onto the hot sidewalk. Not cool. He stared down at the melting pool of vanilla for a minute, then they walked on.

Chocho. Even her name made him lose control. For months now, not even a glimpse of her at a tournament—nothing since that awful day when she saw him lose to Fishface. Nothing since that sigh-inducing day when she sent him the congratulatory note, the note he kept in his pillowcase and inhaled the scent of whenever Torakiba gave him a particularly painful beating.

"Because she will. And she told the sponsors to make southern barbecue."

"What? Whatever, man. You're just funning me."

"No, seriously. I hear things—you know." Dude horked down the last of his second cone and chucked his napkin in the trash.

Buck switched to his best nonchalant air. "Food sounds good. I might go." Just like there *might* be a fireworks display in Texas on the Fourth of July.

THAT NIGHT, BUCK DONNED HIS sky blue *yukata*—his best color— and he had the *tokoyama* slather enough chamomile oil on his hair to make it shine. He shaved, found a little aftershave stashed away in his ugly, striped bag, and flossed his teeth.

Legs shaking, he entered the hotel. Even if she were there, she might ignore him. He'd rather she slapped him and told him to leap in front of the slam train.

Daydreams rode with him on the elevator to the twenty-fifth floor. *Buck Cooper made a grand entrance through the double doors. Every eye turned to see the blond giant. Chocho spied him instantly and raced into his arms. Resting her head against his chest, she embraced him. "Buck! Take me away from all this!" In one heroic move, he swept her out the door and onto a plane back to Texas, where they found a little ranch to live out their lives in idyllic bliss.*

Who was he kidding? He was an amateur. A nobody. He didn't stand a chance with her. Wake up.

Plus, there was Tiger Fang, the rib cracker, to consider, with those warnings to keep his eyes off her. His lungs still rattled now and then from their run-ins.

Hope sank.

The elevator doors opened, and the world smelled delicious. The sensory feast made him not even regret the cab fare to get to the hotel. Garlic, black pepper, brown sugar and mustards. Yes! Hickory smoke, incense of the purest form. It infused his sinuses and filled his soul. Man, where did the Japanese get enough hickory wood? He'd died and gone to a carnivore's heaven.

He burst through the door.

Meat was piled high on plates. Never in all his months in this place had he seen any Japanese person eat even a single full serving of beef. It was just not being done. But tonight, folks lost all inhibitions. Stacks of shredded roast graced Buck's plate in no time. With a mouthful of tender brisket, Buck sashayed toward an open armchair near the doors to the balcony, where he might catch a breeze on this steamy June night. He settled into his seat, just as a feminine voice lilted near his right ear. "Excuse me. Is that you, Asagohan?" came the soft, alto tones with the British accent.

Chocho!

Buck wrenched around in his chair and surged upward. In a swift motion, he stashed his plate on a side table and bowed to the girl, at the same time pulling at the sides of his *yukata* like a curtseying ballerina.

She bowed slightly, too, and kept her eyes lowered a moment before lifting them to meet his. His insides melted like the ice cream cone on the sidewalk, pooling down at his calves and ankles as he gazed at that face, those gold-flecked eyes, those dimples.

"I hope I am not bothering you."

"Yes. I mean, no. I mean, nice to see you, Miss Chocho." His jaw barely worked. She wore green tonight, and her hair was down, long, big loose curls resting on creamy white shoulders. They looked smooth as milk.

"Just Chocho." A smile wrinkled the corners of her eyes, and the dimples sank, along with Buck's stomach. "Everyone just calls me Chocho."

"Buck Cooper." Not everyone called him that. Most people called him *breakfast.* He dipped his head. Finally! Here he stood, talking to her at last. *She'd* found *him.* His veins coursed with fear and ecstasy.She extended her arm, and he took it. A lover's instinct. She led him through double French doors onto the balcony. The air hung muggy with humidity, despite the late hour.

"Nice view," he managed to say, heart pounding. He walked alongside her to an iron railing, twenty-five floors above Tokyo City. A heavy, warm wind gusted intermittently. The crush and hum of the party dissipated as the French doors swung closed. They were alone, surrounded by the Tokyo skyline, a thousand skyscrapers and a million lights against an orange horizon.

"Mmm." Chocho stared out at the fading sunset and sighed. A bracelet sparkled on her delicate wrist as she pressed a hand to her throat. She looked perfect in green. "Do you by chance recall a day last summer—here in Tokyo? There was a car, a street corner—?" She shook her head as if giving up on the idea.

"That was you?" Buck did his best to feign surprise. He wasn't sure it worked.

A genuine smile of pleasure spread across her face as she turned to look up at him. "Every time I saw you in the *dohyo*, I told myself I was mad for thinking you and Asagohan could be the same person, but you are."

His response caught in his throat. She was right. Sometimes *he* couldn't believe he was Asagohan.

"There's enough of me to be two people." He patted his flank.

She laughed, a vibrant, joyous sound that made Buck fall hopelessly in love. With a smile she squeezed up against his arm where she remained linked to him. The pressure shot electricity through him. Was it hot out here, or was it just Buck? This woman—she could ask him anything and he would do it, give it, make it happen. Alakazam. She even found his marginally funny joke funny. He squared his shoulders. The most gorgeous girl in the galaxy clung to his arm, and Buck was a man—a real man—for the first time.

"Seems to go on forever." She gestured toward the cityscape. "All the way to the horizon. And here we are, twenty-five stories up. If you could go to the end of where you can see, Tokyo's metropolis lights would stretch another horizon, and another. Seven horizons, all of Tokyo."

Whoa. He was a tiny dot in comparison to the teeming masses that must inhabit all those apartment and office buildings cramming the view.

"That day, when I saw you, was my first day in Japan." He drew infinity signs with his fingertip atop the railing.

"Really? You seemed so confident. You've been here before."

"Never. Did I? I wasn't." He chuffed.

"So, you just go about your daily life committing acts of heroism as a regular activity?" Again, the laughter. "Still, Mr. Saito was glad you showed up when you did." She rested her hand on his. His heart might explode.

"Mr. Saito?" The businessman he'd yanked from traffic. How did she know his name? Maybe Tokyo was like Dallas, in actuality a series of small neighborhoods connected together. You saw people you knew everywhere you went.

She pulled away to walk along the metal railing, beckoning him to follow. Buck trailed along like a puppy dog. It took all his will to keep his tongue from lolling as they circumnavigated the penthouse area, passing benches and potted ferns and statues. A helicopter buzzed between two buildings a block away at their eye level.

"That was, in a way, my first day in Japan as well. I'd just got back from England." She stopped at a corner and turned toward Buck. "I had a lot on my mind that day."

"Oh? How's that?" Buck approached her, not sure what distance to leave between them. But she didn't pull away.

"Family matters. My life is . . . complex." Her wistful sigh wafted away, down over the balcony onto the cars and people of Tokyo. "I spent two years away in school and thinking about what matters most. Integrity—so much of our world lacks it. Coming back here I wanted to bring that with me." Her voice trailed off and she closed her iridescent eyelids before drawing a sharp breath, shaking off the intensity of the moment. "You're enjoying Japan?"

Buck didn't have it in him to lie. There was a lot to hate about his own complex life. "There are some very beautiful places." And people.

"Yes, but there are too many buildings. Too close together. I like the sky, open fields. Pure, green earth." She turned toward the cityscape again. "You come from Texas, Buck. You must miss the sky."

"More than I can say." Buck pressed up to the balcony beside her. The farm, the expanse of alfalfa and wheat. He took a deep, cleansing breath, but all he got was a lungful of smog.

"Texas." She sighed. "Everyone has horses in Texas, I think." Her eyes glistened with expectant wonder, which made his sense of balance wobble. "Do you?"

"I loved to ride as a kid. There were—are—some on my grandparents' farm. Rosie and Ninety-nine." He could still feel their gallops leaping the irrigation ditches, taking them through the trees along the fence line.

Chocho's every feature lit up. "Mine are called Vashti and Hopalong."

"There's a place to ride in Tokyo?" A siren blared in the distance.

Chocho's laugh jingled. "Of course not. Back in England. Near Oxford, where I was in school. They're my father's horses, technically. But in my heart they're mine. They're at my mother's place, and I would have failed Chemistry and Economics if my mother hadn't had limited my riding." She closed her eyes and lifted her chin. "I love those horses more than life itself."

"Your parents don't live together."

"Not all married men are husbands."

They started walking again. Only the two of them existed in the hot night air.

"Oh, Buck Cooper. What a gift your young life must have been," she sighed. "You're so American. Baseball and apple pie."

"A whole lot of both." Well, too much apple pie, and not enough *playing* baseball. "I've watched a lot of Texas Rangers games in my day." Buck missed the whole season so far this year, from spring training on down. He wondered how they were doing.

Around a corner they found a stone bench and sat down. Her knees rested against his, only two thin kimonos separating her skin from his. Goosebumps. Everywhere. It was getting hard to carry on a conversation. She smelled like honeysuckle. He was going crazy.

"Texas Rangers? I haven't heard of them. Dodgers, Yankees, Braves, yes. Not Rangers."

"It's the hometown team thing, I guess." He stifled indignation. The big T! They were his team. "Someday, I'm going to get season tickets and never miss a game. Seats near left field, somewhere high enough that I can see all the action, but low enough that I can see the pain on the pitcher's face when he throws, and where I can smell the fresh cut grass." His voice trailed off.

"That sounds great." She had a dreamy, faraway look. "Save me a seat."

Totally. "I will. It's a promise. You like baseball?"

"Like it? You could say that."

"More than sumo?"

"Ah, that's a loaded question." She grinned. "My team is Seibu Lions. My hometown team." She got a sly look. "I bet they could beat your Rangers." She pulled away and nodded.

"Oh, ho, ho! Now you're walking on dangerous ground, madam." He tapped her on her shoulder. "No trash talking my Rangers."

With a little laugh, she stood up and straightened her kimono. It hung so well. He followed her as they continued their lap around the building. They were nearly back around to the French doors now. The magic started to dissipate as party sounds came back. He pulled her to a stop before the final corner.

"It's funny," she said, fingering a leaf of a geranium, then dropping it. "I remember how difficult a time I had in England. Months of feeling isolated—isolated by the language, the culture. I could be in a crowded room and still be alone. I felt invisible much of the time."

Impossible. Chocho Ginza invisible? Not a chance. "I assume it got better. What finally made the difference?"

She paused a long moment. "I made a friend."

Buck's response came out involuntarily, and it caught in his constricted throat. "I could use a friend."

She whispered back. "So could I."

A long moment passed between them, heavy with the steamy night air. He ached to take her in his arms. Her perfections exceeded his hopes. She was real. She stared up into his eyes for a long moment, like she was waiting for him to give her something. For a second he almost felt she could be his.

"Buck, it's been so nice talking with you tonight. It's been an escape. Being around you makes everything look so simple."

Impulse mastered him, and he touched her hand, covering it with his. He memorized its gentle curve. So warm. He, Buck Cooper, fat guy and official lifelong nobody, basked in the grace of Chocho Ginza.

"I should get back." Her eyes darted toward the party. "I've been gone too long, I'm sure, for my father's taste. I hope you enjoy the rest of the party. The food is glorious. We Japanese so rarely eat such sumptuous foods. It's a feast." She glanced back up at him, a delicate flush blooming on her cheeks. "Being around you makes everything look so clear. Stay true, Buck. For me. For all of us." She disappeared back inside.

Buck's knees buckled. He clutched the balcony railing, his lungs filled with the humidity of the summer night, and his head Chocho.

BUCK SPENT FIFTEEN MINUTES IN the men's room trying to get hold of himself. Then he planted himself against a wall at the banquet where he scanned the heads of partygoers and caught another glimpse of Chocho, sparkling and fine, beside her father and his furry eyebrows across the ballroom.

"Aw, not again." The familiar voice of Dude resonated in Buck's ear. Buck didn't want to discuss this now. "Bucko. Believe me. The Ginza girl is so far out of your league you'd need the Hubble Telescope to see her."

"Doesn't matter."

"What? Seriously?"

"Wally Wada, my friend, I am slam-diggity-dog in love with that girl." Saying it aloud, Buck swelled at the truth of it. There was no going back.

"Buck, my friend, she will reach inside your heart and dissect it chamber by chamber."

"Don't care." Buck shuddered. "And that is just way too much imagery, man."

"Still, I'm telling you. It's not just because of how smoking hot she is that you can't think about her."

"What, then? I know she's Ginza's daughter."

Across the room Chocho stood beside her father, nodding at intervals, with her back turned to them. Ginza looked intense, as usual.

"For one, she's richer than Warr-en Buf-fett—put together. Two, she's some kind of freak genius, spent three years at Oxford."

Two years. She'd said two.

"Number three, and most worst-est, she's practically the *property* of your favorite rib-cracking *senpai*, Torakiba. You go after her and it's like poaching on the king's land. I don't care how hungry you are, pal." Dude gnawed a spare rib. "They'll getcha for trespass and shoot you on sight."

Buck stopped listening. Across the room a scene unfolded. Torakiba approached where Ginza and Chocho stood, sidled up to her and handed her a drink. Old Man Ginza's intense face softened as he glanced up at the sharp-toothed menace.

"Naw. No. Not that guy. She's too smart. She can see he's no good." Buck took a swig of lemonade, but it caught in his gullet.

"Torakiba's well respected. Her dad likes him. Plus, the guy needs her." Dude wiped his lips with his sleeve. "Well, he needs her moolah. Ginza's fortune could help the Fujiwaras get back on their feet after that big earthquake."

"What?"

"That's why the guy's in sumo—to restore honor to the family name—and cash to the coffers. For like, forever, the Fujiwaras were a household name. Then, pow. Earthquake. That's the official report, anyhow." Dude swirled his arm in the air. "Now, this big galoot thinks it's up to him to fix it all up."

"I heard he just had a mom in a nursing home."

Dude shrugged.

Torakiba's beefy fist reached up and touched Chocho briefly on the shoulder before dropping back to his side. Ginza grinned at the champion, and a cold blade sliced through Buck's warm plans.

He didn't stand a chance against a champion with a pedigree and a prior claim.

Dude clicked his tongue. "Money solves a lot of problems—especially around here. When he marries the Ginza fortune, he's home free."

Buck suddenly hated the smell of cooking meat.

Dude took a big bite of barbecue and sighed. "Yep, yep, yep. They lost it all when his little sister got kidnapped by some Chinese slavers when she was on vacation in Beijing. Had to pay the huge ransom. Now, they're penniless. Without her, all the pimple meds and trophy payoffs in the sport couldn't recharge his family's bank account."

"Wait. I thought you said earthquake."

"Something like that. Earthquake, kidnapping ransom. Whatever."

Buck's stomach clenched. The man he despised most in the whole world was stealing the woman Buck loved, for *money*. The woman Buck *needed* to *complete* himself, at the very moment she came within his grasp, gone.

He imagined her bestowing a look, gentle and sweet, on that sharp-toothed face. Buck's air supply faucet slowly twisted to a close.

"I'm outta here." He slapped Dude's arm. He had to go, before he lost the few bites of brisket he'd managed to ingest and made an even bigger fool of himself in front of her.

Buck made a beeline for the door.

But it was too late. Torakiba appeared in Buck's path. The jolly, party-time, drink delivering schmoozer face that the champ had displayed to the Ginzas vanished. Now a murderous look remained.

"You seem to think I am blind, Cowboy." His bared teeth gleamed. "I warned you, and you did not hear. She can never belong to you. The Ginza girl will have greatness, not *gaijin* embarrassment. She is mine."

"That's ridiculous," Buck muttered. "That's like declaring ownership over the sky."

Torakiba's frown deepened. "Stay away, *far* away, from Chocho Ginza. No more warnings." He shoved Buck's shoulder and stalked off.

Buck lingered at the door, fuming. In a burst of self-flagellation he turned back to see her. He should have just left. Why did he do these things to himself?

Her whole face smiled, down to the dimples, and she rested one hand on her father's arm and the other on Torakiba's.

Fool.

OUT IN THE STREET, HE sucked in great gulps of humid air. It didn't cool his lungs—or his anger. Defeat gave way to seething, jealous rage. His *senpai's* face burned in his mind. Buck's jaw clenched and unclenched. He cursed the rules of sumo, the ones that didn't let him do what any guy would want to do: punch out Torakiba in the light of day. If only he could run into Torakiba in a dark alley again, he wouldn't sit back and take the punishment. He'd never despised his amateur status more than he did tonight. He felt so powerless.

Buck rounded a corner of the city park, stomping in his rage, and ran belly-first into a huge man made of pig iron.

"Baku Coopah?" The pig iron spoke in a muffled growl, almost metallic.

Buck's eyes rose upward and sized up the Mac truck. Before he could respond, a clenched fist clad with brass knuckles collided with his face.

"I got a message for you from my boss."

Boss? Before Buck knew anything, pig iron wrapped an arm around his neck in a chokehold and dragged him into a clump of trees in the park. The metal knuckles cracked him right between the eyes. Buck heard the crunch of the bridge of his nose just as he slipped into blackness.

LAST MAN STANDING
JULY. TOKYO AND NAGOYA

Bruises darkened his face. Buck cleaned the dried bits of blood the best he could, standing over the running tap water at the sink. The now-stanched blood-flow released its final drops onto the porcelain. Crushed capillaries loosed their river below the surface of his skin, the redness spreading outward.

Stay conscious, stay conscious! Steady, man, steady! His head went woozy. He had to use one arm to cradle the bowl of the sink to keep himself vertical. Clenching his eyes shut, he lifted one brave finger to the bridge of his nose and gave it a gentle nudge. Shattered. A thousand pieces. He couldn't believe the shards of broken bone didn't protrude through his skin.

Luckily the toilet—squatter style though it was—sat nearby, and Buck emptied the contents of his stomach—what was left of the southern barbecue—into it. What a waste of a perfectly good cow. He mourned for a split second before barfing again.

"Wah?" A head appeared in the steel mirror above his eye line. "What happened to you? Geez. I've never seen a pair of eyes so blacked. Except maybe mine the night I first met Miss One Thousand Autumn Leaves." Reggie got a look in his eye Buck could discern even in the steel mirror: rage. Buck rinsed the clotty blood down the drain while Reggie shook his head.

"Got in a fight with a piece of metal," Buck said. The bleeding was beginning to subside. "It's a good thing you're not Torakiba or I'd probably kill you."

"*Si*. Well, you looks like Alice Cooper or Ozzy Osbourne. Not so pretty with your blue eyes that all the sumo fan girls loves so much. And, *ay caramba*, it stinks in here," said Reggie.

"Thanks." Buck wiped up the blood mess and splashed cool water on his face. "Know where a guy can get a good ice bag around here?"

"Frozen *mochi*. That's what you need." Reggie spoke wisely. Japan didn't go in for frozen peas much—the ice bag of choice back home. Instead they had frozen rice paste candy rolled into little balls that resembled frozen peas. That'd work. "Who did this to you?"

"I don't know. Not for certain." But he could guess, though. And man, could he guess. He followed Reggie to the kitchen and they dug through a freezer for something to curb the swelling.

"Sobakubi let you out of your *kohai* slave duties today?" Buck changed the subject to calm his dizziness. He thought of Sobakubi's round, pig eyes, ringed in pillows of fat—a good tangent. The eyeglasses Sobakubi wore when not in the *dohyo* barely balanced on his nose because of the fat of his eyes. Good thing the guy had so much money and a powerful father; otherwise, he would have nothing to claim—no personality, no wit, looks or charm. Just a sour emptiness. A spoiled man, like a stinky, bad potato Buck'd find under his apartment's sink, all hollowed out and black.

"No such luck," Reggie replied. "He sent me on an errand to get a bowl of *chanko nabe* from your stable's cook. Our batch today has the distinct flavor of an old museum. Dust, mold, furniture polish. He hates it and will wait for a replacement. I'm taking my time."

"Any creative torture lately?"

Sobakubi. Despite his expertise at tortures, he was even a

middling sumo wrestler. He'd been perched in the lowest bracket of the professional ranks for more than four years. The jerk treated Reggie like a dog.

"Not unless you count this." Reggie showed a scab nine inches long on his forearm. They dug through the freezer and eventually found the frozen *mochi* for Buck's face.

"We're living the dream, aren't we," Buck said, rolling his eyes. "So. What's up with your pretty sidekick?"

"Aw, man. That girl is a plague." Reggie led Buck down the hall toward the metal first aid box on the wall. "This week, you knows what she sended me? A plant. This little tree. It's about yay big, and it has these spikes on it, but it looks like an old tree, one you could maybe sees out in a desert or growing on a big rock for a thousand years." They walked back to the eating area of the kitchen.

"It's only this little, but the guys back in my stable, they says the papers that camed with the tree tells us the tree is more than four hundred years old. But I don't believes it. No tree that old could be so short."

Buck raised an eyebrow. A four-hundred-year-old *bonsai* tree could cost millions of yen. It had to be a fake. No way did Miss One Thousand Autumn Leaves lavish that kind of money on Reg.

"But back to you." Reggie accepted a big bowl of soup from the soup line, stopped, and briefly stared at Buck's face. "Man that eye is a shiner. Makes me want to sing 'Bark at the Moon.' Tell me how this happened, man."

Buck gritted his teeth and finally let loose with the story over his own bowl.

"That is brutal, man. Look, I know you think it was Tiger Fang. He did threaten you at the party." Reggie wiped his chin. "But that sounds like a darker job than I'd expect from Torakiba, *esse. Si*, he's a jerk. But a thug in an alley? Not his style."

MAKE A
spla

DAY

ale

**ALL YOU NEED
FOR WHEREVER
SUMMER
TAKES YOU**

Buck frowned and shoved back from the table. "I gotta go." How could Reggie trust Torakiba? That idiotic façade of being a "gentleman"—it even fooled Reggie. Reggie, who witnessed daily Tiger Fang's poundings on Buck. Blind! *Everybody in the whole stinking world is blind.*

"WHOA. YOU LOOK LIKE A bad piece of sushi." Dude took a long drag and crushed out his cigarette. Buck had run into Dude in the hallway after supper.

"Thanks." Buck mock-punched the wall. "I'm telling you, Wally Wada. Sometimes a *senpai* can go too far."

"Maybe, but lucky for you, yours got out of Dodge before you could retaliate."

Buck gave Dude a sharp look.

"Yeah, didn't you hear? After the sponsor party last night, your beloved *senpai* took the train to Nagoya. His homeland. He's not coming back until we go over there for the Nagoya *basho* in July. Family business or something. So, dude, you're free as the sea for a week. You could come hang out with me. I'm heading over to Yokohama to a good golf course where the American military guys play. Should I book us a tee time?"

Buck had stopped listening. The very thought of Torakiba overwhelmed his brain. That coward. *Sure, throw the first punch then run and hide in your cave with mommy and daddy.*

"Fine, no tee time for you, but did you hear? The *banzuke* are out, and you're at the tiptop of *makushita*. Way to go, dude. Just one more good tourney and you've dug yourself out of the amateur pit. No more slaving or slobbering, and you'll finally get paid. Totally awesome, man. You won't have to wear those awful *geta* shoes anymore. Think about that. Yeah, that's right. Keep that uppermost in your noggin...and don't do anything stupid."

Buck flexed his toes in the hobbling wooden flip-flops.

"Anything stupid? Like going after Torakiba in the stable or the training ring?"

"Bingo." Dude lit another cigarette.

"It just makes me nutso, Dude. The guy hates me because my skin is white and my hair is yellow. I'm the same fat guy I've always been." And people never let him forget it. Fat guy, we should beat him up. Same mantra since he was five, seven, seventeen. Fat target, fat punching bag, fat lard. He grabbed his hanging belly and jiggled it. "I'm fat. I'm fat! And now I'm *white* fat. So what? Leave me alone, stupid jerks."

Dude shook his head. "You don't get it, do you? When are you ever going to get it?"

"Me? What do you mean *me. I* don't get it? It's the SOBs who won't stop throwing punches at my fat white kidneys who don't get it."

Dude wagged his cigarette at Buck. "No, I mean you, Buck-man. It's not about what you are—fat, white, any hair color, whatever, dude. It's about *who* you are. That's what they can't stand. They hate that *they're* not *you.*"

A light flicked off in the next hallway, making it half-dark now.

"Chuh, right." Buck folded his arms over his chest. "Give me a break." Dude was the one who didn't get it. He wasn't the race-target. He looked Japanese. His blood was Japanese.

"Think about it. They hate that they aren't the guy who helped the old lady carry her groceries up the stairs. They hate that they didn't stop the disrespecting conversation about the woman. They hate that they don't have anything noble in them, none of your chivalry, and that you remind them of their lack of nobility every time you show up. And you're a foreigner, and an amateur, and that just rubs salty, salty salt in their shame-filled wounds."

Buck stared a long time at Dude, not believing, but not

disbelieving either. He just chewed the inside of his cheek and mulled Dude's words.

"Whatever. Fine. I won't pound Torakiba." Bucked waved the smoke out of his face. "Even though he deserves it."

"If we all got what we deserve, we'd be miserable. But don't hate the JSA over it, either. Rigid rules keep them in business—keep us in hairstyles and robes. They can't be letting *kohais* do whatever they want to the *senpais*. The whole house of cards would crumble. Whoa. What would my uncle do then?"

"Take up golf?"

IN NAGOYA, BUCK STARTED FRESH. If he dominated here, he could emerge from the deep, dark woods—ding dong the witch was dead. Escape from Torakiba. Sounded like a movie title.

"Buck! Your lineup in the *banzuke* for the autumn *basho* in Tokyo looks like a who's who of the hungriest animals in all of sumo."

"Are you going to be there, Hiro?"

"Sorry. Nagoya is far, and I have to go to school. I wish I could quit."

"Don't quit school, kid. It's your ticket." He wiped the stable's greasy phone receiver on his *yukata* again.

"You could soon be pro. You ache for that, Buck! But there is bad news. Beasts like Gyunyu the belcher and Guta the hairy Russian ache for it at least as much as you do, if not more."

Guta was Buck's opponent on the last day of competition. They both sat in slots one and two of this level, ready to spring into the pro rank.

"Guta once enjoyed the good life of *juryo*, Buck. He spent five *bashos* there before getting bumped. He wants back in, bad! Only you stand in his way. He *hates* you, Buck! He has been training since his pre-hair days for these very bouts. He *must* defeat you."

Sometimes Buck wished he didn't know these things.

"Guta will not hold back when you face him." Hiro wished Buck good luck, a cold comfort, and Buck boarded the bus for Nagoya.

Two weeks of hard-fought wins and a few sorry losses defined the tournament, and then came Sunday: Buck versus Guta. Russia versus America. In Japan.

Guta's win-loss record matched Buck's identically. It was win and advance, lose and languish.

Buck chugged into the arena. Waves of trepidation rocked him, but the Kokugikan buzzed with energy. Buck flexed his thigh muscles. He'd reviewed dozens of highlight reels of Guta's fights. He'd boiled down the stats. He was loaded for Russian bear.

Across the ring the big Russian scowled, and the black hair on his chest, neck, chin, arms, legs, and back bristled with the rage of his spirit. Buck cringed at the thought of having to touch even one of the millions of prickly spikes on that guy's ruddy frame, let alone the majority of them, which a sumo takedown would require. Guta was even hairier in person than on the videos.

The *yobidashi* did his fancy stuff to start the match. Guta had just come from the upper ranks in the last tournament. Buck saw the loophole: Guta was accustomed to the lax start-ceremonies in the upper ranks. In the upper ranks, Buck knew the *rikishi* often made a false start or two before making their serious attacks, to prolong the show for the fans, for their own cockiness. That was his silver bullet against Guta, even with that scary technique of his.

Guta glared at Buck, unblinking. The Russian's every muscle spasm reflected his animosity toward *makushita* and everyone in it—and at this moment, Buck, particularly.

Buck's kneecap jiggled with fear.

It's him or me. Buck steeled himself. *Guta had his chance there and blew it. Now it needs to be my turn.*

The start signal came. Buck sprang across the line, not waiting a fraction of a second. His body slammed into Guta like a freight train. The speed and force caught the Russian off guard. The human hairbrush stumbled backward toward the edge. *Just one more foot.* Buck needed to shove him that final distance to force Guta to step outside the rim of rice straw bales. *One foot more!* Buck used all his strength to press Guta out.

But Guta caught his balance. He began to shove back at Buck with a force Buck had never known before. The bristling arms encircled Buck's ribcage, and Guta began to execute his signature move, the one Buck had studied in all the video clips of matches, the *gasshohineri*—the clasped-hand-twist-down.

Buck had seen it coming. *Freak!* This must be what professional ranks felt like—a building toppling sans warning. Buck planted his knees and squatted, trying to gain purchase on the clay floor with his feet, but without any traction or luck. He was falling backward, unable to shift the center of his weight forward, drifting toward the floor.

In a last ditch effort, as Guta's weight came pouring down on him like a waterfall, Buck hooked his leg around one of Guta's. It pulled Guta's weight off the floor. If Buck had to go down, he wasn't going alone.

Time stopped as Buck and Guta hung in the air side by side, their eyes meeting in fury and terror. Nanoseconds would separate their falls. Buck gave a final twist of his body, his right foot still on solid ground while everything else remained aloft.

The first to land on the ground would lose, stuck for the next two months in *makushita* purgatory. The second would fly straight to *juryo*.

Buck scrambled to keep his body skyward. But gravity prevailed, as the two Titanics came crushing down, sending a cloud of red dust into the air followed by a the sound of thunder. Buck's head slammed onto the stage. Ringing sounded in his ears. Guta's spiny body hairs prickled against Buck's back, causing him to lurch from the Russian's sweaty frame. And yet he wasn't moving, his body lay pinned beneath the weight of Guta's torso.

Oh, no! Not beneath!

十
四

THRONE OF BLOOD
SEPTEMBER. TOKYO

The crowd screamed. Buck shook his head to get his bearings. Everything in him knew he'd won by landing second—just *knew* it. And yet he still suffocated under Guta's weight. Get up. *Get off!* Buck struggled against the pressure, wrangling himself free.

Dejection flooded him. Where was the referee? What was the call? Who won this match? Buck's eyes shot around, and he could see confusion on the faces in the front row. No one knew. No more than a millisecond could have separated their falls.

A lifetime passed before the referee appeared. Guta struggled to his feet beside Buck. The crowd didn't make a sound. Buck held his breath. He'd never seen a match too close to call—and he didn't know if there was such a thing as a do-over. His blood pounded through him, his head throbbing with each beat. The referee's response was the final word—and it meant the world for Buck.

The referee cleared his throat, bowed to the crowd, to the judges in the front row, and with great pomp, made the call: "Kachikoshi, Asagohan."

Buck caught his breath, adrenaline-fueled joy exploding inside him. *Juryo on the blessed shore.*

"WHAT YOU GONNA DO TO celebrate?" Dude asked him over a

bowl of shrimp and tofu the day the *banzuke* came out. "Should we hit the links, Buck-man?"

"Why don't you join a country club here or something? Stop begging green fees off unsuspecting sumo fans?" Buck slurped the dregs of his hot soup.

"Are you kidding me? Country club memberships and green fees in this country are *through the roof.* Property values costs and all. Do you know? It's cheaper to fly to Hawaii for the weekend to golf than it is to golf in Japan. Seriously. If I had the green to fly to Hawaii for the weekend, you can bet your pink polka dot galoshes you'd find me at Turtle Bay." He mimed, swinging his driver and watching the ball sail.

"That's okay. I have something different in mind." Buck rummaged in his bag and got up.

"Where are you going?"

"Come and see." Buck led a small procession of *rikishi* to the trash barrel in the alley behind the stable. "Give me a lighter." Buck snatched one from a chain smoking Japanese *rikishi* and produced the contents of the parcel he carried—the world's most uncomfortable shoes. "Let's rid the world of this menace."

He chucked his platform sandals atop the pile of combustible trash, picked up a bit of wadded up newsprint for kindling, and lit the whole barrel on fire. "Bye-bye, *geta.* I hope to never wear you again." In no time, a blaze roared and consumed the wooden instruments of torture.

THE NEXT AFTERNOON, THE GOOCH called Buck aside. His bass voice reverberated with pride. "You have arrived at a new level, Asagohan. Much proud you are."

It was all Yoda these days with his sentence construction.

"You must now take your own *kohai.*"

Buck gulped.

A much-battered newcomer, full Japanese, stepped forward from behind a paper door to a connecting room. His eyes were down, and scars and scabs decorated his skin, probably from years of sumo prep schools. The guy couldn't be more than sixteen years old. He reminded Buck of a rescue dog—but with a gold tooth as bonus. "May I present Ohimesama. He will be your *kohai.* Treat him as you must."

Buck swallowed hard—a tough pill, taking a servant. He'd only considered his own emancipation, not the enslavement of another person for his use when he escaped the amateur ranks. Nonetheless, Buck bowed in acceptance, and Ohimesama nearly licked the floor with his bow. He followed Buck out of the office and down the hallway, always two paces behind.

As soon as they were out of The Gooch's earshot, Buck turned around. He patted Ohimesama on the shoulder. "Hey, how you doing? When did you get here?"

He took him out into the sunshine of the practice court, where it took three minutes for the kid to look up at Buck, and when he did, his eyes about popped out of his head. "You is *Amerika-jin.* Oh, New York is dangerous!"

If Buck had heard it once he'd heard it a thousand times.

"New York! They is have guns there. So dangerous."

"You ain't seen guns 'til you've seen Texas." He grinned.

Ohimesama bowed again. "I am come today to Kawaguchi stable. My English bad."

"Sounds better than a lot of guys I knew back home. We're going to have a good time, friend." Buck flashed a smile when Ohimesama looked up. A light flickered in the kid's face.

"This is going to be new, having a shadow. I think I probably won't like it. You'll have to find other stuff to do all day. Like training. And sleeping. You know, other stuff. Somebody else dressing me doesn't exactly float my boat either. Or wiping my sweat. Any of that. I like to take care of myself."

Ohimesama looked confused.

"Look, kid. I don't know what you've been used to, but hey. Take a deep breath. You got nothing to fear from me."

Buck let all Ohimesama's scabs heal.

YES! THE PRO RANKS. BUCK basked in the perks. He let Ohimesama help him now and then, but mostly he reveled in the freedom he enjoyed—no kitchen duty, no being bossed here and there, sleeping late and getting straight to the practice ring in the morning. In sumo realm, this was the life.

Reggie and Dude showed up just as practice was winding down and Buck was coming out of the training room. "Hey, Dude. Reggie, pal. What's going on?"

"Oh, I just got another problem," Reggie said.

"The girl again?"

"Again. Why won't this girl leaves me alone?"

"Not another four hundred year-old tree," Dude chortled.

"Trees! I forgot to water that stupid tree. It's getting all yellow now and dried out. I need to get rid of that thing. You know anybody who wants it?" said Reggie.

They left the other *rikishi* behind and went out into the sunshine of the fall afternoon. The light slanted against the Tokyo buildings. Red maple leaves shivered in a breeze.

"Probably." Buck looked up and saw flying geese that formed a V overhead. "Who's on your roster for tonight?"

"New guy. Named Umeboshi," Reggie answered. "Hey, Buck, Dude, you wanna go with me over and see Umeboshi training? Check out his technique, see what he's got?"

"Uh, is that even ethical?" Buck bent down and picked up a fallen gingko leaf, yellow and shiny.

"Coach told me to go."

"Don't worry, dudes. It happens pretty often. I know some guys from my stable went to scout you once or twice." Dude lit a cigarette. "It's part of the system. Umeboshi. I heard he's in the same stable as the *yokozuna.*"

"Not Butaniku. That guy sucks. Let's go." Reggie's pace sped up. Buck tagged along as they made their way across the streets to the other training camp.

Autumn air had a tang. It was a pretty day, even if it did look like it was going to rain.

"Have you noticed the food tastes better since a few of the lower tier guys in the stable ended up being from Thailand instead of Eastern Europe? Those Thai guys know how to spice it."

"We're still eating bleu cheese and dirt over yonder." Reggie pointed a thumb in the direction of his stable.

"What have you heard about Umeboshi?" Buck asked.

"Yeah. Umeboshi. Young kid, only been in the ranks about four tournaments. He's doing pretty good, but I hear his heart isn't in it, so I might have a good shot against him. I just gotta get out of these amatueurs."

"Sobakubi still using you as his karate chop lumber?"

"Only on days when the sun comes up. I'm telling you, *amigos, my* scar tissue now gots scars."

"The weird thing is," Buck said, "Sobakubi doesn't seem to do it out of a personal vendetta or spite, or even out of a bad temper. The ratfink just does it because he can. And nobody stops him. That guy is everything that's wrong with the sport."

Reggie led the way through the maze of alleys and buildings near the Kokugikan. All the stables tried to get training facilities as near to the arena as possible.

"No kidding." Dude spat on the ground and stomped out his cigarette. "Every time I hear of some poor kid getting beat up in an alley, they always say Sobakubi was there—even if he's only stand-ing nearby holding the thuggy leather jackets of other bullies."

"Somebody needs to teach that guy a lesson." Reggie held the door for them.

As a member of *juryo*, Buck would be in the same rank as that overgrown troll. In *juryo* the numbers thinned. Sooner or later every *juryo* faced every other. Time would take care of it. Buck would make that bout count.

"Umeboshi is in this stable, I thinks. I saw a picture of him before so I can recognize that *hombre*." He pressed open the front door of a low building, dark with narrow hallways like so many of the stables. Plaster walls painted a hundred times—and still dingy—pressed against their shoulders as they made their way toward the training rooms. "He's from Okinawa, and Dude told me the kid's parents flew in to watch him compete this week. I hate to burst their bubbles," Reggie smacked his fist into his palm.

"Weird. It seems like I hardly ever hear of full Japanese guys coming in these days."

"I know, right?" Dude said. "It's because all the Japanese par-ents think sumo is totally unsafe for their kids." He stubbed out his cigarette against a wall. "Those parents are smart."

Buck could hear the sounds of training drills behind door after door, hup, hup, hup, as the *rikishi* from every other stable honed their skills for the September tournament. After passing a dozen or so closed rooms, they came to an open one.

"Umeboshi gets to train with the warthog, the lucky dog."

"Uh—" Buck didn't know if lucky covered it. In the far corner, Buck couldn't mistake the form of the human warthog, Butaniku. *Yokozuna*, the great grand champion. Beside him, and about half a mile from his assigned stable lurked Sobakubi, his eyes their usual concentric circles of fat with dark slits in the middle. He sneered a vicious grin downward at a pile of wounded flesh on the ground at Warthog's feet.

And then Buck saw it: an aluminum baseball bat hoisted high in the air above Butaniku's head. The hog gripped it with both hands and brought it hurtling down onto the limp body.

Reggie gasped.

The victim, wearing only a white *mawashi,* bellowed in pain but barely moved. Bruises spread on his back. Blood flowed like oil from a laceration on his neck, making a dark stain on the ground. Sobakubi gurgled something to urge the thrasher onward, a broken beer bottle in his fat fist, shards of brown glass strewn near the victim's head and shoulders.

Butaniku brought the baseball bat aloft again, twirled it with a diabolical guffaw, and prepared to bring it down on the kid again.

"What the hell are you doing?" Buck didn't stop to think. His legs propelled him forward, moving with greater speed than he'd ever forced himself in the *dohyo.* Buck hurtled and seized Butaniku's arm, smashing into him, shoving him hard toward the wall. Sobakubi dropped his weapon and made a beeline for the door. Dude went after him.

"Get off, you *gaijin!*" Butaniku called Buck a foreigner like it was a curse, like he wasn't one himself. "You don't know anything!" Blows started undercutting into Buck's ribs and neck and head, like a paddlewheel of fists. Buck didn't feel any of them—his adrenaline surged too furiously. This guy deserved a broken neck, but Buck's first duty was to protect the inert kid on the floor. Just a few punches here and there should distract Butaniku—get him off the victim. Buck landed one on the Korean's jaw, but pulled a second to the solar plexus.

"Buck! It's Umeboshi, all right. I recognize him." Reggie leaned over the victim, taking his pulse. "I gotta get him out of here."

Reggie dragged the injured boy away while Buck wrestled the bat out of the *yokozuna's* hands. The so-called champion. If this was champion behavior, Buck wanted no part of it.

"You defile the sacred sport of sumo, *gaijin*." Butaniku spat blood at Buck's eye from his bleeding lower lip. "You know nothing! This *rikishi* is weak. He defiles the sport with his fear. He tries to quit. He is soft. He must be taught!"

Reggie glanced up, his face petrified in horror. He shook his head, pressing his fingers to Umeboshi's neck. Buck let go of the Warthog and ran to Umeboshi's side.

"Call for help, Reggie."

"Look out, Buck!" Reggie hollered.

Buck craned his neck around just in time to see Butaniku loom up and wield his bat right at Buck's melon.

"You must learn to keep your tall nose where it belongs, Asagohan."

十
五

THE OUTRAGE
NOVEMBER. FUKUOKA

"Where am I?" Grogginess clogged Buck's brain. His hair matted on his forehead and neck in sweaty gobs. His brain pounded like a freight train had run through it. The backs of his eyes were on fire. His brain rattled. "Whoa." He felt a lump the size of a grapefruit at the base of his skull.

Reggie and Dude bent over him, concern clouding their faces. "You're at the sumo *biyoin*. The hospital. You took quite a beating, pal." For once, Dude's accent didn't sound surfer. "They said you're out of danger once you woke up, so hey. Good to see you awake."

"Thanks," Buck said. Hospital. No wonder it smelled like rubbing alcohol in here. "What happened to Butaniku? How long have I been out?" Buck rubbed his hand lightly over the painful area. Nothing could be worse—he'd just barely healed from one major injury, and now he'd incurred yet another round of pain. In a flash of memory, he relived how it all went down. "How's the kid?"

"You've been out a day and a half. Butaniku left you for dead on the floor of the stable after the one smack. Reggie started yelling and some people came," Dude said.

"That long." Buck's stomach made the sound of a grizzly bear. "Bring me something to eat, would you?"

Dude produced a takeout bag, and from it pulled a clamshell of food, food that smelled like actual food. Inside was a hamburger—without seaweed on it—with cheese. Wow. But Buck's appetite wavered.

"And the kid?"

Dude looked at his feet.

Buck shot up to sitting position. His bedsheets crackled. Buck's stomach burned. "Where's Sobakubi?"

"Gone. With Butaniku. Presumably off to assault someone new," Reggie said.

"I don't know about that," Dude said. "A dead kid might make them lay low a while."

Dead kid? Buck caught his breath. The words screamed in his mind. "You mean the kid's dead and nothing's been done about it yet? What about the police? Who is investigating this?"

The Hawaiian produced an English language newspaper and shook it in Buck's direction. "Hata Junichiro (also known as Umeboshi) of Okinawa, lately of the Ryogoku district of Tokyo, died last Wednesday at the Hakabata sumo stable of undetermined causes."

"What?" Buck hissed. "Bludgeoning isn't obvious enough?"

"Coroner's report states heart failure, but Hata's family is requesting an autopsy."

"Darn straight they should." Indignation brought Buck to his full sitting height and a surge of pain to his head.

"The JSA, however, is urging an immediate cremation. I might not be a rocket surgeon, but even I can smell a rat there," Reggie said.

Anger began to replace nausea. "Covering themselves? Un-believable. Don't they even care a guy has been killed? Don't they know who did this?"

But of course they knew. And all of a sudden it was clear that the cover-up had to happen—the Hata family would never get justice. Suddenly, it seemed a sumo grand champion needed no conscience after all, for nothing with any consequence applied to him. Buck's blood ran hot.

"What about the *basho*? Did I miss my match?"

Reggie looked grim. "Canceled."

It took a minute for this to sink in. "Canceled? When does that ever happen?" Buck gasped.

"First tournament cancellation in the history of sumo. In a thousand years. Dude. I never thought I'd see this day."

"Whoa." Buck tried to sit up a little higher before falling back. His head pounded. "Is there *any* good news?" The hospital intercom beeped and a voice requested a doctor to a certain room.

Reggie and Dude exchanged glances, and a smile tugged at Dude's mouth.

"What? You've got a girlfriend?"

"Better than that," Dude said. "Well, almost. Besides, I only like blondes with beach bodies, and they're not hanging out in Tokyo anywhere I can see. I'm talking about the government."

"Government?" Government never meant good news to Buck the Texan. The JSA served as more than government around here. They were the pantheon. Buck lay on his face to let his biceps rest.

"Nope, nope, listen. Saito got elected. Mr. *Saito.*"

"Yeah, so?"

"Come on, bro. It totally means everything. Saito is a fan, a big fan of the sacred sport. Yesterday, right after I was done missing the best windless day my golf buddy in Cape Town ever saw, His Awesomeness took his oath of office, and today he launched a full government investigation into Umeboshi's death. The JSA is running like scared little girls, and the edict came down to all the stable masters—'Hazing is dead.'"

Buck dropped to the bed, suddenly tired again. "Seriously?

But wasn't that the rule before? They never enforced it in the past. Why now?"

"They're scared witless, dude. The Japanese people don't dig the Umeboshi thing one smidge. It has some people all suspicious-like, and in this country, public sentiment can make or break any institution at all."

"Even sumo?"

"Even sumo."

"I like this Saito guy." Buck glanced furtively at Dude. "He gets my vote, whoever he is."

"Yeah, well, you better get it together soon, Buck. Funeral Tuesday. Attendance mandatory."

Buck and his friends had better keep a low profile there, and everywhere else.

BUCK TOSSED AND TURNED IN his bed, as much as a man with a bump the size of a baseball on the back of his head could toss and turn. Night fell, but sleep escaped him. Anxieties stretched his soul on the rack, and each aspect of the situation ratcheted the pain up a little higher.

He had witnessed a murder.

He'd punched the grand champion of sumo.

He had let Reggie move an injured body—and possibly precipitated the death of a poor kid. Did that make him an accessory to the crime?

He had come close to being deep-sixed himself with the baseball bat of doom. Lucky for him, he had the noggin of Hank Cooper—eleven inches thick in some spots—to protect his brainier parts. It would crush his parents if he died here.

Just like it must have crushed Umeboshi's poor parents. If only there were some way to console them—the truth would comfort no one. But keeping it to himself wasn't right either. Just because truth brought pain didn't mean it should be hidden.

Buck twisted onto his side. The one advantage of being in the hospital was the actual bed. Funny, though, after fifteen months on the floor, a bed wasn't as comfortable as he expected. Then again, under the circumstances, probably no place physical or emotional could be comfortable anymore. He ought to feel good about himself—for the first time in his life he'd stood up to a bully. *Chuh.* Standing up to bullies wasn't all it was cracked up to be.

He needed to tell someone about the crime. But who?

IT TOOK A FEW DAYS, but Buck got back on his feet in time for the Tuesday funeral. The press and the papers and the stables hissed about the cancellation of the September *basho.* Everyone whispered maybe this was the end of sumo. Buck knew better. There was too much money in it for anyone to let it end. The entire sumo community conducted an official mourning for Umeboshi— Buck saw through the ruse. It was nothing more than a surface-overreaction to the death, a way for the organization to save face, to give a good show. There was no way the main officials didn't know what happened. Buck shuddered at the shallowness of them all. If they really cared, they'd bring Butaniku's crime to light and ride him out of town on a rail.

On the morning of the funeral, the weather took a sudden chill. It was like nature had decided to die, too. Buck donned a black kimono issued to him by the JSA, alongside all his fellow *rikishi.* Crowds thronged the streets between the Kokugikan and the Buddhist temple, where monks hummed a low, penetrating buzz, their bright orange kimonos a stark contrast to the dark wood and dusty interior of the temple. Mourners really mourned here, wails, moans, echoing into the deep shadows of the holy building.

Incense, chanting, and piles of white gardenias stretched to the ceiling. Buck picked the bereaved parents out of the crowd with no trouble, their grief-creased faces a giveaway. He watched them, thinking of his mom, his dad. Someone with authority needed to know what Buck knew. Someone who could make a stand against the JSA.

"Kawaguchi Oyakata? I need to speak with you. It is private." Buck took The Gooch by the sleeve after the services ended. "I need to tell someone what I saw."

THE DEATH CAST A DARK pall over the sport. Diehard, lifelong fans reneged on their allegiance to popular *rikishi*. Gossip rumbled about the cause, and Buck held his breath to hear some action by officials against Butaniku and Sobakubi. Surely The Gooch had taken his information to responsible parties. But nothing.

He mentioned it to Reggie and Dude on a chilly fall evening in an otherwise deserted bathhouse. Steam coated them and muted their whispered conversation.

"I wasn't going to tell you guys this, but I reported the murder to The Gooch," Buck started.

"The Gooch!" Dude scoffed.

"What's wrong with my trainer? He's a stand-up guy."

"Yeah, as a trainer." Dude flicked a mosquito buzzing near him.

"What Dude's trying to say is reporting it to Kawaguchi is like reporting it to the JSA," Reggie said.

"Yeah, because The Gooch *is* the JSA," Dude said.

Buck knit his brows. The Gooch was one of the good guys. "I don't buy that."

"Please. To be a sumo trainer you have to pay your annual *hefty* fee and buy your JSA membership. Sneaking in and telling The Gooch Butaniku and Sobakubi offed that kid is like telling Butaniku's brother or something. He ain't gonna do nothing."

Buck bit his pinky nail down to the nub. "Well then, that puts us on dangerous ground, boys. Butaniku is out there somewhere— and we've got damaging testimony that he's a murderer. If the wrong—er, right—person got this information, his career is in the squatter."

"But not Sobakubi. He's Teflon Boy. Gets away with everything, thanks to daddy." Dude took a long drag on his cigarette, its smoke mingling with the ribbons of steam.

"But maybe not murder."

"I don't like this." Reggie's big Easter Island face scowled. Neither did Buck. A week in the upper ranks, and Buck was amassing enemies faster than the speed of the Millennium Falcon when the warp drive actually worked.

"Hey, Buck. You know how every day has been just awash in good news?" Dude tossed his cigarette against the tile wall and it snuffed out in a hot puddle. "Well, there's more, Buck-meister." He hummed the theme to *Jaws*.

"Surprise me," Buck said as he watched the cigarette butt hiss in the water.

"Did you see lucky day thirteen on your lineup in the *banzuke* for November in Fukuoka?"

Sobakubi.

RASHOMON: THE DRAGONS' GATE
NOVEMBER. FUKUOKA

The November day dawned smoggy in Fukuoka. The south of Japan didn't get as cold as the northern islands, but humidity combined with pollution to create a chill that seeped into Buck and froze him to the core.

"Chop-chop, Asagohan. Your march into the ring begins soon. Put on this *yukata*." Ohimesama scuttled Buck into his attire for the afternoon's event. His gold tooth glinted. Buck might end up hating having a *kohai* more than being one.

"It's your first day, too, kid. Get yourself ready. I can do this." Buck's jaw chattered.

"Really?" Ohimesama's eyes grew wide. "Thank you, Buck."

"And I don't need your help any more today. Good luck. I've seen you practicing, and you're going to plow that guy into the ground."

Ohimesama bowed six or seven times before hustling away as Buck finished dressing himself. The shoes were heaven on his feet after months in the wooden *geta* sandals. He stared at himself in the mirror, the topknot greased to a golden, oily shine, the blue of his eyes looking so out of place in the context of sumo. For the first time in six months he assessed his size—today's weigh-in produced numbers not associated with his body since tenth grade, even if he had to make the conversion from kilograms to pounds in his head. The mirror showed he looked a lot closer to that "after" picture he remembered keeping in his desk drawer back at Eaglestone.

Weird. Those days seemed like *the* dream now.

Game day. The energy surged.

"Asagohan!" Sixteen girls in miniskirts screamed when he passed them on his way to the arena. "Blue eyes!"

Buck's rocket ride through the ranks had made him a celebrity—and with the hair, he was easily the most recognizable low-ranking professional *rikishi*. This had its pros and cons.

Pros: Fans entering the building shouted to him, waved hand-print autograph cards at him—some reached out to pull on his *yukata's* sleeves. Cons: all around him, other wrestlers streamed in, frowning in his general direction.

"Asagohan! Asagohan!" A slew of reporters thronged him as he entered the huge glass and steel arena. Such a modern building for such an ancient sport, it struck him. Fluorescent lights cast a blue glow on everything. Buck recognized the hair-flipping guy, Tanaka, from months back, and gave him a wave.

Then the first shoe dropped.

"Asagohan! What do you think about the death of Umeboshi?" The other shoe followed swiftly: "Asagohan! You must know something about this death. Is sumo still safe?"

Buck stopped in his tracks. His heart thrummed in his chest. He had to do something. He couldn't answer Tanaka. Not now. As soon as he got back to Tokyo, he would do something about it.

Day one, Buck smeared his first competitor like butter on bread. Maybe it wouldn't be so bad here in the pros after all. Maybe these guys were the same as the amateurs, except that they'd just been around longer.

On days two, three and four, however, Buck stumbled. The

professionals fought differently after all. For the first time ever, he amassed a losing record, one win to three losses. Buck stomped down a deserted hallway, punching brick walls as he went.

Torakiba passed him and sneered. "You're in the pros now. You mess with tigers, you get the teeth." He bared them. Buck kept walking. Tomorrow he'd pull out of the death spiral. That jerk would see.

Day five, he redeemed himself, but day six left him lagging behind again. Competing every single day without a rest on the alternate days threw off his rhythm. Every day brought him closer to day thirteen against Sobakubi, and the losing record frustrated him. The bile of it gurgled in his stomach—good old Guta's Russian countryman, Gochisosama, turned Buck into gouda cheese, and a burly Belarusian made Buck look like a pest on the playground.

He analyzed the slumping results so far. It had to be the weight loss. It had started to work against him. He just couldn't leverage his strength here like he could in lower ranks. It peeved him. These mammoths reached this rank for a reason. Suddenly, Sobakubi's persistence in maintaining this tier impressed Buck rather than disgusted him. He could see why getting above all these power-houses would take incredible doggedness, more than Buck had ever imagined when he set foot in the *juryo* rank.

Day nine came and went. He sat down with Reggie at a late night dinner. Buck mulled his three-and-six record and his pile of shredded seaweed atop his greasy Shakey's pizza with disgust. If he didn't get a positive win-loss record in this tournament, he would junk all his chances at staying in *juryo*. Reggie kicked him under the table.

"You gotta step up your game, *amigo*, if you don't wanna get busted back to the minors with us losers." Reggie took a big bite of his pizza decorated with tiny fish—eyes and all.

"What happened to your face?" Buck asked, noticing the bruises across the Filipino's mug. So much for the end of hazing.

"I gotta get out of there. Seriously, man. That guy is toxic," Reggie said. "Ever since Sobakubi's daddy got the big promotion in Saito's government, he has been even worst than ever. And that's saying a lot."

Buck's fist twitched. Four more days, and he could legally crush the spoiled SOB. He threw his crust in the trash and went back to the training room for some extra workouts. He needed them.

Day ten and eleven. Buck found renewed fury and redeemed his record to five-and-six. On day twelve he dominated an Estonian and put his record at six and six.

Six and six. He stared at the lists. A tie. His mouth went sour. A tie smelled like *nat-to*. A winning ratio guaranteed the JSA wouldn't bump him down. A losing ratio put him in jeopardy.

He needed one more win to secure his place in *juryo* for another round. And Sobakubi stood in his way.

Worse, Sobakubi's record was the same as Buck's. Six-and-six. Although they might be in the same kind of boat, Sobakubi's boat had a leak. For days fourteen and fifteen, Sobakubi's schedule pitted him against two guys the jerk had never beaten. Ever. Not in all his months in the tier.

Buck, however, had beaten both of them this *basho*. When Sobakubi lost to them on days fourteen and fifteen, the rankings system assured his demotion—out of the pros. It was going to be more satisfying than a plateful of Charlie Unger's barbecue to see that happen—especially if Buck beat him tomorrow and helped solidify Sobakubi's demise.

Sobakubi was going *down*.

Late that night, a pounding came at Buck's door. He cracked open an eye and saw his worst nightmare: Sobakubi's silhouette.

"What do you want."

"Asagohan. Let's talk. You're going to the *koen-kai.* You like parties?"

"Not much. That's why I'm in bed. Sleeping." *Getting my strength up to crush you.*

"I will meet you near the bar."

"No, sir, you won't."

But after Sobakubi left, Buck tossed in his futon. What could that guy possibly have to say that Buck would want to hear? It was probably a horrible idea to even go. Like Han Solo always said, *I got a bad feeling about this.*

An hour later, Buck's eyes shot around the *koen-kai.* Everyone here partied at the expense of a cigarette company—the billows of smoke showed it. Buck hated himself for following Sobakubi into this hazy lair. Music pulsed, girls in dresses gyrated while people drank and drank and drank around him. Buck stared with narrowed eyes at Sobakubi, who pulled a cup of steaming *sake* from a tray and downed it.

"What do you want from me, Sobakubi?" Buck raised his chin.

"Nice party, right? I love parties. It's nice being in the professional ranks, getting invited to places like this, meeting the women, making new friends."

"I don't have time for your bull puckey." Buck turned to go.

"Your first *basho* in Fukuoka as a pro is going well, Asagohan," Sobakubi hollered. "My father has noticed. With his new position in Mr. Saito's cabinet he finds himself impressed with what is impressive."

Buck rolled his eyes. As a Texan, Buck found himself unimpressed with what was unimpressive.

"I see, Asagohan, that you are not catching my drift. You're too disconnected from the real world, stuck with your head deep in the sand of sumo." He made a sound and gave Buck a patronizing look through those fat-ringed eyes. Buck's skin crawled. "My father's job means a lot to you."

"Look, Sobakubi. You obviously want something. Spit it out."

"I like your record, like I said. Your stay in *juryo* is nearly sealed. You need just one victory." He raised an eyebrow and his second sake cup, this time in salute. "*Kampai* to you for that. I, however, have not fared as well this time."

Buck knew Sobakubi took into account the complexities of the point calculations JSA used to create the ranks. Their win-loss records might be equal, but their footing differed considerably because of whom Buck had beaten and whom Sobakubi had lost to.

"Condolences." Buck scanned the room for the nearest exit.

"You and I compete tomorrow, face to face in the *dohyo.* I have been waiting for this opportunity for a long time, my American friend."

Friend schmend. Buck sat here face to face with a murderer's accomplice, a man who spent the last year thrashing Buck's best friend Reggie into chaff as a pastime. "I wouldn't call myself your friend, exactly." Friends don't wish for friends to spend eternity rotating on Hell's rotisserie.

"I have a deal to offer you."

"I don't want your deals. Take your deals and skedaddle."

"Aha-ha-ha. Not so fast, Cowboy. I'll make it worth your while."

"You have nothing I could possibly want." Buck spat. "You're obsequious and manipulative. You think you're some kind of puppet-master who can control people around him with your 'deals.' Money—I'll earn mine fair and square, thanks. Women? None you would know could interest me. Power and fame? I don't care about any of that. Your deal is worthless."

Sobakubi didn't bat an eye. "First I'll tell you what I want, and then I'll tell you what you want."

"What I want is for you to face justice for what you did to

Umeboshi." There, Buck said it. The threat hung in the air like a frozen breath.

Sobakubi let it crack and fall to the ground, only giving it the dignity of a single raise of an eyebrow. "What I want is for you to allow me to win tomorrow."

Buck choked on his *sake*. "Excuse me? You what?" A low chuckle formed in Buck's belly and worked its way northward through his chest and throat and out his mouth where it emerged as a deafening guffaw.

Sobakubi remained unfazed. "Tomorrow, you will allow me to defeat you." Another sip, and the man's round face hardened into reptilian coldness. "If not, my fate will be sealed. I'll be removed to a lower rank, a place I have no wish to go. I'm not the devil, Asagohan. Allowing me to win does not absolutely prevent you from having a winning record. You can still keep that by winning your last two bouts, which you certainly will." His tongue flicked, serpent-like, to punctuate the flattery.

"Think about it," Sobakubi continued. "The JSA can do nothing about their ranking system, and my win-loss record will require my demotion if I do not win tomorrow. All the fans would rebel if the officials kept me in *juryo*. We don't want the fans rebelling, things being as precarious as they are right now, as you well know. So, you will oblige me."

"Yeah, sure. Because we're such close friends." Buck stood to leave.

"No, because of what *you* did that day."

Buck froze.

"Look, Sobakubi." Buck stared down at the snake. "I have much more damning evidence on you than you'll ever have on me. You and I and all God's angels know who swung the bat that night. And who was holding the broken beer bottle. And who stopped them."

"*Baka!*" Sobakubi cursed. Wild fury burned in his eyes. "You contributed your own chaos to the situation, and you know it. Moving the body? But let's set that aside for now. It's much more than mere blackmail I'm talking about here."

He stood and forced Buck back into a seated position at the table. "I wanted to ask you nicely, Asagohan. I wanted to give you the chance to be the bigger man, to do the generous thing." The words oozed from his mouth. He downed another cup of *sake* when a tray came by.

Hot lava stirred in Buck's innards. The rest of this conversation could only get worse.

"Your father. He's a businessman."

"What does my father have to do with anything?" The hair on the back of Buck's neck stood up, and his hot lava turned glacial.

Sobakubi loomed too close, his breath poured cool and foul at Buck's face. "He has a product to sell, a product that needs approval, a product that his very life depends on."

Buck sat riveted to the spot.

"What *you* want, Buck Cooper, is for your father's deal with the Yoshidas to go through. Nangrimax, right? You want your parents to keep their little mansion in the Texas suburbs. You want them to not be ruined financially. You don't want your father to lose his self-respect by failing—again. And so, Asagohan, I suggest that you allow me to win the bout tomorrow. There's no thought I hate worse than the idea of being sent down to the *makushita* level again. I fought my way out of there years ago and intend to never return. You'll see to it." Sobakubi slammed back a final cup of steaming *sake* and hissed, "Or your father's drug approval is dead."

Sobakubi set his cup on the table, then stood and stalked into the dark and pulsating party, leaving Buck with a heart of ash.

Any breeze might send it filtering away from where he sat at the corner table, his leaden decision throbbing round his neck.

FUKUOKA. BUCK BEGAN TO DESPISE IT.

After a restless night in his futon, Buck rose in the dawn's gray light. His birthday. Twenty-six years old. Weird.

Lumbering through their makeshift stable area, he passed the hapless underlings peeling potatoes and washing vats of rice, and ventured out into the morning air. It was November. Not cold, but not warm either. A storm threatened. Buck pulled his *yukata* close around his neck, wishing he could wear two of them. And while his parents lay sleeping in their beds in Texas, or tilling the garden on a fall afternoon, or getting ready for the holidays, or whatever they might be doing, a vicious, selfish Japanese man a million miles away was plotting their financial and emotional demise.

Buck walked along into the Fukuoka City morning. Fog tendrils beckoned him toward a tea shop.

Sobakubi—the name snaked like a curse through Buck's mind. *Sobakubi.* For a violent, blackmailing murder accomplice, he sure masqueraded well as a spineless wuss. Somebody ought to give that boy a whipping he wouldn't forget.

But maybe not today, maybe not Buck.

So much was at stake—and Buck weighed it all, over and over, on the scales of his mind. To do what was right or to do what was safe. To preserve integrity or to preserve his childhood home, his mother's little kingdom, her whole world, where she sewed and baked and cleaned and served her neighbors. To keep his virtue or to keep his father's self-confidence, his self-worth.

He's only got one failure left in him, his mom's words echoed from what seemed like a lifetime ago in his office. If Sobakubi and his important father in the Prime Minister's cabinet did have the power to create or destroy Hank Cooper's success—

"Hello. Buck. That's you, isn't it?" A soft voice startled him as he sat over his tea in the tea shop. It shook him from the turbulence of his thoughts. He glanced up and saw dimples!

"Chocho? What are you doing here?" He got that weight-lessness again as she approached. He jumped to his feet, almost jostling the teacup she cradled in her palm.

"It's morning, and I'm a morning person." She sat down in the chair he proffered her, and pulled her sweater tight around her shoulders. He steadied himself and sat back down beside her. She was so beautiful in the morning.

"I like the sunrise over the water." She sipped her cup and checked her watch. "I guess I misestimated this morning's dawn by an hour. So much travel, and sunrise changes at every latitude."

Buck nodded. She glowed, radiant, the sun itself to his eyes. Everything that had perplexed him a moment ago faded, like shadows chased away by bright sunshine. Chocho illuminated everything.

"Travel?"

"The usual." She lifted one shoulder and it enchanted him, her every move a poem. "The tuna have been exceptional this year, a huge catch in northern seas and southern. I'm all over the map." She sighed, and it wafted like heaven's breath to his ear.

"I guess I never bothered to ask what you do. Your job."

"Me?" Chocho blushed. "I work for my father." It didn't look like it gave her any pleasure to say this, but Buck waited for her to expound. "One of the subsidiary companies of Ginza Corporation is seafood marketing." She reached into her wallet and pulled out a photo.

"Holy giant tuna! Don't tell me you caught this."

She laughed a sincere laugh.

"No, no, Buck. Of course not. I just bought it. This one happened to be the largest one I'd seen, so I had to take a photo."

"You're a tuna broker. I heard about a tuna broker a couple of years ago. Huge fish. Auctioned for like $175,000. A monstrous fish."

Chocho sat back and beamed.

"Don't tell me you were the buyer." Buck's eyes opened wide.

"I can't believe you heard about that." She sipped her tea and double-blinked.

"Everyone heard about that. It was top Google news." Buck found this girl more and more impressive. "How does that work, exactly?"

Chocho set her teacup down and folded her slender hands.

"When the fish come in on the docks, my people notify me and I race to wherever the new catch is, and it can be at any dock on any coast of all of Japan from Hokkaido to Okinawa. The travel is so stressful. Then, while it's still on ice or hanging from its crane in the salt air, I bid on it, and if I win, all our seafood dealers have the freshest fish in Japan."

Cool. "But the big one. With a price that high, I wondered how the buyer could turn a profit."

"My father always turns a profit." Chocho lifted her eyes to the ceiling for a moment. "Besides," she sighed, "everyone in Japan wanted to taste that particular tuna. It was sensational, and our dealers were able to sell it to restaurants for even more money." A soft lift of a shoulder said she took this all in stride. She fascinated him. "I love my job and hate it at the same time."

Doesn't everyone? But Buck could see she meant something deeper. And it had its roots in her father.

Then she perked up. "It's nice to be here to watch the *basho*. I hear so many good things about you, what you're doing—both in the ring and out." Her face softened and one dimple sank. "It's nice to see you in the professional ranks already, quite a meteoric rise, I must say."

Buck blushed from his *chonmage* to his toes. "Well, like they say—fast ripe, fast rotten."

They sipped their tea in silence and looked out the window at the lightening sky for a long moment. Comfortable silence.

His dilemma settled on him once again—the house mortgaged, his father's life's work, his own honor—all being ransomed by that con man. After all, sumo rules forbade throwing a bout for any reason. A *rikishi* could be expelled for even a first offense. It had happened in the past. With the current crackdown climate, Buck calculated leniency from the JSA as a statistical impossibility.

And here sat Chocho. If he kowtowed to Sobakubi's demands, he risked losing her respect.

"I hate moral dilemmas," Buck said, breaking the silence.

She sipped her tea and looked thoughtful, staring back up at his face. "So do I." She moistened her perfect, heart-shaped lips and looked out at the coming dawn. Then, she turned toward Buck with purpose, half smiling. "You know what I do? I ask myself, 'What would my father do?' and then I do the opposite."

Buck sniffed. "Nice to have access to a moral compass that always points south so you know where north is."

She rested her hands on his, where he held his cup, and whispered, barely loud enough for Buck to distinguish, "You're my north, Buck."

Buck glanced back from the window down at this unparalleled woman, who gazed up at him. "Chocho." His gratitude lodged in his throat. "I'm glad I ran into you here this morning." He gave her a second look, a deeper one, past the beauty that barricaded her true self. And inside, he saw more—much more beauty.

"Buck." She lowered her eyes before looking back up into his, "I think meeting you was a necessary accident."

The door of the tea shop creaked open, and a bevy of early risers bustled in with shouts of "Asagohan!" and "Ginza Chocho-*san*!"

Everybody was a fan at tournament time. Buck tried his best to duck the cameras, but a few shots snapped. Chocho jumped up to leave. Part of Buck began ripping away. His eye willed her to stay. He hadn't even asked her about her horses, or a thousand other things he needed to know. Fans clamored for his attention, and she slipped off into the morning light.

Strength drained from him. The afternoon's decision still loomed.

SOBAKUBI'S FACE WOBBLED IN COCKINESS across the ring from Buck. He arched that single eyebrow, a smile of contempt on his lips. The announcer called for Asagohan and Sobakubi to face off in the *dohyo*, eye-to-eye, gut-to-gut. Buck crouched into fighting stance, just as he must. His body obeyed the commands he gave it, but his mind and heart roiled completely out of his control.

Worry chewed at his soul—this was *the* moment. If Sobakubi possessed the power to know about Buck's family, to do the reconnaissance on Buck's personal life, then he couldn't be a hundred percent bluffing about his power of control over it. Buck's thigh muscle quivered.

Several things shimmered crystal clear to Buck as he stomped away the demons of the *dohyo*, as he spat out his bitter tasting power water behind the power paper. One, he'd never hurt his parents in any way. Two, he would protect them with his very life. Three, they deserved his full respect and honor. Four, Reggie bore the scars of months and months of torture at this villain's hand.

And five, Chocho was watching.

The *yobidashi* signaled the fight to begin. Time slowed to a halt. Buck's mind raced. His breath became heavy, steamy in the humidity of the Fukuoka autumn. Why couldn't they pump AC into these places to dry the air?

The laughing, fat-encircled eyes of Sobakubi danced. A jaunty smirk made him look like a kid who had already unwrapped all his presents on his birthday, and then rewrapped them before the party, liking what he saw.

Buck seethed. This guy deserved the meat grinder. He deserved the wood chipper. He deserved no mercy. Mercy—Buck had tried mercy. He pulled his punches in that awful altercation against Butaniku when the champ killed that kid. What did it get him? A concussion and a hospital stay, plus more months of terrorizing in the stables by that mammoth bully. Mercy was overrated when it came to these two.

With the final flourish the *yobidashi* bid them begin their *tachiai,* their initial head butting. Sobakubi came at Buck, languid, muscles slack, a man of leisure sauntering to the center of the ring. This cocky dirtbag supposed Buck would roll over, take a knee, and step outside the ring, anything to lose in the first second.

Buck's nerves snapped. *You won't like today's gift, you spoiled brat.*

The whole thing happened faster than a jackrabbit crossing a freeway. Sobakubi didn't know what hit him when Buck went from coiled spring to springing lion. The second the signal came, Buck lunged, full-force at Sobakubi's slack posture. The murder-accomplice sailed, airborne, out of the ring and landed on his head in the first row of chairs, rendered unconscious, getting exactly what he deserved.

TKO.

The crowd went nuts. There lay the result of his fury, inert and oily. The paramedic staff rushed to Sobakubi's side, took his pulse, and began a scan. The audience's cheers died down fast. No one made a peep while the medics examined the unconscious hulk, whose only motion was the faint rise and fall of his chest.

Sobakubi wasn't dead, but defeated on full public display as the result of Buck's brutal physical power. Duplicity filled him. He looked down at his hands and forearms. His face burned as his adrenaline steamed out. Without smiling for the first time ever, Buck bowed and lumbered back to the dressing room.

He really hoped he'd done the right thing.

十七

FISTFUL OF DOLLARS
JANUARY-MARCH. TOKYO

Fukuoka's tournament ended. So did November. Buck waited on pins and needles all December for signs of repercussions from his brush with Sobakubi. It was like holding his breath, constantly checking his rear view mirror for cops when he was speeding. It was that feeling he got whenever he watched a horror movie—the monster was around the corner and the idiot in the woods could almost sense it, but didn't have the brains to run.

Christmas came. He dialed his parents, fingers trembling at the possibility of devastating news from the other side of the ocean.

"No news is good news, I guess," his father said, still optimistic. Little did his dad know.

"We're getting so tired of the waiting game," his mom said, her voice revealing a trace of anxiety. Buck didn't tell them about Sobakubi. They wouldn't understand, but her concern rekindled a fire in Buck. He'd sat on his conscience long enough. Umeboshi's parents deserved to find peace. The truth will out, Shakespeare might've said, but sometimes it needed someone to kick down the door first.

"Hey, dude. How about a Christmas Day walk down to the local precinct?" Buck shambled into the nap room of Dude's stable.

"You're gonna try and tell someone? There's no one to tell,

man. The truth won't help anybody." Dude twirled a candy cane in his mouth, lying on his futon, eyes shut.

"That family has a right to know." The mother of the dead boy—how could she sleep at night? "Besides, we have other things to consider."

"What? Like the completely sucky fact that no one in sumo is safe until that warthog is incarcerated?" Dude rolled his eyes.

"Exactly. We've sat on it long enough."

"Look, I admire the mondo depth of your zeal, but there's nothing to be gained by outing the guy, and a lot more than you think to be lost. Do you know how much money is invested in a *yokozuna*? Have you thought about what this will do to the fans, what it will do to the sport, what will happen to the rankings? Remember who is next in line for the grand champion slot. It's not your favorite person. You'll be trading evil for eviler."

"Eviler isn't a word. And if you won't come with me to back my story up, I'm going anyway." Buck put a hand on the door to go. Dude didn't budge.

"You're on your own, crusader. I can't help you."

It was a fifteen-minute walk, and cold. Wind shoved hard against him, pushing him back toward the stable where it was safe. A taxi sloshed the contents of a sleety puddle onto him. His *yukata* was like a sieve for the slush. He struggled to put one foot in front of the other.

"*Konnichiwa.* Merry Christmas." Buck met the policeman at the desk with a bow. He gulped and said, "I have a present for one lucky detective."

JANUARY ARRIVED WITH AN ICE storm. Buck went to lunch with Reggie at his stable. Sure enough, the food here *did* taste like an old museum. Then they shivered their way back to Buck's stable for the beer phase of the lunch hour and to wait for the lists.

"Where are those lists? They're five days late." Reggie took a long pull at his longneck. They stretched their legs under a low table with a blanket covering its top. A heater attached to the underside of the table glowed, keeping their legs warm. It was the only place to get warm in this breath-visible land of no indoor heating. Buck wedged as much of his legs under the table as he could.

"I don't know, but when they do show up, Sobakubi had better not be in *juryo*," Buck said.

"*Kampai* to that." Reggie shook his Kirin beer bottle in Buck's direction. "You better believe he won't be. I ain't seen him in days and days. He's probably crying to his daddy."

"*Kampai*." Buck clinked Reggie's beer bottle with his Lamune, a drink that was also a toy because of the little marble in the bottleneck. The strawberry version tasted better than anything else. Except, maybe, for the melon version. Buck drank about a case of it a week.

Reggie leaned on one elbow and took another swig. "To wax or not to wax, man. That is the question."

"Wax what?"

"My back. The beast from Belarus, forgot his name, he never waxes. But he looks like a furry varmint. I think it's part of his intimidation factor. But I don't want to go there. Not at all, man."

"Waxing, huh. Sounds painful." It would be as painful as for Buck to see Sobakubi's name still in *juryo* and not down in *makushita* where he belonged.

"You don't know pain if you never got yourself waxed."

Buck downed the final drops of Lamune, letting the blue marble plink against his upper lip. "I hope I never find out."

"You're lucky. You're only hairy up here." Reggie pounded his upper chest. "And your back's got nothing. It's not nasty like mine." Reggie rubbed his fingers through the curls at his collarbone. "I guess I don't really got no choice."

Buck winced as he envisioned yet another indignity he was probably going to be forced to endure.

"And your lady friend. She likes smooth skin, eh?"

Reggie winced back. "Come on, man. It's getting real bad. Did you see what she sended me for Christmas, or New Year's, or whatever? That kimono was made all of pure silk, and it had all these huge firebird things stitched onto it, and the guys over in my stable, they said it probably costed like *hyaku man* yen. Do you know how much that is? It's like a car. A little one, but *ay!* I can't shake her. She is calling and calling me and saying I should go with her to see some kind of *kabuki* show, and I don't knows whats to tell her. I'm real busy!"

"Too bad, buddy. Burdened with the trial of a beautiful woman throwing herself at you." Buck flexed his numb fingers. Stupid cold.

"There is some news you should know, though." Reggie downed his last drop and sat up straight. Before he could continue, another *rikishi* came bounding in.

"*Banzuke aru!*" He had the lists.

"Ohimesama. Come here. Can you please translate this for me?"

"You say please, Asagohan." Ohimesama grinned and bowed for the thousandth time. "I like this so very, very much." It sounded like "berry berry mahchi." Ohimesama was starting to grow on him. "I happy translate for you. Ready? I go. Takoyaki—he gone. Oishiringo move to top of *jonokuchi.* He still low rank. You beat Oishiringo many time, Asagohan! He so low now and not you. You top guy!"

"What about Reggie. Er, Futokaba?" Buck saw fear in Reggie's eyes.

Ohimesama scanned the lists and frowned. "Futokaba still same tier."

"*Caramba!*" Reggie kicked the floor. "Ah, well, you know, *muchacho*, it fits how I did in Fukuoka."

"You'll get 'em next time." Buck took a deep breath. "What about Sobakubi?" He'd waited long enough. "Tell me his name is down a level. Say it's in *makushita.*"

Ohimesama frowned. He looked twice at the list. "It is not in *makushita.*" He looked confused. Buck gritted his teeth. "You gotta be kidding me. Look again."

"It is not there, Asagohan. No Sobakubi. You look?"

Buck shook his head and swore. The unfairness of if choked him. For Sobakubi to suffer no consequences, to have *no* rules apply to him—not even the scoring requirements for rank placement—was like an avalanche of "unfair." Buck punched his fist into his palm five times hard.

Ohimesama minced over and whispered, "Ah, yes, Baku-*san*. This is why *banzuke* is takes so long to appear this time." He paused, and whispered, "Sobakubi is not in *makushita*. But he is not in *juryo*, too. Sobakubi is *quit*."

"Quit?" Buck did a double take.

"He is quit! He leaving sumo! He no is like *makushita*, and he no like become *kohai* again after life as *senpai*. I think maybe he not receive 'A-number-one' *senpai* like Ohimesama get. Asago-han is best!" The grin spread wide enough to rival one of Buck's own, and Buck returned it. *Sobakubi is quit?* Best news in forever.

"I thought he was just on vacation again." Reggie made fists and chugged his arms around like the wheels of a steam train. "I guess if you're not good enough to stay in the pros without cheating, you'd better get out."

"Out, out!" Buck did his own invisible victory dance. "Ding dong, the witch is dead." The guy might eventually retaliate against Buck, but at least no one else would be stuck as his whipping boy, like Reggie, or like Buck as his blackmail victim. Besides, the guy's fury might burn out fast before he could concoct any revenge. Maybe he'd even go all sour grapes and wash his hands of the sport entirely.

Yeah, that was it. Three cheers for optimism. Even if it was optimism based on naïveté.

JANUARY'S *BASHO* SHOT INTO ACTION. Buck lined up his opponents and busted them like piñatas. He amassed his best win-loss record in months, and the press started bothering him on the streets again. To Buck's dismay, however, none of them asked any pointed questions about Umeboshi's death. They should have been digging. They *should* have been dogging the police in the force's investigation, if there was one.

Dang it. He kicked himself for trusting that a police force so near to the epicenter of sumo would be anxious to crack open a rotten egg like this. Maybe things were stuck in paperwork. Maybe a sting operation was in the works. Still, he hated the inaction, the lack of swift justice.

He hated wondering what Sobakubi had in mind to punish his family.

March loomed, and still no word about Butaniku coming to terms with his crimes.

"You wanna go to the parade with me? Just kidding," Reggie snickered, taking a bite of an enormous apple as plum blossom petals fluttered to the ground around him.

"What parade?" Buck did another chin-up on the bar in the city park. The air smelled fresher here.

"The parade in Butaniku's honor. It's over on Midori Street."

Buck dropped off the bar.

"What is wrong with people?" He stomped across the park toward the boulevard. Flags with the *yokozuna's* warty warthog image flew on every light pole. Little children chanted Butaniku's name. Disgusting. Honoring evil. It was so wrong.

"You know what, Reggie? I'm done. Done waiting. Japan has freedom of the press, right?"

"I guess so. What's freedom of the press?"

Buck tore off and stuck his nose into every bar in Ryugoku. That guy had to be somewhere. It took an hour, but he located his quarry in a bar notorious for sumo hounds.

"Tanaka-*san*." Buck's voice trembled with anger. The hair-flipping reporter looked up from his drink.

"Asagohan. *Konnichiwa*." He bowed deeply. "This is such a very, very nice surprise. You are ripping it up out there. I loved day six when Hamigaki charged at you with his head like an old man sheep, and you just took a step back and reached out with your big white hand, and *yatta!* You pushed his head down to the *dohyo,* and there he went to the clay so fast. Good show to watch that day. I never forget."

"Thanks, Tanaka. Listen, I need to trust you."

"Absolutely." Tanaka jumped off his barstool and followed Buck out into the light of day, where Buck took him for a walk in the park and explained what happened last September.

"Do you know how catastrophic this information is?" Tanaka let the hair fall in his eyes, peering through the strands of the black curtain with horror.

"I think so." Buck was grave. "The grand champion could go down."

"The grand champion? The whole JSA could go down. Our new prime minister is already in a mood to swing an axe. It could take out Ginza-*sama* himself."

"Look. I know it's a huge risk—"

"I could lose my job, Asagohan—or worse." Tanaka didn't look amused. "Perhaps you want me to go to my editor with a 'secret source.' Not use your name."

Buck shifted his weight. Well, yes, naturally. He didn't want to be the sport's Biggest Snitch of All Time. Not even his professional status could protect him from the all-out hazing storm that would rain down on him after that.

He chewed his lip and his fingernail. "Somebody has to be brave, Tanaka, or the family of Umeboshi will continue to suffer. And Butaniku will get away with murder." Buck took long, slow breaths while Tanaka shifted his weight nervously, possibly sorry he'd ever met Buck.

"However, if you're going to be brave, so am I. Name me as your source."

Tanaka's shoulders fell, nodding. He was in. He wasn't thrilled, but he was in nonetheless.

"And, Tanaka? If that 'or worse' thing starts happening, you come get me. I'll be there," Buck assured.

A FIRESTORM OF PRESS AND hounding erupted when Tanaka's news story broke. Buck got peppered with questions everywhere he went all through the March tournament in Osaka—that did not go without its share of threats from diehard Butaniku fans.

Nothing official happened yet. Buck punched almost every wall he passed. The killer still reigned over the sport with those warthog tusk wrinkles at his upper lip.

"You still want to take me golfing, dude?" Buck had to have a break.

"Too muddy." Dude stomped in a puddle on their way to the AM/PM. "Don't look so dejected, dude. We can still hit spring training. Go get Reggie. I got some sweet tickets for this afternoon—if you like baseball."

Baseball. Yes! Exactly what he needed.

Two hours later, Buck stepped into the skybox flanked by Dude and Reggie.

"Shut the front door!" Buck's jaw dropped as he looked around at true luxury.

The Filipino's eyes bugged out. "This place is bigger than my family's whole house."

The Seibu Lions didn't hold back on amenities for VIPs at Seibu Dome—massage recliners, refrigerators, a wet bar, a plush leather sofa.

"Eleven of us live in that little one-bedroom house. Granny, grandpa, aunts, uncles, and five kids. Their eyes would fall out of their heads if they saw this place." Reggie bent down and sniffed the leather of the sofa.

Buck kicked off his shoe and squished his toes in the high pile carpet. Carpet. It had been ages. Rich and brown, it felt like velvet. The room smelled like leather and apples and spices. Buck grabbed a Coke from the fridge and oozed into one of the chairs. If there weren't a baseball game, he might curl up and sleep. His body could use it.

"Dude, how'd you score these tickets? I thought we were just going to be in the cheap seats with the hot dog and pretzel crowd." Buck stared out the plate glass window into the domed field area. Crowds filled the seats. Just a few minutes now. The crowd's energy was starting to crescendo.

"Hot dogs? Please. Squid on a stick, baby." Dude pulled a steaming barbecued crustacean from the countertop rotisserie and bit off its head. "Yeah, the Uncle-man's pals with the owner of the ball club. Rich fella. He likes sumo, and he likes to stay in good with the trainers and the JSA. They trade tickets and stuff."

And stuff? With the betting scandals between sumo and baseball over the past couple of years, Buck didn't pry about what *and stuff* could mean.

"I don't give a rip about Seibu Lions, meself. I come for the chairs." Dude plunked down. Reggie was already fiddling with the controls on his recliner.

A filtered, silvery sunlight came through the dome, giving it a cool glow. The players took the field, and the Lions fans went wild shaking plastic clappers. Not a bad idea—keeping the palms of the hands safe and unharmed during a good game. The Japanese were sedate and dignified, even at their sporting events.

Buck's brain shifted into high stats-compiling gear. Within a few minutes he was keeping track of at-bats, errors, runs, runs batted in. It was like riding a bike. He hunched forward, breathing on the glass to watch the Lions pitcher's wicked fastball. It burned across the plate eleven out of the first fifteen pitches.

"Yamada-*san's* fastball is shutting the Marines down," a woman's voice fell on Buck's ear. "It's over 160 kilometers per hour."

Buck bobbled his Coke and jumped to his feet. Chocho!

"That's about a hundred miles an hour." His heart rate competed for that speed record, though. "Pretty fast."

"No, your mathematics are fast." She dipped her head. "Lightning fast." The dimples flashed.

Without her formal kimono, she looked different today, wearing jeans rolled up to her calf muscles, little canvas shoes, and a pink v-neck t-shirt that said "Seibu Lions" on it, hugging all the right curves. Her hair hung in a messy ponytail—he'd never seen her look more dazzling.

Dude and Reggie struggled out of their wallows to greet their unannounced guest. Something told Buck that Chocho's father and Dude's uncle had a mutual friend in the Lions' ballclub owner.

Reggie shoved Dude and whispered, "Uh, yeah. Bathroom break." Reggie and Dude bustled out the door, leaving Buck alone in the room with his butterfly. Chocho waved a small goodbye, and Buck reminded himself to breathe.

"This is my cousin, Miki," Chocho said. From behind her, a young girl emerged. Miki was about ten or eleven, and wearing the same t-shirt as Chocho's, but without the same effect. "She's here visiting from the country where she lives."

"Nice to meet you, Miki." Buck bowed. "She lives in another country?"

Chocho's dimples now more apparent flanked her grin. "I said that wrong. She lives outside Tokyo, in the countryside, I should say."

"Hello, Miss Miki. I'm Buck. *Nani ga Tōkyō ni anata o motarashimasu ka?*" Buck asked in his best halting Japanese. A year-plus in Japan and his language was getting better.

"*Ishi.*" Miki's gaze fell on the game, a long fly ball to left field.

Chocho leaned in and spoke softly in English, "The doctor. She's been in and out of the hospital. We're trying to get her well. She needed an outing." Her whisper sent a chill up Buck's spine for a couple of reasons. Chocho switched back to Japanese, her volume normalized, "Miki's a big fan of the Lions."

"Go Lions!" Miki cheered for the fielder who caught a pop fly, using her own plastic clapper.

Chocho took Buck's arm and led him away from the glass toward the wet bar, where she sat on a barstool.

"What can I get you to drink?" Buck went behind the bar, putting on his best charm, flashing her his winning smile. He hoped it won, and begged the heavens to let him win—just this girl, just this once.

"Ah, yes, bartender. I'd like a Lamune. Do you have one?"

"One frosty cold Lamune coming right up." Buck rummaged under the bar and found a glass, and from the fridge retrieved the drink and some ice. "Ice, or none?" She nodded in favor of ice. Buck handed her the glass and watched her sip daintily.

"It's good to see you again, Buck. It's been a long time." Three months, nineteen days, nine hours and twenty-five minutes, to be exact, since their chance meeting in the tea shop, and since he'd fallen hardcore in love with this girl. He poured himself a Pocari Sweat and tried not to gulp.

"You come to all the Lions games?" Because if she did, Buck would be getting season tickets, whatever it cost.

"This is my first one this year—and for Miki-*chan* as well. I'd love to come to all of them, but usually I have to record them and watch them later at my apartment. Not as exciting, but a fan does what she can."

Clappers interrupted them. "Lions! Homerun!" Miki went wild for a full minute. Buck and Chocho strolled over to the other side of the box, where Buck began rummaging through the cabinets and found a box of Twinkies in the cupboard. Twinkies! Real ones. His heart skipped. He tore it open and took a spongy, creamy bite.

"So, Miki. Is she okay?"

Chocho sighed. "Not really."

His Twinkie hand dropped.

"Her liver. She needs a transplant."

"Liver transplant?" His brow wrinkled.

"They're very hard to come by in Japan. Our medical system is not especially efficient. Her mother, my aunt, has a contact in the U.S., and it seems like it might be a possibility, but—"

"But?"

"But it's extremely expensive."

He lost his appetite for cream filling.

Chocho stared down at her tiny, dainty sneakers.

"Money." He winced. His family faced their own money problems, and he understood that type of pressure all too well. But wait. Her family had money. Big money. "Don't—?" he stuttered.

"Yes, I know. It's only a problem because of who holds the purse strings."

Her dad. That guy was building quite a jerkutation. Buck frowned. "And Miki?"

"Is an angel. If I ever have a daughter I hope she's just like that girl. Couldn't be better. I'd do anything for her. Anything."

Another great at-bat for the Lions made Miki explode. Buck caught several number-words in the torrent. "The girl knows her baseball stats." He felt a surge of love for the little girl, too. How could he help it? "I can see why you care."

"Miki's special." Chocho looked at Miki with love in her eyes.

The Lions pulled ahead by three in the bottom of the fourth. Miki went crazy with that plastic clapper. Buck's moments with Chocho—taking about horses and baseball and tuna sales—sped like the fastball. If only those Chiba Marines would come from behind with a couple of grand slams, tie the score, send the game into extra innings. She was slipping away from him. His kneecap started to shake. He could face down the biggest, fiercest goons in all sumo-dom, but when it came to the thought of tiny Chocho walking out of a room, he trembled. It was more than that. Their meetings were so haphazard, so unpredictable—every time she left his presence could be the final time.

"Buck," Chocho said, touching his arm. "I don't really know how to say this."

"Yeah?" Buck whirled toward her. He had some things he was struggling to say, too. A hot wave of expectation sloshed in his chest as he waited for her to speak first.

She bit her lip and stared at the ceiling. "It's just that—I heard what happened with Butaniku. After that young *rikishi* died so tragically last fall."

Oh, that. All the air compressed out of Buck's chest. "You did?" He gulped. If she'd heard about his violent fight with *yokozuna*, as some papers were reporting—albeit inaccurately—if she'd considered him a snitch, hating snitches herself, and planned to tell him so, he would be paying the ultimate sacrifice for justice: the loss of her respect. His stomach burned while he waited for her to explain. Chocho's phone rang, and she glanced at the phone display. A woman's face appeared on it. "It's Miki's mom. We have to get going." She rested her hand on Miki's shoulder and spoke in Japanese. "Okay, Miki-*chan*. Your mom needs us now—at the doctor's office."

Miki protested but got up. She bowed to Buck, who bowed back.

Wait, Chocho hadn't finished. He stared after her expectantly, but her focus had shifted. "Thank you, Buck. We really must go immediately." She tugged Miki out of the room. Buck's feet grew into the floor as he watched her disappear down the hall.

She glanced over her shoulder just once at him.

She didn't finish telling him what she'd heard. Or what she thought of it.

AFTERNOON WANED IN A CHILL, and Buck stared at the March *banzuke* to take his mind off things. Reggie made it. *Juryo* at last. He'd be a pro for the Osaka *basho, which meant* celebration tonight. Buck's own name rested on the cusp of greatness, teetering at the top of *juryo*, almost ready to topple into *maegashira*, the top half of the pro triangle. He just *had* to get there. But first, he needed to—

Dude came yelling into the room and interrupted Buck's calculations.

"Quick! They're taking off Butaniku's topknot! The JSA expelled him!"

Buck and Reggie scrambled to their feet and ran after Dude, along with a thundering herd of sumo wrestlers to a training courtyard strewn with the carnage of half-presentable *rikishi* and officials. An angry spring storm brewed.

"That *baka* killed Umeboshi." one guy muttered as Buck and Dude approached the scene. Reggie was already there, arms folded across his chest. JSA black kimonos—the most Buck had ever seen in one place—made a half circle of judgment around the champ. Butaniku had his head down, his shoulders slumped, his fists clenched. Buck could see his temples pulsating in the spring gale. He was unrepentant.

"The fans want him lynched, so they're shipping him out of the country as soon as they chop off his *chonmage*. He'd better speed." Dude picked a scab on his arm. "No one will be sorry to see him go."

Two *rikishi* walked up, and one spoke, "Look, there's Asagohan." He jostled Buck and stood beside him to whisper. "You got a lot of nerve taking down the JSA's biggest investment."

"Yeah, I can't believe you even show your face here today. You're not the JSA's favorite person today," said the other.

A solemn official in full regalia appeared, and the crowd hushed. He carried a gleaming steel sword on a tasseled cushion. The birds in the trees stopped singing; even the breeze refused to blow.

A few official words were spoken, ancient Japanese Buck didn't recognize, and then the *katana* sword was raised in the air to do the deed. Just as it was lifted, Butaniku caught Buck's eye, anger burning like a volcano. His frown grew more exaggerated, more warthoggish. He leaned forward and the blade came down. The Korean warthog's career ended with a thunk as the blade hit the wood and his topknot fell at his feet among the fluttering plum blossom petals.

BUCK HUMMED A PATRIOTIC TOBY Keith song all day. With both Sobakubi *and* Butaniku gone, life was going to be awesome. Even if the JSA did go around in their black kimonos wearing frowns to the floor, and fans shouted their disappointment with silence, a little jig came to Buck's legs whenever he thought of it. And he was lighter on his feet, too. Lighter than he'd ever been. He could probably even get on those horses back home at this point.

Home. He hadn't called in a couple of months, what with all the bad news. They always taught him, "If you can't say something nice, don't say anything at all," and he'd had nothing nice in his world for a while to talk about. Until now.

"Hi, Dad. Just checking in. I hope it's not too late there." Buck knew the time, but he figured they were still up watching the news. "How are things going? Any news on your invention's approval yet?"

"Buck, nice to hear your voice. Funny you should call today. What timing." His dad's voice didn't sound quite right. A tremor ran through it. "Your mom will be sorry she missed your call, you know."

"She's not there, I take it? Gone out shopping?"

"Gone to take the neighbor to the ER. Just her usual, even on a day like today. Everyone can count on her."

"What's going on today, Dad? What's wrong?" Buck's pulse took an up-tick.

"I haven't even told your mother yet. I don't know how I'm going to." His voice quavered, almost like someone had died. Buck got panicky.

"Tell me, Dad. Maybe together we can figure out a way to break it to her."

"After all, so much of her life is tied up in this." There was a catch in his dad's throat that shifted Buck's pulse another gear higher.

"It's just, I got a call from Yoshida today." Another long pause. "You know, Buck, I've been at work on this product for years. I honestly believe it can help a lot of people. First it's all tied up in FDA nightmares over here, and now—"

Buck's eyes welled up.

"What's happened, Dad?" Buck's own voice cracked. He needed to know if this was Sobakubi's revenge. He could've prevented it. "Is Nangrimax still pending?"

"It's not pending anymore."

"What? Don't tell me—"

"Denied," Dad whispered.

Denied. His drug approval had been denied? The Japanese government denied it after all the quality testing, all the meticulous experimentation and proof of its safety and efficacy?

"No, I can't believe it, Dad. No. That's just awful. Isn't there any recourse, any other chance?"

"Yoshida says there's one last appeal process, but in all his years he's never heard of it being overturned. Unless it gets ironed out in the next hundred-and-eighty days, he's pulling his funding. Buck, we're cooked." His dad's voice broke, and a rogue tear slid down Buck's cheek.

Behind Buck's closed eyelids burned the defiant face of Sobakubi, brash with insolence. The attitude that generated that countenance could commit atrocities of great magnitude. He had to know. "How bad is it, Dad? The house? More?"

"The house. The nest egg I had put away for retirement." A long pause. "Your grandfather's property."

Not Grandpa's farm. Sobakubi's vengeance stung like a scorpion's tail.

"The extended family will probably blacklist us. The property—it was a sacred trust. I never should have talked your mother into putting it on the line for this. But I was sure, so sure." His dad's voice trailed off.

BUCK WALKED A CIRCULAR RUT in the floor. No way could a foreign athlete get any leverage against a bureaucrat, even a corrupt one. Buck knew no one, had no money, influence, or power.

He didn't speak the language, had no legal standing in this foreign country, and barely knew his way around on a subway. He couldn't even drive here.

Powerless, he flopped down on his futon and collapsed under the weight of his own failure. He'd hurt the people he loved most, like he'd always sworn he wouldn't.

DRUNKEN ANGEL
MARCH. OSAKA

"I've never been to a *koen-kai* in Osaka before. I hear they talk weird here. Do they?" Buck shoved coins into the machine that dispensed subway tickets and they headed through the turnstile toward the train platform.

Dude smelled like a cologne shop as he boarded the subway with Buck and Reggie to go to the sponsor-party in the Western Japan city. No parties had been sponsored in Tokyo for a while, due to the rough patch sumo hit, and Dude needed an outing. Buck didn't protest, but Reggie kept looking over his shoulder. Buck understood. They'd all been a little paranoid lately.

"Osaka was famous for being Butaniku haters, so they probably loved seeing him go as much as we did." Dude led as they stepped onto the train.

"Well, almost." Reggie hustled through the closing doors. Buck grabbed hold of the strap hanging from the car ceiling as the train slid into the underground tunnel.

"I'm real sorry about your parents. That bites, dude." Dude grabbed his own strap.

"Thanks." Buck smirked and glanced over at Reggie, who was wringing his hands.

"What's the matter, Reggie?" Buck needed to take his mind off his own sorrow. Reggie looked like he had problems of his own.

"Oh, don't mind him, Bucky-boy. He just got another uber-expensive present from that chick who digs him. Can't believe how much money she wastes on you, pal. Don't tell me you don't even like her a little." Dude gave Reggie a friendly punch in the shoulder.

Buck examined Reggie closer. The poor guy looked like he'd eaten something rotten and was going to lose it. "Are you carsick?"

"I don't know what to do, Buck. This girl—Miss One Thousand Autumn Leaves! She sended me something terrible. Japanese short sword. You know these?" Reggie mimed stabbing himself in the stomach. Buck nodded. They were famous samurai weapons, and Buck understood the suicide ritual pantomime.

"What, she cranked it up a notch and is going to kill you?" And Buck thought he had girl problems.

"No, no, dude. The sword. It came with a note." Dude threw his head back and laughed. "Crazy geisha is taking those do-you-like-me-yes-no-maybe-check-one notes to the next level. Her letter told our pal here that if he returns her affection, he should keep the sword as a present. It even came with a certification so he can legally own it. The thing cost a small fortune, no doubt. I can't imagine what he's going to do with it in the stable now that Sobakubi is gone, but it's a really nice piece of steel."

"And if he sends it back?" Buck had to know.

Reggie leaned forward. "If I don't return her love, I have to send it back."

"And?" Buck asked.

"And she will commit *seppuku!*"

"Suicide?" Buck gasped. "Well, that's that. You can't send it back."

"I know." Reggie gave the hangdog look and wrung his hands again.

"Come on, don't you like her? Even a tiny bit?" Dude had to chide him. "She could be at this *koen-kai* tonight, you know. She gets around for her job, and it's sponsored by Yuzu Lemon. You know, lotions and dishwashing liquid and floor cleaners and automobile paint job polishes. Miss One Thousand Autumn Leaves loves their hand creams, I bet."

"Yuzu Lemon. Oh." Reggie turned to Buck with a growl. "The Ginza Corp subsidiary. Now I get what we're doing out tonight. Ginza sponsor party. You seriously think you could run into that girl tonight, don't you? That's why you're dragging me downtown in nothing but my skivvies in the chill."

"It's not chilly, Reggie, and you always only wear your skivvies."

"Right on, Bucky-boy. You tell him." Dude punched Buck in the arm.

This was cool. Dude and Reggie were pretty good friends to him. Actual friends. People who didn't hit him up for money every afternoon. They joked, went out for food together, had heated rock-paper-scissors tournaments, witnessed brutal beatings together. A satisfied smile stretched across Buck's face.

"See? I knew it. You only always thinking about that Ginza chica. I'm telling you, it's too far. You cannot reach it, man. I mean, you're not big leaguer. You still batting down in just the peewee leagues." Reggie swung an imaginary bat—poorly.

"*Maegashira* is not exactly the peewee leagues, Reggie. Have you seen those guys I'm going up against?" Buck let go of the strap and swung his own imaginary bat. His pretend ball sailed over the fence.

"Aw, come on. It's not that. Reggie's just being realistic. The girl—she's fine. Fi-i-i-ine. No question. It's just that she's out of your price range. Sure you talked to her once or twice. She sent you a note way back when. But seriously, there's been so-o-o-o many high tides since then. Does she even know you're alive?"

Dude's words were a punch in Buck's gut. It was true. He hadn't seen Chocho in weeks. A lot could happen in weeks, love-wise. She could have met a guy somewhere in her tuna-scrounging travels and eloped, for all Buck knew. He hiccupped. Although weeks without any fuel for his fire hadn't made the blaze burn any dimmer, it did contain flickering flames of doubt. He had to see her even if it meant attending one of these hated parties. Some way. Any way. Only her presence could soothe his pain.

"This is our stop. Come on. Those doors shut fast. Gotta be speedy. Like a *gokiburi*." Reggie sniggered.

"Takes one to know one, *la cucaracha*." Buck hustled off the train and onto the escalator. Above ground loomed a glittering hotel with golden lights, the scent of jasmine wafting from its entryway. They took the elevator to the top floor.

"Asagohan!" Girly voices screamed as soon as Buck and Dude stepped into the ballroom. In a trice, a bevy of satin-clad girls clung to Buck's sides. Three planted kisses on his neck, and four more pulled at his *yukata,* slipped pieces of paper—presumably with their phone numbers—into his sleeves. "We love your sparkling baby blue eyes!"

How on God's green earth did Buck Cooper go from fat geek statistician nobody knew was alive to veritable rock star with girls throwing themselves at him and screaming his name when he entered a room?

It took a few minutes, but he was able to flick the girls off himself and get to a table with some good-smelling food piled on it. Buck took a plateful and headed to what looked like a quiet corner with sofas, away from the loud techno-pop band and the stage area. Here he planned to eat in peace and look for any glimpse of Chocho in the crowd. If she was at any *koen-kai*, it had to be this one.

Before he sat he let his eyes race over the scores of faces. No Chocho. He spotted Dude swarmed with girls across the way. Double eagles, all of them. A buxom blonde fed him pieces of fruit. Dude might complain about missing the golf course, but sumo life had its perks.

Over in another part of the ballroom, Buck spied Reggie. Beside him nestled that tiny little waif of a girl in traditional Japanese clothing, hair done up in a perfect knot, staring up at him with adoration. Reggie stared back down at her with a similar visage. Miss One Thousand Autumn Leaves had won, it appeared.

"Asagohan, *sa.*" A young woman in a business suit approached Buck, bowing. "My name is Ichigo. I'm with the company that makes a very popular special Japanese drink, Calpis. Do you know this drink?"

Buck knew it all too well. She blushed when he met her gaze. A guy passing the couches slowed down and called out to Buck. He waved.

"We would like to offer you an endorsement contract. You could be *The Face of Calpis.*" She bobbed her head rapidly with a face that looked like it was meant to encourage him.

"As a matter of fact, I've often thought of my face as closely resembling Calpis." He grinned. "Sounds great."

She had no idea what he meant, but smiled generously anyway. "Wonderful. Thank you very much. We have a contract for you and will come to you in Tokyo soon. By the way, Asagohan, I very much enjoyed your sumo technique of *uwatenage.* It is your signature move now. You are very strong."

"Thank you, Ichigo. You are very kind." He bowed and returned to eat his fried calamari and resume people-watching, nestling down onto the sofa. Suddenly, it dawned on him that he was to be *the* face of Calpis. That meant *money.* Giddy bubbles filled his soul. Calpis was huge, and its endorsement contract could help his parents.

"You having a good time tonight, Asagohan?"

Buck turned and saw a middle-aged businessman sitting beside him, a plate of food on his lap. A couple of men in suits lurked nearby, but they stared off into the distance, not interested in chitchat. Party security.

"Sure. Good food. Are you?" Buck replied.

"I like the Ginza parties. They're usually pretty tame, and the food is the best," the man said.

Buck remembered the barbecue at a similar party months back, and had to agree.

"Look. There's Torakiba. He was your *senpai,* right? Back before you hit professional ranks?"

"That's right." Buck nodded. This guy knew his sumo stats.

"Lucky you. He's the gem of the sport."

Buck sniffed.

"I hope they make him the *yokozuna* now that Butaniku is gone. I guess they'll do that at the final day of the Nagoya *basho* in July. They'll need to wait a couple of cycles because of the scandal, and Nagoya will be the perfect place for it. His hometown."

Buck recognized this guy from somewhere. Grey hair, dark mustache. A unique look, yet Buck couldn't place it. "You like Torakiba, do you?"

"Sure. Everyone loves him."

"Not everyone."

"True. Ginza tried to influence his daughter to marry Torakiba, but she wouldn't have anything to do with it."

Smart girl.

"Can't figure out why. Torakiba is the cream." The businessman leaned closer. "I have a theory: she wasn't ready to marry and wanted to experience life a bit first. Everyone knows about her disagreement with her father, but it might not be about Torakiba. About that time she had already applied for a scholarship to graduate school in England. She left and spent two years there."

Two years of hoping her father's dream for her would die, Buck figured. Or that Torakiba would evaporate.

Wait a minute. England. Buck remembered now—he'd bumped into her on her first day back from England. The British accent, her talk about courage. Pieces of the puzzle were coming together. She'd left Japan and gone to stay with her mother in order to escape Torakiba. *Really* smart move. He smiled as he pictured her curves and dimples.

"Then she came back," the man continued, "and everyone expected her to marry Torakiba, and when she wouldn't, her father made his odd announcement. He makes another announcement soon, I hear."

Buck remembered that "odd" announcement. Something bad was in the wind. He could feel it.

"It would be a smart alliance. Torakiba idolizes Ginza for his business sense. Ginza's flush with cash, and Torakiba is the best Japan has to offer right now. From a distance it looks like a match made at the Nikkei." The businessman leaned back and laced his fingers behind his head. "Personally, I wish the champ would leave it alone, but I can see why the Ginza cash would be attractive. Torakiba's family—the Fujiwaras—lost so much when they invested poorly in a diamond mine in the Congo. Big tribal war broke out and they spent all their money on automatic weapons to fund their side, but the other tribe used money from DeBeers, bought shoulder-mounted missile launchers. Fujiwaras lost out."

Diamonds and missiles? "I heard they lost their fortune in an earthquake."

"Diehard fans want to scrub the true disgrace of it—"

Buck bit his tongue. He couldn't think of anything nice to say about Torakiba or the alliance with Ginza. He could see what was in it for Torakiba—the girl, the wealth, the fame, the superhighway to achieving his ultimate goal in life, all the while taking pleasure in smashing Buck's hope. But what did Ginza have to gain from all this? A connection to a failed family? It didn't sound Ginza-esque. Besides, Chocho played the key role in this and couldn't be keen on this matchmaking. She'd left the hemisphere to escape him before—at least Buck had wanted to believe that.

Unless there was a chance she had feelings for the brute. Buck rejected the thought and set his fried calamari down. He began to work out the puzzle, sliding around the pieces on the tabletop of his mind.

It could be pride—Ginza might simply want to have a son-in-law who was a champion. If so, why not marry her to Butaniku years ago? The Korean warthog reigned for a long time as *yoko-zuna,* and Torakiba wasn't even there yet. Or could it be a matter of status? There could be more than one reason why Ginza would want to be associated with the Fujiwara clan. Even in disgrace, the clan had had its glory days, he'd heard.

Suddenly, a drunken party girl in the world's shortest micro-dress came stumbling into their seating area, followed by an equally intoxicated entourage. She stepped a wobbly foot onto the coffee table then took a dive into the businessman's lap. In a flash, the security guards leaped into action from behind him. They yanked the girl from his body, but they didn't see what Buck saw: another party girl, laughing herself silly as she whipped out her cell phone to snap a picture of her fallen friend.

With uncanny speed, Buck leapt.

"Cheese!" With a grin the width of the Rio Grande, Buck flung himself between camera floosie and sumo-fanboy businessman. His big face blocked her shot. Instead of a sordid face-plus-lap of her drunken friend, her camera captured a garish blond sumo wrestler's wild-eyed mug.

While the security team escorted the tipsy gang out of the area, Buck and the businessman wiped their brows and settled back into their meals.

"Well, Asagohan, that's the second time you've come to my rescue."

"I'm sorry? Second?"

"Surely you remember that day in Tokyo when you pulled me from the path of the speeding car. I think of that moment every day. I have placed many gifts of gratitude in my home's *butsudan* of worship for you."

"That was you?" Buck choked a little on his Yuzu Lemon pie. No wonder the face looked familiar. "Well, what a small world. Call me Buck." Japan—it was a small world after all.

"Sure, Buck, thanks. Now, I must ask again today, since you may have just saved my marriage by keeping that picture from being snapped. Is there anything I can do for you? Just say the word—"

"That's real kind of you, but not unless you know how to get the Minister of Health to stop kowtowing to his vindictive son and actually take a look at—"

"Your father's drug. Nangrimax, isn't it?" The businessman pulled out a smart phone and jotted something down. "Let me see what I can do. I know a guy."

"How? How did you—?" *How did he know about Nangrimax?*

A member of the security detail tapped the businessman on the shoulder, and he made his excuses and left. It struck Buck that maybe—

"Oh, my giddy aunt. Buck Cooper," Dude's voice interrupted. "How the *heck* do you know the Prime Minister of Japan? That guy's Saito! He's, like, totally my hero. Political hero, I mean. Because I have golf heroes too, and astronaut heroes, and big bass trophy heroes, and—wow. What did he say? Did he ask about me? He's a huge sumo fan. What's he doing here?"

"Wait. *That* was Saito? Recently-elected Prime Minister of Japan?"

"You bet your fur-lined underpants it was. Give me the scoop or, or, or I'll drop you from my helicopter onto a hillside covered with jumping cacti."

"What does a Hawaii boy know about cacti?" Buck threw back the banter by rote. At the same time, he was also occupied by a new subject—whether the Prime Minister of Japan could save his parents.

十
九

HIGH AND LOW
MAY–JULY. TOKYO AND NAGOYA

"**B**uck! I have not talked to you for so very, very long!" Hiro Yoshida sounded older on the phone, but still as hyper. Buck could picture him hopping foot to foot. "You done so good in sumo. I tell all my friends about you every time."

"Thanks, Hiro. What's going on?" Buck liked this kid. "How's your family?"

"I don't want to talk about that so much. And not about my father's deal with your honorable father. There is now nothing so nice there. I want to talk about your sumo! We watch you every time. You bash Arisama to smithereens at Osaka. We cry when Ryu-gyunyu squeezed you out at Tokyo in May. So very sad. Wabesama must watch his back. You are coming for him. It is so great you are now in upper ranks." Hiro paused and gasped, his eyes wide with realization. "You can now be friends with Torakiba!"

Right. Besties. "You're getting really good at that sumo reporting thing," Buck said.

"This is almost July and you will go to Nagoya for the summer *basho* and you will fight Kotako and Piiman. Big sumo stars! They say you are the most naturally gifted sumo wrestler in the sport's memory, Buck." Hiro hardly took a breath. "We saw your billboards and posters for Calpis. They are everywhere in Tokyo, with your smiling face so big and holding the blue and white can of delicious, refreshing drink. Your face *is* Calpis. Your parents would be so proud."

So proud.

At least some good stacks of yen were coming in from it. *The things we do for money.*

BUCK STRETCHED IN THE HOT bath, up to his neck in steaming water. The pools teemed with other *rikishi* since it was the place closest to the Nagoya sumo arena. There was no discernable difference between the ambient summer air and the hot water. Long gone were his inhibitions about public nudity—Buck actually looked forward to his nightly scrub-down by these little old ladies with the loofa sponges and Fels Naptha soap. This ritual cleaned the body of all dirt and skin cells before any man entered the bath. At first he'd resisted, feeling squeamish about the shared water, but once he experienced the equivalent of sandblasting on his own skin, he worried less about germs. Besides, the heat of the water would likely kill almost any stray germ.

Tonight he sat in the water, his head reclining onto the tiled floor behind him—he'd been lumbering back and forth between the searing water and the cool tub. After today's bout against Piiman, this was a much-needed routine to ease his aching muscles.

Hiro would have been proud today—Buck turned the Piiman into chopped green peppers. They could sprinkle him on a veggie lover's pizza after that obliteration.

"Asagohan, *sa.*" A woman's voice surprised him. Soap ladies hardly ever spoke in here. "There is a message for you, Asagohan." In her outstretched hands she held a pink envelope.

Buck recognized the linen paper of the envelope instantly and leapt from the water, springing for his bathrobe. He dried his hands quickly and ripped the letter open, pausing to lift the envelope to his nose and inhale the honeysuckle scent. His eyes rolled upward as it filled his whole head. He saw her dimples, her curves, heard her twinkling laugh. Chocho.

Dear Buck,

Would you meet me? I will be waiting.

There was an address, and she signed it with a hand-drawn butterfly. Buck's heart raced. Would he meet her? He'd walk across razors. He'd highjack an Apache helicopter. He'd sell his scientific calculator to pay the cab fare. Even if she were to show up only long enough to tell him to go jump in a lake, he'd be there.

In a better *yukata* and dry, he hustled toward the curb and hailed a cab. He might never get used to those taxi doors that flung open on their own accord, powered by a button on the driver's dash. It whacked him—again. *Dang it.* The bruise on his shin from the last cab ride had barely healed.

The summer sun set late, and the hot air came in and out of his lungs in ragged breaths as the cab tore through Nagoya's winding streets. He really needed to calm down. The driver kept giving him big-eyed stares in his rear view mirror. Buck pasted on his usual grin and gave a nod. The cabbie cackled and swung wildly to the curb in front of a park—a perfect park—with thousands of trees, little streams, several bridges, and a pond where a man sat serenely fishing under the light of the rising moon as daylight fled. That pond—if Buck could just get to the top of the hillock that stood in the center, he might—just *might*—get to see the sunset.

And then, it got better. Out of the next cab emerged Chocho, like the butterfly from her cocoon. Wreathed in the light of the fading sun, her skin glowed. A broad smile spread across her face, and Buck's knees turned to water. She wore her hair down, resting on her shoulders in glossy curls, and her sundress gave him a glimpse of her soft shoulders as she came up beside him.

If he'd been less of a gentleman, he could have caressed their silken smoothness.

This night held possibilities. The air crackled with them.

Chocho linked her arm through his and led him into the bamboo wilderness toward the stream. "Thank you for coming, Buck."

"This place is fantastic. How did it . . . happen?"

"Japan has many beautiful parks."

He'd seen so much concrete lately he'd almost forgotten. Birdsong filled his ears—nightingales, mourning doves. And the sky! It had been so long.

He slid his hand to clasp Chocho's. It was so small and delicate. He grasped it gently. He was too happy to say anything, and she seemed content to stay quiet as they strolled past other park-goers sitting on blankets or pushing strollers or practicing photography.

Soon they came to the stream. It gurgled and surged over a pile of rocks resulting in a small waterfall.

"It seems like three lifetimes ago since we last met." She gazed at the stream, then into Buck's face. "Your eyes look so blue sometimes. Does the world look blue when you look through them?"

He smiled. "How is Miki-*chan*?"

She turned away and heaved a sigh.

"But—what about the transplant?"

She shrugged. "A donor was found, a match."

"Well, that's good, isn't it?" Buck squeezed her hand. A light breeze fluttered the leaves, their shadows sparkling on the water.

"It should be, yes."

"But your father . . ." Buck frowned. What kind of a monster would hold a little girl's life in his hands like that and not take action? His blood boiled. "I have a little money from my Calpis contract, Chocho. It's all yours. Take it."

"No, no. Buck." She shook her head firmly and pulled back. "It's not possible that way. You are too kind." She pressed his hand. The warmth of its pressure spread to his toes. "Really, it's close. I believe we are getting very close with him now. I can feel it happening soon . . ." Her words trailed off, strained.

Buck didn't press the issue, but he would have sold those Star Wars action figures and all his baseball cards for that little girl—and he was talking a Hank Aaron rookie card and a Luke Skywalker still in its original package.

"Well, Chocho, if I can't do you a favor," he said, "can I ask you for one?"

Her eyes brightened.

"I'm dying to see a sunset. It's been forever. Can we just walk up that little hill and watch it over the trees? See how the sky is streaked with red?"

Chocho glanced toward the west. "We'll have to hurry. It's beginning to fade already."

They crossed a highly arched red bridge over a brook, straight from a Japanese postcard. Across a grassy area, they came to the pond, in which sat the island. Buck glanced skyward. Sunset still glowed. "Let's cross this moat of a pond. We'll go up there." He pointed at the knoll of the island. A long, level bridge spanned the pond several hundred yards away and led to the grassy isle.

"But, if it's the sunset you want, isn't it," she glanced at the sky, "we'll never make it down to the bridge and up to the top of the hill in time for the view." She sounded disappointed, too.

Scanning the top of the quickly darkening pond, Buck could make out the faint outline of a trail of black, shiny rocks. But they were spaced unevenly apart.

"There might be one other way." Buck pulled her toward the rock closest to shore. With his long legs, it shouldn't be too much of a problem to cross these rocks. But Chocho might have a harder time—she checked in at just under five feet.

Chocho's eyes slid toward the edge of the stream. Buck leaped onto the first slick rock. It held, and there was room for her feet. He turned back and offered her a hand.

"How's your balance?" She glanced at the water and back at him, hesitant.

"I'm a sumo wrestler, remember?" He smiled.

"Ha—I almost forgot." She gave him a trusting look and leapt to him, teetering in his arms.

Buck moved to the next stone, keeping her hand firmly in his and pulled her to his rock. They shared it for an instant while he steadied her before leapfrogging onto the next stone, a farther stretch. *This is fun—like Frogger.*

Chocho bit her lip. Her dimples were gone.

"Are you doing okay?" Buck turned to ask.

She trembled a little but looked up at him. "If I take your hand we can do it."

Buck nodded. He reached out, grasped her and pulled her across. Despite his size, each rock had just enough room for them to share, but only for a moment. Then there was the fourth rock. The fifth. The sixth. Buck leapt and drew her to him—she was a feather lilting across the water, tugged by a frog with a spider web.

They now had spanned more than two-thirds of the pond, but a large, aqueous gap loomed between the tenth and eleventh stones.

"Can we make it?" Chocho sounded unsure.

Buck didn't answer but leaped before reaching out for her hand.

Chocho kept her eyes focused on Buck's, and with resolution stretched her leg as far as it would go, springing toward him.

But she couldn't make it—her stride wasn't enough.

Buck lunged for her, planting his feet firmly on the slick rock. With all the grasping he could muster, he caught her just under her arms and yanked her toward him, pulling her to his chest.

"You caught me." Chocho heaved, breathless in his arms, clinging to him, light as air. Her sighs fell against his shoulders. She was shaking. He pressed her softness to him, his hand strayed to the silken shoulder, running his palm and fingers across her back.

"Of course, I did, Chocho," he breathed, twirling strands of her soft hair. Her honeysuckle scent conquered his mind again—every statistic and factoid he'd ever memorized now went wafting away out of his brain. Her breathing sounded like a baby's sleep.

"I can't swim, you know." She clung to him more tightly. "Not at all. I sink like a rock. It terrifies me."

"I have you. I promise."

They embraced on the stone in the middle of the moat as nightingales trilled and sunset faded to indigo. His own inner sunset glowed in Chocho's embrace. She whispered something he could barely hear.

"Kiss me."

"What?" His eyes flew open and he double blinked to see if he was daydreaming. Dewy lips and shining eyes repeated the request. A surge of love and hope and foolish giddy manhood rushed through him. Maybe he'd never kissed any woman before, but stopping himself from kissing this exquisite creature now would be like stopping a runaway train.

Ever so softly, Buck dipped his head toward hers, drinking in the sweetness of her face. Chocho's body rose as she raised her heels and tilted her chin upward, parting her lips. Her deep amber eyes fluttered shut, and he closed his own to let his other senses take over. Their lips touched, and the world around them seemed to have disappeared.

"Oh, Buck," she whispered. "Whatever happens tomorrow—please, don't forget this moment."

"Not a chance," Buck said, savoring the moment.

Chocho glanced up at the darkening sky. "We missed the sunset. I'm so sorry, Buck. You wanted to see it so much."

"There will be countless other sunsets. But a first kiss only comes once." And then he kissed her again. On an impulse, he abandoned his plan to cross the stream, and swept Chocho up into his arms. With deft steps he sprang from rock to rock, cradling her back to the shore, where he set her gently down on the ground. "Safer here."

Her eyes filled with appreciation, then sadness. "I have to go." Darkness had nearly enveloped the park. Only a few other patrons remained, and they were heading toward the gates.

"When can I see you again? Will you be at the press reception tomorrow night?"

"I have to be there," she answered.

"I have to meet a reporter friend there, too. Can I see you?"

"Buck, I—" She faltered, wringing her hands. "Please, remember. Today is real." She pulled back, taking a step toward the gates.

"What do you mean?" He reached out to touch her hand.

"I have to go right now, or I'll be missed." Her eyes pleaded with him and she stretched away. "Keep being the best, Buck."

And she was gone, flown away on her butterfly wings into the night.

二
十

ASUNARO: SORROW
JULY. NAGOYA

Buck buzzed onto the elevator, *kachikoshi* envelope in hand from tonight's win. It had thousands of yen in it, enough to buy almost anything—even a ring. He was coming straight from the *dohyo* to the press reception. He hustled, not to miss a nano-second of Chocho's company if he could get it. With a strut he'd never managed before, he strode off the elevator, shoulders broad, chin up, and eyes bright. The girl was his, and he was heading to the party to claim her.

She must want him to—or she wouldn't have mentioned where she'd be tonight. He'd heard girls played games with guys' heads—Chocho wasn't the type.

"Dude. I didn't think you'd be here already. Or at all." Dude jostled Buck's shoulder as soon as he entered the banquet room. Chandeliers sprinkled prisms on the white marble floor of the Nagoya Center. A techno pop band beeped from a stage area across the hall. The air smelled like orange blossoms, and the room brimmed with sumo wrestlers and their entourages, as well as the press, almost a thousand people from a glance. Buck scanned for Tanaka without luck.

"Look. We got matching dresses on tonight." Dude pulled at the collar of his dark blue *yukata,* the sumo off-duty uniform.

"Whatcha doing here so early? There's not even any very good grub this time. Some carrot sticks and a few California rolls of sushi. Ew, right?"

Reggie walked up. "No, he's here for the girl. A-gain."

"Duh, right. I can't blame you. She's seriously freakin' hot. On a scale from one to hot, she's an Albatross," Dude said.

Buck made a fist.

"Come on. Know your golf terms, pal. It's another way to say double eagle. And Chocho, she's like, double-eagle-on-the-eigh-teenth-hole-on-Sunday-afternoon-of-the-Master's-Tournament-hot." Dude teed off and swung his imaginary three wood.

"She's the best, Wally. The best there is." Buck was a goner. "Indeed, boys, that girl is going to be here, and I intend to monopolize her time and attention."

Voices and techno-pop bounced between the ceiling and marble floors. It was quite a ruckus, especially with a hundred interviews being conducted on the floor at the same time. Sumo wrestlers answered questions with animation and bashfulness while cameras rolled and microphones swung back and forth between interviewer and interviewee like pendulums. This press reception crackled—and Buck knew why. Tonight the JSA would announce the new *yokozuna* to replace Butaniku. It was the first good day for sumo in general in a long while.

"Uh, too late to grab *all* her time, *amigo*." Reggie stepped aside and pointed to a columned area near the center of the room. "Your little *mamacita* already found a *papacita* to dance her around the floor."

Buck's spine jerked straight. Chocho and . . . Torakiba. Not *that guy.* He pushed Reggie aside and jostled through the crowd of reporters and cameras and TV crews. Before he could get far, a hush fell over the crowd. Everyone in the room halted activity, even Buck. Someone was clearing his throat at the microphone.

Ginza struck a pose on the stage in his ominous black kimono and fuzzy eyebrows. The words poured forth, slow and emphatic enough that Buck could translate them.

But he wished he couldn't.

"My friends," Ginza began. "This coming year marks the hundredth anniversary of the Ginza family's association with sumo. We are very, very happy. And proud." He sniffled. A smattering of applause rose from the crowd. Ginza air-patted it out. "Months ago I told you our family would make an offering of deep respect to the gods of sumo. Tonight I tell you how."

Whispers scurried through the crowd. Foreboding welled in Buck and impelled him toward the stage, muscling his way through to where he'd seen her. But she wasn't there anymore.

"My daughter, Chocho, is here tonight." Ginza beamed as she stepped onto the stage beside him, her face a stone. "My daughter, as you know and can see, is a young woman of great beauty. I believe she is of the highest quality in every way. Only the highest, the *best*, is worthy of gods."

"This coming January marks our one hundredth anniversary in sumo. And so, at the January *basho,* the winner of the Emperor's Cup will be given my daughter as his wife."

Buck's knees buckled, and he had to grab a nearby marble pillar for support. Chocho was up for *auction.* Human trafficking, right here? Buck searched Chocho's face for a sign, any sign of how she felt about this, but her face was granite.

Buck whirled around, gauging the reaction of the crowd. No one spoke. A few mouths hung open in shock. Women clutched their hearts. No one cheered. No one even gasped. But they didn't shout Ginza down and stop him. How could they be so complicit?

This is so wrong! Selling her to the highest bidder, awarding her as the prize for a sparring match—what kind of meathead would do that? Buck watched Ginza lick his pinkie finger and tame each ferocious eyebrow meticulously.

Wait. She could be won. By *anyone.* A spark of hope sizzled in him. Ginza's announcement did suddenly look completely democratic—and anyone, even a foreigner with "the whited skin of a dead eel" had a shot at winning Chocho in this setup, though the whole concept may be wrong.

It could work. He could outsmart Ginza and get the girl. Who cared that if the *maegashira* rank was still small potatoes. Six months remained—July to January. Buck could do that; he could climb to the top if it meant Chocho waited for him there. He clenched his fists and relaxed them, tossing his head from side to side to loosen it up for battle. *Ginza, watch out, buddy.*

Lack of crowd support didn't faze Ginza. "I have one more exciting piece of news for everyone." He chuckled, rubbing his hands together with glee. "Also, here tonight is our strong champion Torakiba."

Torakiba jutted above the heads of the crowd and bobbed toward the podium. A virtual rug came ripping out from under Buck. *I got a bad feeling about this.*

The crowd parted for Torakiba, who bustled toward a grinning Ginza.

Buck's spark of hope extinguished. His heart slammed in his chest. This couldn't be happening.

Ginza bowed to Torakiba, who sported a smug expression and a cocked eyebrow.

"I am happy to make another grand announcement," Ginza continued. "Our very own Torakiba, champion of the Kawaguchi stable, who has served sumo well as *ozeki* for these past months, will be our new *yokozuna.*"

The crowd erupted in cheers of worship. Sickness rose in Buck's stomach.

"We are proud to have such a gentleman at the top of our ranks," Ginza gushed.

Torakiba, *yokozuna*. The Prime Minister had predicted it, but Buck didn't want to believe. Worst of all, Torakiba as designated champ greatly increased his likelihood of receiving the coveted Emperor's Cup. The JSA played favorites that way. Buck began to see—this game of Ginza's was a sham. Chocho was being sold.

"We are so proud of him, and the whole Kawaguchi stable should show him their respect." Ginza shouted this over the unending applause. His eyes met Buck's from across the room, boring into him. He gave a snarky frown, wiped his hands twice down the lapel of his black kimono in self-satisfaction before patting out the clapping again. "Attention, please. Torakiba himself has a surprise announcement to make. What will it be? We shall see, we shall see." Giddy, Ginza bowed to the crowd and handed the microphone to the new grand champion, whose fangs gleamed in his smile, a frightening contrast to Chocho's emotionless stare.

"Good evening." Torakiba bowed very low and put on a mask of contrition, as TV camera operators jockeyed for the best position. "I am so blessed to be here. Miss Chocho is kind to allow me to stand beside her." His eyes flashed toward Chocho, whose lips pulled to one side in an approximation of a smile. There were no dimples. Nausea gushed through Buck's gut.

"I know this is premature. I know I should not ask this. But Miss Chocho and I have known each other a long time. As you are aware, I have won the Emperor's Cup for the last five tournaments. I am now your *yokozuna*." Torakiba bowed with a humility that did not match his words, and Buck sniffed in derision. "When I win in January, I will win a greater prize than any that has ever been offered in sumo history: the hand of Miss Chocho Ginza, princess of our national sport."

The crowd screamed in joy. Buck gawked at the fools. Couldn't they see this was garbage? Stinky, rotting meat and Stilton cheese and three-day-old refried bean garbage? He spun around, gawking at their happy faces, suppressing the urge to give them all a big wake-up slap across the cheek.

"And so, with her father's permission," Torakiba continued, "I ask Miss Chocho Ginza to marry me in January, the day after I win the Emperor's Cup."

Hot lead dropped into the pit of Buck's stomach. He might vomit. Torakiba had just proposed to Chocho on national television.

二十一

STRAY DOG
JULY. NAGOYA

Everyone began to whisper and point at Chocho. Buck couldn't breathe. His soul stretched out toward her, but his feet were welded to the spot. He could do nothing.

Buck's lip curled in derision. She deserved rubies, and that Tiger Fang deserved Texas Root Rot. How could Torakiba even think of defiling her like that?

Chocho lifted her hand to her throat and rested it there, her eyes wide. Ginza, however, broke into a smile of unmitigated pleasure.

"Wha! What a surprise," Ginza exclaimed.

Buck almost wished he couldn't understand the lies.

"Torakiba. You have surprised me, too, completely. I am shocked." Ginza bowed to the champion. "Ladies and gentlemen. Your *yokozuna* has just offered his hand to my daughter for marriage." The crowd exploded in rupturing applause. All eyes were on her. What would Chocho say? Would she say yes?

Every muscle in Buck's body tightened. Betrayal. It would cut Buck to shreds. He couldn't swallow past the dry patch at the back of his throat. But no words came from her. Ginza gripped his microphone and rattled on about sumo's history and how his family was a landmark, and what a great man he was. Self-aggrandizing baboon. Buck wanted to twist his head off. Anger supplanted fear.

Ginza chortled, "But, seriously, I note Torakiba's suggestion with joy. In fact, I will go so far as to set the preparations for the wedding into motion. When he wins the Emperor's Cup in January, he can have my daughter the very next day."

Torakiba beamed.

"I said *when*, but I do mean *if*," Ginza backtracked. "Torakiba must still win the Emperor's Cup,"—a laugh—"however, I will make it sweeter. When Torakiba wins—or *whoever* it may be—he will receive my daughter; but he will also receive fifty percent of Ginza Corp's stock."

Voices exploded in gossip. Torakiba looked like he might faint for joy. Every single razor tooth gleamed. One marriage could be the architect of the Fujiwaras' rise from the ashes. And Buck's disintegration into them.

Buck's stomach soured. Forget this. He was getting out of here. And not just out of this building, or Nagoya—he was getting out of sumo. He was heading to Narita for the next plane to the good old U.S. of A. Forget these people, this sport, this sham, this whole seaweed sucking country.

Disgust drove his steps toward the double doors. *Come on, Chocho. Why would you go along with this tripe?* Hot puffs of anger expelled from his nose.

His hand touched the door. He turned to take one last glance at her gorgeous face between those two chuckleheads on the stage. Her face still wore the emotionless mask, but her eyes met his for a split second before returning to their original post, staring straight ahead into the audience.

Buck halted his steps. He shot a laser stare at Chocho, willing her to look his way again so he could be sure what he'd seen—what she'd said—was real. But no more glances came. He didn't know what to make of it. Perhaps a flicker of the eyes was all the good-byes she could bother to send him. It meant, *Give up, you sap. Fate made you fall for me but there's nothing I can do about that now; move on. Sorry, pal. This is the way it is.* One thing for sure, there was resignation in her stoic look, which meant there was at least a sliver of a chance she wasn't happy about the situation. And if there was even a one percent chance she didn't want to be stuck with that human grizzly, Buck wouldn't give up on her. But he had to get out of there.

He stepped out the door and into the down elevator. A nasty vision seared into his imagination: a gruesome beauty-and-the-beast wedding night scenario should Torakiba get his wish. Buck banished the horrifying thought.

Six months until that dreaded tournament. "Six!" Buck cursed. From where he ranked now, it would take a miracle for him to get into position to even *compete* for that Emperor's Cup. Winning looked beyond impossible.

But Chocho deserved a man who fought through the impossible for her. He replayed what she'd said to him last night in the park. *Whatever happens tomorrow, today is real.* She walked across water for him when she couldn't swim—so he could see a sunset.

A countdown clock to January began to tick in Buck's soul. He was going to do it. Fixed odds or not, Buck intended to play Ginza's game against Torakiba.

For Chocho.

THE TAXI LURCHED TO A halt outside the stable.

"Let me get this straight." Buck quizzed Dude. "Only the top four tiers fight for the Emperor's Cup,"

"Right-o, my big blond friend." Dude hefted himself out of the cab, still groggy from the party. "That'd be your old pal Torakiba, official King-o'-Sumo now, and all his bodacious buddies in the top four levels. All ten of those handsome charm school grads."

Buck winced. Four exclusive tiers towered above Buck's current rank. Nine men, plus one *yokozuna* named, constituted Chocho's pool of possible husbands. Buck had to shove his way in there. Literally. Or take a flying leap like he had at the public bath. No matter what, he'd be making a splash of colossal proportion, and they'd all better duck and cover.

Buck piled out and followed Dude into the throng of photo-snapping fans where he pasted on his usual smile and signed a few *tegata* handprint autographs before disappearing into the Kawaguchi stable's temporary training quarters.

Once inside, Buck sat down with his list, his films, and his brain. Tonight he devoted himself to studying the competition, both his immediate division of *maegashira* and the realm of champs. He needed to know their ins and outs. All his years of sports facts mental cataloging came in handy as he scrounged up film clips of their moves, scoured magazines for articles about them, analyzed their techniques and strengths, plus their weaknesses. The past two years of intense training had taught him how to practically apply the data to his body. He was on the job.

For the remainder of the Nagoya *basho*, his strategy worked.

As Hiro would report, Buck made borscht out of a Russian named Yokoso. He made Kotako look like a flailing octopus. That Estonian who sprouted a beard between the time of the march-in and the time of their bout went running for his shave and a haircut under Buck's mighty wallop. Eight other competitors also bowed to Buck's perfect record, the only *maegashira* to do so in the past two years.

They headed back to Tokyo, Buck a conquering hero.

All the buzz was for Buck, now that the hubbub about the

new *yokozuna* had tapered off. Reporters hounded him as he got off the bus. The Gooch shook his hand—which freaked Buck out. Handshakes—they seemed so unsanitary now.

Voice resonant with praise, The Gooch bowed. "You have done honor to the stable of Kawaguchi this *basho*, Asagohan."

As Buck and Ohimesama stumped back to their barracks, Buck thought of his name. Asagohan. He despised his sumo name. Now that he'd earned a victorious reputation, to be called "breakfast" just didn't seem appropriate anymore.

"What do you think, O-man? Should we play Texas Hold 'Em or Five Card Stud tonight?" Buck asked his *kohai* as he went for his deck of cards. They slid back the paper door to Buck's room, and Buck's jaw dropped.

On the ground near Buck's folded futons sat an enormous silver tray stacked high with a sumptuous gift: crates of exquisite Japanese fruit.

"What's all this?" Buck's eyes about boinged out of his head. Fruits. Fresh and perfect and beautiful. Nobody on God's green earth produced fruit more exquisite than the Japanese. Each apple, each pear, each morsel was a masterpiece. He stood agog at the haul. "Square watermelon?" His mouth watered. It had been far too long since he savored his favorite fruit—for a change, it was not pre-chewed up and spit into his face.

"Exactamente." Reggie leaned in through the door behind them and marveled, too. "Excellente!" He bustled in and picked up the basketball-sized cube of a fruit and hugged it to his chest. It made him look like a totem pole with legs. "Nothing better than a sweet *suika*." He sniffed it and set it down.

"You're going to share this, right?" Dude entered after Reggie, equally impressed. "I mean, they do cost over *sen man* yen apiece." Dude palmed a kiwi the size of a softball.

"*Sen man* yen. That's like a hundred bucks. You're not serious."

Buck shuddered in disbelief as he stared at the stack of watermelons, ten or so high. Surrounding them were cartons of enormous apples, each fruit ensconced in its own white styrofoam net. Then there were Asian pears, also in styro-nets, and star fruits, and kiwis—the biggest Buck had ever laid eyes on—and other melons he'd never seen before. He made a quick estimate: on this table lay about 2,500 dollars worth of produce.

"There's a note." Reggie plucked it from the top of the watermelon pyramid and handed it to Buck, who summoned Ohimesama.

The *kohai* came over. He browsed the message then frowned.

"So sorry, *senpai*. You will not like note."

"Tell me anyway," Buck demanded.

"It is to say *omedeto*. Congratulations."

Buck remembered back to his days as *kohai* when Torakiba was presented with a similar array of fruits, cut and arranged in beautiful shapes. Buck now ranked with the fruit basket champs. Yes!

"Why wouldn't I like that?" Buck asked.

"Because it is congratulations for your retirement from sumo."

二
十
二

RUNAWAY TRAIN
JULY–NOVEMBER. TOKYO AND FUKUOKA

"Wait a cotton picking minute." Buck stepped back from the offering.

Ohimesama's eyes grew wide, and as the seconds passed, they welled with tears. "Buck-*san*. You can *not* choose retirement."

"No siree," Buck chuffed and snatched at the letter. "Who wrote this note, Ohimesama?" He peered over it, but the characters still eluded him for the most part. Stupid pain of illiteracy.

"No one owns the note," Ohimesama blurted out in relief, and the welling receded from his eyes.

"Well then, that settles that." Dude hoisted the giant platter onto his shoulder like a waiter. "I'll be right back."

"Where are you going with my watermelon?" Buck chased after the Hawaiian. His stomach longed for juicy watermelon. This heat parched him and watermelon sounded like heaven.

"Get back here! Believe me, Wally Wada. You do not want to come between a hungry Southern boy and his watermelon."

Dude moved too fast, and before Buck knew it, the watermelon and all the other pretty fruits landed in a heap inside the compost barrel alongside the putrid stench of leftover tofu and mollusk shells in the stable's back alley.

"What is wrong with your brain?" Buck croaked. He'd never wanted to punch Dude before, but this was outrageous.

"Dude," Dude said, hands on hips. "You are not going to eat even one itty, bitty, teeny, tiny bite of retirement." He tossed the tray like a frisbee into a trash can, then clap-brushed his hands together and wiped them on his *yukata*.

"I cannot believe you just did that." Buck's mouth watered at the scent of the fruit, even over the stench.

"I can't believe you'd do otherwise." Dude stalked back into the stable, calling over his shoulder, "Don't you get it? It's *symbolic*. You wouldn't want to disappoint your butterfly."

Back inside, Ohimesama greeted Buck with the low bow as Buck flung himself onto his nicely spread futon. The Mongolian shifted his weight back and forth, and finally spoke in a troubled voice, eyes lowered.

"Akabaka was right to throw out the gift." The *kohai* frowned, and Buck opened a single eye to peer out at him. After a moment he whispered, "In days gone by, a *kohai* would taste all the food of the *senpai*." He cleared his throat. "Thank you, Buck, for not demanding I do that for you today."

"What are you talking about?" Buck opened both eyes.

"Now, we must watch for the birds." Ohimesama's gold tooth glinted.

Uh, birds. Right. Whatever. Buck had too many other people and situations on his mind to watch the birds. But wait. Buck gulped. "You mean poison?" It finally sank in.

Ohimesama kept steady eye contact with Buck, breathing in and out for a long time. "You are good *senpai*, Buck. Wally Wada is good friend to you."

BUCK DIGESTED THE INFORMATION ALL afternoon and night—since he had no juicy fruits of paradise to digest. His mathematical mind made a dozen connections, most of them wild. Poison? Naw. Supremely unlikely. But not impossible. Memories of being a kid at Halloween, the urban legend of razor blades in the apples still made the roof of his mouth hurt, but he'd never heard of one single real case of it. Besides, who wouldn't notice that? Please.

On the other hand, a hypodermic needle filled with poison and inserted in a watermelon—well, that would be virtually undetectable.

Worse, he hated how easy it was to make a list of possible suspects: Torakiba had pummeled Buck into near oblivion in a rage in the past; Sobakubi still had every reason to hate Buck; Butaniku from his distant cell in Korea still had contacts in stables and the sport; a random fan of any higher ranked *rikishi* might not appreciate Buck's success. And fan obsessions could be deadly, as Jodie Foster and John Lennon found out the hard way back in the day.

Enemies buffeted Buck round about. Doing the right thing had made him a target in a dozen ways. Buck dropped his skepticism. Ohimesama might be right. It could very well be poison. The realization fully dawned on him—someone had wanted him dead.

Tiger Fang floated to the top of Buck's suspect list. Past behavior warranted it. Even though Buck had no actual proof that Torakiba had hired the brass-knuckled thug who broke his nose—the jerk did threaten Buck right before the knuckles struck.

Curse words ping-ponged around in his mind. That scum sucking moron. The image of Chocho in the clutches of that monster made Buck's blood freeze in his veins.

Buck needed a dozen miracles.

And to stay alive.

"BUCK! I CANNOT BELIEVE YOU!" Hiro hopped up and down beside their table in the sushi bar. He'd grown a foot taller since the first time Buck saw him almost two years ago. "You are such a sumo megastar now. Thank you for inviting me today!" Every sentence that came from the kid's mouth ended with an exclamation point.

"Glad to have you, kiddo." Buck patted Hiro's shoulder and sent him back to the sushi bar for another plate from the conveyor belt. "Grab me a fresh tuna, would you? With some wasabi." He loved that green horseradish.

Hiro returned to their table balancing six or seven plates of varying sushi selections, all beautifully filleted atop mounds of sweet rice. "I like the eel."

"It's all yours." Buck knocked back his tuna in a single bite. Good stuff.

"So, I've been working on my Buck report. I get a lot of hits on my video log online after the matches. Have you seen it?" Hiro cleared his throat, his tone and expression more grave. "In the past three months of *dohyo* match-ups, Asagohan has proven himself the gem of the Kawaguchi stable, as long-predicted by this reporter. His rise has been compared to a rocket, shooting into the sky. Fans watched him get perfect win-loss records in Nagoya in July and in Tokyo in September. Even his exhibition matches on the road in cities throughout Japan have been stellar."

Hiro broke out of character for a minute. "Stellar. Do you like that word, Buck? I found it online."

Buck responded with a nod as he wolfed down another tuna slab.

Hiro grinned. "Now, the golden-headed bomb from America will certainly stun fans again in Fukuoka starting tomorrow. We hold our breath for anticipation." He looked expectantly at Buck.

"Nice. Gotta say, Hiro, you're my good luck charm. Last time, before Nagoya, I met with you right before the *basho*, and it was my best *basho* ever. I'm going to have you visit me before every tournament. Deal?"

"Deal." Hiro's grin stretched from ear to ear. Then it fell. "There's just one thing, Buck."

"What's wrong?"

"Your name. Your sumo name. It is not strong. It does not fit you now. You need new sumo name."

Nobody hated the name Breakfast more than Buck. "Yeah, well, what can I do about it? Kawaguchi Oyakata gave it to me. It's what I got." Breakfast. Forever.

"No." Hiro stood up and started his hopping again. "You can change. All you must do is choose a new name and ask your trainer. You are so good now. He will agree." Hiro stopped short. Looking directly into Buck's eyes, he said, "Your new name. I know what it must be. It is *Baku*."

"You mean my old name is Baku." Everyone pronounced Buck that way here.

"No. Baku. It is special Japanese spirit, 'destroyer of dreams.' You are taking so many dreams away from other *rikishi*. It is perfect. Now go! You tell Kawaguchi Oyakata this is your new name."

BUCK MULLED THEIR CONVERSATION THAT night at the stable. Hiro might describe the past four months as a whirlwind of sumo fun, but Buck couldn't smile. Doing five hundred squat-and-kicks with searing thigh muscles, he agonized over his dad's broken dream. Stomps thundered out his anger over his mom's home on the chopping block, along with grandma and grandpa's farm. Acres of alfalfa, the old farmhouse, the fields, the stand of poplars, the vegetable garden, the horses—just dessicating, blowing away from his life like the dustbowl in *The Grapes of Wrath*.

Buck had socked away all his winnings from sumo, mostly in Japan's Sumitomo Bank. He hadn't spent a single yen other than an occasional butternut squash flavored ice cream cone at the AM/PM Market and regular baths at the local bathhouse.

He had a duffel bag stuffed with cash from his winnings and the Calpis endorsement that he kept in the stable's safe, but even those wouldn't cover the cost of waiting out another bureaucratic runaround. Besides, his parents would never accept his money to ransom their house. That, he knew.

It had been one hundred and seventy-five days. The calendar was his enemy. He started in on his pseudo-push-ups—sumo style—and kept stewing about his parents' problem. He should call them tonight. With five days left to the deadline, they were probably a mess.

AT PRACTICE THE NEXT DAY, Buck moped.

"Look, dude. Just because you didn't make *komusubi* rank doesn't mean you failed. There's next time." The surfer voice did not comfort Buck, who was agonizingly aware of the passage of every day, for his parents' sake and his own. And Chocho's, too.

"No, there's not. This is *it*. I'm not ranked high enough. Even if I ace it at Fukuoka, I'm not qualified to compete for the Emperor's Cup in January." Buck punched the air and grabbed a towel to wipe the sweat from the back of his neck.

"Come on. Let's go again. I'm gonna take you *down*." Buck squatted and put his elbows on his knees, hands open, doing spirit fingers. "You're dead meat." He put on his game face, but inside he was dragging. Five weeks to Fukuoka, thirteen weeks to January, and no hope glimmered anywhere on his horizon.

Before he knew it, Dude had slammed him onto the dirt. Buck stared up at the ceiling with a smirk.

"Phone call for Asagohan," Ohimesama interrupted. Buck trotted out into the hallway to the Kermit phone.

"Buck Cooper-*san*? Please hold for the Prime Minister."

"DAD? ARE YOU STILL UP?"

"I'm up. It's been a while since I slept well."

"Well, Dad. There's good news." Buck explained the result of his phone conversation with the Prime Minister as succinctly as possible, leaving the firing of Sobakubi's cabinet minister father for another day. "And from what I hear, the appeal has been granted, so the new Minister of Health will be contacting Mr. Yoshida tomorrow morning to begin the fair review of your product. The data's clean, Dad. I think Nangrimax is a shoo-in for the Japanese markets now." Buck knew clean data. Eaglestone taught him that.

Buck's dad gushed with relief, calling his wife to the phone so Buck could tell the whole story all over.

"Oh, Hank." his mom exclaimed. "Isn't this wonderful! Now you'll have to follow through on that Christmas gift you promised me. Buck, we said if the deal did go through we'd catch the first plane in January to come over and see you do what it is you do. We've been dying to go, but everything has been on hold, as you can imagine. So when do you compete next? We'd love to be there."

AS BUCK MEANDERED BACK TO his quarters—the smile from the conversation with his parents still warm—he saw Ohimesama's ashen face at the door.

"What is it, pal?" Buck put an arm over his *kohai's* shoulder and guided him into the room. "You look like you've seen a dead man."

"*Honto desu.* Not dead man, but death itself." Eyes wide, Ohimesama pointed at a window, exposing the back lot near the trash heap. Buck peered to see what could be disturbing Ohimesama so much. Nothing different out there today, except—

"Ninety-nine dead birds, Baku-*san.* Death in the plenty."

THE BAD SLEEP WELL
NOVEMBER. FUKUOKA

The authorities investigated the bird anomaly, the death count reaching over two hundred in the months since July. Newspapers described it as an unexplained phenomenon, but it was no mystery to Ohimesama, or Buck and Dude. It was clear that the fruits were indeed poisoned.

The out of town *basho* in Fukuoka came as a welcome relief.

"Great show tonight, Baku." Reggie jostled Buck's arm as they exited the Fukuoka Sumo Arena. "They're gonna wanna interview you for the JSA web page, so start brushing up your quotable quotes, man. Give them something juicy, I think."

Buck didn't do juicy, but he wanted to sing about the win. Tonight's victory solidified his record for this *basho*. He wasn't going to get bumped down a level next time, and that rocked. He'd resigned himself to taking joy in the small things, since the big things were beyond his reach.

Bitter winter air snapped at his legs below his thin *yukata*. He steered through Fukuoka past the tea shop where he saw her last fall. Wistfulness washed through him, deflating the happy feelings of triumph because despite tonight's win, he still couldn't compete for Chocho next *basho,* even if he won all his remaining matches in this November tournament. Stupid, stupid, stupid.

"I like your new sumo name, man. It is a lot easier to say than that lame breakfast name. The fans, they loves it, too. It makes you even stronger. I should change mine? What you think?" Reggie asked.

Reggie's name, Futokaba, meant Fat Hippo, and it fit well enough. "I like it, Reg," Buck said. "After all, they do say the most dangerous of all the animals in Africa is not the lion or the rhinoceros. It's the hippopotamus."

"You lie."

"I speak truth, friend. They're territorial, aggressive, the heaviest animal other than the elephant, and they are known to attack humans, even boats. They're the animal responsible for the most human deaths on that continent."

"Besides other humans."

"Right."

"Okay, I'll stick with it. Plus I like how it sounds—fu-to-ka-ba. Almost like *futtoboru,* my favorite sport, soccer."

Buck sniffed. *It's happening, I think we're turning Japanese.*

The two turned onto a side street on their way back to the Kawaguchi stable's Fukuoka headquarters. After tonight's bout, only a miracle would let him compete for the Emperor's Cup in the January tournament. Where was he going to come up with a miracle? Thunder clapped, and lightning zig-zagged through the sky.

"Iya da na!" Reggie hated lightning. "I'm ducking into this ramen shop. You coming?"

Buck shook his head. "I need a bath and a good night's rest." But as soon as Reggie peeled off, a chill went through Buck. A crack of thunder rolled across the tops of the buildings on either side of him, rattling the glass in the skyscraper windows. Ominous. No rain yet, but wind came in gusts. Lightning flashed again, this time much closer. A lone leaf tumbled past his foot like a scurrying animal. Buck picked up his pace.

About halfway down the alley, he noticed it stretched much longer than he thought. Something felt off. He glanced over his shoulder, first right, then left. No one. The backs of his arms began to tingle, his upper lip twitched.

A human-made noise sounded behind him. He whirled around to see who it was. Nothing. He picked up his pace, ducking his head from the thunder, which cracked with deafening roars. Uneasiness dogged him. He made a quick dodge down an alley, and the storm quit as quickly as it had begun, leaving an eerie, crackling mist in the icy air. A moment later, a bank of fog rolled in from the nearby ocean, chilling his bones. Yellow light from sodium lamps filtered through the mist, creating an eerie glow.

"*Dareka ga iru?* Who's there?" Buck tried both languages, glancing up and down.

Out of nowhere, a dark figure sprang to the concrete smack-dab in front of Buck. Before Buck could think, the man in black attacked. Buck felt a leg connect with his jaw—a roundhouse kick—and then a second, and a third.

Buck blinked, his hands flying to where the pain throbbed. The man bounded backward. And without thinking, Buck gave chase. Small karate boy bounded over trash heaps, moving like a gazelle. Buck followed, his moves much more like a water buffalo, but a water buffalo enraged. Seriously, he'd had enough of getting smacked in alleys by strangers. This twerp would pay.

The alley opened up into a slightly broader cross-street, and Buck saw it blur past him as he sped after the assailant, his feet pounding the pavement as he hurtled after the ninja man, out to where huge freight boxes stacked fifty feet in the air came into view. They'd arrived at the docks.

The sodium streetlights lit the waterfront, giving a yellow cast to the steel and concrete in the cold night. Thunder cracked again, and Buck looked back and forth, then upward but couldn't spot his quarry.

No sign.

Buck's chin ached. A goose egg was already forming on his jawbone. His breath came in quick gasps. He bent over and held his side.

Curse the weasel. His eyes searched on.

Two soft footfalls pattered behind Buck. He wrenched around and saw the attacker again, this time flanked by two more fighters, hands balled into fists, knees bent, ready to spring.

"What do y'all want? I take it someone sent you." Obviously Torakiba. Again. This had gone too far. Buck didn't fight his way to the top of the sumo food chain to keep eating knuckle sandwiches in dark alleys—and Torakiba should quit the cowardice and fight Buck himself if he had a problem with him. Buck seethed. He'd teach these toadies a lesson they could take back to their boss.

Buck crouched into fighting stance. Nothing stood between him and his assailants but his thin kimono and the bitter winter air. Night enveloped him, but the streetlights gave faint yellow outline to the three black-pajamaed henchmen. Their eyes pierced the night in steely hatred.

Buck's poundage shivered like Jell-O on his mother's table—not so much from fear, but from the winter night. He prepped himself to spring on them full force. Their boss'd get the message.

The tallest of the three advanced first. Something like this had to be courtesy of the *yakuza*. The walls formed by the freight began to slide together. Buck had never fought three men at once, and certainly never triumphed in a three-on-one battle.

A gust of icy air constricted his throat. The first hitman circled him at a short distance, and Buck rotated to keep him in sight, even though it meant turning his back on the other two.

"Come on, boys. Surely you're not simple disgruntled Buta-niku fans. Spill it. Who sent y'all?" Puffs of exhaled steam hung stagnant in the freezing air.

With blinding speed the first assailant attacked. Buck struck out his right hand in hopes of catching him by the throat. It sent the first man backward, as if the assailant had been treed while riding a horse. The impact seared through Buck's shoulder. Good thing, too, because right then the second attacker advanced, and Buck was forced to immediately jut his left elbow into the man's neck. Being the tallest person in a fight had its advantages.

From above, the third man swung from a ladder and pounced onto Buck, landing on Buck's back. Ninja number three thrust his arms around Buck's neck and began to pull. Buck's Adam's apple pressed against the back of his throat, his airway collapsing. He twisted and flailed to shake off the choker, but to no avail.

Meanwhile, the other two men struggled to their feet and gathered their wits. The first sent the heel of his hand straight up against Buck's nose, breaking it—yet again. Blood oozed southward.

The second assailant landed a kick on Buck's left side, ripping through Buck's ribcage in searing pain. But it didn't last long— Buck's mind was beginning to darken for lack of oxygen.

They want to kill me. These guys want me dead. His peripheral vision was fading to black.

"Buck!" a voice shouted from afar as he sank to his knees.

Suddenly, he could breathe again. The suffocating force behind him had left. The remaining two continued to pound on him in full force. Buck pulled himself together and regained his balance. He ducked his head, and with the strength it would take to push against a wrecking ball, Buck shouldered both of his assasins to the ground, smacking them hard onto the concrete.

Buck spun around and saw a looming figure.

"Reggie? Is that you?" Buck's swelling face made his speech muffled.

Reginald the Fat Filipino Hippo had the third assailant upside down by one leg, pounding the attacker's head onto the ground. It didn't look good for the human.

"Stop! Man, don't kill him." Buck lunged for Reggie.

Reggie dropped the assassin, gave him a good kick. "What are you going to do with that one? You have to incapacitate him." Reggie pointed to one of the assailants, who was still writhing on the floor. Buck had a foot on his throat.

Through the opening on the man's black mask, Buck could see fear and a hint of surrender. "No, he's too afraid. We have to let him go." Buck stepped back.

Without warning, the eyes in the mask immediately narrowed. The fighter sprang back into action, grabbing Reggie by the neck, slashing it faster than either of the *rikishi* could react. His knife flashed in the yellow lamplight.

Blood spurted out onto Reggie's *yukata* and he stared down in horror. Buck gasped helplessly as he watched blood pool on his friend's *yukata*.

Buck couldn't lift his arms—the sight of blood pinned them to his side. Time ground into low gear, ticking by audibly with each pulse of Reggie's heart. Buck stared in horror as the knife now came flashing toward him.

Buck suddenly snapped back to life. With speed he'd never exhibited anywhere before, Buck's hand whipped out and snatched the arm of the slasher. He hurled the man around in a circle, wrapping his arm behind his back and yanked it skyward as hard as he could, squeezing the forearm until the fingers gave way and the knife clattered on the cement. He gave the assailant a second yank, dislocating the man's shoulder, and shoved him to the pavement where his head hit with a crack.

Buck bent down and felt Reggie for a pulse.

"You're going to live, Reggie." Buck pleaded with his friend; his own pain numbed in the waves of fear he had for his friend's life. "And, pal? I owe you one. You're one dangerous hippo."

Reggie gave a weak nod and sank in a heap to the pavement.

"YOU LOOK AWFUL," REGGIE MUMBLED through a mouthful of hot cereal, before washing it down with a swig of wheat tea served by the hospital.

"Speak for yourself." Buck rubbed his jaw. "Those stitches are going to leave a mark."

"You almost makes me wish I just quit sumo and marries Miss One Thousand Autumn Leaves. Painful, but not as painful as knife fights in the alley with *yakuza* henchmen."

"You think they were *yakuza*, then?" Buck looked out the third story window of the hospital onto the morning landscape of Fukuoka. It looked deceptively peaceful from up here.

"No question. That was the mafia." Reggie frowned. Then he winced, feeling the stitches on his neck. "You saved my life, Buck."

It was Buck's turn to frown. He never should have spared his enemies' lives. Those men were there to kill him, and he'd endangered the life of his best friend trying to be merciful.

"Look, you was just doing what a man with honor does, Buck. I can't never blame you for that." Reggie took a deep breath and turned away. "I just wish the doctors weren't going to make me sit out this *basho* because of it."

"What? What are you talking about?" Buck asked.

"Now the blood is gone and I don'ts have enough," he shrugged, "I can't fight again until maybe the next *basho* in January, or maybe even until March. But I don't know if—"

"If what?" Beads of sweat formed on Buck's upper lip. This was all his fault. His stupid principles.

"I don't know if Miss One Thousand Autumn Leaves will still want to marry me if I'm an amateur."

"What? You're getting married?"

"I think I maybe wants to ask her now. It's either that or the short sword, you know. And I'm so busy as *rikishi*, too busy for girlfriend, but not too busy for wife." His eye twinkled. "She also is very rich, you know. I never been rich before."

Buck chuckled, "Oh, I think she'll still want you. She sent you all those origami roses and that fancy silk kimono before you hit the pro ranks, after all. Am I right, Reg? I'm right." He raised an eyebrow, but Reggie still looked concerned.

"I don't know. I really think she liked the idea of being wife to a professional sumo wrestler, and she chose me because I had a good chance to go up to the pros. I don't know what she will think, if she will want me now." He looked shattered. "Besides, man. I really hate to go back to amateurs and be a *kohai*. It's a bad life. I don't know if I can do it, you know?"

"At least you're not in the Kawaguchi stable. You can't get assigned to Torakiba. If you were, we'd have to join forces and incapacitate him for what he did to you." There were a hundred ways he'd like to chop that animal into pieces. Anything to prevent him from harming anyone else—including Chocho.

Reggie sighed in exasperation. "When are you going to get it, man? This attack? It was no Torakiba thing. Look around you."

A nurse came in—the one who could speak English and Spanish—which shushed them. Buck's eye caught the clock. He had to go. He had to get on the train back to Tokyo. But he looked back at Reggie. He couldn't strand his friend here in Fukuoka hospital, not in this state.

"Go on. I'll be fine," Reggie said.

"You're injured because of me. I can't just leave you here." It tore at his chest to think of it. "No. I'm not leaving."

"You have to, Buck. For *her* sake. I saw the photo of you two. It's all over the Internet." Reg made a kissing sound.

Photo. What photo?

"She needs you, man. If you don't go now, your girl is as good as married to that Tiger Tooth jerk."

Torakiba and Chocho. Buck double-blinked. No matter what Reggie thought, Torakiba was responsible for all this—for the knifing, for making Reggie bleed. Anger blazed in Buck.

"You're a true man, Reggie. Miss One Thousand Autumn Leaves will be one lucky geisha."

THE TRAIN BACK TO TOKYO bumped and jostled. Buck's bones ached. His chin was the size of a grapefruit. The area beneath his eyes swelled up, and he could almost feel it getting blacker by the minute.

"Asagohan. *Ossu.*" A large figure thunked down in the empty seat beside Buck. At first he assumed the seatmate was Reggie, as usual, and didn't look up. A second later he realized how impossible that was and turned to see none other than Torakiba.

The *yokozuna* recoiled when he saw Buck's messed up face. "Whoa, Cowboy."

"Came to see your handiwork?" Buck sneered. All the hatred simmering over the past two years now came to a steaming hiss as he turned toward Torakiba. "You like what your three henchmen did to me? Snuck up on me in the dark, waited until I was alone. You're too much of a coward to do your own dirty work." Buck stood for emphasis. "So you hired thugs to take care of it? You disgust me," he spat and bustled past Torakiba into the aisle of the moving train. "And Reggie who came to save my life is taking a real punishment for it. Did you hear that, too? "Know this, Torakiba. His blood is on your hands."

Torakiba stood and crossed his arms over his chest. "What are you talking about?"

Buck couldn't bear to be in the same enclosed space with this murderous liar. He stood up and stalked toward a different car.

"Come back, Asagohan." Torakiba lumbered after him. "Baku!" He caught Buck by the shoulder, the one that seared with pain at the slightest movement.

Buck's hand flew to the injury, and he wrenched around to face his enemy. "I'm a numbers guy. Don't you think I did the math? You're behind them all. Three times you had me pummeled in the night. First with your own fists, then you sent a thug with brass knuckles. I really hated that, and my nose did, too—until I found out how it felt to have three trained assassins try to wax me in a dark alley."

Torakiba looked incredulous. Buck couldn't bear it.

"I'm going to prove it was you, Torakiba. Then your reputation and career will go flushing away. Watch them circle the drain, pal. Gnash your sharp teeth at me all you want. Your hero days, are *numbered*." Buck didn't even mention the poisoned fruit.

"I didn't hire—no. Never!" Torakiba spluttered. "Yes, I tortured you as my *kohai*. It is expected. But I never hired someone to hurt you. Certainly not twice! What do you think I am? A monster?" Torakiba shoved his arms into his armpits then lowered his voice. "I won't say I never thought about beating your face. That smile. It didn't quit. A sumo wrestler must be stern. But the people *loved* you. The more they loved you the angrier I got." He trailed off.

Buck steeled his jaw. This guy was so full of garbage and lies. He made a fist, ready to punch those long teeth right off.

"Believe me, Baku. I never sent anyone to attack you. I saw your beaten face when we were in Nagoya. I didn't ask—it wouldn't be fitting for a *senpai* to ask such a personal question of his *kohai*." Torakiba motioned for Buck to sit. Buck seethed a moment, but complied. Torakiba folded and unfolded a map from the seat pocket. Finally he spoke.

"At the time when you came to be my *kohai,* my family became especially troubled at home. The House of Fujiwara was in great danger. I could not make things better. I became very angry in all parts of my life." He hung his head. "The words I spoke to you that night, they would bring shame to my parents." Torakiba looked up again. "Many years I have worked to restore the honor of the Fujiwara family, honor that was lost in a single heated moment by my father, a shame that still lives with everyone in the family."

Torakiba seemed pretty ashamed of whatever his father did, even now. So it wasn't a mom in a nursing home or a natural disaster that drove him, but a man-made disaster. A lot of those were floating around these days.

"I left that *koen-kai* and went straight to Nagoya," Torakiba continued. "I found my parents' home had been sold, their possessions taken from them, and they had exhausted the patience of relatives. My father needed work, but he needed to look respectable first. I took all my sumo winnings and set things back into good motion. Very soon I was myself again."

Buck, wary, weighed the sincerity in Torakiba's voice and his countenance. "You didn't send a man with brass hands to break my nose? Even though you admit you wanted to kill me?"

"No. I promise on my family's honor."

Another sweep of Buck's memory showed that Torakiba did stop abusing him long before the sumo-wide "no hazing" crackdown. Family honor—it struck a nerve. After a long pause, Buck acquiesced. "But if you didn't send those men after me, who did?"

Torakiba stared at him a long moment. "Have you seen the photos?"

Buck's pulse took an up-tick. "What photos?"

Torakiba's eyes narrowed. "I didn't think you'd lie about such a small thing. In something as important as this, the least you can do is tell the truth."

"Truthfully, I have not seen of any photos." But as soon as he said the words, Buck remembered—the photo from the tea shop. Or worse, that photographer in the stepping stone park. His face fell as blood drained from it. "Oh, maybe—"

Torakiba nodded, satisfied. "Even greater than my own wish to marry Chocho Ginza is her father's wish for her to marry me, a full-blooded Japanese man with power, strength, and skill. Someone who can make his future secure, and pure."

"What are you talking about?"

"Ginza wants a pure heir. If his daughter, offspring of a sumo champion, marries a pure champion, their child will be pure, a fitting offering to the gods. He will be trained from his earliest age, and, with the power of genetics and pure blood, will reign forever as a sumo legend. And *I* am to be the sire."

Buck snorted. "You clowns may have convinced yourselves that this imaginary future child is Ginza's grand offering to the sumo gods, but the reality is, *Chocho* was the sacrifice. Her life for your pleasure." His eyes narrowed to slits. "Chocho is nothing but a rent-a-womb to her father." Sick hatred flooded him.

"That's right, perhaps, but it is also why you, Baku, will never, ever be an acceptable match for Chocho."

A frown contorted Buck's chin and lips. "You and your family money problems be hanged. Chocho deserves love! What would make me give up on her now, after all I've been through? Even if I only have the ghost of a chance at that Emperor's Cup, I'll fight."

Every single domino in the whole January tournament may have to line up exactly right, but Buck was sticking it out like he'd never stuck anything out before.

Suddenly, another thing became crystal clear: Torakiba really didn't try to off him. Ginza did. But why? At the time of the first attack, Buck was nothing but a newbie *rikishi*, so low in the ranks there was no way he'd pose a threat to the big Ginza-and-Torakiba-marriage-and-money scheme. None.

Unless Chocho was already in love with Buck, and her father knew it.

"Tell me, Torakiba, why you want her. Not the money, the *girl*," Buck asked.

"No. You tell me why *you* want Chocho Ginza." The fangs flashed.

The last thing Buck intended to do was lay bare his innermost feelings to this brute. Still, he had to make it clear. "It's not a want. It's a need." Without her, he'd suffocate.

"What, a need to stop your lonely feelings? Because you have been fat all your life and no American woman will look at you?" Torakiba scoffed. He'd hit the mark with searing accuracy. Chocho was the antidote to decades of pain. She absorbed him, made him vast, not small and afraid. He was a snowflake melting in her ocean.

Torakiba's eyes gleamed. "You cannot win this, Baku. Stop fooling yourself. Ginza will have a pure Japanese heir, the beginning of a long line of champions. I will have his money, and the House of Fujiwara will rise as the House of Ginza rises, just as Japan itself—the rising sun!"

"Asinine. You're the two most selfish men I've ever met." The train barreled into a tunnel, and all the windows went dark. Buck turned toward Torakiba, who'd merged into that darkness. He spoke in a fierce whisper. "The house of Fujiwara may be your future, but *she* is *my* future. We will each fight for our causes." He turned back to see Torakiba's eyes and teeth glowing white in the darkness. "And believe me, *I will fight*."

Torakiba's voice lowered to a tiger's growl. "So will I."

THE MEN WHO TREAD ON THE TIGER'S TAIL
JANUARY. TOKYO

Six weeks later, Buck plodded toward destiny in the January wind. Tokyo. The January *basho*. D-Day. Bitterness filled his throat. He may have just won his first fourteen bouts and have a perfect record, but reality remained. He wasn't going to compete for the Emperor's Cup tomorrow. There was no way he could ever face Torakiba in the ring.

It didn't matter that on day six, Buck trounced the steroid-happy Estonian, Wabesama. The judges almost made them re-do the match, but it ended with good news for Buck. Afterwards, none other than Ginza approached the judges' table wearing a dark cloud of fury. The instant replay confirmed the judges' decision, which darkened Ginza's brow even further.

No matter how many Wabesamas he ate for lunch or how dark Ginza's brow clouded, the fact remained—the system didn't allow two guys from the same stable to face each other. So even though Torakiba—whose roster pitted him against Wabesama tomorrow—had no losses this *basho*, either, which should theoretically make them even and destined to face off for the Cup, rules were rules. Rules dictated that Buck's whole existence was a lost cause.

For all his stout talk on the train, the truth was, unless Buck went head to head against that sharp-toothed freak, Chocho Ginza was doomed to be Torakiba's wife. His heart turned to wax and melted down around his internal organs.

Maybe he should just go home. He had enough cash saved up to buy a plane, not just a ticket. He might as well spend some of it. His parents were coming to watch him in a couple of days, and they'd understand. They never wanted him doing this in the first place anyway.

"Asagohan!" A reporter bipped along after Buck as he entered the double doors of the Kokugikan. "Now you have perfect record for this *basho*. Fourteen and zero! You compete for Emperor's Cup."

"That's real nice of you to take note. I'm doing my best." What he didn't want to explain, and shouldn't have to explain to a sports reporter of all people, was that he could never amass enough points to go for this tournament's Emperor's Cup.

"But you *must* compete. There is so much at stake, Baku."

No kidding. But he just wasn't the man to do it, it seemed. "I'll give a hundred and ten percent." Pat answers to the press—he was so sick of them. He headed for the bath house to get the chamomile oil washed out of his topknot, now shaped like a gingko leaf as part of his new rank, which was even more annoying to sleep on.

"But, Baku Coopah-*san!*"

"Oh, Tanaka, that's you?" Buck turned around and double blinked when he heard his given name approximation. Tanaka had gotten a haircut. Talk about prisoner of his hairdo—without the shock in front of his eyes he'd never be recognized anywhere. Buck fit the same category: if he dyed his own hair black, he could go incognito anywhere he wanted.

Buck tried to keep the tiredness out of his voice. "Don't write a story on the loser who doesn't know when to give up." Like General Custer. Or Rocky in the first film.

"You've got to listen to me. Chocho Ginza can still be yours."

Buck's motives were an open book to all of the world. He blushed crimson and stopped, as his ears pricked up.

"What do you mean? Torakiba has a perfect record this *basho* so far, and his roster pitted him against stronger men than my roster. That gives him more points. The end. Finito." Put his name on the list of the top ten most hopeless causes of all time. "Besides, I'll never go up against Torakiba. We're in the Kawaguchi stable together. We don't ever face each other. That's the rule. You should know that." Buck started walking again.

"Tiger Fang is strong, yes." Tanaka lowered his voice. "But what *you* don't know is if your *basho* points are even, they will pit you against each other to break the tie."

Buck caught his breath. Points weren't the same as the win-loss record. Points he might be able to manage. *If* Torakiba were to lose to Wabesame tomorow. "Even though we're in the same stable?"

"Yes. It's the only way that ever happens. And it has not happened since 1922 when Mushi battled Hazumatto. Not since 1922— until *now*, Baku."

Buck stopped walking right over a subway vent where it was warmer.

"Baku, baku, baku." Tanaka nodded like it was growing on him. "I like this new name. Destroyer of dreams! It is so much better than breakfast!"

Tanaka had that right. But was Tanaka right about the rules? If so, that was a game-changer. Especially if Torakiba's match-up against Wabesama this afternoon didn't go as the grand champion planned.

Because Buck had already beaten Wabesama on day three, and because the yokozuna could very possibly lose to the Estonian, a wisp of hope remained. Holy smoke. Now Buck realized that single win had unlocked the door for a potential miracle. For the first time in days, a spark of hope ignited in his chest. A win for Buck today against Kaminari—and the far outside chance of a loss by Torakiba to Wabesama—could mean the whole game, the whole *world* shifted for Buck.

"I saw this photo of you with Miss Chocho. Everyone has seen this online. She loves you, Baku. Do not let her down."

Photo? What photo? His heart clenched.

"I CAN'T BELIEVE YOU'RE HERE!" Buck embraced his mother, and she hugged him back, long and warm. It had been too long. His mom and dad were like a drink of cold, fresh water after months of sucking warm pond scum.

"What have you done with yourself?" His mom gave him the once-over a few times. "I hardly recognize you, son. I thought becoming a sumo wrestler might be, well—"

Clearly she hesitated over mentioning his weight. Hallelujah. Finally, someone with tact! After two years' plague of people constantly mentioning whether he'd gained or lost weight, he threw his arms around his mother's neck for joy. Crazy Japanese—sometimes they were the least tactful people on earth. Poor Ohimesama fielded I-see-your-acne-is-much-worse-today comments all the time.

They walked toward the lower chairs in the Kokugikan, where the Yoshidas were saving their seats. His eyes searched the filling room for Chocho. No sign of her yet.

"Sure, Ma. I've lost a little weight. Most guys start out smaller and have to put it on. Luckily, even though I was big, I still had good enough balance to even things out. Actually, some commentators say the weight was what gave me the advantage in my early bouts." They came up to where the Yoshidas were sitting.

"Commentators? What are you talking about?" His mom

pressed her hand to her heart. "You mean someone reports on these games you're in?"

"Sweetheart," Buck's dad interrupted, "it *is* the national sport of Japan, after all."

"And my buddy Hiro, here, is going to be one of the best sumo commentators of all time." Buck ruffled Hiro's hair. The kid beamed back up at him. The Yoshida parents and the older brother stood and bowed.

"I'm just glad we made it to see him compete on the final day. Luckily, Mr. Yoshida's son has filled me in on Buck's success. He says you could be a big winner this tourney." His dad smiled proudly. "Mr. Yoshida has been really impressed with your stick-to-itiveness in sumo. I don't know where Nangrimax—or your mother and I, for that matter—would be without your determination to succeed at this wrestling venture, son." He patted Buck firmly on the back.

"Now, what's this you're wearing?" Buck's mom fingered the collar of the *yukata*. "And who does your hair?"

Buck fell into a description of sumo life—with some choice exceptions. Hiro could explain the rest of the ins and outs of rankings later, including the big if of whether he and Torakiba would ultimately face off at the end of this tournament.

"Buck has fourteen wins, no losses!" Hiro enthused. "His score matches Torakiba's, and Torakiba is the grand champion!"

"Really? You're competing for the grand prize? Against a champ?"

Buck pulled back. "It's called the Emperor's Cup. And possibly." He didn't want to jinx himself. It was all based on Tanaka's theory anyway, which may or may not have merit. "It really depends on if I win today, and if my former training partner,"—how could he explain the concept of *senpai* to them—"loses."

"But that would put you one up from him, wouldn't it? Or are there weighted scores depending on rank?" Buck's dad got it. "Well, I have no doubts, son. You'll make it happen. You've always made us proud."

Wonder and ease and warmth flowed through Buck. Ever since he made this leap, he'd waited for this moment of their approval. His buttons would burst—if he were wearing any.

Just then, a familiar face appeared. Buck did a double-take as Reggie skipped up, beaming. His cuts had healed, even his neck. The Filipino wore the fancy silk kimono from Miss One Thousand Fall Leaves and a smile as wide as the Pecos. Buck introduced him to his parents, then to the pretty woman nestled under Reggie's arm.

"Here she is. What do you think, Buck? She agreed to be my wife."

"Wonderful!" Buck's mom beamed. "You will make a lovely bride." She asked the geisha about wedding plans while Buck pulled Reggie aside.

"So, you finally did it! When did this all happen?" Buck punched him in the arm.

"She came and found me in the hospital in Fukuoka, brought me all kinds of things to make me feel better, and then she said she didn't care if I was a professional or not. Before I knew it, I was down on one knee." Reggie swiped his hands down the silk kimono as they returned to his fiancée's side. Reggie took her by the hand and left to go spread the good news.

"And is there a special lady in your life, Buck?" His mom winked at him. "I mean, besides your dear old mom."

"Not yet, Mom."

How could he count Chocho as being in his life—no matter how desperately he ached for it, or how often he'd relived that kiss in the Nagoya park—when she could be another man's wife less than forty-eight hours from now?

His eyes scanned the crowd for her, hungry for a glimpse. Nothing. He ached.

"I have to go now." He hugged them goodbye, waved to Hiro, and made his way up the dim tunnel to the dressing rooms. He needed mental preparation to face his opponent: Kaminari, the Lightning-Fast Man from Northern Japan. His bout came near the end of the day, before Torakiba's match with Wabesama. He bit the inside of his cheek and swilled Calpis backstage for three hours while the lower-ranked *rikishi* shoved each other around down front.

At last, Buck climbed onto the clay stage with a trepidation he hadn't felt in months. *Breathe, breathe.* This win mattered the same as every other win in his whole career. It was a cumulative thing. Every win was necessary. But if he lost to Kaminari, and if Torakiba defeated Wabesama, it was all over. He could kiss Chocho good-bye.

Or not. In fact, he'd never see her again, let alone kiss her.

It weighed on him like an anvil.

BUCK'S MATCH AGAINST KAMINARI BEGAN with the ceremonial ritual. Buck stomped hard and angry, warning off those evil sumo spirits. Demons out! Begone!

In a bolt, Kaminari zapped toward Buck, his fat hands slapping at Buck's chest, shoulders, face. Each contact stung. Buck slapped back as hard as he dared. Kaminari backed away. Buck won the slapping contest. Yes!

Buck lowered a shoulder and hurtled at him like a missile, but Kaminari dodged. Really, the guy was fast.

Buck didn't let him off easy, though, and he shot after his

opponent. Kaminari's feet of speed were stepping outside the ring after this shove for sure.

But no. Instead, Kaminari wheeled around and crouched. Buck lurched to a halt and planted his feet. Kaminari came at him, head down, like a bullet. Buck sniffed. He had *this* technique under total control. Before Kaminari's head could reach its target—Buck's ribcage—Buck reached out a steady arm and, with his palm, thrust Kaminari's head straight down. Mr. Lightning sounded a lot like thunder when his forehead thudded onto the clay.

"*Kachikoshi*, Baku!"

The crowd flew into a frenzy. Shouts of "Emperor's Cup" and "Baku" came chanting across the breeze. Buck smiled, bowed, and searched the crowd for Chocho, but the spotlight blinded him. He did see his mother grasping her throat, though, and his dad beaming beside her. He waved to them then stepped off the stage and went up the gangway to breathe.

ONLY ONE BOUT REMAINED. WABESAMA versus Torakiba. Buck clenched and unclenched his jaw. He calculated again and again the JSA's scoring algorithm. It had to be correct. Buck had beaten Wabesama already. Now, if Torakiba won today's final bout against the steroid king, his prize was Chocho. If Wabesama won, everything went up in the air, because a win for Wabesame would make Torakiba and Buck's point totals equal. Equal points between two *rikishi* from the same stable could go any which way the JSA decided. They held Buck's entire future in their hands. They'd either allow him to compete for Chocho, or they'd give it to the higher-ranked wrestler—the *yokozuna*—by default. It boiled down to the JSA's decision—*if* Torakiba lost to Wabesama. Which was doubtful. The champ was the champ for a reason. For a lot of reasons

Buck stood in the *hanamichi* and bit his nails—the inside of his cheek hurt too much to keep chewing there. If he were a drinking man, he could use a stiff one right now to calm his nerves. Instead, he'd taken a walk outside where rain was falling and turning the sidewalk into a sheet of ice. Now he was back to watch fate unfold.

Wabesama and Torakiba approached the *dohyo*. The crowd sat in silent deference while the champs performed the choreographic stomps and spins, spits and waving. They both wore the black *mawashi* of the champion level, with the dozens of white rickrack win tassels dangling from their belts. Between them existed over fifteen years of sumo experience. Despite the prowess of his opponent, Torakiba exhibited no fear.

It began. The two powerhouses slammed into one another with all their force. Heads locked, and both men pushed with mighty torque. Veins came bursting from Torakiba's neck. Shove, shove, shove. Wabesama edged closer and closer to the out-of-bounds line. Torakiba moved toward victory, toward wealth and fame and marriage to Chocho. Buck gritted his teeth and sent a thousand prayers lofting heavenward, willing Wabesama to power.

Suddenly, Wabesama wriggled out of the headlock and twisted free. The steroids kicked in, and the Estonian scuttled around behind Torakiba. With a flat palm, he skewered the grand champ in the back. The force sent Torakiba reeling around and around, falling in slow motion, his elbow grazing the clay. He dropped with a swish-clunk onto his side. Buck felt the quake all the way up the *hanamichi*.

Victory, Wabesama!

Buck nearly swallowed his tongue. His breath constricted.

The crowd cheered and jeered, mocking the *yokozuna* for getting whupped. The hubbub lasted a couple of minutes.

All Buck could think about was the final win-loss record: Torakiba fourteen and one, Buck fifteen and zero. His heart began to rev like NASCAR in the summer. If Tanaka was right, Buck *could* really compete for the Emperor's Cup. In fifteen minutes.

Where was Chocho? Was she even in the stands?

The announcer boomed over the din of the crowd, "Final match for Emperor's Cup. Torakiba versus Baku. Fifteen minutes." The audience went crazy, and Buck's blood pressure made him go momentarily deaf. It was really going to happen. He was going to face Torakiba at last.

Torakiba descended the stage and came thundering up the *hanamichi* toward Buck. Buck collected himself and steeled his gaze. Torakiba's eyes burned back, huffing from his gargantuan but losing effort. "You started this sport too old. Too fat. You were soft. I wanted to break you. And I still will, when I face you in the *dohyo* at last." He sneered, staring Buck down. "You may be Baku now, but you will not take my dream."

Buck refused to blink. He kept his breathing steady. They locked eyes for another dragging moment, and sparks flew. Buck would never let the tiger sink his fangs into Chocho. Buck's eyes followed Torakiba's stalk up the ramp never straying until his nemesis vanished into the dressing rooms.

Buck stomped down a couple of deserted hallways to decompress and brew before turning back. Out of nowhere reporters swarmed him at the mouth of the ramp to the *dohyo*. The crowd's roar was deafening, and the air smelled of fermented soy and fish. A dozen microphones and TV cameras were thrust in his face.

"Baku! We likes your new sumo name. You are first *maegashira* in so many years to compete for Emperor's Cup. How does you feel?"

"Baku! You now go fight for Emperor's Cup against former *senpai*. How can you fight against you best friend?"

"Baku! This first time big *America-jin* with the blond hair is maybe final day champion and winner to the Emperor's Cup, and it is you. How do you like that?"

"Baku! If you wins this big Emperor's Cup today, you will marry with Japanese woman Miss Chocho Ginza. Can you love Japanese woman?"

At last, a question he could answer with confidence. "With all my heart."

Suddenly, from the dark end of the *hanamichi* tunnel, a snarl erupted, and Ginza-*sama* himself loomed forth. With a wave of his hand and a piercing scowl he dismissed the fray. The reporters and cameramen melted away, leaving only Buck in his iron grip.

"Walk with me, Baku." The command brought back a thousand memories of being followed, being dragged into dark alleys, being punched with brass knuckles, being kicked in the face by ninjas, and watching his best friend being slashed in the throat.

"If you have something to say, you can say it right here." Buck raised his chin.

A few lingering reporters inched their way up behind the black kimono, but Buck didn't let his eye stray toward them, keeping his gaze locked on Ginza. Smoldering in the official's face he saw hatred and fury unlike any he'd ever seen before. Ginza's eyebrows became one angry monobrow.

"You refuse to accept well-meant advice. You continue to defy the tradition of sumo, and insist on defiling it with your foreign ideas and genetics." Venom dripped from every word. "Like every American, you think you have a monopoly on intelligence. You think whatever *you* do is right."

"On the contrary, sir. I try to do what's right no matter the situation." Buck used his most humble form of Japanese to make this reply, but he didn't let his eyes waver from Ginza's stare.

"Bah!" Ginza barked. "You and your integrity! This integrity is what led you to defile my daughter in the dead of night?"

"Whoa there, partner. Just a darn minute. I never did one ounce of dishonor to your daughter." He reverted to English in his gut-reaction. "We had a cup of tea together. We went for a walk in a beautiful Japanese garden. If you call that dishonor, I say you're no true Japanese man yourself."

Ginza's mouth began to foam at the corners. "Warning after warning I sent you to stay away from her!" he hissed, the foam more apparent.

"Warnings? Like the man you sent to break my nose before the Nagoya *basho* year before last? Or the huge delicious tray of special Japanese fruit you poisoned for me after last year's Nagoya *basho*?" Buck heard his voice rising a pitch with an edge of irony. "Oh, wait, or maybe you're talking about the warning you gave me when you sent three men with knives to stab me on the docks at Fukuoka two months ago, the attack that broke my tall American nose and nearly killed my friend, Futokaba, when your henchmen slashed his throat. Do you feel good about that? About almost killing an innocent and honorable bystander? Or because we're *gaijin* we don't matter?" If Buck's eyes were lasers he could sear Ginza's face with them. "Just like your daughter's happiness doesn't matter to you."

Ginza's eyes blazed.

Meanwhile, the press had crept in closer and closer. Extended microphones began to pick up some of the discussion. Ginza, too intense, didn't notice.

"My daughter matters. She is everything in my plan."

"Oh, right. She's a pawn in your measly chess game. You don't love her."

"Love! What do you know about love? *Gaijin!*" The sneer deepened. "You just want the Ginza fortune, and to foul our country and our sacred sumo."

"Ha! You have it so wrong. I don't want a single yen of your

Ginza fortune. It doesn't mean zilch to me. Keep every *hyaku en* of it. But the daughter of yours, the one you don't deserve, means everything. You yank out a contract and write your precious Torakiba's name on the line as your heir right now. See if I care. But if you dare to take your daughter out of what you promised for the winner, you'll break your word and have all of Japan hating you for the rest of your days." Buck lowered his voice to a threatening whisper. "You'll be a liar in their eyes. They won't forgive or forget that disgrace. Your shame will seep so deep into your bones you can never get it out. You'll never set foot in the sumo world again. The Japanese people will see to that."

"It's true!" a familiar voice shouted, and Buck glanced up to see Tanaka. Ginza swung around to face the reporter in shock. "All of Japan is waiting for the wedding of the winner and your daughter. It will be national sumo holiday. If you promise it and take it away, we will never forgive. Shame will heap onto your head for being a liar." Tanaka wore a look of triumph.

Ginza fidgeted, his temples pulsing in and out. He paced a tight circle of fierce unhappiness. Finally, he exploded at Buck. "You will lose today! Torakiba will destroy you!" He balled his hands into fists and shook them in Buck's face. The words came out as a hiss, but it signaled deflation of his determination.

"You ought to know this, Ginza." Buck jutted his chin. "*Chocho* is the prize. If I defeat Torakiba, you will have no choice but to give her to me. But don't fear for her happiness. Chocho is the reason for all I have done, every hour of every practice and every tournament of every day I've been in sumo. It's been for her. Now watch me win." Buck marched back down the *hanamichi*.

"Baku!" Ginza shouted after him. "If you attempt to take from me what is dearest to me, I will take from you your dearest treasure."

Buck stopped in his tracks but didn't turn around, his ears pricked to listen.

Ginza continued, "Your parents are here. Lose today or lose your parents."

Buck's fists clenched. More than anything he longed to haul off and flatten this meathead. He spun around and faced the threat. Words turned to flames, burning his throat.

"Ginza—" Before Buck could finish, the familiar loudspeaker shouted his name, *"Baku!"* and he stopped dead in his charge toward the old man. It was time—his final bout against Torakiba. His very soul began to tear at its seams. Ginza was threatening his parents now—their very lives. Their lives versus Chocho's happiness. How could he make this choice?

"Baku!" The loudspeaker called again. Buck could not protect both of them. Something had to give.

And then something budged.

His stop created a vacuum of space between him and Ginza, and the waiting press swarmed forward to fill it. Questions fired like gunshots, and Buck eased back on his heels, catching his breath and letting the flame lower.

"Ginza-*san*! Ginza-*san*!" Reporters thronged the old man. "Is what we just heard true, that you hired *yakuza* to kill Baku as far back as Nagoya *basho* two seasons ago?"

"Is it also true your hitman slit the throat of crowd favorite Futokaba the Filipino?"

"Ginza-*san*! Did we just hear you threaten Mr. and Mrs. Cooper-*san* who are our American guests here to see their son compete for the Emperor's Cup? What do you intend to do to them? Should they hire protection to save them from your connections in the *yakuza*?"

"Do you like being connected to the Japanese mafia? Will the

JSA allow you to stay a sumo official when they find out these connections?"

"Is it true, what we are guessing, that your fruit basket to Baku was the cause of the poisoning of hundreds of wild birds in downtown Tokyo last summer?"

Buck marched toward the *dohyo* and Torakiba. He'd left Ginza to the wolves.

二
十
五

TORA! TORA! TORA!
JANUARY, TOKYO

"Final match. Torakiba, Baku." The announcer's voice bounced off the high walls and all around the open steel beams of the Kokugikan's ceiling. Buck lifted his eyes, as if he could see the sound ricocheting above. Torakiba versus Buck, face to face in the ring. His heart throbbed. The announcer continued, "This match is unprecedented. Not since 1922 have two from the same stable faced off for the Emperor's Cup after a tie score. Never before has a former *senpai* faced a former *kohai* for the championship. Never has a blond American stepped foot in the ring to fight for the biggest prize in sumo—and a *maegashira* rank at that. If he wins, it will make sumo history."

And if Buck threw up, it would really add to the drama.

Buck thundered down the *hanamichi,* focused on the crowd. Reggie and Dude stepped in front of him.

"Hey, buddy. Good luck out there." Dude gave him a man-hug.

"Thanks. Can you guys do me a favor? Go flank my parents, eh? One of you on either side?" Buck slapped them each on the shoulder, relieved he could trust the two biggest bodyguards the *yakuza* would ever encounter.

There, a stone's throw away, sat his parents, their eyes bright with wonder at the surroundings, the drums, the flags, the pomp and circumstance. He prayed they were safe. Beside them, young Hiro Yoshida's mouth jabbered in perpetual motion. If only he could see Chocho. One glance of her face—

An official nudged him. Time to climb the *dohyo*. Across the ring, slapping his shiny skin and looking as mean and gentlemanly as ever, Torakiba frowned, his upside down sausage more pronounced. Buck stomped, stretched, twisted. He was ready for this battle. Sort of.

The *yobidashi* appeared, waving the fan. The crowd sounded like the tarmac of an airport, whirring and screaming. Buck blocked it all out—pressing himself into silence with his concentration. The required ceremonial moves began, and all the lights around him went dark, except for the spotlight. Buck saw nothing but his opponent across from him.

A sudden vision of the last two years flashed past him—a slide show set on high speed, showing all the most intense moments of his unexpected career. His first step in the *dohyo* as comic sumo, the faces of the Kawaguchi brothers when they recruited him, the fear in his mother's eyes when he told her he was taking their offer, the elation on Hiro's face, his first encounter with Torakiba, the beating in the alley, seeing Chocho on the street, at the parade, at the party, and then at the tea shop, the stepping stones in the park, all the matches against other *rikishi*, his friendships, his allies, his enemies, standing up to Sobakubi and Butaniku and Ginza, becoming so much more of a man than he'd ever guessed he could become—all these moments culminated here, now.

This moment.

He'd never fought Torakiba, even in practice; however, he'd watched him every day his first year in Japan. He knew Torakiba's techniques by heart, better than any other *rikishi* in the league. And more—Buck knew the secret weapon Torakiba harbored: the *mitokorozeme* technique.

And Buck was ready for that should Torakiba pull it out of his arsenal.

With deadly accuracy, Torakiba bent forward, curved his back and charged toward him. "Chocho *no tame!*" Torakiba shouted. *For Chocho!*

Buck screamed against it and hurtled forward. They slammed into one another like a car wreck, instantly putting each other in headlocks. Torakiba's breath fell hot against Buck's ear; it sounded like an angry bear's bawling. Buck squeezed the man's neck, his ribcage. Torakiba squeezed back harder. Buck pressed up onto his toes, pushing forward with all his might, driving his opponent backward.

It lasted a full twenty seconds. The painful grip broke, slid apart on each other's sweat. Buck gasped to catch his breath.

Torakiba immediately hooked his right heel behind Buck's and yanked on his oft-injured right arm, trying to pull him down. The signature move. Buck had expected it—had been expecting it since the first time he witnessed a sumo match—and with a deft move twisted fast and lifted the hooked heel out of danger. Yes!

Torakiba didn't stop. In an instant the total weight of the enormous powerhouse shoved Buck backward, the *yokozuna*'s shoulder slamming full force into Buck's white chest. Pain ripped through him, and he heard a snap. His clavicle.

His right shoulder seared from an old injury to his deltoid muscle. It burned all the way down into hi ribcage. The clavicle might pop through his skin. His chest rattled like the bottom of a bag of potato chips.

Buck couldn't quit now, no matter the pain. He gritted his teeth and lunged back at the *yokozuna* only to reel against the brick wall that was Torakiba. Buck's head snapped backward, pulling all the muscles in his neck, making even the edge of his tongue tingle. Buck saw stars.

The titan force sent him backwards—at least the top half of his body—into a near backbend. But Buck's feet held firm—the traction from his weight pressed down on them. He gripped his toes against the ground. Torakiba had the strength of ten other *rikishi* put together.

From his hips down, Buck kept it all in one balanced location on the clay. The impact made tremors from his hips to his knees to his ankles. An eternity passed before he could sidestep the force, but he did it, and Torakiba swished by without grabbing Buck's torso or *mawashi*.

Buck twisted back around, ready for another assault, but Torakiba paused to regain his own balance. Buck seized the moment and struck, coming at the *yokozuna's* unguarded back. He was a T-Rex going after a wounded Brontosaurus. At last, he saw Torakiba not as predator but prey.

They collided, skin slapping.

With full strength Buck clenched his arms around the back of Torakiba's ribcage, and twisted to the right. He wrapped his left leg around Torakiba's and drove it forward at maximum force, hoping to send the *yokozuna* toppling to the ground in a thunderous face plant.

But it was no good. Torakiba had already wriggled free, turning around for Buck's *mawashi*. Buck saw desperation in the champion's eyes, and it made Buck stronger. He could take him. One more move and this *yokozuna* was going down.

A voice came hissing from near the officials' table. "*Mitokorozeme*," it commanded. Buck knew that voice. *Ginza*.

Then it happened: three things at once. Torakiba reached around Buck's left thigh and made a grab to lift it. At the same time, he thrust his other leg hard against the inside of Buck's right knee, pulling him off balance just as Torakiba's head began to barrel into Buck's chest. It knocked the wind out of Buck as he felt himself topple backward, a collective whisper rushed through the crowd: *"Mitokorozeme!"*

So, this was what it felt like to get triple-whammied by that lost technique—awful. Buck had never felt so wobbly in all of his life. Earthquake-worthy unbalance rippled through him as he struggled to gain purchase on the ground with his single standing leg.

Mitokorozeme. But Buck had this one. He was prepared, or so he thought. All those months of imagining what it would feel like to combat it never compared with reality. His toes scraped backward across the clay—and unless he could right himself and force his core forward, it would be all over.

In the midst of desperation, Buck's eyes fell on Chocho in the crowd. He shouldn't have looked out there; he should have stayed firmly focused on the task. Perhaps it had been accidental. Perhaps not. Still, he caught a glimpse of her, the way she bated her breath and held a hand to her heart.

Then, their eyes met.

That same electrical pulse he felt the first time he saw her in the street surged through him. His eyes conducted a current between the two of them. He felt her. He felt her soul. Her lips parted to form a single word: *Please.* It was the only encouragement Buck needed.

Reinvigorated, Buck hoisted his core forward, pushing Torakiba's head hard into his own clavicle, the broken bone forgotten. Torakiba's head snapped backward, and Buck wrenched both hands free, using them to twist Torakiba's arms away from his waist and leg, down and away. It broke the bruising grip on Buck's thigh, which brought his leg down hard, planting it firmly on the soil. Buck's colossal tread would've sent any existing demons in the *dohyo* scurrying away.

Torakiba, caught off guard by the retaliation, stumbled

backward, his face shocked with alarm. Buck strode into the *yoko-zuna* with power, resolve, strength. He was a stomping, Tasmanian devil, a snarling, whirling dervish of pain-inflicting force.

Before Torakiba knew what was happening, Buck had him in a chokehold. Mass, gravity, torgue, thrust—the elements of sumo power combined to assist Buck in his attack. All two hundred and eighty-five pounds of solid muscle on Buck's frame lurched into action. Buck appreciated each and every ounce of his body as it bulldozed Torakiba backward. Torakiba resisted with ferocity, but Buck made use of his every sinew and attacked, shoving, mauling, wrestling. Torakiba retreated as Buck pressed forward, claiming the upper hand.

This bout could last all night.

Then, in a flash of inspiration, Buck knew what to do: *uwatenage*. It was the technique he'd used the very first time he'd set foot in this ring. Using every remaining iota of strength, Buck heaved Torakiba downward at a sharp angle and turned away. Torakiba's legs flew out from under him and his shoulders lurched sideways, his gargantuan body suspended in mid-air. Buck spun around and stared as it hovered horizontally, Torakiba's eyes wide with surprise. Time stood curiously still for what seemed like a lifetime—before the body came slamming hard onto the ground, first the hips, then the shoulders, followed by the rest of Torakiba's defeated form. The *yokozuna* shuddered and lay still.

"Victory, Baku!" the announcer shouted over the roar, penetrating even Buck's concentrating ear.

"Victory, Baku!" The crowd exploded. It sang, high and long. It penetrated his soul. "Victory, Baku!" *Buck, the Victorious!*

Buck fell to his knees and clasped his hands to his heart, his head thrown back in gratitude to the heavens above. His heart pounded hot, and he shook with exhaustion.

He'd won.

THE CROWD WENT BERSERK. *ZABUTON* seat cushions flew into the air and onto the *dohyo* in celebration of the triumph of a low-ranked *rikishi* over the *yokozuna*. Torakiba's head bowed, crushed by his defeat.

Buck's parents and the Yoshidas jumped to their feet, cheering in fan mania. Buck heard Dude's voice magically sailing over all the shouts, "Way to go, Buck! Awesome, dude!" He saw Reggie lean back and pound his chest with a Tarzan yell.

Eventually, Torakiba creaked to his feet. Buck reached out a hand to help him up, which Torakiba accepted with a gracious nod. Once on his feet again, Torakiba bowed.

"You have been a worthy opponent, Baku. You deserve the title Gentleman *Rikishi*." Torakiba clapped Buck on the shoulder.

Buck bowed in return. "Torakiba. There's a reason you're the *yokozuna*. You have a champion's heart."

Torakiba held his head high, but his voice came low and dejected. "I know what happens next. She will be yours." His eyes dropped. The last word caught in Torakiba's throat, and he bowed to the audience in each direction before stepping off the platform. Maybe Torakiba was like every other guy on earth—he would be lying if he wasn't at least a little in love with Chocho Ginza. For a split second Buck pitied Torakiba for what he'd lost.

A JSA official hoisted himself onto the stage. A hush settled the crowd, and in uneven layers they returned to their seats for the announcement. Buck's breath bated. He didn't dare look in Chocho's direction for fear he couldn't contain his emotions.

"Ladies and gentlemen. We will now present the grand prize, the Emperor's Cup." The official bowed and the crowd pealed in joy. "After the awards ceremony, JSA Grand Sumo Association Official Ginza-*sama* will come to the platform for a final presentation. We await that very much."

Yes, we do. Buck's eyes glanced Chocho's direction. Tears

streamed down her cheeks, her shoulders shook. Panic flashed through him.

From the long *hanamichi* hallway emerged the most enormous bowl of metal Buck could ever imagine. All these months he'd seen it on TV from back in the dressing room, but never up close and in person. A family of four could use the trophy's basin as a hot tub. It took two officials to hoist the Cup onto a dais on the stage where Buck stood. With the help of an official in a yellow kimono, a man in a business suit presented it to Buck, who bowed and accepted it with all the grace he could muster at the moment.

The trophy weighed as much as he did. Well, almost. He gave his best grin and bowed to the audience. Then, in a bursting release of pent up emotion, Buck threw his arms around the neck of the trophy and gave it a big kiss. Using all his remaining muscle power, he raised it aloft, holding the whole hunk of silver and wood over his head, and shook it in joy.

The crowd erupted.

Buck set the trophy down, careful not to smash any toes, and the moment fled. All he could think of now was the real prize in question.

Ginza glowered at the edge of the *dohyo*. A look at his face, and Buck rumbled inside. Worries formed hot tremors in his stomach. Ginza couldn't be trusted. No matter the cost, Ginza would act in his own self-interest, shoving aside everyone else's safety and prosperity like a *yokozuna* before his prey.

The crowd continued to roar, although the volume seemed to have gone down. Ginza stood frowning but ready to rise up and crown the victor. Or not.

Suddenly, Buck knew what he had to do. Even if it ruined everything.

IKIRU: TO LIVE
JANUARY–JUNE. TOKYO AND TEXAS

He bit his cheek again, right where it was already raw. The pain sharpened his focus and gave him the nerve to do what he needed to do: cut Ginza off.

In a surge of awkward bravado, Buck snatched the microphone out of the JSA official's hand before he could pass it to Ginza. The audience gasped and hushed.

Ginza halted in his tracks, his face frowned into deep crevices. The mic-seizure was the first brazenly American thing Buck had done in a while—other than kissing the Emperor's Cup, which was just the giddiness of a glorious moment. It was strange being back in his American skin, but it was time.

Buck cleared his throat, too loudly, into the microphone, and the echo of it resounded through the hall. The crowd's remaining whispers hushed.

In his best Japanese—rough but passable—Buck spoke, "Ginza-san. I am deeply grateful to receive the Emperor's Cup in this January *basho*." Buck used the most humble forms of Japanese. "Last autumn, you made an announcement. Tonight's winner would receive another precious prize, which is your daughter." Buck left out the Ginza Corp stock offer. "I believe you have come to honor me with that gift." The crowd applauded. Ginza's face was a stone, and Buck's stomach twisted in a hard knot.

"However, Ginza-*san*, there is a problem." Buck's knees quivered. "Although I revere your daughter—" Buck choked. Love, it was a risky word in any language, and extremely risky in Japanese. *I can't believe I am doing this.* Color drained from his face as the words tumbled out. "Your daughter is like her name: she is the butterfly and belongs to no one but herself. If she wants to marry me, it must be her *own* choice. She deserves happiness. If she chooses me, she will come and find me."

Buck's soul wrenched. He'd said it. His kneecap began a tremor that threatened to bring his whole frame down. He sought her in the audience, but the faces swam together. The truth was, if he simply left, she could go on and live her life in peace. She could find herself a nice, native Japanese man and live happily ever after. This was the merciful thing to do, for so many reasons.

And he despised himself for it.

Now, Buck dropped the mic and spoke only to Ginza, whose mouth hung agape. "Please, sir. She's not a product to be bought or sold. She's a woman. She's your daughter. I love her with all my heart." There, he'd said it. It echoed and filled the immensity of the Kokugikan. "Please do the right thing here." He stared into Ginza's eyes, pleading, but they stared back, hard as ice.

It left Buck no choice. He steeled himself to do the most shocking thing of the night—possibly the most shocking thing the gods of sumo had seen in all their millennia of godhood.

First, Buck gave the audience a wave and the biggest smile he could muster, his parting gift. Then, with trembling hand he reached over to the stand where all the awards were sitting. From the stand where it was perched, Buck slid forth the ceremonial sword—the *katana,* sharpest sword of a samurai, sharp enough to slice through human hair.

It glinted in the spotlight. When his hand touched it, the audience gave a collective gasp. He raised it from its setting and brandished it. The steel sang. In his mind Buck heard the soft *hum* of a light saber as he swung the *katana* over the *dohyo*.

A terrible, heavy silence fell across the entire Kokugikan.

Buck raised the sword high above his head. It was surreal. He must look like a cartoon with just the loincloth, the blond hair, and the sword aloft: *By the power of Greyskull!* With his left hand he lifted his topknot, stretching it high. With his right, he gripped the sword. He'd better not miss.

Every eye in the stadium lasered in on Buck. Women covered their mouths in fear and horror.

Buck let the sword drop with a single swish. His topknot fell onto the *dohyo* at his feet. *Sayonara.*

BUCK WAITED AT THE KOKUGIKAN'S doorway.

"That's okay, Mom and Dad. I'll meet you back at your hotel room in a little while. I'm waiting for someone." He spoke the words like an automaton, numbness buzzing through his head. Exhaustion racked him.

She didn't show.

The fans filtered out through the front doors. Buck signed a hundred autographed handprints, faked his way through smiles and photographs with scores of fans. Some even wept on the lapel of his *yukata.* He wanted to comfort them, to be the jolly blond giant for them, but his soul was an empty cavity of ache.

She didn't come.

The last fan trickled out the door, and a janitor approached.

"*Gokurosama desu,*" Buck robotically congratulated him for working so hard and being so diligent, as was the custom.

"I am turning out all lights now, locking doors. You go home, Baku," the janitor said. But Buck stood firm.

"I'll just be a minute."

"She is not coming, Baku. I saw her take a taxi many long time ago, right after match."

The words sent a jolt of despair through him. She didn't come, and she wasn't coming. She didn't choose him. He lifted his hand and ran it across his shorn hair, all silky from the chamomile oil but spiky from the sword cut. He wished he'd kept the sword and sliced it into his belly.

BUCK CLUTCHED HIS UGLY STRIPED duffel bag, the one he brought his first day in the *dohyo* a lifetime ago. None of the clothes in it fit him anymore. He hugged it to his chest against the cold of the taxicab. He and his parents lurched through the Tokyo streets on their way to the airport.

In spirit, Buck was still waiting outside the Kokugikan, where he stood the night before in swirling gales of snowflakes. Two hours in the snow with only his *yukata* as a shield against the chill, he hummed, *She'll come, she'll be here.* With every face that appeared and every body that passed, he knew the next one could be Chocho, coming around the corner to tell him she was ready to run off with him, or to at least say something. Anything.

"What I don't understand is why a haircut meant you quit." His mom craned around from the front seat. "Or why that girl shrieked and ran out of the arena. I noticed her earlier—so pretty. People really get caught up in things, don't they?"

Buck was too blank to reply. Shriek or no shriek, she hadn't come.

"What I don't understand," Buck's dad said in his seat beside him, "is what Yoshida's son kept saying about you. That you're the face of cow piss? Son, is there a cultural joke I'm not getting?"

"Hank, I'm sure there are thousands of things about Buck's life over here that we'll never really understand." His mom reached for his dad's hand, and they shared a look.

Buck tried to swallow, but his mouth was too dry. His eyes were dry from the wind. They scraped against his eyelids when he blinked, so he shut them. He huddled back against the leather seat and hunched against the cold, letting a tingling cocoon of numbness encase him, one he didn't know how long it might take to emerge from. Weeks, maybe months. Maybe never.

He'd gambled everything. And lost.

"WELL, SON, I GUESS THE first thing we need to do is get you some real clothes. That dress is not going to work here in Texas." Buck's dad pulled the car out of the parking garage at the airport and headed for the freeway. It was warmer here. "You'll get beat up faster than you can say Sam Houston in that thing."

"I can handle myself, Dad." Buck hefted his mom's suitcase from the trunk.

Even in the comfort of home, their voices came at him from down a long, hollow tube. Buck needed some sleep. The world here, all tract housing and sky, looked stark and briar-filled and strange.

Buck retreated into his man-cave to think. And think. And think. Days passed, thinking. Still no plan. He couldn't find a plan. Not without her.

He found the picture of the two of them online. It wasn't hard. He printed it out and pinched it between his fingertips, lying in fetal position on his bed and staring hour after hour at the two of them kissing on the stepping stone in the park.

A week passed. From outside the bedroom door he could hear anxious whispers, "Well, he's home now. What's he going to do?" which mirrored his own sentiments. Fortunately, both the internal and external pressure to make a move exerted equally on him, so he didn't burst. He had to think some more.

He needed a job. He didn't know how to get a job. His résumé was too weird. Nothing seemed right. He was fit for anything and nothing. He needed to work, but if it meant Eaglestone or anyplace like it, he'd rather pass a kidney stone.

He needed Chocho.

Another week passed, the jetlag and travel headache and "eau de Japan" scent wore off, and Buck stood in front of the mirror and stared at the crisp oxford shirt and dark jeans, the size fifteen loafers and thirty-eight inch belt. He ran a hand through his hair. Shorn. Gone. For the first time in six years he'd lost the long brassy waves. Everything felt lighter. Even his head.

"Really, son. Make yourself a to-do list. It's time to get yourself going again." His mother came in early in the morning and pulled back the curtains. She looked surprised to see him showered and dressed. "Wow, the haircut looks good." She assessed him with her eyes. "All of you looks good."

All of him felt good. At least on the outside. He might not ever feel okay on the inside again, but he'd have to keep breathing.

"Anything you need me to do for you today, Mom?" He shoved his wallet in his back pocket. It was nice to have pockets again.

"Great of you to ask, Buck." Genuine pleasure sparkled in his mom's eyes—her son was back at last. "There's a box in the basement of stuff your job sent over a year or so ago. I'm heading over to Aunt Phyllis's."

"Baseball? Already?" Buck didn't think spring training started until the end of February. His mom and Aunt Phyllis were diehards. It was probably where Buck got it.

"We're getting online to order our tickets together. There's a three game series against the Astros in June and we don't want to miss any of that. Do you want to come over there with me?"

Buck chewed a fingernail. "I think I'll go through that box in the basement. But do me a favor, would you?"

LATER, IN THE DANK OF his parents' basement, among the piles of boxes that contained his childhood and his parents' entire married life, plus a few dozen boxes containing his grandparents' lives as well, Buck rummaged for the Eaglestone box. The single dangling light bulb made his dad's makeshift lab along the south wall look almost mad-scientist-like. He was glad his dad could now afford a formal lab with actual lighting, thanks to Prime Minister Saito.

At last, he located the box labeled "Mr. Buck" with his parents' address. It was in Alison Turner's handwriting, with her signature purple Sharpie marker. Strange, his heart didn't even bother to skip a beat when he saw the lettering. He lifted the lid.

Inside the box were a few personal items: a dead philodendron houseplant in a terra cotta pot; some books; the before and after photos he'd doctored and left in his bottom drawer. Great. He could see everyone in that office passing those around and getting a real laugh. Funny how he now weighed close to that "after" picture of himself. Then again, chances were nobody passed those pictures around. Nobody would have bothered to notice him then, even to joke at his expense. A memory of Ranjit's face made his lip curl.

But what was he going to do? It wasn't like he could take all of his sumo winnings and slip away into retirement somewhere, even though he could afford to. He was twenty-six, and he had more energy than he'd ever had. He needed to do something—something active. Something fulfilling.

Then, under the *Rock Hard Abs* book, he saw his answer. In a flash he chugged up the stairs two at a time, yanked the yellow phone off the wall and dialed his Aunt Phyllis's number.

"Hey, Mom?" He gripped the picture of himself at his grandparents' farm and stared at the blue skies and rolling fields and his own happy face. "Do you think Uncle Joe would like to get back to his landscaping business full time?"

"HON, I'VE GOT YOUR AUNT Phyllis in the truck with the motor running. Are you finished yet?" His mom called to him up the stairs of the old farmhouse. "I don't want to miss any of the game. You've missed the last three."

Buck was upstairs in the bathroom putting on his jeans and shirt. It took until just ten minutes ago to get the water pressure right in the sprinkler pipes so the fifty acres of alfalfa in the field west of the house would get their irrigation turn. June was dry in Texas outside Midlothian where his grandparents' ranch lay. *His* ranch now, and water turns mattered.

"Sorry, Mom. I know the opening pitch is important to you." He checked his teeth after towel-drying his hair. The size eighteen neck of this dress shirt hung a little loose. Sixteen-hour days of farm work with no Charlie Unger's barbecue for fifty miles, was starting to take a real toll on his waistline. And his neckline. And all of his other lines. But it meant he could ride the horses out to check the sprinkler lines.

A big slice of heaven.

But not the whole pie. Like a guy who lost a limb or an eye who always felt the absence of the missing body part, he'd learned to cope. Life had to go on, not as pleasant or fulfilling as it might have been with Chocho at his side, but he was dealing with the new normal.

"Come on, Buck. It's the Astros series. Your Aunt Phyllis is going to wet her pants if'n we don't get going." Her voice trailed off and her jaw fell open as Buck appeared at the top of the stairs and smiled down at his mom. "Well, shut my mouth. You look like some kind of surfer god, Buck. Blond, all tan and trim. What's the matter? Too busy farming and no time to get the grocery shopping done?" She gave him a hug when he got to the bottom of the stairs and headed out to Aunt Phyllis's truck. "Well, I left a peach pie in your refrigerator, so there's no excuse not to eat. Peaches right off our tree."

That sounded great. Fresh food, fresh air, and fresh start as owner of a big Texas farm. Well, small by Texan standards, only six hundred acres, but he loved the early mornings—the wide fields and the hard work—and the sky, broad above him every day. And the horses—Rosie and Ninety-Nine were liking their new corral mates his Calpis earnings had bought. Those funds also paid off the mortgage on his grandparents' farm. He was as happy as he ever might be, under the circumstances.

A half hour later, Buck held his mom's arm as she climbed the stairs to their seats at Rangers Stadium in downtown Arlington. Summer heat pulsed off the concrete outside in the parking lot, but here, over the left field, the cool of the grass with its perfect hash-mark mow lines wafted fresh breezes. It smelled like summer. Popcorn, hot dogs, the corny guy on the baseball organ. "Charge!" the gathering crowd shouted after the organist's fanfare.

"I'm so glad you decided to get season tickets, Buck. You ought to bring a date one of these times so the other seat doesn't go empty. Lots of girls would go with y'all. Give my neighbor girl a call. Not the sharpest knife in the drawer, but she's cute as can be." Aunt Phyllis nudged him hard as she passed, almost spilling her Coke on his chilidog. "Anyway, this is going to be the greatest series all season. The Astros are going *down*." She wedged into to the seat on the other side of his mom.

These days Buck didn't mind coming to the games instead of staying home in his La-Z-Boy. His backside fit fine in the stadium chair, and his shoulders didn't overflow into the seat of the person beside him. Sure, he might still block the view of a small child seated behind him, but what can a six-foot-six guy do? For sure he was no worse than a guy in a Stetson—and there were bound to be several hundred of those here tonight anyhow.

"Maybe I missed a couple of games, but it's nice to be here with two lovely ladies for the Astros game tonight. I'm feeling pretty lucky." He took a bite of his chilidog and settled in.

A different female voice in the empty seat on the other side of him responded to that comment. "Oh, lucky, huh? How lucky?"

Buck turned and saw a half-drunken blonde with a huge cup of beer staggering toward him. "Is this seat taken? Because if it's not, I'm gonna set myself right down beside y'all and find out what your name is, hotboy. Ooh! And check out those baby blues. Mm-mmm."

She looked a little familiar. The face. Then he saw the hot pink fingernails.

"Alison Turner?" Waves of memories, of all different colors and tones, resurged. His cheek felt hot, and not just from the weather.

"That's me!" Her hand flew to her chest. "Totally! Like how did you know that?" Her beer breath floated up to Buck's nostrils. Her legs stuck out beneath a too-short white miniskirt, and she'd cut her long hair and bleached it almost white. But he'd know her face anywhere. "Totally! Like, this must be destiny." She touched her cheek and then ran her finger along her bottom lip.

Buck watched her, a mixture of wonder and disgust brewing in his stomach. "This is my mother, Alison." He sat back in his chair so Alison could see her. His mom merely gave a double blink of acknowledgement and nothing more before returning to a conversation with Aunt Phyllis. His mom could see at a glance what it took Buck a year to discern.

"So, like, your name, Destiny Boy?"

"Buck Cooper." He looked back out at the field. "How are things at Eaglestone?"

She gasped, combined with a hiccup, and slapped her cheek. "Oh. My. Gosh! That's where I know you from? Like, wow. Seriously. Tonight, after the game, me and some of my girlfriends are, like, going to dinner, and there's, like, this *contest* of who can bring the best looking guy, and I'm so totally going to smoke them when I show up with you, *blue eyes*." Buck swallowed down a little bit of bile that rose up from his stomach. Maybe it was from the chilidog, but judging from the situation, probably not.

Like, wow. Mentally negligible and chronically shallow. Weird. Not that long ago, he would have traded his scientific calculator for a chance to sit at a ballgame with Alison Turner, with her begging for his attention. Now, looking at this Alison was akin to looking at a caterpillar he'd just discovered in his salad. He shifted in his seat and turned his knees away from her.

"Alison, I'm so flattered. You're a very pretty girl," even though all the gloss had dulled, "and I'm sure you'll find yourself a great guy to take tonight, maybe even one to marry someday."

"Oh, I'm not ready to settle down, Buck. That's your name, ain't it? Such a Texas name. Buck. Did I ever know a Buck?" She glanced at the sky, thinking. "Oh, yeah. There used to be this guy at our office. Mr. Buck. He was *so* huge, you'd run out of gas trying to drive your Ford around him if he were lying in the road. But he was super nice. Too bad I had to fire him when he went to China." She sighed and smirked. "But about you and me. Tonight. Seriously. You have to come. I am *not* gonna lose to Trish this time."

Buck smirked. How could a woman who had captivated him so completely swing the pendulum so far into revulsion? His temples throbbed slightly. This discussion had reached its saturation point.

"Naw. But thanks. Hey, there's a guy I knew from Eaglestone. You could ask him. Ranjit?"

"Ew! Did you see what he eats for lunch?" Her eye spotted someone else in the crowd a section away. "Well, gorgeous, if I really can't convince you, I guess it's your loss. Well, buh-bye. See you around." She flounced off, vacating the seat once again.

Buck slowly let out a long breath of relief when she walked away.

"How did you know that tramp, Buck?" Aunt Phyllis asked.

His mom raised a suspicious eyebrow at him and leaned in. "I know you've been lonely, but good for you for giving her the brush. Sweep her into the dustpan with the dead bugs, son. You don't need any of that."

Maybe not, but seeing Alison go, he got a resurgence of loneliness. Maybe he should have said yes, or maybe he should go on the blind date with Aunt Phyllis's ditzy neighbor. At least then he wouldn't be alone. Was an occupied seat beside him—no matter by whom—better than an empty one?

The Rangers took the outfield and threw out the first pitch. Buck's mom and Aunt Phyllis pulled out their fan paraphernalia and got obnoxious. The next nine fastballs were on fire.

"I bet that isn't over sixty kilometers per hour," a familiar voice sounded in his ear. "Yamada could smoke him on the mound."

Buck jumped to his feet and shoved his ball cap into his armpit. Chocho!

She stood in the aisle, hair in a ponytail, wearing cutoff jeans and a pink Seibu Lions t-shirt. Her dimple-flanked smile sparkled in the waning daylight.

"Yeah? Maybe, maybe not. This guy's still a rookie. Still has years to perfect his craft. Yamada's arm is bound to wear out soon." He cocked an eyebrow.

"Randy Johnson's arm lasted twenty-one years in the pros. Yamada is Japan's own Big Unit—not some flash-in-the-pan, two-year-career rookie." Chocho said, one hand on her hip. It was probably the sexiest thing she'd ever said to him. *Talk baseball to me, darling.* Buck motioned for her to sit down. His heart would beat any fastball.

"You know your Yankees." Buck sat beside her, and the rest of the world disappeared, again.

"There are some things a girl needs to know." Her eyebrow arched and a smile toyed with her lips—the only lips he'd ever kissed. He itched to take them right now, but there were so many things he didn't know—how she found him, why she never came to him on that awful night, or why now.

Still, she was *here*—or was she an apparition? Just a hope-ghost? He reached over to her knee and covered her hand with his.

The baseball organist played "Take Me Out to the Ballgame."

"Buck?" his mom's voice jerked him out of the spell. "I think I recognize this young lady, do I?" She pulled off her red foam Rico the Ranger antlers and extended a hand.

"You do, Mom. Mom, Aunt Phyllis, this is Chocho Ginza." He instinctively bowed to them as he said this, then felt stupid.

"Chocho. Now that's an unusual name." Aunt Phyllis took a deep breath, but before she could launch into one of her interrogations, Buck reached for Chocho's elbow and hand.

"Would you like to go for a walk? There's a beautiful arboretum between here and the lake. Mom, keep stats on the game for me, would you?"

"The Astros are gonna eat turf!" His mom waved her big red foam hand toward the field and winked at Buck as he escorted Chocho down the hundreds of stairs to the greater outdoors.

"The sky here—how do you stand it? It's so huge." Chocho's arm made a broad stroke against the expanse. It was a cloudless evening, warm and muggy. Her skin glistened in the humidity. Shimmered. Buck thought he might explode.

"This is nothing. You should see it when you get outside the city." They wandered around the far side of Rangers Stadium to where it met up with the park at Lake Arlington. A flock of geese waddled across the grass, honking, quarreling. Screams from the nearby Six Flags roller coasters squealed intermittently. The bluebonnets were gone, but clover smelled like honeysuckle on the air.

No, that was Chocho's hair. He closed his eyes and inhaled. Her sweetness lodged in him, and he ached to take her in his arms—but his questions made him hesitate.

"How did you find me?" They entered the park area. Trees of all kinds dotted the grassy knolls flanking the lake.

"It wasn't easy. I remembered your season tickets to the Rangers. The stadium is pretty huge, and you've changed—a lot."

"I saved you a seat."

"You did?"

"Every game. I promised. I don't break that kind of promise, you know." Warmth flushed to his face.

"I know." She cleared her throat and clutched his hand, pressing it firmly in her tiny hands. "Your Rangers. They're not too bad—I've been to three of their games now."

Three games! His heart fell into his stomach like lead. He shouldn't have skipped even one game. He told her he'd be waiting, and he wasn't. It was agony.

However, all the unknowns about her arrival were even more agonizing. She either came to make him the happiest man in the world or the most miserable. Her arrival had reopened a wound that hadn't properly healed, but had at least stopped. Now she was either going to run a magical healing hand over it or rip him to shreds. At the edge of the lake, Buck halted and turned to face her, resting his hand on her shoulder. He couldn't take the suspense anymore.

"If you're here to tell me bad news, tell it quick, Chocho. Don't try to spare my feelings."

"Buck. No, I have great news. Miki-*chan's* surgery was a success, and she is a healthy, happy little girl now." Her eyes glistened with tears. "It couldn't have happened without what you did, Buck."

"What *I* did?"

"When you quit sumo, an investigation was launched into my father's business practices, and while his companies are still in his control, though limping, the JSA removed him from his post. A news reporter dug deep enough to find out why I'd gone along with the arranged marriage, and the people of Japan were so appalled at my father's refusal to fund her transplant unless I agreed to marry Torakiba that they donated enough to help Miki-*chan*. It was beautiful. All because you dared to stand up to him."

"You stayed to see the operation through?" His mind was going like a hamster in a wheel—she'd only agreed to go along with the forced marriage because of Miki-*chan*. He could cover her with ten thousand kisses. Still, he had to play it cool. He picked up a smooth stone and skipped it across the water's surface. Nine skips before it sank. Not bad, Mr.-Playing-it-Cool. Whatever. He knew the facade was thin.

"Her parents were the main caregivers, but she's so special to me, I couldn't leave her. I'm sorry I didn't contact you sooner." Chocho's voice strained. She stooped and picked up her own stone. Sixteen before it sank.

"Why didn't you?" The question blurted out before he could filter it.

"My mother's place in England has a pond." She trailed off, and then turned to him, eyes glistening. "I thought when you left, when you said to all the world you didn't want to receive me as your prize, perhaps you didn't want me."

"Didn't want you?" Buck said, throwing his arms around her tiny frame, pulling her to him in a powerful embrace. "Chocho!"

She buried her face in his chest. "You left, Buck. You quit, and you didn't come to find me, and you didn't call. I thought—"

Buck stooped down and stopped her mouth with a kiss. He swept her up into his arms and breathed the honeysuckle scent of the nape of her neck and whispered with intensity into her ear. "Impossible."

She set her hands on his shoulders and gave him a long look, which soon softened, and a tear glistened in the lower wells of her eyes. She reached up and ran her fingers through his shorn hair.

"I've wanted to do that since the second I saw you." She tiptoed and kissed him with a passion that sent him flying. He pulled her tiny ribcage to him and felt the softness of her curves and the warmth of her skin. Her heart rate sped alongside his. The coil of suspense between them had sprung at last; it sent him soaring.

Buck set Chocho on her feet again, and they began strolling along the bank of the lake.

"How is your grandparents' farm? You will take me to see it, won't you? I want to see the sky there," Chocho said.

"Actually, I bought it," Buck said.

Her eyes grew wide, and the lashes that framed them almost touched her eyebrows. "You did? Oh!"

"The fields of hay smell like springtime all year round."

"And Rosie and Ninety-nine?"

"All the horses are doing fine." Buck grinned—she remembered their names. "I ride them most days." They shuffled through the green grass and listened to the birds and the distant sounds of the game winding down. "And yours? Vashti and Hopalong?"

Chocho stopped, her eyebrows knit together. "My father—he is nothing if not vindictive. When he couldn't hold Miki's health at ransom anymore, he tried another tactic to force me to marry Torakiba."

"No." Buck clenched his teeth.

"Oh, I refused—again. But my father followed through on his threat and sold my horses. My mother was there and said some

American buyer had purchased them with a phone bid. She had to watch them get loaded into crates and hauled away." Chocho's words caught in her throat.

"That must have been awful." Buck embraced her. "Don't worry, Chocho. I'm sure they're in a good place. I mean, I *know* they're in a good place."

"What are you saying?" She drew away and searched his face.

"I'm saying, Chocho Ginza, I have something to show you out at the farm."

"Oh, Buck!" She threw her arms around him and squealed. "You were the buyer!"

"You crossed a stream on stepping stones for me, just so I could see a sunset."

"There's only one problem, though, Buck."

Problem? Oh, no. His heart stuttered.

"If I come out to your farm," she rested a hand on his shoulder, "I might never want to leave."

The heart-stutter returned with a thousand friends—and they danced in his chest. "I'll never want you to."

A muffled roar rose from the stadium behind them—someone had hit a homerun. On another evening, Buck would've sat in the stands cheering, tossing Coke with all the spectators. But this evening was different. This evening he wasn't relegated to being a spectator sitting on the sidelines—of life, of love, of anything. This evening, and every evening hereafter, he was living it. And it was all *"Kachikoshi,* Buck!" all the time, with Chocho encircled in his embrace.

His butterfly had flown back to him.

PRONUNCIATION GUIDE

Japanese pronunciation is very simple: pronounce each vowel syllable separately, even when they are paired. The pair makes the blend. For instance "ai" is pronounced "ah-ee" but when slurred becomes the long I of English. The letter "r" is more of a tongue flap, as in Spanish. Vowels are pronounced as follows:

a—ah

i—ee

u—oo

e—eh

o—oh

The letter *g* always makes the hard *g* as in *gag*. The letter *j* always sounds like *j* in *jump*.

GLOSSARY

akabaka—red idiot.

asagohan—breakfast.

banzai—a war cry.

basho—tournament.

beri—very.

butaniku—pig meat, pork.

butsudan—a small Buddhist shrine placed in a person's home where offerings are made to gods and ancestors.

chonmage—the sumo hairstyle, a topknot created with great care with chamomile oil.

Dareka ga iru?—"Is anybody there?"

dohyo—training and competition ring, a clay platform about three feet high and covered with reddish dirt, and a painted ring with two starting lines; measures about fifteen feet in diameter.

Doshita no—"What just happened?" or "What happened?"

Fukuoka—a large city on Japan's southern island of Kyushu, location of the annual November sumo tournament.

futokaba—fat hippo.

genkan—a small cement foyer, lower than the rest of the house, where Japanese people leave their shoes before entering the house-proper.

Ganbare—command form of a phrase meaning "hang in there."

geta—shoes made of a wooden slat and a thong of fabric and having two wooden dowels attached to the bottom of the slat, one at the ball of the food and one at the arch.

gochisosama—phrase used at the end of a meal to thank the preparer of the food.

hajimemashite—"I am pleased to meet you."

hamigaki—toothpaste.

hana-michi—the aisles that lead from the dressing rooms toward the ring.

honbasho—an official sumo tournament, one of six throughout a calendar year, where wrestlers compete for rankings and prizes; held in Tokyo in January, May and September. March is in Osaka; July is in Nagoya; November is in Fukuoka.

honto desu—truly so.

hyaku en—one hundred yen, about a dollar, depending on the exchange rate.

ike!—go! (but in a rude command form).

inukaze—dogbreath.

-jin—suffix meaning person, as in Amerika-*jin*, meainng an American person.

jinbeizame—whale shark.

jonokuchi—the lowest amateur level of sumo.

kachikoshi—victory.

katana—a samurai long sword.

kessho mawashi—the ornately embroidered silk apron worn during opening ceremonies.

kimono—a more formal robe, often made of silk; literally "the thing you wear."

Ki wo tsukete kudasai—"Take care, please."

kohai—junior.

Kokugikan—The National Sumo Arena, located in the Ryugoku neighborhood of Tokyo.

maegashira—the fifth highest level in sumo.

makushita—the fourth lowest level in sumo; the highest of the amateur ranks.

matte—the command form of "to wait."

mawashi—loin covering, made of heavy cotton; amateurs wear white; professional ranked wrestlers wear black.

Nagoya—a large city in western Japan, home of the annual July sumo tournament.

Nan senchi desho ka na—"Wow. How tall are you?"

oishiringo—delicious apple.

oki nasai—"Wake up!"

Osaka—a large city in western Japan, location of the grand sumo tournament each March.

ossu—phrase meaning "hey, there," much like "what's up."

ozeki—champion, the second highest level in sumo.

pachinko—Japanese pinball, vertical machines with steel balls.

piiman—green pepper.

rikishi—a sumo wrestler, either amateur or pro, part of a sumo training stable.

sakananokao—fishface.

-sama—highest level of honorific suffix attached to the end of a person's name to show respect or honor.

-san—standard level of honorific suffix attached to the end of a person's name to show respect or honor.

sen yen—one thousand yen, about ten dollars.

senpai—senior.

sobakubi—noodle neck.

sugoi!—great! or wow!

taiko—special Japanese kettle drums.

takoyaki—cooked octopus meat.

uwatenage—a sumo technique in which the attacker establishes an outside grip then throws his opponent by heaving him down and away at a sharp angle.

yobidashi—the ornately dressed referee.

yokozuna—grand champion, the highest level in sumo.

yukata—thin woven cotton robe, usually with a pattern, tied around the waist, usually worn by Japanese people in the evening. Standard uniform clothing for sumo wrestlers.

謝
辞

ACKNOWLEDGMENTS

First, all love and thanks to Gary, my muse and my true love, who, when I was telling him about my experiences in Japan and people I'd met, said, "Hey, that would make a great novel!" and helped me flesh out the story. He's the best! I married so very well.

Thanks, too, to the great and talented women in ANWA, my unparalleled writers group, who are endlessly supportive and cheer one another on to victory.

I had some fabulous beta readers: Paul Johnson, Whitney Larson, Donna Hatch, Corey Sanders, and Chris Stewart, all fine writers, the cream of the crop. Thank you for sharing your skills to improve this book from draft to draft.

Megan Collins Oliphant is the best vision-expanding critique partner I could have asked for. She took this book to the next level more than once.

All the staff and editorial team at Jolly Fish Press deserve three cheers of appreciation. Thank you so much for believing in Buck and for your constant enthusiasm.

Boundless thanks to my parents for teaching me to love to read, for encouraging me to write, for getting me through college, for supporting and encouraging me, and for being the best examples of everything.

ABOUT THE AUTHOR

Jennifer Griffith grew up on a farm in Idaho, a far cry from the crowds of Tokyo. While spending a year and a half in Japan during college, she grew to love the people, language and culture of that country. Plus, being 5'1" tall, Jennifer found Japan fantastic—she could reach everything on the shelves at the grocery store.

Jennifer is a book geek, forever buying books and always needing another bookshelf. Besides sumo, she also loves demolition derbies, art, politics, and cold cereal.

Big in Japan is Mrs. Griffith's fourth novel. She and her husband live in the rural Arizona desert, where they are raising their five children.

You may visit Jennifer's website at:
www.authorjennifergriffith.com